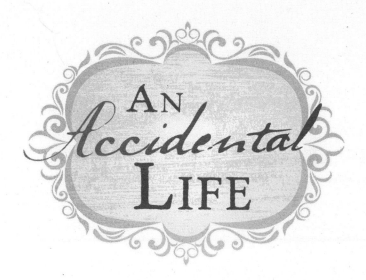

AN Accidental LIFE

PAMELA BINNINGS EWEN

PUBLISHING GROUP

Nashville, Tennessee

978-0-8054-6432-0

Published by B&H Publishing Group,
Nashville, Tennessee

Dewey Decimal Classification: F
Subject Heading: ABORTION—FICTION \ LAWYERS—FICTION \
TRIALS (HOMICIDE)—FICTION

1 2 3 4 5 6 7 8 • 17 16 15 14 13

To the Survivors

Prologue

WHY DID SHE EXIST, IF NOT for the news that she was waiting to receive? She glanced over her shoulder at the silent telephone on the credenza behind her. Then she turned back to the document on which she'd been struggling to focus her thoughts.

Rebecca Downer Jacobs mulled the question over as she sat at her desk in her office on the sixteenth floor of the law firm of Mangen & Morris gazing out over the Central Business District of the city of New Orleans. It was May of 1982 and she'd been waiting for this day to arrive for six years. She supposed we are all seekers of some ultimate goal and light—we all have a human desire to understand and find our singular purpose. And then make it count.

Hers was about to be fulfilled. For now, at least.

Glancing again at the phone, she willed it to ring.

In the resulting silence she leaned back, winged her elbows and clasped her hands behind her neck, acknowledging her worst fault—a driving ambition that sometimes tested her patience. And, she was conscious that sometimes she had a tendency to drift toward the glitter, the false lights. But those moments were small rewards, the riches that kept the difficult challenges entertaining. She fought always to keep her primary focus on her latest goal.

Now, waiting for the phone call that would change her life, she sat gazing through her office window at the windows in the building across the street. She guessed it would be difficult to know when you'd finally made it to the top, because so far, each time Rebecca had won what she'd been seeking, something better popped up ahead and she found herself at yet another crossroads, with yet another decision to make, yet another difficult choice turning her life upside down.

That's one reason she and Peter had agreed there'd be no children in their marriage.

She swung the chair around and stared hard at the phone, blaming it for the churning in her stomach and the billable hours that she was wasting. With a glance at her watch and a sigh, she swiveled back to the desk and picked up the contract that she'd been reading, staring down at the black type. With an exasperated click of her tongue, she reread the paragraph her client had decided that he now wanted to renegotiate. Here she was waiting for that phone call and teetering on the edge of an abyss or great success—and she was forced to try to focus on this minutia.

If she'd been certain that someone was listening, she would send up a prayer for patience. Still, she wondered if it was true, as Peter sometimes mused, that prayers unspoken might also be heard.

This made her think of Amalise—Amalise Catoir, her closest friend. There was a woman who knew how to pray. Amalise was certain that when she prayed, someone was listening. Abba, she called him: Father. That relationship between Amalise and her God was tender; one she'd often wished that she had too. But you can't force your mind to accept ideas that your heart shuts out. Still, she recognized that Amalise derived comforting strength through her faith. And, assisted by her husband, Jude, Amalise seemed to have achieved balance between her career, and her marriage and raising their son, Luke.

Amalise and Rebecca began their careers practicing law together at Mangen & Morris, the first women lawyers ever hired by the firm. And now, here they were six years later and both up for the same prize. A sudden thought made her heart race. What if Amalise had already gotten the call, and she did not? Surely by now she should have heard.

The thought made her shut her eyes.

When she opened them again, the sunshine pouring through the window made her blink. Amalise was her best friend, but there were limits to loyalty. She loved Amalise, in the strange way that friends who are also competitors sometimes do. But if, in fact, the partnership choice today came down to only one between them, she had to win.

To keep things in perspective, she ticked off prior wins in her mind one at a time. High-school homecoming queen, "most beautiful" girl in her class, and valedictorian at graduation. Magna cum laude at Newcomb College. Her grades in law school at Tulane ranked in the top five percent.

But, Amalise's class ranking had been close to hers at Tulane, she had to admit.

Still, it was Rebecca, and not Amalise, who was described by the magazine *New Woman* as one of the IT Girls to watch this year. That cover was now framed and displayed on the wall outside the large conference room on the firm's executive floor. The reminder made her smile. She swiveled back to the desk and looked at the document she'd been reading. Of course she would get the call.

But—if not?

The nausea rose again, and she dropped her head into her hands. How would she tell Peter, if the call didn't come? The husband she adored was certain, unwavering, waiting to congratulate. He was fast approaching his own goal, already a Senior Assistant District Attorney for Jefferson Parish. The Parish, as it was called, equaled the power and wealth of the city of New Orleans, to which it was geographically attached.

No. She couldn't think that way. Not yet. For Peter, and for her, their careers were their lives. They'd agreed to this from the very start of their relationship. Together they'd reap the rewards of their hard work, unencumbered; free to travel on a whim, to live the way they wanted to live. A child would be a hindrance. Work, love, and marriage were enough for them, they'd both agreed.

She glanced at the silent phone. There was too much to lose to fail now.

Rebecca looked down, twirling her thumbs in her lap as a shadow she'd been forcing from her mind for over a week slipped through to a conscious level. A different problem altogether and one she'd not yet mentioned to Peter.

Annoyed by the intrusion, she yanked open the bottom drawer in her desk and pulled out a mirror. She touched the corners of her lips, smoothed her hair; told herself that she was worrying for nothing, that such injustice could not exist.

Just then the telephone rang.

Part One

Secrets

1

AMALISE STUCK HER HEAD INTO THE office and Rebecca, who'd been lounging with her feet on the desk and hands clasped behind her head, reliving the day, looked up.

"You certainly look comfortable." Amalise laughed as she leaned a shoulder against the door jamb. Glancing at her watch, she crossed her arms. "Are you coming? It's six thirty and I'm going home to dress for tonight. Jude's already gone for the sitter."

Rebecca smiled and, lifting her feet, dropped them to the floor. She sat up straight and ran her hands back through her hair. "I've brought clothes," she said. "Peter's picking me up here in an hour."

Amalise's face lit. "Can you believe this, Rebecca? We finally made it."

Rebecca laughed. She curled her fingers and looked at a cuticle near her thumbnail. This would have to go before tonight. "Always knew we would."

When Amalise had gone, she stood up and went to the closet in the corner of her office where she pulled out the clothes she'd brought to work in that morning.

Changing into the dress she'd bought for this occasion, a long-sleeved, knee-length black velvet sheath with a V-neckline, she turned, inspecting herself in the long mirror hanging inside the closet door. Comfortable now that partnership was a certainty, she smiled, thinking of the look of sheer joy she'd just seen on Amalise's face. In her stocking feet she turned one way, then the other, smoothing the velvet over her hips, musing on how different her life was from Amalise's.

Amalise was a mother now. She shook her head at the thought of how time had flown since Amalise had first met Luke. He'd been a foster child, an orphan rescued in 1975 during the Vietnam War. She'd married Jude four years ago, and they had adopted Luke, who was somewhere around twelve years old right now. Not much was known about the child's life before he'd found Amalise and Jude.

Even with a child, Amalise had been a tough competitor in their race up the ladder at the firm. Fleetingly the thought crossed her mind that perhaps she'd been lucky the firm had chosen both. But Amalise had held on through the years because always, always, Jude was there for her—he had her back. Before their marriage, Jude was a river pilot down at the mouth of the Mississippi. But he'd rearranged his life for Amalise and Luke; had given up one job for another to share the responsibilities at home. And now, today, Jude was a successful contractor in the city, his own boss, with flexible hours, freeing Amalise for the long hours her own work required. Unlike Peter, whose days were scheduled minute by minute on trial dockets.

Rebecca adjusted the folds on the neckline of her dress and turned away from the mirror, satisfied.

Both Peter and Jude did have had one thing in common though, a deep certain faith in a God who reaches down and touches our lives. Peter lived his faith through his work, and his relationship with her. But he would never give up his demanding career to take primary responsibility for a child, she knew. He just could not.

As a rule Rebecca avoided children—they were generally a nuisance. But Luke was an exception. After the war in Southeast Asia, Luke had somehow found his way to New Orleans and into Amalise's and Jude's hearts.

Reaching down into the closet, she picked up the shoes she'd brought to wear tonight. Then, closing the closet door, she sat down in the chair to put them on.

Yes, Luke was a special kid. Unusually bright—she wondered what his IQ would be if Amalise ever had him tested. She slipped one shoe on, fitting it over her heel. The twelve-year-old was brilliant, Rebecca thought; he had a fascinating talent for understanding logical connections. She slipped on the other shoe. Standing, she strutted in a circle, trying out the shoes. The heels were higher than the ones she wore to work, but they were stylish.

But children were such a responsibility.

Glancing at her watch, a slim diamond Patek Philippe that Peter had given her for her birthday last year, she saw there were still a few minutes left. She walked back to her desk and sank down in the chair behind it as the thought thrilled her once again: she'd made it. She smiled in the empty room. Rebecca Downer Jacobs was a partner in the firm of Mangen & Morris, L.L.P.

Rebecca spun the desk chair around and around, exhilarated, thinking how things change in life over time. She wished her mother could see her now. It suddenly struck her that they hadn't spoken in over a year, and she made a mental note to try to remedy that. Mama and her new husband, Anthony, had moved out to California a few years ago, to San Francisco. And there, the two seemed to have forgotten that she even existed.

Well, so what. That was nothing new. She was tempted to leave things just as they were—to let Mama go. The bond between them was smashed long ago—the spinning chair stopped and the images flashed before her eyes: her little sister Elise's pink bike on the sidewalk before her, suddenly swerving off down the driveway. Elise had loved the feel of swooping down that driveway, the steep slope leading into the street, and sometimes she'd throw her arms out to her sides, balancing, and . . .

Ah, no. No. Not tonight. Holding onto the edges of the chair seat she closed her eyes and forced the thoughts away. Not tonight. This was a night to be happy, a night for celebration, a night to share her success with Peter.

Still the memories came, as though they'd been waiting back there in the darkness for just this moment, and they reeled on through her mind. The screaming brakes, the sickening sounds, the pink bicycle blurring, and then . . . everything, everyone just disappearing.

She opened her eyes, looking off, unseeing. Mama had turned to stone after that day when Elise had died—consumed, completely consumed with her own grief. And there was something else to this. Rebecca had seen it in her eyes; even at the age of ten, she'd known. The accident was her fault. She was riding right behind her little sister; she should have seen the car coming; should have realized what might happen.

She was responsible for Elise when they were out together.

She remembered standing in the front room of the dark house a few days later. Elise was gone. The little sister she'd loved so much had simply disappeared. A neighbor was with her then, Mama was somewhere else. After Elise died, Mama was always somewhere else. Rebecca never knew where.

God had taken Elise, the woman had said.

And, oh, how she'd hated God for that.

She rotated her thumbs as the resentment built and burst through her carefully constructed wall. When that happened, Rebecca was an expert at rebuilding. But for now she let herself think of how nice it would be to call Mama out in California and dangle this shining new success before her. *See Mama? Elise may be gone, but I am here. I am here and look at what I've done! I'm a partner in my law firm, and after that?* Who knows . . . maybe politics, or maybe Wall Street, or maybe she'd just hop on one of those shuttles and shoot for the stars.

Elise is gone. But I am here.

Perhaps she would make that phone call.

And then, she shook it off. She'd never been able to compete with her mother's memories of Elise, and year by year Mama had made that more and more clear, as though in Mama's eyes, Rebecca's each success was an affront, a deliberate slap at Elise's unfulfilled potential.

Rebecca bit her bottom lip as the memories stirred feelings that she thought she'd buried long ago. Turning back to the desk, she pulled her calendar toward her. Next week she was scheduled to talk with the CEO of Roberts Engineering, a new client she was bringing to the firm. The company was considering an investment in a gold mine in Nevada. It occurred to her for the first time, that as a partner in the firm, she could now open the file under her own name.

She closed the calendar book and pushed it away. She fixed her eyes on the rows of books across the room, directing her thoughts, reminding herself again of what she'd achieved; that she and Amalise were the first women partners ever in the firm, and that her name was probably being mentioned at cocktail parties around town tonight.

And that Peter was probably now waiting downstairs.

Feeling better, she stood. She walked down the well-lit hallway toward the elevator. It was Friday night. Her own secretary, Rose Marie, was gone, but a few of the secretaries were still at their desks, and she told each and every one good-bye and to have a nice weekend. They'd all celebrated together earlier, when the news had spread about Rebecca and Amalise.

Partner. She tried out the word.

Rebecca stepped into the elevator, pressed the button, and gazed at her reflection in the metal doors as the elevator descended. There was no limit to what she could accomplish if she worked hard enough. And already the worry that had haunted her earlier was submerged beneath the possibilities that lay ahead.

2

ANTOINE'S RESTAURANT, ESTABLISHED IN 1840 AND located in the heart of the *Vieux Carré*—the French Quarter—is an elegant, busy, and colorful reflection of the city's past. As always, when Rebecca walked through the ornate doors opening from St. Louis Street, she was transported.

The huge restaurant was like a woman, she thought; queen of a Mardi Gras Krewe. There were thirteen dining rooms in Antoine's; some were large and opulent, some small and intimate. Some of the rooms hid secrets, like women do. She looked up—the sparkling crystal chandeliers were the queen's crown; the wall of mirrors and the embroidered silk panels alongside, her robe. The crisp white linens covering the tables, her mantle. And the flowers and candles, and the long-stemmed crystal, rows of shining silver forks and knives and spoons of every size, those were her jewels.

To her left in the large front room, just before a mirrored wall, Rebecca saw the many partners of the firm and their wives gathered around a long table. Raymond caught her eye and gave her a victory sign. She smiled and waved.

Clarence, their usual waiter, ambled up and caught Rebecca's hand in both of his and said how happy he was for her tonight. Rebecca's face lit with a smile. On any given night if a line had formed on the sidewalk outside, she knew that Clarence would meet Peter and her at the side door in the alleyway and let them in.

Peter's hand warmed her back as Clarence guided them toward the table. Sitting just before the front windows looking out over St. Louis Street, Doug Bastion, the managing partner of the firm, put his napkin down and stood as they approached. Beaming with excitement, Rebecca glided toward the group. Hands extended, Doug was first to greet them. Through the windows behind him lights from the streetlamps and passing cars cast a ghostly glow in the fog, even though spring was now drifting into summer.

Amalise and Jude had already arrived, and they sat across the table on one side of Doug. Places on Doug's other side had been saved for Rebecca and Peter. At the opposite end of the long table, Alice Bastion, Doug's wife, was holding court. And in between were the men that Rebecca and Amalise had worked alongside as associates for the past six years and their wives.

Catcalls, congratulations, and high fives rose as Rebecca and Peter arrived. Everyone stood to greet them. Preston's wife came down from the other end of the table and hugged Rebecca tight. Raymond slapped her on the back, and pumped Peter's hand. Across the table Jude called out something that made Peter laugh, and Amalise gave her that look.

We're the silver girls—our dream came true.

Rebecca tipped her chin, a little nod. From a distance she could hear the clarinet and sax and drums of a second-line band moving down Royal Street toward the square.

As Clarence took her coat and Rebecca and Peter were seated, Doug remained standing. He lifted his glass and tapped it lightly. For Rebecca, the thin, bell-like tone sounded a new beginning. But as calls of "Speech! Speech!" arose so did the half-formed worry that she'd been holding at bay for almost a week. The question came unbidden—what if that tinkling sounded an ending, and not a beginning.

She shook off the vague fear. Not tonight. Beneath the table Peter rested his hand on her knee, and her husband's touch was warm and comforting. She turned her head and smiled.

Doug clanged the spoon against the glass again and gave a little speech welcoming Amalise and Rebecca into the partnership of the firm.

From someone at the far end of the table: "Did I hear we've now got girls in the firm?"

There was laughter all around.

Raymond stood and raised his glass. "A toast, please, to our lovely new partners!" He took in both Amalise and Rebecca with his eyes as he said with a grin, "On your first day with the firm, Preston and I took you to Bailey's for lunch to welcome you. Do you remember what I said that day?"

Rebecca glanced at Amalise; they both shook their heads.

He laughed. "Well, you can't say I didn't warn you, but guess what, girls. You've now reached the bottom of a whole new food chain."

Groans and laughter erupted. Amalise met Rebecca's eyes, and Rebecca saw a reflection of her thoughts. The competition is never over; not really. But Amalise didn't care as much as she, Rebecca knew.

After the toasts were finished, everyone talked and laughed, as always, Rebecca loved the chatter, the noise, the ambient hum of a crowd—the music of her life. Exuberant, triumphant, she turned to Peter, smiling and lifting her face for his kiss, forgetting all about that fear in this moment.

He slipped his arm around her shoulders and leaning close, whispered, "Enjoy this night, Beauty. You've earned it."

As the kitchen doors burst open and a platoon of Antoine's tuxedoed waiters marched toward the Mangen & Morris table in double lines, each waiter balancing a silver tray at shoulder level, Clarence appeared at Peter's side. A hand slipped a plate of steaming Gulf oysters before Peter just as Clarence whispered in his ear—"Telephone for you, Mr. Peter."

He nodded, and with a longing long at the Oysters Rockefeller, folded his napkin and placed it on the table near his plate.

"I'll be right back," he said to Rebecca. She looked at him and nodded.

Clarence led Peter to the small office and left him there. Peter took the phone, said hello, and heard the voice of Fred McAndrews, detective first class, homicide division, known as Mac. Mac was the detective he preferred to work with on cases. Mac got right to the point. Peter listened.

"Who signed the warrant?" he asked when Mac had finished. He turned, sitting on the edge of a desk as he spoke, studying the array of photographs covering the walls of the little room. Framed sepia shots of family over the years, and some of diners, celebrities he supposed.

"Judge Florant." Mac sounded tired, beaten down. That was unusual—Mac was usually unflappable.

"She made the complaint this morning?"

"About nine or ten, I guess."

"You moved fast."

"Yeah. Her story was pretty convincing. And it was exigent circumstances. We had to get out there before they moved the body." Peter heard him blow out his breath. "Still, they'd already put it in the freezer."

"Any idea how long it was in there?"

"Other than what the complainant told us, no. Not yet anyway." Seconds passed. "There's no way to tell. Stephanie says after it thaws, she'll try to fix a time line. But, you know, all around this is a very strange situation."

Peter's voice was harsh. "You got that right." It was hard to believe, in fact. Good that Stephanie Kand had gone along with them. She was the best forensic pathologist in the Parish coroner's office in his opinion. No question she'd do a thorough job. If anyone could work out the mystery, Dr. Kand could.

"Sorry to bust in on the party," Mac said. "I know this is a special night."

"I'm glad you called. Keep me informed, will you?"

"Sure."

Peter dropped his chin and closed his eyes. His was a violent world. He'd never gotten used to the cruelties, though, and he hoped he never would. The world was sad. So much pain, and the malevolence—he saw it, lived it every day as a prosecutor. But he'd chosen this path in the DA's office just for that reason—to clean things up.

Could what he now suspected really be happening? If so, and if he decided to take the case to trial, it would be the biggest challenge he'd ever faced. And one, he was sure would keep him up at night.

He stood there, hand on the cradled telephone receiver, thinking about the complaint that Mac had described. It didn't make any sense. But the evidence doesn't lie.

Love, when she'd finally found it with Peter, was everything Rebecca had always dreamed. They were made for each other, both had set goals early on in life and both were passionate in their drive to make these dreams come true. Both were ambitions, albeit for different reasons. She adored her husband, and her love was fully returned.

Peter's goals were different from hers though. Since she was a child, she'd known that she could accomplish great things, but in her most honest moments with herself, she acknowledged that what propelled her was the idea of success, glittering top-of-the-world achievement, and the rewards that go along with that. She loved living the good life.

Peter, on the other hand, was motivated by his desire to make a difference in the world. He'd graduated with honors from Loyola Law School and had his choice of firms. But instead he'd accepted the Jefferson Parish District Attorney's offer right away because he loved the idea of being in the trenches, fighting the battles. He'd once said that he believed that right and wrong, good and evil, must be understood and recognized if we're to overcome. Consecrated was the word he'd used. Good must be consecrated.

Peter's dream was to spend his life making the world a little safer. She'd loved that about him.

Not that they didn't have their disagreements. They were both strong-willed. And stubborn. But, oh how she loved him. She admired him. They sometimes teased each other about their choices. She was a bird in a gilded cage downtown, he would say. He was just a gladiator, she'd reply. But with both of them, for different reasons perhaps, work came first. Like her, Peter was completely focused on his career.

And so, with Antoine's glittering around her, she finished the soup, lifted the napkin from her lap and patted her lips, then folded it and placed it back down on her lap. Peter had not yet returned from that phone call.

Doug leaned toward her and they began talking about the new office that came with the partnership, more room, several large windows instead of one, and new furniture that she could choose. She beamed as he talked, nodding and listening, once in a while adding that she'd like this or that—a larger desk, for example; made of walnut. And she preferred a conversation area in one corner instead of the usual small conference table. She'd been thinking about this for years. The office should look crisp and sharp, efficient, but elegant.

Across the table Jude was telling Preston about a house he'd just renovated for friends in the Foubourg Marigny, the district bordering the downriver side of the French Quarter. The house was one on Kerelec Street where Luke had lived as a foster child.

"Luke's working with me on that Marigny job," Jude was saying. "I'm teaching him how to lay tile."

"That's a good area," Doug replied without missing a beat.

Amalise caught Rebecca's eye and they exchanged a secret smile. The house on Kerelec house had been involved in a strange transaction five years ago that had cost the firm some time and money, and caused Doug plenty of heartburn.

Peter touched her shoulder as he slid into the empty chair beside her. "Trouble?" She turned to him, hoping they wouldn't have to leave.

He shook his head. "Mac's taking care of it. I'll talk to him tomorrow."

Conversations continued, the buzz increased, and all thoughts of work were left behind as waiters carrying huge trays of Baked Alaska overhead arrived.

3

REBECCA TIPPED BACK THE CHAIR AS she read. The small type in the Offering Memorandum seemed to swim before her eyes. A vague sense of nausea swept her now. It was nine o'clock in the morning and she told herself that she should have just stayed in bed after last night's celebrations. It was Saturday and the office was deserted so she jumped when a voice nearby whispered, "Hello."

"How long have you been here?" Rebecca put the document down and rubbed her eyes.

"Not long." Amalise dragged over a chair and sat down. "What are you working on?" Leaning back, she eyed the document that Rebecca had been reading.

Rebecca looked down at the papers, and back at Amalise. "This is a new client. Roberts Engineering."

"You brought that work in?"

"Yes." She pulled back her hair, twisted it, and let it fall. "I met the CFO at a party a few weeks ago. He's a friend of a friend of Peter's. I've got Sydney Martin on it, and a couple other associates, and we're meeting in half an hour to set up a schedule. I'm just trying to grasp the big picture right now."

A fleeting look of envy crossed Amalise's face, and then it disappeared. Rebecca studied her friend, who, she reminded herself, was also her competition. Mixed emotions rose. It was a real coup for a young partner to bring an important client to the firm. Amalise was turning this news over in her mind, she knew. But in an instant, Amalise managed a smile.

"Congratulations," she said. Her tone was sincere. She tapped her fingers on the end of the armrest and let a beat go by, staring through the window. Then she turned her eyes back to Rebecca. "Do you suppose that now we're partners, we're on our own? Expected to bring in all of our own work?"

"I don't know." Rebecca's reply was honest. Bringing in a new client wasn't easy. And even though it was 1982, in the business world, 99 percent of decision-makers were men; this was unexplored territory for Amalise and Rebecca.

Suddenly, nausea sent the room spinning. Holding on, she looked at Amalise. "I suppose we'll soon find out."

"Maybe Raymond was right that we're starting over now." Amalise smiled. "Maybe I'll take up golf."

Rebecca braced her hands against the edge of the desk and pushed back, stretching her arms. She flinched, pressing one hand over her forehead.

"What's wrong?" Amalise's voice was sharp as she rose. Rebecca bent and felt the cold dampness on her face, her neck.

"Rebecca?" Amalise stood over her, her hand warm on Rebecca's shoulder. "Can I get you something?"

She managed to hold up one hand, pressing her lips together as she shook her head. The nausea was winning. *Please, please, she thought, let Amalise leave right now.*

"I'm fine," she said, struggling to keep her tone casual. "I'm all right. Didn't sleep well at all last night." Glancing at the door, she swallowed. Ten steps to the doorway, a short walk down the hall to the restroom. Amalise cautiously backed up, her eyes on Rebecca.

With a rap on the door, Raymond walked in. She straightened as he halted just behind Amalise. "Twenty-four hours as partners and you're both still here. That's a good sign. But you're looking a little wan, Rebecca."

"Don't get your hopes up." Smiling, she waved him off. Amalise seemed to get the message. Hooking her arm through Raymond's, she turned him toward the door. As they entered the hallway, she looked back over her shoulder and mouthed to Rebecca, "Call me."

That nagging suspicion that she'd carried around for the last few weeks deepened now. She would have to make an appointment, she knew. And then, if her suspicion was confirmed? The room seemed to dim, almost as if clouds had covered the sun.

When she could no longer hear Amalise's and Raymond's voices, she hurried toward the restroom. First thing Monday morning she'd make the call.

At the same time, on that same morning, Peter was in his office in Gretna, a small incorporated city in Jefferson Parish, just across the river from the edge of the Central Business District in New Orleans where Rebecca worked. The district attorney's offices were housed on the upper floors of the Parish courthouse building near the foot of Huey P. Long Drive. The first four floors above the lobby of the building housed the courtrooms. The street ended at the levee and the Mississippi River and the ferry landing, and the blocks just before the levee constituted the courthouse area. Peter's office was on the tenth floor, on the side of the building that faced the river and the city of New Orleans through a wall of green glass.

Peter's office was five hundred square feet and, like the two other senior assistant district attorneys, the ADAs, he enjoyed a private office with a view. Just outside the row of senior ADAs' offices was a large open room where the junior ADAs had their desks. The cavernous room was brightly lit and noisy. Molly, the secretary that Peter shared with the other Senior ADAs, had her desk there as well. The district attorney's office suite was one floor up.

Unlike Rebecca's office across the river, the furnishings in Peter's office were utilitarian, and he liked it that way. There was a large oak desk with lots of drawers, and two wooden club-style chairs for visitors. Most of the wall space was taken up by three army-green filing cabinets containing files for his open cases. On any given day, Peter might have over a hundred cases moving forward on his schedule. Simple. Efficient. Everything he needed.

On this Saturday morning, things were quiet and Peter's door was open. He heard footsteps and looked up. Mac was standing there.

He'd been reading a defense motion in a hearing scheduled for Monday morning. Bullets from guns shot off celebrating last New Year's Eve along Lake Pontchartrain had rained down on citizens in Metairie, killing one.

With a nod, Mac pinched the cigarette from the corner of his mouth and walked in.

"Figured I'd find you here," he said, pulling out a chair before Peter's desk and taking a seat. "You sure know how to waste a Saturday morning."

Peter tossed the papers down, nodding toward them. "The raining bullets case. It's coming to trial soon."

"You'd think people would've learned that whatever goes up must come down."

Peter tipped back his chair. "How are thing coming along on the case you called me about?"

"It's insane." Mac stubbed his cigarette into the glass ashtray on the visitor side of Peter's desk. "Everything's backwards. And it's gonna break your heart."

"The complainant's a young girl name of Glory Lynn Chasson." Mac pushed out his lower lip, hesitating before he went on. "Says she's twenty. I'm pretty sure she's younger, but we haven't got to that."

His eyes wandered to the window. "Like I told you, when she first showed up at the station yesterday morning, she was upset. Hard to understand what she was saying at first, until her father calmed her down some."

Peter nodded. "What exactly did she allege?"

The detective gave Peter a long look and drew in his breath. "She went to the Alpha Woman's Clinic out in Metairie for an abortion. The abortion was performed, but the baby lived." He paused. "Have you ever heard of that?"

"No, never."

"Well. She says she heard the infant crying and then, doesn't know what happened to it. This was during the procedure and she was groggy from some valium they'd given her. She'd thought the abortion was all over, but then she claims she heard an infant's cry. Clear as a bell, she heard a baby cry, she says." He dipped his chin, looking at Peter from under his brows. "She claims when she heard that cry, everything in her changed. She realized that something had gone wrong and her baby was alive. Says she remembers screaming that she wanted to see the baby; that she wanted to hold it. That she'd changed her mind and not to hurt it."

"She remembers all of this?"

"Yep. Says they wouldn't let her see it. She remembers struggling with a nurse. Then another nurse, by the name of Clara Sonsten, came in while she was fighting with the first one. She was trying to get out of bed and the doctor was telling her to keep still, not to move." He shrugged. "That's all she remembers. Thinks she might have fainted or something."

"That's it?"

Mac nodded. "Doesn't remember a thing after that, not until she woke up in another room a few hours later. By that time, they told her the baby had died." He paused. "In her words, they just let it die."

"She's claiming homicide. Says the doctor killed her baby after it was born. Paul Rusher and I took her statement; it took a while to make some sense out of what she was saying."

Peter nodded. "And with the warrant you found the body."

"Yeah. In the freezer, like I said."

Peter frowned. "But, she went voluntarily to the clinic for an abortion?"

"Right."

Peter picked up a pen, rolling it between his fingers. "She consented to the abortion?"

"Yes. But she says this is different, says she didn't consent to what happened after. Apparently this is called a live birth."

Peter dropped his hands and thought about that. He'd never heard of such a possibility before, a live birth. An infant surviving an abortion. He looked at Mac. "How far along was she, the mother?"

"She's not completely sure. Says she thought she was twenty-two weeks, and the doc examined her and said he thought twenty-three. Stephanie Kand's autopsy will give us more information."

Peter stared, unable to fix the facts and the images in his mind. "All right," he said after a moment. "Let's go back a little. Did Miss Chasson give us any details?"

The detective who'd seen almost every crime in the book now hiked his shoulders in answer to Peter's question and gave him a helpless look. "According to Miss Chasson, they started the whole business on Tuesday last week, sent her home and told her to come back the next day. Said the procedure would take about twenty-four hours to complete, and that it would be easy and pretty painless. She says no one told her this could happen."

"And she'd signed consent forms?"

"Yes. She was really upset and so was the father. Her old man is Frankie Chasson."

Peter raised his brows. "Import-exports?"

"That's him." Mac heaved a sigh.

A minute passed while Peter thought about that. He knew the name. Everyone in the Parish knew that name. Then he rose and walked to the window. Beyond the levee he could see the Mississippi River, as busy this morning as any highway with freighters, tugs and barges, a paddle-wheeler heading upriver, still just below the Greater New Orleans Bridge—the GNO—that linked the Westbank, including Gretna, to the business district.

He clasped his hands behind his back, watching the ferry moving away from the landing toward the Eastbank. "Who told her that the baby died?"

"The nurse who was with her in the procedure room, that day." He looked down at his notes. "She said the nurse told her the infant died almost immediately, within a few minutes of birth. She asked, so the nurse told her it was a boy. Glory Lynn says they told her most women don't want to see the baby."

"So this has happened before?"

Mac shook his head. "I don't know. Like I said, I've sure never heard of this before. She says the same nurse drove her home. Glory Lynn lives in an apartment by herself. She called her father. They came down to the station . . . You know the rest."

Dropping his head, Peter rubbed the tops of his eyeballs. Then planted his elbows on the desk and dragged his fingers down his face as he looked at Mac. "So you got the warrant. How'd that go?"

"Her old man has some pull, let me tell you. At first we—Paul and I—didn't think we had enough, but Glory Lynn was bound and determined to find that baby, and the judge signed the warrant. She still thought there was a chance he might be alive. Old man Chasson was in a rage; said he was going to find his grandson one way or the other." He shrugged. "Glory Lynn was wild to find out what had happened to that child."

"Well, you know how it goes. We got the warrant. Best we could make out from Miss Chasson, it had been about twelve hours since she'd left the clinic. The search objective was limited to locating the body, and the procedure room that she'd occupied. Dr. Kand came along for forensics.

"We got there before they'd closed for business yesterday. Nurse Broussard was there, apparently in charge; the doc had gone."

"Only one doctor practices there?"

"Yes. Charles Vicari. I imagine we'll find he owns it. Anyway, Broussard wouldn't cooperate. Said she'd talk to her lawyer. Eventually we found the body in a freezer, back in a storage room."

"That's so hard to comprehend." Peter stared. "Broussard said nothing?"

"Nope. Tight as a clam. Just stood by watching while Dr. Kand did her thing. We took the photos. Bagged the body . . . it was so small, man." His voice was thick with sorrow and he shook his head. "And then we transported it to the morgue. Kand said she'd get on the autopsy and the forensic analysis soon as she can."

Peter bent forward, staring at the desktop, hands shielding his eyes. "Let me know as soon as you find anything, Mac, cause and manner of death."

"Should have that by Monday, she says."

Both of them fell silent. Minutes passed. Peter knew nothing about children. He wondered if the child, the fetus, whatever it was at that point, had fingers and toes, and facial features. Babies had never been a part of his life, nor were they a part of his life plan.

Mac broke the silence. "Like I said, it's a crazy case. But if Glory Lynn's right and there was someone else in that room—that second nurse, Clara Sonsten—we might get a break. I'll find her; get her statement.

"I'll talk to the receptionist again," he added. "We'll need another search of the place, and we'll want to search those records."

"Healthcare privacy issues won't make that easy." Peter chewed his lower lip. "Mac, check out this doctor's background, and his connection with the clinic. Find out how long he's been there, any ownership interest. Where he was before. Like that."

Mac nodded.

Peter straightened, mulling over the contradictions. Glory Lynn Chasson choosing an abortion and then changing her mind when the infant was born alive. Laws governing abortion prior to birth were clear. But what happened here? And where does the law draw the line? Did a woman's choice extend to an infant born alive?

That was only one question.

He roused himself. He needed more facts. Peter looked at Mac. "I'd like to see the autopsy and pathology reports as soon as Stephanie completes them."

4

SUNSHINE STREAMED THROUGH THE WINDOW OVER the kitchen table where Rebecca sat brooding. It was Monday morning and she was attempting to read the paper but couldn't concentrate. A slice of toast lay untouched on a small plate beside her. Beside the plate, an almost translucent fluted china cup of chamomile tea waited, steaming. She'd thought it would settle her stomach; better than her usual coffee.

The *Times-Picayune* was folded in half and then in quarters, and Rebecca struggled to focus her eyes and thoughts on the article she'd begun reading before the words had seemed to move. A sheen of perspiration shone on her forehead and cheeks as she fought to relax. Peter would be down soon and he'd spot that something was wrong right away. She didn't want to think about what was causing this nausea. She only had forty-five minutes to get to work and prepare for the meeting today and she wasn't feeling well. She didn't have the energy to put on an act that would convince Peter that nothing was wrong.

The article, which took up a significant portion of the front page, covered Peter's current trial, a death by raining bullets last New Year's Eve. Drugs were involved. This case had been stuck in the black hole of pre-trial preparation since then, and she knew that Peter was glad it was finally in court. The longer a defendant stalled, the more frightened and forgetful witnesses became. They were picking the jury this morning, she read, and glancing at the clock, she knew she'd gotten a reprieve from an inquisition. He was running late and he'd fly through the kitchen this morning at the speed of light to get to the courthouse.

Rebecca wrinkled her nose and turned the page. As a general rule she viewed litigation as a zero sum game—in order for one to win, someone else had to lose. She picked up the cup and sipped the tea, feeling the soothing warmth as it went down her throat. Shaking a crease from the page, she refolded the paper, and sipped the tea again, realizing that she was already feeling better.

When Peter strode in a few minutes later she could see that he was feeling good. Relieved that the nausea had disappeared, she set the paper down beside her and turned her face up for his kiss. He wore his first-day-of-trial suit, dark gray, with a white buttoned-down collared shirt and a blue and gray tie. She'd given him the tie for a present on his last birthday. He claimed it was his favorite.

He greeted her in a cheerful tone and planted a kiss on her cheek, and as she drew back, smiling now, her eyes followed him. His smile was contagious. She picked up the newspaper again, thinking how lucky she was to be married to this man that she loved so much. Two years of marriage with Peter had been just about perfect.

"I see you're picking a jury this morning," she said, peering at him over the paper.

"Yes, but my bet is they'll want to cut a deal." He went to the counter where the she'd left a thick mug there, the one he liked to use. "We're hoping anyway because our main witness has disappeared."

She shook her head, reading on. Witnesses terrified into silence; that was an ongoing problem. "You'd think there'd be some way to protect them."

"It's tough." He poured coffee into his cup and added a teaspoon of sugar. "Witnesses usually live in the same neighborhood as the perp. When he's picked up, they're still there, still living in the same place surrounded by gang members, and families and friends. Lots of animosity. It takes courage to talk." He gulped down the coffee.

"Can't you protect them?" She put down the paper and sipped the tea. She could feel it returning again, that wavy, foggy feeling.

"Only if they want to move out of the neighborhood, change their lives." Rinsing the cup under the faucet, he set it in the drain. "I'm letting Sam try this case. I'll be there with him, but he'll take the lead." Sam was a young assistant district attorney that Peter was training. He was aggressive and smart, a good combination, Peter had said. "The experience will do him good."

Settling back in her chair, Rebecca picked up the toast and took a cautious bite. *Please, please don't let that nausea return. Not now.* "I'll be home around seven or so tonight, I think," she said. "Will you be late?"

"I'll let you know. I'll call later." He left the room and she chewed the toast and sat very still, hoping this strange feeling was her imagination. She heard him going through the living room and the hallway and into the study they shared. When he returned a moment later with some files, he picked up the pace, heading for the door that led to the garage. At the door he stopped and picked up his briefcase. Then he turned, looking at her.

"Say. I've been thinking of something."

She turned, looking at him.

"We should celebrate your new partnership. If I'm right and the defense takes a plea this week, I'll be free in a few days. What's your schedule like this weekend? Could you get away for a couple days?"

Ah, to get away. To rest. Rebecca mentally scanned through her schedule. It just might be possible.

"We're closing the bond offering next week, but it's in good shape and Sydney could manage that for a few days." Sydney Martin, her favorite associate, was a hard worker. Both Rebecca and Amalise had taken the younger woman under their wings when she was hired five years ago, the third woman lawyer hired by Mangen & Morris.

With a broad smile she looked at him, brows high, and nodded.

He grinned.

She cocked her head. "Where would we go?"

"How about Italy." He smiled. "A quick trip to the Amalfi Coast? Maybe Positano for four or five days?"

Memories lit her mind—they'd spent their honeymoon in the village of Positano two years ago, staying at the hotel *Le Sirenuse*. Visualizing the small horseshoe cove at the foot of the town and the green blue water stretching all the way to the horizon, she could already feel the warm sun soaking into her skin. They could lounge on beach chairs for hours and think of nothing but each other.

"Peter, I would love that," she breathed. "I'll check my calendar and make it work if you can."

"Good," he said. "Let's plan on it."

Through the window she watched him back the car out of the driveway. Then, turning back to the paper again, the room spun. She braced her elbows on the table and covered her face. No. No. No.

Not again. Closing her eyes, she let a few minutes pass. And then she shoved back the chair and hurried through the kitchen and down the hallway, walls swaying around her.

5

WHEN SHE REACHED THE OFFICE, REBECCA looked up the name of a doctor. She looked at the number she'd written down and put down the pen thinking she was feeling better and perhaps didn't need a doctor after all. But then her stomach churned.

Resigned, she picked up the telephone and dialed.

The appointment was confirmed for four o'clock the following afternoon.

Just then Rose Marie hurried into the office, breathless.

Rebecca hung up the phone, turned back to her desk and looked at her secretary. "What's got you all riled up?"

"*Spin-it*—that new magazine everyone reads?" Rebecca nodded her head. "Well, they want to interview you. They saw the firm's partnership announcements, and want to fit you into an article they're doing on ten women in law to watch. But they're just about to go to press, so the schedule is tight."

Rose Marie threw up her hands. "They've chosen you as one of the group."

Rebecca stared. "Me?" *Spin*-it was a national magazine, very *avant-gard*. Her mind spun with possibilities. "What about Amalise?"

"They didn't mention her."

"Oh."

"They're on the phone right now. They want to schedule the interview day after tomorrow. Asked if that would work for you." Rose Marie smiled and glanced at the credenza where Rebecca kept her calendar. "Check the date, they're holding."

Rebecca picked up the calendar, still open, and put it on her desk, scanning the schedule. "I could do it Wednesday morning." If she was to escape to Italy with Peter, she'd need time on Wednesday afternoon to transition the bond deal to Sydney. She smoothed both hands over the pages of the calendar, then looked at Rose. "Is this for real?"

Rose Marie glittered. "Oh yes. They said they also saw the article in *New Woman* a few months ago. They want to send a reporter and a photographer and they've asked which hotel to book, one that's close. I told them the Roosevelt." Rose Marie spun around. "I'll go confirm it now." Looking back over her shoulder just before she disappeared through the door, she laughed and said, "Rebecca, you're going to be a star."

Rebecca, smiling, waved her off and pulled a file across her desk. But when Rose Marie was gone, she looked up again, her mind racing. She looked around the office, wondering if it would be possible to get into her new partner's office before the *Spin-it* people arrived. The managing partner could make it happen, she knew, and he'd be thrilled about the publicity for the firm.

Picking up the phone, she dialed Doug Bastion's office. Wanda Stanford replied that Mr. Bastion was busy at that moment, but that he would call back.

Rebecca knew better. Hold onto control. She said she'd wait.

Leaning back in the chair, Rebecca envisioned Doug's face when she told him of the article that would reach every client's desk. She was certain Doug would find a way to get her moved into the new office before those *Spin-it* people showed up.

For a moment she entertained the thought of inviting Amalise to join the interview. But, quickly she discarded the idea. That could complicate her request for a quick office move. And besides, they had chosen her, not Amalise . . .

⟡

Two hours later, carrying an armload of documents, Rebecca strode into the conference room on the eighteenth floor of Mangen & Morris for the meeting on the bond offering. Today, as an antidote to the anxiety that the brief nausea had wrought, she'd worn a gray silk suit that she especially liked, one tailored to fit her curves. The waistband was a bit snug today, but a day or two of eating only salads would take care of that.

And now she was feeling fine, just fine. The tone she'd heard in Doug's voice when she told him of the *Spin-it* request told her what she needed to know—she was number one in the new partner ranks. Moving her into the new office was not a problem, he'd assured. By Wednesday morning when the reporter arrived, she'd be ensconced in new furnishings. And the promise of the trip to Italy with Peter this weekend had lifted her spirits too. So as she walked into the conference room there was a spring in her step and a smile on her face and she shifted her thoughts to work, resolved to focus on nothing but this transaction for the rest of the day.

The large conference room featured a row of long windows on the outer wall of the room. Sydney and the other Mangen & Morris lawyers on the transaction team had arranged themselves along that far side of the table, with the sun at their backs. They'd saved the middle seat for her. In a large meeting this was generally the power seat. From Doug, Rebecca had absorbed the workings of power in this man's world; how to win it, hold it, and use it.

Four lawyers from the Dallas office of Johnson, Morris & Field sat facing the Mangen & Morris group. When she entered the room, she greeted Wilson Hanover, a partner in Johnson, Morris, and then she stopped and shook hands as he introduced her to the other lawyers from his firm. As she rounded the end of the long table and took her seat, Wilson congratulated her on the recent partnership announcement.

The Johnson, Morris team had arrived late yesterday afternoon they said, in time for dinner at Mr. B's on Chartres Street. They were staying at the Monteleone Hotel just across the way. Listening and smiling, Rebecca rose and walked to the credenza along the wall to her right, where coffee and ice and cold drinks were. Sydney volunteered that Mr. B's was one of her favorite restaurants, and then Wilson added they'd spent some time investigating the history of the Napoleon House, too. In 1821 the café, a local landmark, was the focus of a failed attempt to rescue Napoleon from exile on the island of Elba.

Oh well, someone said—not everything goes according to plan.

Rebecca filled a glass with ice, picked up a Tab and a napkin, and returned to her place at the table. She watched the drink foam as she poured it into the glass. "I think we're close," she said to Wilson, across the table. Her voice was casual, but she knew that if he agreed, the trip to Italy on the weekend would become a distinct possibility. "How do the changes we made last night look to you?"

"We've got a few points to discuss, but they're minor. Basically, I think we're on the same page."

Nodding, Rebecca slowly exhaled.

Sydney said that she'd ordered lunch to be brought in around noon. "Let's get started," Wilson said. Then, heads bent over the agreements, and pages turned.

Rebecca remained quiet as Sydney took over. That's how she'd learned when she was a young associate, too. "We'll start with the Offering Memorandum," Sydney said. Papers shuffled around the table. "Page by page. Does everyone have copies?"

As Sydney took the lead, working her way with the group through the pages of the first document for review, Positano rose before Rebecca—the sunshine, the sparkling water, languid days. The romantic nights.

Then, forcing herself to follow the discussion, Rebecca followed along as Sydney noted each Mangen & Morris change on each page, explaining the reasons and answering questions. Once in a while she made a comment or two, but Sydney was doing fine. She couldn't wait to talk to Peter, to assure him that she could go.

When lunch arrived at twelve thirty, they took a break. Rebecca left as the lunch cart rolled into the room. She took the elevator down to sixteen, and alerted Rose Marie that the move to her new office would take place that evening after everyone went home.

"Everything will be exactly the same when we arrive?"

"Yep." Rebecca snapped her finger. "Except the furniture will be new, and my office will be twice as big."

"How do they do it?"

"They take pictures."

Rebecca went into her office. Glancing down at the open calendar, she shivered as she saw the appointment with Dr. Roger Matlock jotted on the page for Tuesday afternoon. That worry wound through her again, like a thread, pulling tight.

It crossed her mind again that perhaps the appointment with Dr. Matlock was unnecessary. But she might as well see the doctor and rid herself of this fear once and for all, so that she could enjoy her weekend in Italy with Peter.

At three thirty that afternoon, the lawyers completed the review of the bond offering memorandum. The company's chief financial officer announced that he needed a break for a telephone call, and Sydney directed him to a small conference room down the hall where he could make the call in private. They would all take a thirty-minute break, Rebecca announced, and gradually the group dissipated, checking messages, stretching their legs.

Rose Marie looked up when Rebecca arrived. "Mr. Bastion's office called. Everything's arranged for the move tonight. And Peter called. He said he'll be very late. The jury selection is going slowly."

Rebecca's smile disappeared. If jury selection was going forward, the trip to Italy was unlikely. *Voir dire*, the process of selecting a jury, sifting the prospects with questions and observation was a critical and tense process. This was a bad sign. She swallowed her disappointment.

In her office she checked the stack of pink message slips near the phone, noting that Case Roberts, the CEO of Roberts Engineering had called. She put the rest of the slips down and picked up the phone. Just then, the room began to spin. With the dial tone buzzing, she lowered her forehead to her hand, pressing the phone between her shoulder and her ear. Seconds passed and then she placed the telephone receiver in the cradle before anyone answered and fell back against the tall soft back of the chair, closing her eyes.

When at last she opened her eyes, the room had quit spinning. This was driving her crazy.

But she planted her hands on the armrest and said to herself, *Self—this is your life.*

With a glance at her watch, she slowly turned the chair around, holding her head very still. Then she picked up the telephone, and dialed Amalise's office. "How about taking a short break," she said when Amalise answered.

"All right. The coffee room?"

"Yes. Five minutes." Rebecca hung up the phone and leaned her head against the back of the chair, thinking that maybe she should try again to return Case Roberts's call before going off to meet Amalise. But another wave of nausea ran through her like a ripple in still water. She closed her eyes, and within a few minutes it disappeared.

In the firm's coffee shop on the seventeenth floor she poured a cup of coffee, added a little milk, a spoonful of sugar, and chose a table near the windows to wait for Amalise. From across the room she watched Amalise walk in and reach into the refrigerator for a Tab.

"I'm glad you called. Work's still slow and I was getting bored." Amalise lifted the cold bottle and sipped the Tab, eying Rebecca. "Plus, Jude fixed a huge sandwich for my lunch, ham and Swiss cheese on rye with avocado—a lunch like that tends to make me sleepy." She grimaced. "Well, I added the avocado and the cheese." Then she set the bottle down on the table and sat back. "Maybe I'll start eating salads for lunch."

Rebecca snorted. Amalise had been saying that for years, and yet she never gained a pound. She looked at Amalise, smiling. "How's my best kid doing?"

"He's waiting for summer. And he's the star of his sixth grade class. At least we think so. Jude says Luke's somehow gotten his genes."

Rebecca laughed, since Luke was adopted that was impossible. But despite having a child almost in his teens, Amalise managed to keep up with her fast-paced life both at work and at home. How did she do it? She'd always had the ability to compartmentalize. She prioritized her home life and life at the office. And at work, Amalise took each problem as it came, focused and solved it before moving on to the next.

The question popped from her mouth. "How do you do it all, Amalise?"

Amalise wrinkled her brow. "How do I do what?"

Rebecca set the coffee cup down on the table, longing to confide the fear that was haunting her right now. In her mind, she tried to put the fear into words—responsibility.

No. It wasn't that. But, a baby would bring her life to a screeching halt. Her dreams would disappear like smoke. She'd always thought that Peter agreed with her that a child would be an encumbrance, but—for the first time, now really thinking the question through, she found she wasn't certain. The only thing she knew for sure was that, unlike Jude, Peter would never give up his work to stick around the house and help raise a child.

When she looked up, Amalise was studying her.

"How do you manage being a mother and . . ." She chewed on her lip, casting about for words—"And handling a demanding career like ours;

working nights, weekends, traveling?" With a self-conscious shrug, she added, "Do you ever have time for yourself?"

Amalise tilted her head. "That doesn't sound like you, Rebecca. You know as well I do that the reason this works for me is Jude. With his own company he has a flexible schedule that he can arrange around Luke's. He picks Luke up at school, takes him along with him to work. Cooks when I'm not there. He goes to the soccer games. And the housekeeper's around for the times when Jude's not free."

She gave a little shrug. "I wish I *could* do it all. But you and I both know that superwoman doesn't exist. We all have to make choices. And, even then, you've got to have a plan . . . and a back-up plan."

Rebecca nodded, leaning back. That was the sum total of the answer, of course. At least for Amalise. Rebecca had fallen for Jude years ago, before he and Amalise had finally recognized what had been right before their eyes since they were children: that they were meant for each other.

Rebecca thought of Peter, bound by his deadlines in court, so engrossed in each case. So dedicated to his work. What was possible for Jude would be impossible for Peter, no matter how much he wanted to be involved. "What if you didn't have Jude?" she pressed. "Would you still be practicing law?"

"No. At least, I don't think so. But lots of women do." Amalise clasped her hands and leaned her chin on her knuckles, still watching Rebecca. "And some don't have a choice. And then, think of all the women with children in other jobs who have to work; and single mothers with no one at all to help. Some working shifts, sometimes two jobs at a time." She dipped her chin and looked up at Rebecca. "So, what's going on?"

"Oh, I was just wondering how you managed." She smiled, feeling foolish. Peter had gotten it right—she did live in a gilded cage. "I've always thought I didn't want children, because they'd interfere with my plans, my career."

"Nothing wrong with that, if that's what you and Peter want. That's certainly a valid choice."

Amalise turned the bottle sitting on the table before her, watching it. "I'll admit something, Rebecca. I've curbed my ambitions some because of Luke. Like I said, we make choices. But I'm happy this way." With a little smile, she tucked her hair behind her ear. "I've finally managed to obtain some balance in my life."

But, balance takes compromise, Rebecca mused, and she'd never been good at that. She'd learned early and well from Mama that no compromise, no sacrifice, would ever be enough . . . you just had to keep on plowing. Since those days, since Elise had died, she'd figured it out for herself. You had to win to be best, and whatever it was you were shooting for, you had to win it on your own and then learn how to keep it.

"Now you, on the other hand . . ." Amalise was saying. Amalise's eyes sparkled as she pushed back her chair. She stood and picked up the empty bottle. "I fully expect that one day you will hold the office of managing partner of Mangen & Morris."

With a stiff smile, Rebecca glanced at her watch. Suddenly she realized that she was late; the meeting in the conference room upstairs had started long ago. They continued chatting as they moved toward the elevator.

Rebecca pressed "Up," and Amalise pressed "Down." With relief, Rebecca realized that the nausea was still gone. Maybe this time it wouldn't return. When Amalise's elevator arrived and the door opened, as if sensing that something was still wrong, she turned and gave Rebecca a quick little hug before stepping on.

6

ON TUESDAY MORNING THE JURY WAS empaneled. Peter gave his opening argument, and the defense offered theirs.

The testimony moved quickly. The State's case was strong, the evidence clear and tangible. The jury seemed entranced. The missing witness showed, to Peter's great surprise. The detective had dispatched a team to find him. Several other witnesses testified that they'd been present when the shooting took place and one identified the shooter. And, they all held to their stories even under cross-examination. Peter was elated. If things kept up this way, he anticipated resting the State's case in a day or two.

So it was no surprise when the defendant's attorney Johnny Wilcox wandered up to him at the beginning of the lunch recess and asked if they could talk. They used an empty witness room for the discussion. When at last they agreed and announced this to the court, the judge left the jury outside the courtroom while he went through the motions with the defendant and Wilcox confirming the deal, and the defendant's understanding. The defendant was subdued, but Peter knew that twenty years without probation or parole wasn't a bad deal for the State.

Afterward, Peter took the elevator up to his office, thinking that he would call Rebecca immediately and tell her they could pack. The trip this weekend was on. Striding through the outer area, feeling good, he said hello to Molly Brown, his secretary.

"Detective McAndrews left something on your desk," she said.

"Thanks." She handed him a slew of messages and he went into his office.

The large brown envelope was sitting on his desk. He hung his jacket on the coat rack in the corner, set the briefcase down on the floor beside his chair, and dropped the messages on the desk. Picking up the envelope, he saw that Mac had attached a note with *Hand Deliver* scrawled across the front in red.

Peter loosened his tie and took a seat. The package was labeled "Baby Chasson." He unsealed the envelope and pulled out the paper and photographs inside, the autopsy photographs and preliminary report from Dr. Stephanie Kand on the infant found in the freezer last week. Photographs were taken all along the way through an autopsy. The forensic analysis would come later.

Baby Chasson. Just the tag evoked the picture of a healthy child, alert and alive. Peter's good mood evaporated. With a feeling of dread he set the photographs aside and picked up the report.

The report was objective and thorough. The infant body, a male—as Glory Lynn Chasson had said—arrived at the coroner's office in a clear plastic bag to preserve the evidence. The infant had been wrapped in a small blue towel inside the bag. In the report Dr. Kand had set forth her conclusions first, before the details: The decedent was 11.80 inches, crown to heel. Weight, one pound, eight ounces, or 680.4 grams. Probable gestation: 24 weeks. Time of death was uncertain, due to the fact that the time of birth was uncertain—but she estimated that the small body had been found approximately nineteen hours after birth, with a margin of error of one hour.

Cause of death was respiratory failure.

Peter picked up the photographs before reading on, bracing himself as he looked at each one, fighting off emotions and attempting to maintain some objectivity, some distance. Photographs of the small body after cleaning showed no obvious evidence of malformation that he could see. But his was a meaningless evaluation. When he'd gone through the stack, he set the pictures down and skimmed through the detailed autopsy report.

Stephanie Kand had concluded that Baby Chasson had breathed on his own for some time after birth, before he'd died, but as yet she hadn't pinpointed exactly how long he'd survived. He hoped that she'd be able to come to a conclusion on the time in her forensic analysis. Peter leaned back in the chair when he'd finished reading, closing his eyes. What had happened in the time between birth and death, and how much time had passed? Mac had said Eileen Broussard refused to cooperate, at least so far. He wondered if Mac had been able to talk to the second nurse, Clara Sonsten, yet.

He placed the reports and photos on the desk, and then, clasping his hands on top of the desk, he looked at the walls before him. The sun outside was going down. Minutes passed, and then he read through the report again. In the gloaming, typewriters and telephones and voices faded, until, at last he was left alone in the silence, still turning the information over in his mind.

Glory Lynn Chasson's baby boy had been born alive. That much of her story was corroborated by the autopsy. So, why hadn't the infant been given medical assistance? It seemed clear to him that even if the clinic didn't have the facilities on site, they could have called an ambulance to take the preemie to neonatal intensive care.

Why hadn't the physician in charge, or one of the nurses, called for help?

Glory Lynn Chasson was entitled to answers to these questions. He sat there looking at nothing for a long time and thinking of those pictures. Suddenly he smashed his fist down on the desktop. And then he dropped his face into his hands. *Dear God,* he prayed. *Help me understand.*

7

ON TUESDAY MORNING, EXCITED ABOUT THE office move, Rebecca left home early, before Peter woke. When she walked through the doorway into her new office on the seventeenth floor of the Merchant Bank Building, she halted just inside and looked around. Three long windows across the outer wall let in sunlight. The bookcases she'd used in her old office were there on her left against the wall, stretching from the doorway, around the corner and ending two-thirds of the way toward the windows. She walked to the bookshelves and surveyed the rows of books. Sure enough, they were in the same order as in her old office.

She turned, inspecting the furniture placed in the corner, as she'd requested. There was a smooth cushioned beige sofa and two chairs. They weren't exactly what she'd have selected had there been more time, but they matched the carpeting on the floor and she could jazz them up with color-ful pillows. There were small square tables at each end of the sofa, and these tables were placed at an angle to the chairs. Someone had placed some of her Lucite transaction mementos on the two side tables and now they glittered, catching the sun. Each table held a lamp. And finally, a small, rectangular glass-topped coffee table was placed before the sofa, atop a pretty blue and white woven rug that tied everything together.

She stepped back, looking at the area as one would see it through a *Spin-it* camera lens. The lamps were too plain, she decided. They'd do for the interview tomorrow, but she'd probably replace them. She'd find some pretty antiques on Magazine Street, or down in the Quarter.

Then, she pressed her hands together, smiling. It was all just perfect for the interview.

Rebecca turned around, looking at the large desk on the other side of the room, facing the wall of books and the sofa and chairs. Walnut, as she'd requested. There was an elegant blue leather chair behind the desk now, the same shade of blue as in the rug. Behind the desk from wall to wall was a credenza, with cabinets underneath. The telephone was placed in the same spot as in her old office, near the chair behind the desk, along with her open calendar.

Walking quickly, she rounded the desk and sat in the chair, swiveling this way and that. Minutes passed as she stopped and gazed around in disbelief. She shook her head. The moving teams must have worked all night to get this done. The phone rang and she swiveled. Peter was right, she thought as she picked up the phone. She might be a bird in a gilded cage; but it was a very, very nice one.

Sydney was on the phone. The group in the conference room had an issue they'd like to discuss.

This had been a long day already, but the worst part of the day was just ahead.

Rebecca picked up her purse and, taking a deep breath, walked out to her secretary's desk. She told Rose Marie that she was leaving and that she might not be back today. Just to take her calls and she'd return them in the morning. "Is everything set for the magazine people tomorrow?"

Rose Marie assured her that everything was ready.

St. Charles Avenue was not yet overtaken by traffic and she made it to Dr. Matlock's office uptown with five minutes to spare. As she walked into the building where his office was located, the whole event seemed surreal. She'd made the appointment yesterday, but she'd banned it from her mind since. And now, here she was. She would get this over, and then move on with her life.

The examination had gone quickly. But now she had to wait. Dressed in the soft pink cotton gown the nurse had handed her, Rebecca sat at the end of the examination table, legs dangling, waiting for the doctor to return. The nurse—Alice Hamilton was her name—had said the lab test wouldn't take too long. Alice reminded her of someone from an old movie in the 1940s, the years after the war. Mulling this over, she guessed the nurse's age at sixty years old, or so. Her hairstyle fit that era, the old pin curls and finger-wavy hair just reaching her chin. And with the little white nurse's cap, she could have been starring on the battlefields of France in a scene with Audie Murphy.

She liked this woman. Alice had helped her get through this ordeal.

The room was cold after the doctor and nurse had stepped out. She hugged herself, rubbing the gooseflesh on her arms, wondering if the chilly feeling was some kind of premonition. She'd been unable to read the doctor's expression after the examination. She'd always prided herself on her ability to read faces, even under stress in negotiating sessions. But this. This was a kind of stress that she'd never had to face before. Usually, when she recognized tension, the tension rose from a situation over which she had some control.

But not now. She'd never felt so vulnerable to fate, so helpless, before.

She told herself to shake this off. Rebecca had always believed that worrying about something before it happened was a waste of time and energy, unless you could do something to prevent it. This in her mind was a universal dilemma: If nothing happens after all, you've worried for nothing.

Still. This time was different, she knew. Staring at the door she could almost see her perfectly ordered life coming apart. Cold fear radiated through her and she couldn't bring herself—no, she didn't want, did not want to name it. Because in the deepest part of her, Rebecca knew that if she was carrying a child, she had no answer. No plan, as Amalise had.

The fear turned to bitter impatience as Rebecca sat at the end of the examination table in the small room waiting for the verdict. The hands on the yellow clock on the wall pointed to numbers circling a happy face. But they seemed to have stopped. Four thirty-three and you're stuck, the clock said. It seemed she'd been sitting here all day. Still hugging herself, she tore her eyes from the clock and looked about. The pale yellow walls—neutral for unknown gender, she supposed, were irritating. Such an optimistic color. The walls were covered with framed, glossy pictures of couples unlike her, unlike Peter.

She squeezed her eyes shut and pressed her lips together, wanting to pray and not knowing how. And, indeed, not knowing whether anyone was really listening. The thought slipped in—if Peter were here, he'd know the right words to pray; and he'd be certain that God was listening.

Opening her eyes, with a flash of irritation she dropped her arms to her sides and bracing her weight on her hands, leaning forward, letting her hair fall around her face as she looked at the floor. Second passed, and then she arched her back and her neck and tilted her head far to one side, then to the other. Where in the world was Dr. Matlock?

Just then she heard heels clacking down the hallway, and she froze as the sound stopped just outside the door. As the door handle turned, her heart began thumping. She sat up straight, fingers gripping the edges of the table, the paper crackling beneath her as she waited.

Dr. Matlock, stethoscope still hung around his neck, walked in followed by Alice. One look at their smiles told her the fear was real. The thumping in her chest became a drum beating double-time while she sat waiting, unable to breathe. She sat very still as Dr. Matlock turned to his right and tossed the clipboard onto the table near the door, and wheeled back to her, smiling, slapping his hands together. And then he said the word that she'd been dreading.

"Congratulations."

She closed her eyes.

"You're going to be a mother, Mrs. Jacobs."

In his voice she heard the celebration, expectation—like the optimism of the yellow paint on the walls, the happy faces in the pictures. When she opened her eyes, she found him swinging his hands behind him, feet spreading apart, and then he planted himself before her with a wide smile on his face.

She had no backup. She had no plan.

From the corners of her eyes she saw that Alice was beginning to comprehend. Her expression remained blank, but her brows lowered until they were flat above her eyes. When Rebecca turned her head toward Alice, the nurse gave her a knowing look.

"I'd say you're about eight weeks along." Hands still caught behind him, he began rocking gently back and forth, brows lifting and falling as he spoke.

Shaken, she looked at him without moving, without saying anything as reality descended. Seconds passed before his smile began to fade. She saw his quick glance at the wedding ring on her finger, and she realized that she was an alien in his world.

Rebecca dipped her chin, blinking as tears pooled in her eyes and one slipped down her cheek. Immediately Alice—perceptive Alice—handed her a Kleenex. Crumpling it in her fist, she pressed it to the corner of each eye. When at last she looked up, her eyes fixed on the doctor behind him, as if by walking through she could undo the afternoon's events, like rewinding a reel of film. The doctor gave her a final, quizzical look. But Alice met her eyes. Alice understood.

She heard a wooden creak and turned to see Doctor Matlock lowering himself slowly into the chair beside the little desk. Knees spread, he leaned forward, letting his hands dangle between them as he gazed at the floor, contemplating what had just begun to sink in. Seconds passed, and then lifting his head with a long sigh, he said, "Let's have some straight talk, shall we?" Without waiting for a response, he picked up a calendar from the desk and studied it. "I take it this baby wasn't planned?"

She shook her head. He looked up. She said, "No."

"Would you like to have an ultrasound?"

"What for?"

He remained silent, watching her.

"How could this have happened?" she suddenly burst out. Flinging her hands in the air, she wiped tears from her cheeks. Alice handed over another Kleenex and she took it.

"We were always so careful; took precautions." Her throat tightened and shaking her head, she looked at him for answers. "How could this have happened?"

He shrugged, holding her eyes. "I can't answer that. Accidents occur. Now you must accept that this has happened."

"But, when?" Her voice moved up the scale with the question. She fought to stop the tears, blinking them back, weak with this feeling that everything, everything now was beyond her control. "I mean, when is it due?"

"Let's see," Dr. Matlock's voice turned gentle. He studied the calendar in his hand. "Today is May 18, so counting the date you gave on the forms as the beginning of your last menstrual cycle . . ." He pressed his lips together and flipped the calendar pages. "I'd say you're due on December 15. That's a Wednesday." He looked up and his tone was decisive.

"How can you be so precise?"

"I'm usually very close on the date, but it's not an exact science." He gave her a look, then grasped the prongs of the stethoscope around his neck.

She could think of nothing but the fact that she, Rebecca Downer Jacobs, was two months pregnant. How could she not have faced the obvious? Thinking back she realized that for the last few weeks she'd been ignoring telling changes in her body; skirt waistbands feeling snug, jeans a little tighter, the nausea. "I'll have to go on a diet," she thought aloud.

"No diets." Matlock wagged his finger at her. "And no alcohol or smoking. Not good for the baby."

Baby!

She stared in disbelief as he went on about vitamins and things she couldn't eat, or foods that she should, and the physical changes to expect in the weeks before her next appointment. The *It* girl's feet might swell, and then what would she do with all those lovely high heels, and she'd be gaining weight, of course. And through this barrage of information and thoughts of the consequences tumbling through her mind, one question stood high above it all: How could this have happened?

As she sat silent, listening, gradually the doctor's voice turned brisk. His smile had disappeared sometime during the last few minutes and now she saw the look of disappointment in his eyes. When he finished giving her the information that he thought she'd need and still she had no questions, at last his face went blank.

He pushed up and stood before her as he fingered the stethoscope and tightened his lips. "You're still in the first trimester, Mrs. Jacobs. There are options, of course." He said this as though the options were unthinkable.

She gave him a challenging look. The doctor averted his eyes, turning his wrist and checking the time.

"If I decide not to have it, do you . . . ?"

"No." His tone was abrupt. His grip tightened on the stethoscope as he frowned at her. "I hope you'll seek counseling before you make such a decision, Mrs. Jacobs. It's the law, I know, but it's a decision that you won't be able to go back and change. You'll talk it over with your husband, I know. But the two of you should really think that through before you make a decision."

"Yes. I know."

His brows met over his nose as he turned and plucked a colorful brochure from a plastic pocket hanging on the wall over the desk. He held it out and she took it.

"Take a look at this and if you decide to have the baby, come back to see me in two weeks. Or, make an appointment with your usual physician." She said nothing and he pulled a large bottle of pills from the pocket of his white coat.

"In the meantime, these are neonatal vitamins. Good for you, and the baby." He held them out, and she reached for them. He handed them to her and stepped back, nodding toward the bottle now in her hands. "That's enough for one month, but you should see a doctor before then. You'll need a prescription for the rest."

She watched in silence as he turned toward the door and Alice stepped aside. As the nurse followed the doctor from the room, she turned and glanced over her shoulder, giving Rebecca a reassuring look that everything would be all right.

8

DRIVING HOME FROM THE DOCTOR'S OFFICE, Rebecca put the top down on her British Racing Green Jaguar convertible and let the wind blow through her hair. She switched on the radio to station WTIX and listened to music from the sixties, turning the volume up high. The news did not seem real.

Bracing her elbow on the windowsill, she raked her fingers through her hair and thought about the *Spin-it* interview scheduled for the next morning, and then considered what she'd look like in comparison by the time the article was published, and then she imagined how Raymond and Preston and Doug and everyone else at the firm would react to this situation, what they'd say when she wasn't around. With only three women lawyers in the firm, she could hear it now—hire a woman, and that's what you get.

When she reached home, she parked the car on her side of the two-car garage. Inside, holding onto her purse and the booklet that Dr. Matlock had given to her and the vitamin bottle, she walked up the stairs to the master bedroom suite. There she kicked off her shoes. She took off her suit jacket and tossed it on the foot of the bed. She slipped the booklet into the drawer of the table on her side of the bed and deposited the vitamins in the cabinet behind the mirror over her sink in the dressing room.

For a moment Rebecca studied her reflection in the mirror, wondering if she was still looking at the same person she'd looked at this morning as she'd readied herself for work. At last she turned away and walked back into the bedroom.

Slowly she lowered herself onto the edge of the bed, hands on her lap, feet flat on the floor. She could feel her heart beating, pounding as she opened the table drawer and pulled out the brochure. Opening it quickly, before she could change her mind, she began paging through it, looking at the pictures and descriptions underneath. Each page had a photo of a blurry

sonogram with captions underneath for week one, week four, week eight . . .
she stopped there. She couldn't make out much from the sonograms, but
there was an artist's rendering on the page opposite that gave detail.

She began studying the picture, and without thinking, dropped her
hand down over her midsection. She studied the spine curving protectively,
tucking in for the adventure. She studied the tiny arms and legs, and feet with
toes already distinct. So soon? The fingers curled near the mouth and nose.
And she could see an ear growing on the side of the profiled head.

She looked at the picture for a long time. It was a personal choice, she'd
always replied when asked what she would do. Her own personal choice.
Then she shut the booklet and stuck it back into the drawer.

There are options, Dr. Matlock had said.

She went downstairs to the kitchen and pulled a Tab from the refrigerator, then wandered back through the living room, drinking from the bottle.
Crossing the living room and the hallway, with the stairs to her right, she
stopped in the doorway of the study that she and Peter shared. She leaned
against the doorframe drinking the Tab, looking over the room without
really seeing it as she tried again to absorb the news and what it meant. There
was a choice to be made now, or so she told herself.

When does life begin?

She closed her eyes, not wanting to think of this.

And, whose choice was this to make—hers, or theirs?

Peter loved her as she loved him. But, as she stood there staring into the
gloom, slowly, slowly the truth rose—who was she kidding. Peter had gone
along with her choice not to have children so far, but now she was pregnant,
all bets were off. His entire career was devoted to protecting the innocent, to
the sanctity of life in all its forms. There was no choice now to be made. Not
if she wanted to hold on to Peter's love.

Shaking her head, she pushed off the doorframe and turned, walking
slowly up the stairs, holding onto the neck of the bottle as she ascended,
wishing that the trip to Italy this weekend were still possible. She needed to
get away; needed time to think.

In the bedroom she set the bottle down and sat once again on the edge
of the mattress. Her entire life was turning upside down—her relationship
with Peter and their marriage, her ambitions and career; in her mind she saw
all of this flittering away like feathers on a breeze. She sighed. Consumed as

she and Peter had been by their careers for the past two years, neither had ever contemplated this situation. And even now, still, it didn't seem real.

She fell back on the bed, arms flung out to her sides and stared at the ceiling. Peter was the only man she'd ever really loved. And once she told Peter the news, this would all be real. What would happen after that? Her life would be forever altered. That bitter resentment that had begun in Dr. Matlock's office now filled her. This was her body, her career at risk—and regardless of his good intentions, Peter would leave her behind with the baby every morning when he left for work.

She would be the one responsible for raising their child.

Responsible.

With a groan, she scooted back on the mattress, pulled the pillow toward her, and stretched out. There she lay until at last, she fell asleep.

The sound of the front door opening downstairs woke her. She squinted into the dim light of the bedroom, confused, then abruptly sat up and looked about, remembering. A cloud of gloom enveloped her as she sat there without moving, absorbing the news all over again as it rose new and shocking.

Slowly she realized that Peter was home.

"Rebecca?"

"Up here," she called.

Her stomach lurched. Should she tell him now?

She looked at the clock and saw that it was early, still. He couldn't find her like this, disheveled, half-asleep at a time when she was usually downtown working. Scrambling for her shoes, she slipped them back on, and tucking her blouse into the waist and smoothing her skirt, she looked about. She needed time to think. She couldn't tell Peter just yet, not yet.

Time. She needed time to think things through before everything came tumbling down around her.

"What are you doing home?" His voice came from the bottom of the stairs and then he started up.

Hurrying into the bathroom, she flicked on the lights in passing and sat at her dressing table. She picked up the hairbrush and swiped it once through her hair. When he walked in, she was holding it midair watching him in the mirror.

"My calendar was free," she said. "So here I am."

He braced his hands on either side of the doorway and looked at her. She resumed brushing her hair.

"That's not like you, Rebbe. Did they clear the building for some reason?"

She tilted her head and looked at him in the mirror. "It's not that early." She put down the brush and turned to face him. "How's the trial coming along? Any chance we're going to Italy this weekend?"

He grinned and circled his finger and thumb. "They took a plea, looks like we're on. I'm ready if you are."

Relief flooded her. "That's great," she said. "I'll get things settled with Sydney. She'll take over at work while we're gone." Instantly she felt better. Time, she just needed time to get used to the idea that she would be . . . was . . . a mother before she announced the news to Peter. Surely there was a way to work this out without sacrificing her career. She would put the thoughts aside. For now.

"Let's go out to dinner, Rebbe. I'm already in vacation mode. How about Pascal's Manalefor barbecued shrimp?"

She turned to him, smiling. "Yes. Let's do that." Suddenly she was hungry. Swinging back to the mirror, she began brushing her hair again and planning what she'd pack to take along. Despite the dull lump of worry that lodged in her chest, she smiled at Peter in the mirror. "We'll plan the trip tonight."

He pushed off the door and glanced at his watch. "Give me half an hour. I've got some calls to make. I'll be down in the study."

As he turned away, she longed to reach out, to call him back and unburden herself right then and there—to let him hold her and tell her that everything would be all right. That their lives wouldn't change all that much; that her career could remain intact, even with a child. That they would work this out together. She twisted around, and called to him before she could stop herself.

With one hand still on the doorframe, Peter swung back into the doorway, brows lifted, smiling. Their eyes met, and for a split second she almost told him. And then she lifted one shoulder with a little shrug, and put down the brush.

"Never mind." She said. "It was nothing."

Pascale's Manale on Napoleon Avenue was, as always, crowded at seven o'clock, even on a Tuesday night. The tiled oyster bar near the door was busy. Customers sat waiting on benches in the corner of the front room under the celebrity photographs and behind the place where the oyster bar stood. The maître d' looked at them when they came in and nodded, then entered their names on the list. Peter located two seats at the bar for the wait.

"Busy tonight," Peter observed. He'd decided to put the case that Mac was working on a back shelf in his mind, for now. It could turn out that this was all just a terrible mistake. He didn't want this case to put a damper on the excitement about their weekend vacation.

Peter leaned close to Rebecca, his eyes shining. "I asked Molly this afternoon to make plane reservations for Thursday, late in the day, around five or so."

"Sounds great," she said.

He pulled back, grinning. "Well I'm looking forward to getting away for a few days. We haven't done this in a while."

She told him about her new office, how large it was, and how quickly the firm had moved her in, and all about the new furniture someone had picked out for her because of the magazine interview.

"You haven't told me about that! What magazine?"

So, she told him all the good news of the day—about the *Spin-it* people coming down from New York to interview her tomorrow, and about the article, how she'd been picked as one of the top ten women in the legal profession to watch on the national scene.

With a huge grin he opened his arms wide and pulled her into a hug. "I knew you'd make it in a big way, Rebbe. You're one amazing woman." He drew back, looking into her eyes. Then he tipped up her chin and gave her a soft, quick kiss before letting go. "I'm so proud of you."

Smiling, she pulled back her hair, twisted it, and let it fall. "Thanks, my love. And I can't wait for this weekend. I'm ready to go someplace far away, just the two of us." She paused and picked up the glass of water. "I'll have to be back by Wednesday next week at the latest though."

Peter swung his stool around, facing her. Fingering a lock of her hair, he gazed at her. "No problem, Beauty. We'll stay at *La Sirenuse* and relax." Their honeymoon hotel.

She saw her love reflected in Peter's eyes.

Someone called to Peter from across the room, breaking the connection between them. He waved and shouted something as she turned back toward the bar, eyeing the glittering rows of bottles near the mirror. Perhaps the place, the village, and the same hotel would bring good luck when she broke the news to Peter. Suddenly she couldn't wait to leave. Four days alone in Positano. She would confide in Peter there, and together, perhaps they could work this out. After all, help could always be hired.

Picturing the terraced buildings on the sides of the steep cliffs rising from the Tyrrhenian Sea, she let her thoughts flow to the ancient quiet village in Italy that for a few days would be a refuge. At a distance, from a boat in the water looking back, the town had a dreamy Moorish look, the buildings and houses all built close together and rectangular, all washed in white almost blinding in the sun, one atop the other. Then, at dusk, when colors deepen when the sun goes down, the vertical village turning amber, almost golden, like a scene on a Paul Gauguin canvas.

She slipped her hand into Peter's. He looked at her and smiled.

"Your table's ready, Mr. Peter." The voice came from behind them. They both turned. The elderly waiter stood a few feet away.

"Thank you," Peter said, standing. He placed his hand on the small of her back as they followed the waiter to a table.

The waiter brought white bibs and they ate barbecued shrimp, peeling back the shells and dipping the shrimp into the spicy buttery sauce while they planned the trip. As they ate and laughed and talked, waves of emotion swept through her, laughter and happiness and anticipation, warring with a clandestine feeling of despair and creeping desperation. But, she concealed that part from Peter. The only thing that she was certain of from moment to moment right now, she realized, was that she could not imagine living the remainder of her life without Peter at her side.

Oh how she loved him. She would have to have the child, because she could not lose him.

She could not.

9

THE NEXT MORNING, WEDNESDAY, REBECCA TOOK an early phone call with Warren Williams, chief financial officer of Roberts Engineering, the new client that she'd brought on board. They were discussing his idea of investing in a gold mine in Nevada. Rose Marie stuck her head in and signaled that the New York people were here from the magazine. Rebecca nodded and held up one finger, listening. A moment later she hung up the phone and turned back to Rose Marie. "They're already here?"

"Yes."

"They're a little early." Rebecca stood and smoothed her skirt. "Do I look all right?"

"You look fine. Great, actually." Rose Marie headed for the door. "They're upstairs in reception. I'll go get them."

A few minutes later Rose Marie guided two men through her office door. Both were dressed for cold weather. She stood and the first one, the smaller of the two, stuck out his hand and introduced himself as Tom Marfrey. She said she was glad to meet him and shook his hand, looking over his shoulder at the man trailing behind him carrying a light on a tall stand.

Tom Marfrey turned and said, "This is Arthur Timmons, our camera."

"Art," the cameraman said, giving her a nod. She watched as he stepped into the office, sweeping his eyes over the angles and corners, the shadows and light with a purposeful look. Turning back to Tom, she caught him inspecting her. She supposed she'd passed his test because he began to shed the heavy coat. "We'll set up and get a few shots before we do the interview," he said.

She took Tom's coat and put it in the closet near the door.

Closing the door and turning around, she bumped into Art. "Excuse me," he said, pushing past her with the light. She stepped aside to give him room. He set down the light, then tossed his own coat over the chair in front of her desk, and then went back out into the hallway.

She walked to her desk and sat on the edge to get out of the way, bracing her hands behind her. "Just tell me what you need."

Rose Marie appeared in the doorway. "Just watching," she said when Rebecca glanced her way.

Tom stood in the middle of the room, hands on his hips, turning, studying the area. "It'll take us a few minutes to set up." He glanced at Rebecca. "This is a nice office. Good light."

"Would you like coffee or Coke-Cola?" Rose Marie asked.

"No thanks. We had breakfast at the hotel."

Rose Marie shuffled aside as Art reappeared carrying a camera tripod this time. Tom motioned to his right, toward the windows. "Can you shoot from there?"

Rebecca wandered out into the hallway with her secretary while they discussed the lighting. Leaning against Rose Marie's typewriter, she folded her arms and looked down the row of desks outside the attorney's offices.

Tom came to the doorway and motioned. "Let's get started." As she entered the office, he gestured toward the sofa. "Sit right over there. Art will do the shots with you sitting on the sofa first, and around the office. Then, when we're ready to start the interview, you'll sit in this chair, and I'll sit here on the sofa, facing you and we'll just talk."

"All right." Rebecca took the spot he'd indicated on the sofa and sat down. She crossed her legs and watched Art setting up the camera near the windows.

"The light's fierce in here," Art said, peering through the lens. "We weren't prepared for this sunshine. We left gray skies and cold wind behind yesterday out of LaGuardia."

"The weather here is always like this," Rebecca said.

Tom let out a laugh. "We sound like tourists, huh? I've been here in August." Hands on his hips, he looked at Ray then studied her position, then turned in a circle taking in the entire room. At last, facing her again, he said, "Oh, and we'll need some shots in a conference room. Can you arrange that?"

Rebecca said sure, and stepped out of the office to tell Rose Marie. Art followed her out and walked on down the hallway. She asked Rose Marie to try to get the executive conference room on the eighteenth floor for the pictures, if it was free. Walking back into the office, she had to step aside again for Art, who came in this time carrying two large silver-looking umbrellas. To filter the light, he said. He opened the umbrellas in the middle of the room, and angled them around the interview area they'd chosen.

Tom and Rebecca sat together in the corner while Art looked through the camera and moved the umbrellas around several times. When Art said, ready, Tom stood up and walked to stand behind him, telling her the photographs would take about twenty minutes. Art said he'd do a few test shots. Then he'd take a series of photos with her sitting on the sofa, first.

Tom sat behind her desk scribbling in a notebook while Art took the first pictures. He guided her into different poses, talking and clicking, sometimes with a small camera and sometimes with the larger camera set on the tripod, which he moved around. They took shots of her in front of the bookcase, and then Tom moved and Rebecca sat behind her desk and pretended to be writing, talking on the phone, and Art took pictures there.

When the photography was finished, Tom walked toward her, waving his hand at the rows of leather bound books. "What are all those?"

She moved to the chair, as he'd earlier instructed and looked over at the bookcases. "Oh, that's my work." Tom took a seat on the sofa beside her. "Six years of transactions I've worked on here at Mangen & Morris are recorded in those." She smiled. "Each one brings back memories."

He set a black-cased tape recorder on the coffee table, and looked at her. "Do you mind? This is more efficient."

"That's fine."

He checked the tape, then turned it on. "Okay. We were talking about the books in your office and you said that each one brings back a memory. Are they good ones?

She grinned. "Yes. Great memories." The camera clicking surprised her.

From behind the camera, Art gave her a thumbs-up. "Good smile," he said. Leaning around the camera, he twisted the lens. "You're the first one we've interviewed for this article who's smiled when explaining that."

"Well those volumes represent six years of my life." *Doug will love this,* she thought. An article in *Spin-it* was such good publicity for the firm. And for her, too.

"That's a good quote, about the books." Tom settled back and crossed his legs. "We'll use it. That's what readers what to know, how you like your work. How you feel about things. What's it like to be you, and what it took to get here." He looked at Art and Art nodded. "Let's get started, shall we?"

The first question was no surprise; it was the one everyone asked first. "When did you decide you wanted to be a lawyer, and why?"

She gave him her best smile, knowing that she'd never tell the whole story. In fact, she'd called Mama on Sunday to give her the news that she'd made partner, thinking maybe this once, just this one time there'd be a response, something more than, "Oh, that's nice," before launching into a stream of regret over the loss of her baby twenty years ago, and how Elise would have chosen another path . . . or something worse.

Unspoken were the words—Elise was gone, and that was Rebecca's fault. Now, she roused herself, looking at Tom and holding onto the smile.

"Mostly," she said, folding her arms and settling back, "it was just good luck." That wasn't true either, of course. She'd worked nonstop for thirteen years to get here, four years undergraduate, three in law school, six as an associate. But her tone, practiced and breezy carried her now. They talked for an hour about how it was to be a young woman partner in a major law firm when, at times, she was the only woman in the room.

"What do you like best about practicing corporate law?"

She pursed her lips and thought about the question. After a few seconds passed, she said, "I've worked on so many different areas of business over the years and my practice is constantly challenging. One day you could be financing a new resort hotel, the next you're working with investors in gold mining, or international shipping." She spread her hands. "The variety is fascinating."

"You like the challenges."

They talked about the little problems women still had to face—the private clubs where clients dined at lunch and women were not yet allowed. Problems that men in the profession had probably never given any thought, but that she and Amalise had worked through over the years. And they talked about the psychological rewards, the feelings that you've accomplished something, that your work has helped clients reach their goals at the end of a transaction.

Tom said that he could see in her manner, in her tone of voice and the expressions on her face when she talked about her work, how much she loved what she was doing.

And he was right, she replied.

Rose Marie stuck her head through the door and informed them that the conference room was reserved only until noon.

Rebecca glanced at her watch and then at Rose Marie. "Thanks," she said. It was eleven thirty. "We'll take the elevator. It's on the eighteenth floor," she said to Tom.

Tom glanced at Art. "Are you ready to go on up?"

Art was packing up the umbrellas. "Yep. You take the tripod and camera. I'll carry these, and come back for the rest."

Tom leaned toward the tape recorder, and then suddenly straightened up again, turning back to her. "One more thing. Before we wrap this up I have a question: Thinking back to the time when women first got the vote, and some struck out on their own. Back in the 1920s. How would you compare the issues that generation of women faced in the business world, in comparison to your own?"

"Today?" Rebecca looked around at her lovely new office, and then back at Tom. "It's kind of like the moonshot, you know. Once NASA got things going in the sixties, we landed on the moon within the decade. That's where we are today, we women. We're on the moon. Now we'll shoot for the stars if we want to. Or some of us will choose to work at home. But either way, because our grandmothers and mothers got things started, now we have choices."

"Any tips for making it in a man's world?"

She smiled. "Keep wearing lipstick. It's our world, too."

Tom laughed and wrote that down. Then he switched off the recorder. Art picked up the closed umbrellas and they followed him out.

"Are you free to have lunch with us after this?" Tom said as they walked toward the elevator. "Our flight's at four."

"Sure. I'm free until one thirty. My secretary can book us a table at Brennan's, or we can take our chances with the line at Galatoire's." She gave him a sideways look. "I'll treat. I have my own credit card now."

10

THE NEXT MORNING REBECCA AND PETER each packed for the trip and Peter put the suitcases in his car. She would spend the morning in her office and he'd wrap things up in his and pick her up downtown at two o'clock. Their flight left at four in the afternoon, giving them plenty of time to check in and relax.

At the office she was happy to find that Sydney was already working with the transaction team to finalize the bond documents for the closing. Changes to the Offering Memorandum had been agreed on by all parties. After a quick call with the chief financial officer of her client, the issuer of the bonds, Rebecca strolled down the hallway to Amalise's new office.

She stood at the door before entering, watching Amalise. She was fully absorbed in her work, reading and making notes in the margin. She thought about the differences between the two of them. While she, Rebecca, put all her energy into a transaction until it was completed, Amalise seemed able to divide hers up between home and work. That talent had helped Amalise make it through the darkness of an earlier marriage that had left her a widow. And, she guessed, maybe that's what made her arrangement with Jude such a success.

With a quick series of raps on the door, she walked into the office.

Amalise looked up and Rebecca could almost see her clearing her mind, shifting her attention completely from one thing to the other as she put the pencil down on the desk and smiled. "Hey. Come on in." She straightened and leaned back in the chair.

"I came to take a look around." Rebecca meandered about. Against the far wall near the windows, Amalise had arranged a conference table instead of the sofa and chairs that Rebecca had chosen. But there was the same L-shaped bookcase and the same leather-bound deal books, and the same Lucite mementos.

Here, however, the wall behind the conference table was covered with pictures of Luke and Jude, and Amalise's mother and father—Maraine and Judge Catoir—at their home in Marianus. And there was a picture of Amalise and Rebecca standing together on the steps of Tulane Law School in their gowns on graduation day six years ago.

"Nice." Rebecca walked over to the conference table and picked up a small glass sculpture in the center of the table, turning it in her hands, feeling the smooth surface and sharp edges.

"It is nice. Fun to have so much space, isn't it? And, you were right about not worrying about getting work—Preston's just asked me to head up a transaction for one of his clients." Amalise massaged the back of her neck as she looked at Rebecca. "As usual, we've got a short deadline. But at least I've got plenty to do now."

Rebecca put the sculpture back down on the table and turned to Amalise. "Do you have a few minutes to talk?"

"Sure. I've got a meeting later on this afternoon, but I've got time right now. What's on your mind?"

Rebecca crossed the room, closed the door, and took a seat in a chair before Amalise's desk. Church bells from Jesuit's down the street tolled eleven and the bells stirred something in her now. A melancholy feeling; the exuberance she'd felt after the *Spin-it* interview, and the excitement of the trip to Italy vanished as everything now came swooping back, bringing an acute sense of the dilemma she was facing. The thought of having a child terrified her, she suddenly realized. And those bells just made things worse, taunting her with comfort in a faith that she didn't have, the comfort of knowing that an absolute truth existed, like Amalise believed.

Right now, she wanted a guide. She needed something like a menu with the choices labeled and stars placed near the favored dishes. She looked down, scratching at the fabric covering the armrest in an absent manner. "I've got a free weekend coming up, so Peter and I are taking off this afternoon. We're going to Italy for a few days."

"Oh, I love the way you two just take off like that. You're like Scott and Zelda. It must be fun." Amalise leaned back with a dreamy look in her eyes. "Sometimes I wish Jude and I could do things like that, just for a day or two."

Rebecca was silent.

Amalise sat up straight and crossed her arms. "My idea of a weekend off these days is Audubon Park with Luke." Then she added quickly, "Not that I really mind."

"I imagine Luke could make a trip to the park unique," Rebecca said. "Remember when I took him to see the meteorite a few years ago?" Local lore was that the large stone in the middle of a fairway in Audubon Park was a meteorite which had fallen from space long ago. Luke was fascinated with science, especially anything from outer space.

Amalise laughed. "He talks about that all the time. Now he's begging to go to the NASA museum in Houston. He wants to see the moon rocks." She rested her elbow on the chair armrest and her chin on her fist.

Luke was a curious child, blooming under Jude and Amalise's constant love. He was inquisitive and dug into things until he found answers and understood them. Much like Amalise, she thought. Despite the depression, Rebecca smiled at the thought of Luke. He loved to read, and most of what he read was science and biology and physics, not the usual children's stories.

Amalise brought her back. "But what did you want to talk about? Is something wrong?"

Glancing down at her skirt, Rebecca brushed a piece of lint from the fabric. Yes, she had a problem.

Amalise waited, clasping her hands before her on the desk. Outside the office typewriters clacked, phones rang, footsteps passed.

It took a moment to begin, but once Rebecca began the words spilled out. Amalise listened in silence. Rebecca was vaguely conscious that her voice had turned monotone, as if none of this was real, as if she was telling someone else's story. She told Amalise of the visit to Dr. Matlock, and the news that she was pregnant.

Looking up, she caught the beginning of Amalise's smile and held up both hands. With a start, Amalise's smile died.

Rebecca went on. She told Amalise about the agreement she'd wrung from Peter before they'd married—the promise, so far as she was concerned, that had been at the core of their marriage vows—a pledge of the heart each to the other that there would be no children in their marriage. Never. No children would ever come between them or distract from their careers.

No child would ever be harmed by her again. Like Elise. But that she kept to herself.

"It was our choice," she said, conscious that her voice was growing thick with gathering tears. She swallowed.

"I understand. Like I said the other day, you had every right to make that choice, you and Peter." Amalise gave her a knowing look. "Have you told him yet?"

"Not yet."

Amalise leaned forward, arms on the desk. "Hmm. Well, how are you feeling, physically, I mean?"

Rebecca folded her arms and looked off through the window. "I'm in good health, the doctor says. There's been a little nausea." A second passed. "And I'm getting fat."

"You're not." Amalise smiled and gave her a sideways look. "At least, not yet. But I'll tell you if it happens."

Rebecca swung her eyes back to her friend, and Amalise added, "And besides, your skin is positively glowing. I don't know how I missed this."

"It's just hormones, Amalise."

"So, when will you tell Peter?"

She squeezed her eyes shut for an instant. "I guess I'll have to do that on this trip. But, Amalise, he's not like Jude. Peter works into the night most evenings. His life is structured; every minute on his calendar is filled." She hesitated, watching Amalise. "I don't even know if he'll be happy about this surprise. This will change our lives completely."

Vehemently, Amalise shook her head. "I think you're wrong. You're underestimating Peter, Rebecca. He's a good man. He's—"

"Men have a right to their choices, too, you know." She drew a long, deep breath. "I know my husband. The moment Peter understands that I'm pregnant, he'll see me as a different woman. Over time our relationship will change."

"The word is 'we.'"

"What?"

"You're both parents of this child. The operative word is 'we.'"

"I'll be the one with all the responsibility."

Amalise brushed her hand over her eyes. "Oh Rebecca." She leaned forward, fixing her eyes on Rebecca's across the desk. "Look. You can do this. There's a life growing in you, Rebecca. A baby, a gift from God. A special blessing."

Rebecca ducked her head. "I don't have your kind of faith, you know. I wish I did. I wish that I had a star to follow, like you."

"Then look for it! Find it."

"What?" She looked up.

"If anything should convince you there's more than we can ever hope to understand, it's that little spark of new life inside of you." She held Rebecca's eyes. "Medically, scientifically, a baby is a miracle. You're a lawyer. Check out the facts."

Rebecca leaned her head back against the chair, closing her eyes and remembering the pictures in that pamphlet that Dr. Matlock had given her, imagining the baby inside of her. Suddenly, with the force of lightning new images arose, submerging the beauty of the infant in a raging storm of emotions. She could see the pink bicycle mangled under the wheel of the car. She could hear someone screaming in the distance, she could hear the car horn blaring. And she could see that one little shoe near the curb.

Her hands flew up to cover her ears; and the images disappeared.

Embarrassed, she looked up. From across the desk, Amalise stared. *Amalise would never understand,* she thought as she brushed back her hair, lifted it from her neck, and let it fall around her shoulders. No one could ever understand the desperate panic filling her, and the need for something solid to hold onto. Rebecca Downer Jacobs, a woman who'd always prided herself on overcoming emotions, found herself drowning in them now. Suddenly she realized that she had to leave.

Pushing back the chair, abruptly she rose. With a bright smile, she said to Amalise, "Listen, Peter will be here soon."

Amalise stood, silent, still studying her face.

"Our flight leaves at four, so I'd better get back to my office. I've got a lot to do." Heading for the door, she said over her shoulders, "You know how it is when you're trying to get away, Amalise. Sydney's got questions; Rose Marie has questions."

But Amalise had reached her. Rebecca turned and was swept into a hug. Tears rose and she blinked them back as she rested her head on Amalise's shoulder for an instant. Just for one moment.

"I'm always here, you know," Amalise whispered in her ear.

"I know." Rebecca nodded as she pulled away.

But Amalise pressed both hands on Rebecca's shoulders, gripping them, holding her eyes. "Talk to Peter while you're on this trip. Give him some credit, Rebecca. I know you'll make the right decision. And the moment you feel that baby move, your life will change," she said.

Rebecca turned away. "That's just what I'm afraid of."

11

PETER SPENT THE MORNING IN SEVERAL hearings, but was able to reschedule most for the following week when he'd be back from the trip. Anything active and moving toward the head of the line he sent on to some of the junior ADAs to handle in the interim.

He was reviewing files, closing the ones to be sent to archives, when Mac showed up. He stood in the doorway, looking at Peter. "Will I be able to get in touch with you over the weekend if anything comes up in the Chasson case?"

"Molly has phone and fax numbers for the hotel. Any luck finding that second nurse?" He set down the file he'd been reading. "The one Glory Lynn says she saw in the delivery room after the baby was born?"

"Clara Sonsten. She's quit, no longer employed. Got another job. There's a talkative little receptionist at the clinic though." He stuck his hands in his pants pockets. "Girl named Melanie Wright. Says she doesn't know where Clara might have gone and wouldn't give out her address. But I'll find her."

"Wonder what happened there."

"Could be interesting. At least this might make it easier for her to talk. And get this, Eileen Broussard and Charles Vicari are married, so the receptionist says. I didn't even think to check those records, but that means we just lost one witness who was in the room."

"Sure. She'll hide behind the privilege. Let's think about that. She could be an accessory; maybe we could work out a deal." Peter rolled his lips together, thinking this over

"What's the receptionist say about her?"

Mac tilted his head. "That bird sounds a little strange. She's a cold one, Melanie says. Came down from Chicago about six months ago, same time Charles Vicari arrived. They both worked at New Hope Hospital up there. New Hope's a private hospital. She thinks they haven't been married all that long. Thinks they only got hitched a few months ago."

"Bad luck. Did you call the hospital?"

"Talked to a couple people up there. But you know how that goes. You have to have a source in a hospital; they're tighter than clams with employee and health information."

Mac shrugged and strolled into the office. Stood at the window, arms hooked behind his back, looking out for a moment. He turned, facing Peter. "I'm gonna have to go up there to get anything done. Spent the morning on the phone while they switched me from one office to another. They'll give you the dates of employment, but not much else."

"You think the receptionist, this Melanie Wright, knows anything?"

"She might. She's a talker, too."

"Good."

Peter leaned on his elbows and massaged his temples and forehead. "This case is keeping me awake at night." He wouldn't have confided this to anyone but Mac. "That photo of the baby in the towel in a freezer. I can't shake it."

He dropped his hand on the desk before him and straightened. "It's hard to imagine what could have happened. Glory Lynn Chasson says she hears that infant cry, and then it disappears. The next time anyone sees it is in a freezer." He clamped his hands behind his head and looked off, past Mac and through the window. A thin layer of dust coated the glass, making the day and the scene on the river look slightly hazy.

Mac shook his head. "You sure you want this case on your back, Counselor? It's not too late to get it into the system."

Peter's eyes flicked back to Mac. "You bet I want this case. I'm going to find out what happened here. I want to know if the baby was alive, and if it was, whether that doctor, Charles Vicari, intentionally let it die."

"And why," Mac added in a laconic tone.

Peter nodded. "And why."

Alice Jean Hamilton, Dr. Matlock's nurse, had had a long day. She slipped off her shoes, leaving them in the usual place near the front door of the living room, and walked in stocking feet into the kitchen. Finally, Thursday afternoon had arrived. With a sigh of relief, she filled the teapot with water, set it on the burner and turned on the fire underneath. Then she retrieved the china cup and saucer from the shelf—a delicate flowered pattern, she'd found the set on Magazine Street—and she took the tea bag from the box in the cupboard and set them both down on the counter.

She heaved a sigh as she pulled out a chair at the kitchen table in the corner, and prepared to wait for the water to boil. What a day. Her feet hurt. You'd think a doctor's office would be easier than working in a hospital. Well, perhaps it was, but the work was boring in comparison, and she was still on her feet all day. Here she merely trudged up and down one short hallway all day long behind the doctor, instead of hustling up and down those long corridors at New Hope where something was always going on.

And the files that Matlock kept. Is this what she'd come to after thirty-seven years of nursing? All in all she'd rather be in hospital pediatrics with the newborns, but . . . that part of her life was over. Done. And just as well. Stretching her legs, she wiggled her toes under the table, glad to be finally off her feet.

Behind her the phone on the wall began to ring. For a moment she considered not answering. Friends from the early years here were long gone by the time she'd moved back. And she had cut all ties but one with people in Chicago and at New Hope. But the phone kept on ringing, so, with an air of resignation and irritated at the interruption, she stood and walked over there.

"Hello?" She leaned one shoulder against the wall.

"Alice?"

Instantly she recognized the voice and tensed, ducking her head to speak directly into the mouthpiece, as if someone else might hear. "Is something wrong?"

"I said I'd call if anyone was asking."

"Oh no." Gripping the receiver, she pushed off the wall, pressing the telephone close to her ear. She pressed her hand against her forehead, looking at the floor.

The voice on the other end said nothing.

Seconds passed and then Alice said, "I'd hoped . . . Well all right then, tell me."

"Listen, calm down, it's not that bad. I was on desk duty this afternoon and took a call. I think it was the police down there, Alice. He said he was a detective something or other with the Jefferson Parish Sheriff's department. Down there near New Orleans."

"Did he ask for me by name?"

"No. Let me finish. He wasn't looking for you. He wanted to know about Dr. Vicari. And Eileen."

Alice was silent, struggling to put the pieces together in her thoughts. What did Charles Vicari have to do with New Orleans? The last she'd seen of him was in Chicago, at New Hope Hospital.

"Are you there?"

"Yes. Yes, I'm here." The room seemed to sway as she dealt with the idea of Charles Vicari in the vicinity. Leaning back against the wall, another worry took seed. Dr. Matlock. What would happen to her job if he knew? Those doctors all stuck together, she knew. She'd lose her job if he found out, of course. Nobody wants to be involved with trouble. She wondered if he'd go after her license, too.

She took a deep breath. "You say he didn't ask for me. Do you know why he called?"

"Like I said, he wanted information on the doctor, and Eileen Broussard, too. How long they were here, things like that. I told him I couldn't give out any information. Told him to call personnel. Say, did you know those two got married?"

Alice said nothing.

The voice turned soothing. "Look. Whatever's going on, he didn't ask a thing about you. There's no way anyone could know, so just stay calm. I'm just letting you know someone called about Vicari, like you asked—like I said I would."

Alice nodded. Then remembering her manners, she said, "I appreciate it."

Slowly her lungs filled again with air. Her grip on the phone relaxed. "Thanks for letting me know. And you'll call if anyone asks again? About either of them, or if anyone mentions me, or if you find out what's going on?"

"Sure. You know I will."

"Okay. Thanks again." She hesitated. "Really, thank you, sweetie."

"You're welcome."

She hung up the phone, and stood looking across the room at the tea pot on the stove. Just then it began to whistle. Just in time—she could really use a hot cup of tea right now.

12

THEY TOOK DELTA TO NEW YORK. The first class seats in the Pan Am Boeing 747 Clipper to Rome—the sleeperettes, as the pretty hostesses in their crisp blue and white uniforms called them—reclined all the way back. She could forget everything and doze through most of the trip. Beside Rebecca, Peter was working. He'd pulled a brief from his briefcase that he said was due next week. The case was coming to trial in two weeks. While the business and tourist class passengers filed onto the plane behind the curtain, the hostesses began passing around drinks and hors d'oeurves.

A hostess halted before Peter and Rebecca's seats with the tray of appetizers and both Peter and Rebecca shook their heads. Rebecca asked for a glass of ginger ale, and Peter, tomato juice with lemon. She returned with the drinks right away. Dinner would be served in about an hour, she said.

Peter put down his brief. He picked up his glass and proposed a toast. "To our weekend."

Rebecca lifted her glass to his. "To sleeping late in the mornings."

Peter gave her a deep look and a long, slow smile. "To late evenings."

The glasses clinked. She smiled at the thought that rose. "Remember the little beach at the foot of the steps where the fishermen keep their boats, their *barcas*?"

"I sure do. And I remember it's a long way down the cliff from the hotel, and steep."

"Yes. But that's easier than climbing back up."

Peter looked off, puckering his forehead.

"What are you thinking about?"

He shook his head and the corners of his mouth grew tight. "I can't get my mind off a complaint that Mac's been investigating. It's gotten under my skin."

"A new case you're taking on?"

"Yes. That is, if we go forward. It's too early yet to tell. We've just received the autopsy report."

She held up her hand. "No autopsies on this trip."

He didn't laugh, as he usually would.

She studied him. "Want to talk about it?"

"Not now. Not this weekend."

Peter set the glass down on his tray-table and returned to work. Rebecca pressed her hand over the little bulge that she'd discovered that morning. She wasn't certain if the bulge was real, or just her imagination. But the waistline of the loose pants she'd worn for the long flight did seem snug. She'd worn a long matching sweater to cover it up, and now, with a glance at Peter that told her he was still engrossed in his work, she unfolded the blanket the hostess handed her, gave it a shake, and spread it across her legs. Then she yanked it up high enough to hide the waistband that she was unhooking.

When the button was undone and the blanket was in place, she reached for the large purse she carried when traveling, and pulled out a novel. The nausea seemed to have disappeared. She hadn't felt the sickness in the last day or two. Maybe, just maybe, that torture was over.

At cruising altitude over the Atlantic, dinner was served. Peter put away his work and she, her book, and they turned their attention to each other and the food—lemony smoked salmon sprinkled with capers, and after that— salad, filet, with a béarnaise sauce, steamed broccoli, and snowy whipped potatoes. Afterward, Peter took coffee, Rebecca passed. Neither had dessert.

When the dinner trays were gone and Peter reached again for his brief-case, she lowered the back of her seat, raised the footrest, and closed her eyes. The dim light, the close quarters, the steady hum of the engines flying thousands of feet above the earth and Peter beside her, all of this provided a comforting sense that time was suspended. Closing her eyes, she resolved not to think of anything right now but the muscles in her body beginning to relax one by one. She would not think of the baby; not right now. Not yet.

Turning her head, for a few minutes she watched Peter writing notes in the margins of the brief. In this relaxed state, Rebecca pondered the time change between Positano, Italy, and New Orleans, and then wondered if babies in the womb have any sense of time, and then wondered whether a newborn baby had any sense of time. And then she stopped those thoughts.

When she yawned, the hostess brought a soft pillow. Fluffing it, she placed it under her head, turning to the side away from Peter's reading light. She pulled the blanket up to her shoulders and stared at the darkness through the small window, wondering what was just below right now. The Atlantic Ocean, she decided. Drifting off to sleep, she let herself remember the beautiful coastline along the way from Sorrento to Positano, where it's said Odysseus's sirens still sing.

And then the gentle vibration of the plane put her to sleep.

In a private car sent from the hotel, Le Sirenuse, Rebecca and Peter were whipped away from the airport in Naples toward Positano. Dazed from the trip, they were quiet. But the driver kept up a stream of conversation in Italian without ever seeming to expect a response. Sometimes he interspersed the Italian with an English word or two, which he seemed to think made him bilingual.

The car first raced through the streets of Naples, a dense teeming city, and then up onto a busy highway. And then for reasons known only to the driver, the car swooped back down into the city, racing along narrow, winding streets under clotheslines strung with colorful laundry, veering around small Vespas and farm trucks, bicycles, lumbering buses, livestock of all specie, market women, barefoot children darting in and out of the traffic, past stalls of heaping fish and fruit, past tourists decorated like Christmas trees with their wide-brimmed straw hats and fanny purses and cameras.

"There's no anarchy like Naples traffic," Peter observed.

The taxi driver chuckled. Surprised, Peter gave him a quick look.

Half-hour later, once again the taxi burst onto the highway toward Sorrento, the beginning of the Amalfi Coast. The road curled around the Bay of Naples with Vesuvius looming on the left and the bay on their right. They watched the ferries and catamarans, and the small fishing boats trailing in their wakes, all heading for the docks in Naples or the marina at Sorrento. Sailboats and great white yachts drifted lazily in the deep blue water.

At last the car entered the town of Sorrento, and they saw the signs announcing their arrival in the *Campania*, the mountainous region bordered by the Tyrrhenian Sea. The driver negotiated their way through the Sorrento traffic until, at last, they were released onto Via Guglielmo Marconi, the coast road leading to Positano, after which it would continue twisting and winding on down through Salerno and Amalfi to the tip of the Italian boot.

Here, with the Lattari Mountains rising on the left, and on their right a sheer drop from the towering cliffs to the sea below, the winding road narrowed and human instinct for survival at last forced the traffic to slow. The drive from Naples airport to Sorrento had taken just about an hour, but it had electrified both Peter and Rebecca, and they were now shot full of adrenaline and fully awake.

Rebecca had the scenic side of the vehicle, and now, she peered over the sparkling water at one of the most beautiful vistas in the world. Below, waves crashed against the rocky coast. She watched a ferry leaving the Sorrento marina—bound for the island of Capri, she guessed, or Ischia. Here again, the sea was alive with fishers, hydrofoils, sailboats, yachts, and small boats bouncing in the waves near the shore.

Twenty minutes later, Rebecca spotted a small green island, the first of *Li Galli*, an archipelago which legend claims as the home of the mythical sirens. The island was just off the coast of Positano and it marked their arrival. She pointed and Peter leaned over to see, peering through the window. They'd gone swimming out there, not far from the island, when they'd last visited, but had never ventured all the way around. The place was private, the home of Rudolf Nureyev, the famed ballet dancer who'd defected from Russia in 1961, foiling the KGB. From the road atop the cliff, the dancer's island was now almost hidden under decades of lush green foliage.

Just before reaching Positano, the car passed a familiar fruit stand built on a perilous point at the edge of the cliff. Rebecca squeezed Peter's hand; the stand had been there the last time they'd come. Then the car hooked a right, leaving the coast road and dipping down toward the village, to Via Cristoforo Colombo, past a parking area at the top of the cliff, and then swinging around and up again to their hotel.

Hotel Le Sirenuse clung to the cliffs, as did every other building in Positano. The hotel car stopped at the entrance. The driver turned off the engine and came around to open the car door on the passenger side, and Peter slid out behind Rebecca. While the driver retrieved their luggage from the trunk and handed it off to a porter, Rebecca and Peter stretched and yawned in the warm May sunshine and looked about. The air was fragrant with the scent of lemons.

Shops across the street were bustling. At the rise of the road just ahead where it curved left on past the hotel, Rebecca saw the usual gathering of young mothers and their strollers and toddlers, all enjoying the sunshine, talking and laughing. One dark-haired woman balanced a baby on her hips, bouncing it gently as she leaned against an old stone wall between the road and the edge of the cliff. Rebecca's eyes lingered on that one, wondering how old the baby was, wondering how she'd learned to hold the child like that. The other women leaned on the parapet, gossiping while they peered down at the beach far below, and the marina, and down the coast toward Sorrento.

Nothing had changed since their last visit, and that made her happy. Peter touched her arm and they strolled into the hotel. Their luggage had already disappeared, having been whisked off to their rooms by the porter. The tiled lobby they entered was open and airy and bright. While Peter checked them in, Rebecca wandered over to the long windows. To her left was an open archway leading to a terrace with white iron chairs and tables, still set up for lunch. Beyond that area she could see the swimming pool and white portico with tables, and past that, the emerald sea and the eternal blue sky.

Waiting for Peter, Rebecca wandered out onto the terrace looming high above the town. Turning her head to the right, she looked out over pastel roofs and the tops of flowering trees, and past the green and yellow dome of Santa Maria Assunta, the village Catholic church gleaming in the sun. The majolica tile on the dome of the church seemed sometimes to change colors in the light. Right now, it was a coppery-green, almost blending into the sea. Toward Sorrento she saw the white foaming waves crashing against the high cliffs. One rocky cliff jutted far into the sea.

Peter had reserved the suite for four nights. A porter took them up in the small elevator and unlocked the door. Looking around, Rebecca felt as though she'd never left and wondered if this might be the same set of rooms they'd had before. This hotel kept records of their clientele, she knew, so that was possible.

While Peter checked the luggage and tipped the porter, Rebecca strolled through the living room, looking ahead through the broad archway to the bedroom where French doors opened to the terrace. The blue and white tiled floors and the stark white of the walls pulled the sea and sky right into the room. Dark mahogany furniture and ceiling fans provided a nice contrast, giving an old-world feeling, cooling the light.

She walked on through the soaring archway into the bedroom, where delicate white flowers in small sparkling glass vases had been placed around the room. Again, the light. The room seemed lit with sunshine—a bright, white light. On a table in the far corner there was a silver ice bucket in which stood a cold bottle of *Limoncello*, the local aperitif. There was a breeze, and freshly pressed white linen curtains billowed from their ties at each side of the open terrace doors.

She heard the porter leave, closing the door behind him, and then she walked out onto the terrace and into the sunshine and dazzling colors of southern Italy. The terrace, high on the cliff overlooking the town, seemed to jut out over a massive forest of trees below—the tops of the trees just touching the terrace. Overhead white clouds streaked the clear blue sky. Scarlet and purple fuchsia bloomed everywhere, even cascading over the white parapet balcony of the terrace, and purple and yellow and red bougainvillea grew wild in the trees.

There were citrus trees, with fruit hanging from the limbs, and bottle brush and cypress, and smaller flowers springing up, winding everywhere— orange and red and pink and yellow—seeming to explode from thick vines and bushes, peeking out through the larger, darker, greener leaves. And beyond all this were the coastline and the sea and the dancer's green island, and then nothing further on but the horizon.

Peter came out onto the terrace and stood beside her, taking in the view.

"Beautiful," she said.

"Like no place else."

Suddenly fatigued, she rested her hand on Peter's shoulder. Although it was already late afternoon, a few fishing boats, small enough to be local, still bobbed offshore. She pointed and Peter followed the direction. "Look how the sun catches the nets, that flashing silver way out there?"

"All as advertised."

"And the water, green close in, then blue." She turned to look at him. "Can you hear the waves?"

"All I can hear right now is that bed calling. I worked most of the way over. Need a quick nap." He slipped his arm around her shoulders and she leaned against him. This was the land of dreamy dreams, the land of the lotus. They'd come here to relax. She could forget everything here for a while.

"You coming?"

She smiled. "Yes. I'll be right in."

Peter kissed the top of her head and released her, going back inside.

Holding onto the top of the parapet, she swung back, stretching her arms, arching her back, and looking up at the sky. She took a long deep breath of the fragrant salt sea air. After a few minutes she turned around and went into the bedroom. Peter was already fast asleep. So she took off her shoes and lay down beside him and fell immediately asleep with her hand unconsciously resting over the little bulge.

The nap helped. But with the time change from the trip and still somewhat fatigued from the long flight and drive from the airport, they decided on an early dinner at the hotel. Since he'd woken up, Peter seemed somewhat distracted, Rebecca thought. She watched him in the mirror as she brushed her hair and he dressed for dinner. Something was bothering him. It was that case he was working with Mac, she knew.

When he stood in the doorway, hands in his pockets jingling change and looking out over the terrace, she put down the brush. "I'm ready," she said.

He turned and she felt his eyes on her as she walked to the table where she'd left the small purse. She wore an apricot-colored silky slip of a dress that she'd always liked with her long red hair, although still she worried that he would notice the new thickening of her waist. But he merely walked toward her, taking her hand in his and saying that she looked beautiful tonight.

Le Sirenuse was once, not too long ago, the summer home of an aristocratic Italian family. The new owners had managed to retain that intimate feeling of old-world elegance, blending it with an open, airy look. They wound their way down the stairs and through the spacious rooms, every room having long windows open to the sea, the terraced pool, and on to La Sponda, the hotel's dining room. The restaurant, like all of the rooms in the hotel, swept the outside in with high ceilings and graceful archways. Vines wound through the room from the jungled forest below, winding up the inner walls and doorways and creeping above the tables, across the ceiling.

The maître d' led them to a table near a window and pulled out a chair for Rebecca. The windows were all open now for the evening breeze. They had decided to dine early tonight and get a good night's sleep. But even now, at dusk, with the sun still a glowing ball of fire on the horizon, the room was already lit with hundreds of flickering candles.

"Would you like water?" the waiter asked.

"Yes," Peter said. "Still, please; not sparkling."

The waiter nodded and soon returned with the bottle, and two menus.

"What is that?" Rebecca asked the waiter, pointing to a bulky stone structure she'd just noticed atop the parapet, the jutting cliff she'd seen earlier from the pool terrace. The waiter bent and looked in that direction.

"Oh, that was a watch tower in the old days, Signora," he said, straightening. Wrapping the water bottle in a napkin, he opened it and bent to pour water into their glasses. "It was built to warn villagers when barbarians or the *saracens*—the pirates—came calling." He set the bottle down on the table and stood beside her, draping the napkin he'd used to hold the water bottle over his arm.

"Up there," he waved his hand in the direction of the watch tower, "when the watchmen spotted the ships, they would light a fire to warn everyone in our village, and others along the coastline too. Each village watch would see the fire and light their own, all the way along the coast from Sorrento to Positano to Praiano to Amalfi to Molare . . ." He rolled his hand as the musical names rolled from his tongue.

"My grandfather told me the stories. And when our people saw the fires, they would run up into the mountains, carrying their valuables with them."

"That's a good early-warning system," Rebecca said, thinking of the steep stone steps climbing the mountain that substituted for roads in the village. The steps would be difficult climbing for those not used to them. Still today, Positano was a warren of alleys and passageways and steps. The road at the top of the cliff past their hotel was the only one for automobiles around.

The man handed her a menu, and gave one to Peter, and then straightened, smiling.

"*Si, certo!*" His face crinkled with amusement. "The saracen's sea legs couldn't handle our steep mountains. They could climb the masts of their ships, but our mountains defeated them."

After he left Peter leaned close, pointing out to sea. "Look at that."

She gazed at the hundreds of dancing lights in the darkness all the way to the horizon, where they became almost indistinguishable from the stars. Those were the *lampara*. The small boats with lanterns swinging from the bow were fishing for anchovies and cuttlefish as they'd done for hundreds, maybe thousands, of years.

Peter rested his hand on her shoulder as they looked at the beautiful sight. "Already I'm letting go. I'm glad we came."

"I don't know," she said, shaking her head. "I kind of miss the old purple K&B signs and Whitney clocks."

Just then the waiter arrived with a dish of sweet local olives, and warm bread, and a hunk of Parmesan cheese. They ordered a large plate of escargot to share. Neither were very hungry since their body clocks still warred with the local time.

Despite the nap and the surroundings, Peter was still tired and wound tight, his mind caught between thoughts of the trial starting in two weeks and the Chasson case.

He'd promised himself that he would not become embroiled in details of the Chasson case, not yet, not this early. The facts he'd seen so far had created a dark emotional pit, and if he allowed himself to sink into the pit this early, he suspected that would shadow his judgment when time came to make a decision on charges, and whether the State could sustain the burden of proof at trial. He empathized with the young Chasson woman's rage, of course he did. But Peter knew that he couldn't afford to let his emotions get in the way. The State's prosecution of Glory Lynn Chasson's complaint depended upon a clear evaluation of the evidence in context, not merely reviewing an autopsy report and pictures. He would wait until Mac came up with more. Meanwhile . . .

He blinked, realizing that Rebecca had asked a question. "Sorry." He picked up an olive from the bowl the waiter had left on the table and turned to her. "What did you say?"

"I asked if you'd like to walk down to the cove early tomorrow morning to watch the sunrise. Like we did before."

Without thinking, he groaned and bit into the olive. The olives of southern Italy were plump and sweet, not briny, like at home.

She laughed and rolled her eyes. "Never mind. I'm tired too. We've got plenty of time."

13

REBECCA WOKE EARLY AND LAY IN the bed beside Peter, orienting herself. In the distance she could hear sea gulls calling, and closer, in the trees around the terrace she heard songbirds. Rolling her head toward Peter, she saw that he was still asleep.

So she lay there for a few minutes, drifting in the half-light between dreams and reality, thinking that maybe she'd get up and dress and walk down to the cove. She could watch the fishermen coming in with their catch. Then again, she told herself there was no reason to move from this soft, comfortable spot beside Peter—this was not a workday, there was no morning traffic to fight—

And then, suddenly she remembered.

She slid her hand to the little bulge as it all came back, the conversation that she must have with Peter, and the knowledge that when she told him, this would all be real. But, at the same time, inside she felt something disconcerting, a strange new feeling—a strong instinctive feeling that above all else she must protect this child. The conflicting emotions were almost overwhelming. And yet the baby was still so small; she could hardly feel a thing.

Pushing the covers away, gently, without waking Peter, she slipped from the bed. They'd left the terrace doors open last night to hear the waves below. Barefoot, she walked silently out onto the terrace and stretched. Her spirits lifted a bit as she put her hands on her hips and looked out to sea, inhaling the crisp morning air. She told herself to get a grip, that this was the time alone she'd longed for, time to think about the problem with no interruptions, no telephones ringing, or clients waiting in the conference room. Turning, she padded back into the bedroom to dress. With a glance at Peter, still sleeping, she pulled on some loose flax-colored linen pants, a white T-shirt, and slipped on some sandals. She would probably be back before he even woke.

But the thoughts that she'd been fighting off since they'd flown out of New Orleans all surfaced at once, suddenly demanding attention. Arms hanging at her sides, Rebecca halted in the middle of the room and looked at Peter, finally—at last—facing facts. She was almost nine weeks along, now. Nine weeks, and the due date was just ahead, in December. She had to break the news to Peter.

Thoughts of Elise rose. She could hear her mother weeping in the church. She could see the little coffin just before the altar. With a sudden sense of desperation, she quickly ran a brush through her hair, twisting it and winding it into a knot at the nape of her neck. She secured it with one more twist, holding it tight with a pen that Peter had left on the table last night.

Then, turning, she stared at Peter, her love, thinking of the responsibility that she would have as a mother, and the havoc this would create with her career. And what if, as with Elise, she failed? She'd learned the hard way what a momentary lapse could do. She would never admit this to Amalise, or to anyone else, but despite the façade that she'd fashioned for the world, she was frightened. She'd never held an infant, never changed a diaper. She could handle a multimillion-dollar financing transaction for a client, but she knew nothing at all about raising a child.

As she watched her husband breathing, his chest rising and falling, his eyelids fluttering in his sleep, fear gripped her. Her mother had never forgiven her for that one instant in time, and she'd never forgiven herself. She turned, heading for the door. As she picked up the room key from the table, she accepted at last that the baby was real. She was a mother. And that everything in her life would surely change.

From the hotel Rebecca turned left on Cristoforo Colombo, heading back toward the top of the town where steps down to the cove began. The air was crisp and cool, carrying the scents of lemon and fresh baked bread and flowers and the sea. At the turn of the road, she started down the long stone steps which had been carved from the cliffs many centuries ago, shading citizens from the beating sun with thick grape arbors overhead. The steps were slippery, still moist in the early hour.

The passageway down to the cove was steep and winding. She hurried between the little shops and markets and galleries, all still closed. Sunshine filtered through the vines overhead creating dancing patterns of light on the shaded pavestones beneath her feet. In places the steps joined with other passageways winding off through the village, but she ignored those and kept walking down and down and down.

When she reached the terraced plateau forming a small piazza before the church of Santa Maria, the steps divided and she looked about, momentarily confused. And then, remembering, she turned to the right and continued walking down again, until she reached the base of the village and the sandy beach.

The sand in the small horseshoe cove was beige and pebbled. From the steps looking out over the scene, it was just as she'd remembered. Behind her the village of Positano ended at the base of the cliff in a terraced swath of cafés, restaurants, and open bars—so that from where she stood and looking to her left or right, they appeared to be built one on top of the other, all vying for views of the sea. In the evenings this area was alive with music and festive colored lights and the sounds of laughter and shouting and dogs barking and plates and glasses clanking.

Bending, she slipped the sandals from her feet and dangling one in each hand, she walked over the sand to the edge of the water where gentle waves lapped the shore. Here, water that had appeared green high up from the terrace of the hotel, now was translucent. She could see every stone and shell on the sand underneath.

Digging her toes into the cool wet sand, she stood there, letting the water wash over her feet. Colorful *barcas* dotted the water far out to sea, far past the dancer's green island. Golden sunshine caught the tips of the dark blue waves. She glanced to her right, to a small paved area, a concrete pier and a makeshift dock bearing a huge black balancing scale suspended from an iron tripod with heavy chains. The fishing boats would come here to weigh the catch later on. Above the pier a boardwalk ran the length of a stone jetty that curved into the cove like the inner side of a crescent moon. A small two-storied hotel was built on the jetty, too. The jetty protected the beach area from the surf pounding the rocky shoreline on the other side, stretching toward Sorrento.

An old man was fishing on the pier. Sitting on the concrete, legs dangling above the water, he wore a rumpled straw hat that had seen better days. As she watched he reeled in a fish, worked it off the hook as it wiggled, then he tossed it into a bucket beside him. She hoped there was some water in the bucket. He didn't seem to notice she was there.

Turning left, she ambled along the pebbly shore. In an hour or two the beach would be fully stocked with rows of wooden lounge chairs facing the water, and bright colored cushions and umbrellas, and an hour after that every chair would be occupied. She strolled along, kicking at the shallow water with her toes, past three chairs that were left on the beach from last night. She walked on past the open-air restaurant at the back of the beach that she and Peter liked. Further on she saw the storage hut where the chairs and umbrellas were stored, and past that the beach swerved out around a rocky jut of the cliff. On the other side was another, narrow straight beach. She could walk on, if she wanted. But here she stopped and turned back.

Dragging one of the abandoned chairs right to the edge of the water, Rebecca sat down, folded her hands behind her head, and stretched out. A dog barked and she turned her head as the dog ran up to her, slid to a stop, spraying sand, and then spun around and sat back on his haunches, tail whipping back and forth. Turning, she saw an old man coming down the steps holding a stick. He held it up, waving it, and the dog jumped up and raced toward him.

Shielding her eyes from the rising sun with her arm and elbow, she watched the man and the dog for a while. Then she relaxed again, closing her eyes and shutting out the sunshine and the world. And with the waves lapping against the shores and the dog barking and the old man's laughter in the distance, for her alone a thought came—unspoken words that were not her own: *I have called you by name; you are mine.*

As she thought these words, a new kind of love swept through her, a love so powerful that it seemed to radiate from her very center into every cell, filling her. Committing her to the child created long ago in the most ancient of days. And, like a prayer, she spoke to her baby, because she knew that this time she must not fail:

I will always be there for you, she promised. *I will always love you. I'm your mother. I am yours, and you are mine.*

And then she rested her hand over the little bulge, feeling the new bond, the powerful attachment between a mother and child. For a long time she lay there on the chair beside the water taking all of this in. And she knew, now, that she was strong enough to make things work.

14

IN THE HOTEL LOBBY REBECCA STOPPED at the reception desk to retrieve the key she'd dutifully left there on her way out, and was greeted by a desk clerk who appeared, as she spoke, to be stunned. "Signora Jacobs! There you are. We have received thousands of faxes for you!"

"Thousands?"

The woman threw up her arms, spun around, and hurried through a door behind the counter.

Rebecca stood waiting, wondering if Peter was awake. Now she couldn't wait to tell him the news. The hotel driver from yesterday hurried through the lobby toward the front door and gave her a cheerful wave. She'd seen the car parked outside—on his way to the airport again, she supposed. She waved back.

The clerk returned clutching a stack of slick paper about an inch thick. "We're not used to this, Signora. Most of our visitors here are on vacation." She gave Rebecca a grim look as she handed them over. "Mamma mia, these took some time on our little machine." Turning, she pulled the Jacobs room key from the slot, and handed it over.

"Thank you." Rebecca smiled at the woman. "I hope this will be all the faxes."

"I hope that also. Anyway," the young woman's expression smoothed and she dropped her arms onto the counter. "Perhaps our machine is now broken."

Rebecca nodded, looking down at the Offering Memorandum she thought she'd handed off to Sydney.

Swooping up the key, she headed for the elevator, reading the fax cover sheet as she walked. Some new issues had come up, Sydney had written. She'd marked the changes in the document, but some would have to be approved by Rebecca, and they were hoping to finalize everything over the weekend.

The date and time stamp on the top of each page told her that the fax had been sent late last night, New Orleans time. A note on the first page suggested a time for a phone call. She glanced at her watch. She'd have about three hours to review this. She clicked her tongue against her teeth, then told herself that would still leave most of the afternoon for Peter. She would tell him this afternoon.

Peter was dressed and sitting on the terrace when she arrived. She called to him, and he turned and waved her out. Clutching the fax, she walked out onto the terrace.

"Did you get my message?"

"Yes. Woke up about twenty minutes ago. What's that?" He eyed the papers in her hand.

"From Sydney." She grimaced. "I'll need to read this and give her a call. Have you had breakfast yet?"

"No. I ordered room service. Thought we could eat out here."

A knock at the door interrupted.

"Breakfast is here." Peter smiled down at her as he rose. Rebecca put the papers down on the table as Peter hurried to the door. "Out on the terrace, please," she heard him say.

A small bird landed on the parapet, as if it knew that breakfast was coming. Peter followed the waiter and tray out onto the sun-glazed terrace.

She would prepare for the conference call with Sydney this morning. And then, later on, she would tell him.

The morning sun was still low in the sky, and the terrace was shady and cool. Rebecca sat outside, working at the table after breakfast. Peter had not minded and was inside now, working on his brief. Sydney had scribbled comments that were in contention on the margin of pages. As Rebecca thought about each one, she made a note on the same page, preparing for the phone call in—she glanced at her watch—two hours, now.

Just then the telephone rang. She heard Peter pick it up, and then he began talking and she bent over the document she was working on again. From his tone she knew the call was business. For something like the hundredth time, she thought about how much she and Peter were alike.

Peter sprawled on the bed with pillows plumped behind his back, talking to Mac on the phone. Outside he could see Rebecca, bent over her work. His eyes roved over the beautiful scene—his wife and the foliage and sea and sky behind her, and the coastline and the church. All of that beauty created a strange juxtaposition against the darkness of the case they were discussing. Following up on Glory Lynn Chasson's complaint, Mac had tracked down the nurse, Clara Sonsten, the second nurse who'd been in the delivery room on the night Glory Lynn's infant was born.

"I found her this morning. She's working pediatrics at Baptist Hospital, and . . ." There was a pause. "We haven't had time to really talk, yet. But I have a gut feeling she's going to confirm everything that Glory Lynn said, Pete. She wouldn't talk to me at work."

"You think she'll be able to help us with the time line, birth to death?"

"I'd bet my life on it."

"Well, I'm not telling you how to do your job, Mac, but don't lose her."

"When do you get back?"

"Next Tuesday."

"I thought I'd give her a few days. Thought I'd see what I can find on that other nurse, too. Eileen Broussard. The one married to Vicari. If she's been working for Vicari for any length of time, I bet she knows plenty. I'll see what I can find."

"I've been thinking about Eileen Broussard. Let's get that marriage certificate just to verify, but I'll bet Vicari will claim the privilege and won't let her testify against him for a deal." Wind moved through the treetops near the terrace. He watched a flutter of scarlet petals floating onto the terrace near Rebecca.

When they'd finished the conversation and he'd hung up the phone, Peter stared unseeing at the walls before him. In his early years as a prosecutor, he'd learned to distance himself from the terrible facts that emerged in the cases he tried. But what he'd begun to think of as the Baby Chasson case didn't allow it; that trick didn't work with this one.

He told himself that as of now this was not yet a case—it was no more than a complaint filed by Glory Lynn Chasson. But one word kept rolling through his mind and he couldn't let it go: *Intent.* Glory Lynn's intent when she entered that delivery room was to abort a fetus. Charles Vicari's intent when he began the procedure was to carry out to a conclusion the choice that she had made.

But what happened after the baby was born and separated from his mother? Had Vicari's or Chason's intentions changed after the birth when they realized that the infant was alive? Had Vicari's duty to the Hippocratic oath kicked in so that he made the decision to try and save the child and something went wrong? And had Glory Lynn's change of heart, as she claimed, invalidated her original consent?

So many questions to be answered. But Peter's biggest fear, the question that underlay everything was whether this case was unique—an isolated incident.

He walked out onto the terrace. Rebecca looked up.

She saw misery in his face. Pushing aside the document that she'd been reading, she stood and met him on the other side of the table. Placing her hand on his cheek, she studied him. "What's wrong?"

He pulled her into his arms, resting his chin atop her head for an instant, then, he stepped back. "It's a case that Mac's working, Rebbe." He pulled out a chair. "Let's sit."

She sat down in her chair again. Peter slouched in his, legs stretched before him, elbows on the armrests, chin on his knuckles as he looked over her shoulder at the treetops and beyond that, the water. "The one you've been worrying about all week?"

He turned his eyes to her. "You noticed."

"Sure. Tell me."

He nodded and looked off again as he told her about the Chasson case, what Mac had found out so far. Immediately, when she heard about Glory Lynn hearing the infant's cry right after birth, she crossed her arms and rested them over the little bulge. And then she listened, remaining quiet as he told her of his fear that this wasn't an isolated case, his face taut with strain as he glanced at her then and wondered aloud how this could possibly be true.

And yet.

She listened, and she asked a few questions, offered a few words, trying to comfort him. But this case had struck Peter in some deep place and her words had no effect. Prosecutors were used to dealing with unthinkable crimes against innocent people, she told herself. Day after day they faced such horrors.

"It's all just so sad," he said.

She knew her decision to wait until the afternoon to tell Peter the news was the right one. There should be space between the Chasson infant case and her news. The two subjects should not be intertwined.

In the afternoon, after the call with Sydney was done, Rebecca and Peter wandered through Positano, trudging up and down the winding steps that spread in every direction through the village, while elderly men and women, locals used to the terrain, walked briskly by. Gradually Peter seemed to pull out of the earlier melancholy mood he'd sunk into after that phone call. Once, on a pathway, they stopped to admire an especially pretty view of the dancer's island, and Rebecca found herself wondering whether they'd have a little girl who would love to dance. The thought caught her off guard, surprising her. Pondering this new perspective on life, she linked her arm through Peter's and they walked on.

Yes. She decided. Something told her the baby was a little girl.

They went into a pottery studio and Rebecca fell in love with the large hand-painted urns. She ordered two. They could be shipped, the clerk assured. It would take three weeks.

They were almost back at the cove when Rebecca pulled Peter aside to admire the window display in a small shop. There were some pastels painted in the area that she pointed out to him, and straw hats and silk scarves, and a corner boutique of tiny, hand-embroidered dresses, and little playsuits, blankets, bonnets, and infant hats. After a moment, with a quizzical look, Peter tugged on her arm. She relented, walking on with a new spring in her step. Because, at last, a spark of excitement had taken hold, controlling Rebecca now. This was something new; something she could never have imagined. She was a mother.

She picked up her pace, swinging along, feeling revived, anticipation pumping fresh energy through her veins as she thought about how, and when, she'd break the news to Peter. She would take her time. It would have to happen in the perfect place, someplace completely unconnected with work, or indeed the outside world.

Smiling up at Peter, she thought how foolish she'd been to think a child would ruin her life, her career. She could make this work. With good help, she could have it all, she knew. It was only a matter of planning and coordination.

Yes. She could make this work.

They turned to the left this time, following the stairs out onto the beach where the open-air café stood. They'd enjoyed sitting here watching the scene on their last visit. The place was really no more than a roof and a floor, with wooden partitions waist high on three sides, separating rough-hewn tables and benches from the sand. The fourth wall backed up to the cliff and there was a long bar against that wall where you could order sandwiches and drinks and take them to the tables.

Peter ordered Coca-Colas—no Tab, the proprietor said in an irritable tone when Rebecca refined the request. No ice, either. But the bottles were cold. Peter carried them to the table beside the partition facing the sea, where Rebecca waited. There he sat down and handed her the drink, keeping one for himself.

The sand on the beach glistened in the sunlight. They drank the Cokes, taking in the scene. Forty yards offshore a large sailing yacht was anchored, and they watched people diving from the deck into the clear, blue water. He pointed the Coke bottle toward the pier where the catch was weighed and told Rebecca they should rent a skiff tomorrow afternoon. He wanted to paddle around the island and see what was on the other side.

"There's nothing there at all," Rebecca said, smiling. "Like the moon." She gave him that look that he loved, a sleepy, heavy lidded look that said perhaps it was time to go back to their rooms.

As they rose, leaving the bottles on the tables, and walked toward the opening onto the beach, a tall lean man sitting on a stool at the end of the bar, a man with graying hair who'd been watching them, took note. He'd recognized the red-haired woman, although he couldn't remember her name. It had been five years. The man, in his mid-to-late sixties, was muscular, in the kind of good health that comes from living in mountains and near the sea. He wore a loose white linen shirt, pressed, with short sleeves, and white linen pants, sharply creased, and an old, weathered, wide-brimmed straw hat. Once when Rebecca glanced back over her shoulder, as if sensing his presence, he tipped the hat down over his face.

"Aldo." He turned, motioning to a man sitting nearby. He spoke in Italian, the local dialect, but with an American accent.

Aldo turned his head and looked at him. "Do I look like a waiter to you?"

"I want you to look at someone." He nodded his head in the direction of Rebecca and Peter. "Do you know them? Ever seen either of them around before?"

Aldo turned to look, then shook his head. Turning back to the counter, he picked up his beer. "American tourists," he said, shrugging. He lifted the beer and took a gulp. "With that hair I'd have noticed her if they'd been around before. Every tourist shows up here sooner or later. Must have just arrived. Why do you want to know?"

"Just wondering," he said. They were out on the sand now, near the water's edge. He tipped the hat to the back of his head again. For a few minutes he watched as the couple wandered across the beach, tapping a rhythm on the bar with his fingers. Then he glanced at his watch. "When does the next ferry arrive?"

Aldo shifted his eyes to his friend. "For Capri? How would I know—do I look like the time-keeper?"

"Help me out. I never go back this time of day. Don't know the afternoon schedule."

Aldo lifted a shoulder and said that in half an hour or so the ferry would arrive. The man thanked him and, sticking his hands in his pockets, walked through the framed opening facing the water and out onto the sand. He would go down to the pier and wait for the ferry, he decided. Just in case; it was best to be cautious.

15

SHE'D FIGURED OUT WHEN SHE WOULD tell him.

So with patience, she waited. They slept late the next morning. For lunch they ate gnocchi, Sorrento style with tomato, basil, and Parmesan, and the cheese was so sharp and crunchy that they ate chunks of it alone, too. Positano is famous for its bread, and tearing off big pieces, they dipped the bread in local olive oil while they ate.

After lunch they rented a small boat and motored out about a quarter mile, near the island, but not too close. Peter anchored on the other side and shut the outboard off. The sudden silence was peaceful. The boat rocked gently, barely disturbing the sea. The sun beat down. They'd worn their bathing suits under their clothing, and Peter said he would like to swim.

Rebecca agreed, lazily swishing her hands through the water on each side of the skiff, watching the spray sparkling in the sunshine. But inside excitement, and joy, and terror whipsawed because this was the moment she'd set to tell him. And because she knew that by telling him she was sealing the deal, and underlying everything, floating amoeba-like through her subconscious was the glittering image of Mangen & Morris and her career, not necessarily one and the same, and all the unanswered questions that a child would bring to that mix. After all, who knew what might lie ahead if she worked smart, and hard enough. But with a baby?

Well, all of that had yet to be figured out. And the other worry shadowing her mind was this: men had choices, too. Yes, she'd been the one to set the ground rules before they'd married, no children. But that was several years ago. Perhaps Peter was happy with that arrangement. What then?

They stripped down to their bathing suits, and Peter wondered if anyone was on the island today. The shore of the little island was about fifty yards from where they'd anchored, and the only sound they heard was birdsong. There was a narrow strip of beach, and then a forest, thick with undergrowth.

She knew there was a house on the island, but from here it was well hidden by the trees.

Peter was ready before her, so he lounged back in the boat, arms spread across the stern, closing his eyes and turning his face to the sun. Ready at last, Rebecca perched on the little seat across the bow with her back to the sea, hugging her knees. Now was the time.

She looked at him and whispered, "Peter?"

He opened one eye, half-smiling.

"I've got something to tell you."

The eye closed. "Good news, or bad?"

She didn't reply.

"Because if it's bad news, just save it, Beauty. This day's too beautiful to spoil."

"Well." She tilted her head and her heart raced. "I guess that's going to be up to you."

He opened his eyes. Then bracing his weight on his elbows, he lifted his head and shoulders, looking at her. He'd heard something in her tone. She recognized that look of his, the dawning suspicion of a prosecutor facing a witness possibly turning hostile on the stand. "What's up?" he said. His tone was cautious as he smiled up at her, hand over his eyes shading them from the sun.

She took a long deep breath and rose, standing now, causing the boat to list slightly starboard. "I'm pregnant," she said. "We're going to have a baby." And then, without thinking, she twisted to her right, lifted into the air and dove, barely leaving a ripple behind as she entered the water, letting it stream over her, cool, soothing. Peaceful. She swam for a few seconds, then turned, arching for the surface, kicking up and up and up.

When she broke through, she tread water, shaking her head. Then she wiped her eyes clear and got her bearings, and turned her head, looking for Peter. She found him, staring, wide-eyed, straddling the middle seat in the boat, leaning toward her. Turning, she swam toward him. Then she grasped the side of the boat and looked up.

"Did you just announce that we're having a baby and then jump in the water?" he said.

"Yes. That's what I did."

"Well." He paused looking up, inspecting the sky for a moment. Then he looked back down at her. "Is it true?"

With water streaming down her face, she nodded. "It's true."

In the silence she gripped the boat and waited.

"Are you certain?" he said at last.

"Yes. I saw a doctor on Tuesday, this week."

"Well, I'll be." Seconds passed. Then, "Are you happy?"

She smiled. "I'm so happy, Peter." She lifted a shoulder, just a bit. "At first, not so much. But now . . ."

Before she could finish the sentence, he arched back his neck, looked at the sky, and roared. When he stood, the boat rocked and she hung on, and then he jumped in, too. Hanging on with one hand, she turned, waiting for him to surface. And when he did, he swam back to where she waited and caught her in his arms.

She let go as he grabbed the boat with one hand, and held her close with his other arm. His face was inches from hers as he looked down, his eyes shining. "Are you all right? Are you healthy, how old is he and when is he due?"

"Yes, yes, I'm fine," she said, laughing. "But he's a she, and she's arriving in December. I think I'll call her Daisy for now."

"December." Seconds passed as he absorbed this news. "Daisy as in Gatsby?" And then, "How do you know we've got a girl?"

She smiled. "Mothers know."

"Is that what the doctor said?"

Rebecca laughed; she arched and pulled back, splashing him. "No."

And then she moved close again, and lay her head in the curve of his neck, and he said, in a tone of sheer wonder, "We're going to have a child."

We. He'd said "we."

That evening, with bells ringing, they attended mass at Santa Maria. The small Baroque church was narrow inside, white and gold, with high arches overhead. Originally this was the abbey of a Benedictine monastery in the tenth century. Golden cherubs above the arches watched as Peter and

Rebecca knelt to pray. Behind the altar was an icon, black and gold, of the Madonna and her child.

The service was similar to their own Methodist church at home, Rebecca thought—Rayne Memorial—although the liturgy was in Italian. She knelt when Peter knelt, and stood when everyone stood. Peter bowed his head in prayer; Rebecca bowed her head too. From her inner depths she thanked Peter's God for the baby, and for Peter's love, and for everything that was good in her life, all the while wondering, as always, if anyone was listening.

How she wished that he was real, and that he was her God too. Still, she thought of the intricate pictures she'd seen in her book at home, the artist's renditions of the baby's growth week by week, and something stirred. She slid her hand over the little bulge, and looked at the painting over the altar, feeling a connection while Peter prayed.

He coddled her the rest of their time at Positano until she finally begged him to stop. She was fine, she told him. The baby was fine. She was perfectly able to walk up and down the steps of Positano by herself, she insisted. She could still swim, she could dance.

"Pfft," she said at last. "I'm fine; stop all that."

16

BACK IN HIS OFFICE IN GRETNA the next week, Peter looked out over the river. He had a trial in one week and needed to focus all of his attention on that case. And yet, the case of Baby Chasson was interfering with his thoughts. Even with his excitement over the news of their baby, the Chasson case haunted him.

He looked around his office, so different from the one that Rebecca inhabited downtown. It was a small office, but he had earned it. Next to Rebecca, and now the baby, his work was his life. Peter had made his choices early on, before he'd even entered law school he'd known exactly what he wanted to do for the rest of his life. Peter was passionate to his bones about his work.

And he was passionate about his marriage and that's what he was thinking about right now. Through the glass window panes he gazed out over the levee and the river, reflecting on the new turn of events. In Italy, he and Rebecca, drifting in sweet anticipation of their coming child, had not once talked about how a child was going to impact her career. Or his. Unspoken between them was the assumption that Peter would continue prosecuting in the district attorney's office just as always. And also left unspoken was any mention of the conflict between the inevitable needs of the baby and the long hours that Rebecca worked downtown, the travel, and her driving ambition.

Usually a glance at the busy river would have made him feel good, like he was on top of the world. But nothing—not the impending trial, not the colorful river traffic, not thoughts of the baby, nor of Positano and Rebecca, none of that pulled his attention from Glory Lynn Chasson's complaint.

With resolution he turned his eyes back to his desk and looked at the files that Molly had stacked on the corner of his desk last week before he'd left for Italy, cases to be closed and sent downstairs to the archives. Work that would keep him busy without requiring much thought. Pulling the files toward him, he picked up the one on top and set it down before him. Nothing went into archives until he'd reviewed the file and signed and dated it.

The intercom on his desk buzzed, Molly's line. Her voice was grim. "Did you forget the bail hearing this morning?"

He started, and then groaned. Glancing at his watch he saw that he had ten minutes to get downstairs to the courtroom.

"I've pulled the file," Molly said. "You've got Judge Benson."

"Thanks." Peter hung up the phone and headed for the closet for his jacket. Slipping it on, he hurried through the door.

Across town, in the conference room on the eighteenth floor of Mangen & Morris, Rebecca leaned back in her chair, balancing a pencil between her fingertips as she listened to Case Roberts, the Chief Operating Officer of Roberts Engineering, describing the company's problem. Beside her sat Bill Brightfield, a senior partner in litigation with Mangen & Morris. Roberts was interested in investing in a gold mine, Nevada Auriel, located in the Sierra Madres just over the California border in Nevada. But Auriel was involved in some ongoing litigation that worried him. He wanted Brightfield's opinion on the potential liability in that lawsuit, and he wanted Rebecca to head up the joint venture team if he moved forward.

Case Roberts looked like he'd just ridden out of the Sierra Madres and hadn't quite settled into city life yet. He'd worn a suit for this meeting, but when Rebecca first met him at a party thrown by some of Peter's friends, he'd worn old jeans, albeit with an expensive looking white dress shirt, and cowboy boots. His hair was brown, with flecks of gray, and his skin was tan and weathered and his eyes held a permanent squint from looking into the sun. Thick gray brows bristled over his eyes. She could almost see the dust rising up around him when he'd introduced himself at that party.

"Don't let the simple name fool you," Brightfield had said. "Roberts Engineering is a holding company for a conglomerate of subsidiaries. That group's always looking for the next acquisition. Good management, sharp investments. They own copper and silver mines all over the world, some natural gas pipelines, offshore drilling rigs in Norway, South America, and here in the Gulf."

So she should be thrilled right now. She was the billing partner on a new transaction for a large company that could—if she handled things right—turn into a long-term client. She should be sitting on the edge of her seat right now, wheels spinning in her head pumping out ideas, questions . . . she should be flashing her smile and controlling the conversation.

But now that she and Peter were home and back at work, she'd begun wrestling with the problem of the career woman's eternal conundrum, how to work full time and raise a child. She was certain that she was carrying a little girl—a woman's instinct, she'd decided. For fun, privately, she called her daughter Daisy. But Amalise was right. She would have to make some choices.

So now, instead of the excitement she should be feeling at this meeting, the shining star that was Rebecca was suddenly in danger of collapsing in upon itself.

Case Roberts was looking at her. She forced herself to tune back in. "The strike was unexpected," he was saying. "We're a little worried about that, too. Already got our geologists on it."

"You're worried about the assays? Salting?" Brightfield tapped his pen lightly on the yellow legal pad on the table before him.

Warren Williams, the chief financial officer, chimed in. "We just want to make certain they're clean. The company's planning to list the shares soon and then make the announcement. If we're going to invest, we've got to move quickly."

"They're listing on the penny exchange?" Rebecca asked.

"Yes." Roberts frowned. "So we'll need the due diligence handled quickly. We'd like you both to handle this preliminary work personally, though—especially on the litigation, Bill." His eyes stopped on Brightfield. "We'll need your analysis of the lawsuit before we make a move."

He leaned across the table, looking at both of them. "Once we've heard back from the two of you, we'll make the decision. If we go forward, we'll need to have the purchase agreements drafted right away. We'll finance the purchase. It'll be a rush project. Our bank group's already been notified."

This is what Rebecca loved, a fast-paced, interesting transaction. "That's not a problem," she said. All thoughts of babies and her career disappeared for the moment. She didn't know a thing about mining, but she could learn. She loved finding out how different companies worked, their operations, their products, learning how management solved problems.

Warren Williams pulled a small stack of papers from a file on the table before him and handed these around. "These will familiarize you with our corporate structure."

Rebecca looked at the chart, a matrix of companies below the parent company at the top—Roberts Engineering. As Warren began explaining the organization, she picked up a pen and began taking notes. She realized the meeting would extend into the evening. Beneath the table she rested her hand over the baby. She'd call Peter and let him know. Meanwhile, Rose Marie could order dinner for the group in the conference room tonight. And she'd have to cancel that follow-up appointment with Dr. Matlock, too, she supposed. Guilt pricked her at that last thought.

But she smiled and picked up the new file that Warren tossed across the table. Time was ticking for the company, but it was also ticking for her.

It was ten o'clock at night and the meeting with Case Roberts and Warren Williams had just concluded. Feeling exhausted, Rebecca had returned to her office for her purse. Once Brightfield finished his analysis and gave the go sign—if he did—this transaction would move forward quickly. She pulled the purse from the desk drawer and slung it over her shoulder, then stood.

"Got a minute?"

Standing behind the desk, she turned to see Brightfield in the doorway. "Sure," she said.

He carried a thick file folder under his arm as he walked in and lowered himself into the chair before her desk. Then he looked at her. "Ever hear that old saying—Mark Twain said it, I think—a gold mine's just a hole in the ground with an idiot on top?"

She laughed. "Warren said they'd be sending boxes over tomorrow. I'll go through them first and send anything pertinent up to you."

He nodded. "That's fine. Congratulations. You've brought in a good client, maybe a real keeper."

"I hope so. Thanks for your help, too, Bill." Her eyes touched on the file folder.

"Glad to oblige," he drawled, sweeping his hand toward her. "I'm here to collect, though."

"Collect?"

"Quid pro quo." He grinned and tilted back the chair. "I need some help. I've got a proposition for you, Rebecca."

She sat back, clasping her hands over her middle, suppressing a sigh. This was all she needed now, more work. But she smiled and said, "Okay. Shoot."

"I want you to write an appellate brief on a case I've been working for two years." As she opened her mouth, he held up his hand. "Hear me out. Just hear me out."

She would hear him out, of course. But she knew nothing about writing an appeal.

He told her about his case that had just gone through trial. A verdict had been rendered against the firm's client, an energy company charged with fraudulent pricing. Daisy chains, they called it. When he'd finished talking and the room went silent, she leaned forward, elbows on the desk, hands clasped under her chin.

"Look, I'd like to help you out, Bill. But I don't think I'm who you need. I've never written an appellate brief in my life."

He shook his head as he lifted the file and plunked it down on the desk. "You're smart, Rebecca. I know your work, and I know that you can do this. You write better than most lawyers in the firm."

He leaned back in the chair. "Listen, there's an opportunity here for someone with foresight and talent. The firm's got no one specializing in appellate work. I've seen what you can do, the way you dig into things . . ." He flicked his wrist toward the file, now before her. "You have, what some might call, a convoluted mind. But I like how you work things out, and that sort of thinking is what I need to clarify the issues in this case."

"Bill, I don't have the time right now."

"You're just what the firm needs, Rebecca. Someone smart, young enough to stick around for a while, and if you like it . . . perhaps develop an expertise."

She looked at him, stunned. He was talking about pure research and writing. She was a transactional lawyer. She loved dealing with people, clients. That was her milieu.

"Anyway," he added, heading for the door. "Give this one a crack. One good turn deserves another. If I've got to trudge around those mountains in Nevada looking for a gold mine, the least you can do is help me out on this." At the doorway he paused and turned, one brow arched high. "Correct?"

"Sure," she said. Raymond had been right; she was on the bottom of a whole new food chain.

When he'd gone, she dropped her head and groaned.

17

WHEN PETER ARRIVED HOME THAT NIGHT, as soon as he opened the front door he knew that the house was empty. When Rebecca was home, every light in the house was on. He glanced into the study to his left, at the overstuffed chair that she usually occupied near the fireplace and the handy table, with a good reading light.

With a flash of disappointment, he walked on through the living room and into the kitchen, switching on lights as he went. He opened the refrigerator door and stood before it for a moment, inspecting the contents. Then he pulled out a package of ham, and jars of mustard and mayonnaise, and the loaf of bread that Rebecca insisted on keeping in the refrigerator instead of on the counter. He disliked cold bread. He stuck two pieces of the bread into the toaster, put the rest back into the refrigerator, and pulled a plate down from the cabinet overhead.

When he'd put it all together, releasing a long sigh, he sat down by the window and picked up the sandwich. He bit into it and chewed, gazing at nothing as the images he'd bottled up until this moment slowly emerged.

He'd managed to push aside thoughts of Glory Lynn Chasson's complaint since he'd left his office for the hearing that morning. As usual he'd spent most of the day in court on one thing or another, working his way through the docket. He often thought of his caseload as a train rattling down the track, cases up for trial soon were in the first car, those still in preliminary proceedings and investigation and motions and depositions and negotiations were in the other cars, each according to their schedules.

Glory Lynn Chasson's case was still in the caboose and he shouldn't be spending so much time on it right now. She'd made a complaint and Mac was leading the investigation. The investigation would take awhile. But still he couldn't banish those autopsy photos from his mind. What on earth was happening at that clinic?

He shook his head at the entire range of legal possibilities raised by an accidental life and bit into the sandwich again. Never in his wildest imagination had he considered the possibility that an infant could survive an abortion. In fact, he reflected, he'd bet that no one on the Supreme Court when *Roe v. Wade* was decided nine years ago had ever contemplated this situation.

The telephone rang. He lifted the receiver and heard Mac's voice on the other end. In the background he could hear clattering dishes, the hum of conversation, some laughter, music from a jukebox.

"Listen, I'm over here at Cisconi's with someone you should meet," Mac said. "Come on over. I'll buy you a pizza."

Peter glanced at his watch. "It's nine thirty, Mac, and I'm beat. Just tell me what you've got."

"Can't, my friend. Get over here. This won't take long. It's important."

"Not tonight."

Mac's voice took on an urgent tone. "Peter. I'm at the payphone in the hallway and Clara Sonsten's here with me. She's waiting at a table and she's got a lot to say about that night and Glory Lynn. Sonsten wants to talk. Wants to waive her rights."

"What? Back up. Are you talking about the nurse from the clinic?"

"That's right. So, get over here quick."

Peter grimaced and shook his head. "What are you doing, Mac? Does she know Chasson's filed a complaint?"

"Yeah. We're okay. She understands what's going on and she says she just wants to tell us what happened." Seconds passed and he heard Mac's exasperated sigh. "Just get on over here. Give her immunity in exchange, but I'm telling you, you're going to want her on that witness stand."

Peter was silent. An offer of immunity could be arranged.

"Look, right now we're having a friendly conversation. I'll fill you in later. Just get over here. You know where this place is?"

Peter rubbed his forehead. "Yes, sure." He knew the place, the usual red and white checked plastic tablecloths and Chianti bottles covered with candle wax. "Give me ten," he said, looking at the half-eaten sandwich on the plate.

"Got it."

Walking toward the front door, he rolled up his sleeves and unbuttoned his collar. He'd call Rebecca if this took more than a half-hour.

Through the large plate glass window in front of the restaurant he could see Mac inside, talking to a nice-looking woman about fifteen years his junior. Mac sat at the end of the table with the woman he assumed was Clara sitting beside him.

They hadn't noticed his arrival, and for a moment he stood near the door, just inside, assessing the nurse as a potential witness, envisioning her as a jury would if she were seated before them. Her plain brown hair barely touched her shoulders, curling under at the ends. Her head was down as she listened to something Mac said. She wore a flowered dress with long sleeves, a straight skirt, and a belt at the waistline, instead of a nurse's white uniform. Beside her, Mac had shed the jacket and tie he usually wore. Between them was a large, half-eaten pizza.

When Mac finished talking, Clara straightened and nodded. Peter started toward the table then. Mac saw him first. With a word to Clara, he pushed back his chair and stood, extending his hand. From the corner of his eyes Peter saw the nurse giving him the once-over.

"Peter," Mac said. "Glad you could make it." He turned to Clara and introduced them.

Peter shook Mac's hand and said hello to Clara. He pulled out an empty chair across the table from them and sat. Mac slid the pizza tray toward him. "Have some. It's still hot." He twisted around. "Where's the waitress. We need another plate."

"No thanks," Peter said. "I just ate. But I'll take a cup of coffee."

The waitress approached and Peter ordered the coffee. As she departed, Mac leaned toward Clara, jabbing his thumb at Peter. "Clara, Peter here is the district attorney I was telling you about."

Clara studied him in silence.

He turned to Peter. "I've explained everything to Clara, Peter—advised her of her rights. She wants to waive them. She wants to tell you what she knows." He glanced at Clara and she nodded, then turned to Peter.

Arms on the table, Peter leaned forward, eyes fixed on Clara. "Are you certain this is what you want?"

"Sure I am. I know what I'm doing. Immunity for my testimony, right?"

He nodded.

"All right then." She picked up a piece of pizza from the plate and took a bite. Chewing slowly, she held her eyes on Peter. "Let's get on with this. I don't have all night." She dropped the pizza onto her plate, picked up a napkin, and wiped her hands.

"Glory Lynn is convinced that baby was born alive," Peter said. "I'd like to hear what you have to say."

"Glory Lynn was a sweet little thing."

Mac turned his eyes to Peter. "Clara here was on duty that night." He looked at Clara. "Just go ahead and tell Peter what you've told me." He picked up a glass of water and took a drink. "Just tell it the same way."

Clara Sonsten pushed her own plate back, away, and knotted her hands together before her. When she finally spoke, Peter had the impression that she was choosing each word.

"Eileen Broussard was the assisting nurse that night," she said, looking at Peter. Mac leaned back now, one arm stretched to the table, listening. "She and Dr. Vicari were in the procedure room with Glory Lynn."

"What was the procedure?" Peter struggled to infuse some warmth into his voice.

She shrugged. "I wasn't assigned to the case—she wasn't my patient. So I wasn't there at that point, but I assume it was induced labor. That's usual when the patient's so far along. It's safest for the client."

"The clinic performs late-term abortions?"

"Sure they do. Well, if the fetus isn't viable. And even after that if the woman's health is involved." She glanced at Mac. "Like high blood pressure, or depression, or . . . whatever."

"And how far along was Glory Lynn?"

She lifted her chin and her voice rose. "I don't know. I already told Mac. She wasn't my patient. You'd have to look at the records." Frowning, she swung her eyes from Peter to Mac, and back again. "Listen, I was only in that room a couple times. It was the last time when Eileen rang for help that I was telling Mac about." Her voice caught on the last few words.

Peter nodded, softening his expression. "Okay. Just tell me what you saw."

Clara's eyes pooled with tears. Peter pulled a napkin from the holder on the table and handed it across to her. "I know this is hard for you, Miss Sonsten."

"Clara." She dabbed her eyes.

"Okay. Just tell me what you saw. Start from the beginning."

She nodded. "The first time Eileen rang I went into the room and Glory Lynn was in labor."

"Was she awake?

"Yes."

"Having a hard time?"

"Not too bad. It's not like that when the fetus is so small . . . not like at full term." She looked down, twisting the napkin in her hands. "Eileen needed some instruments and I went to get them. Brought them back, and handed them to her." Her eyes dropped to her hands. "Dr. Vicari was beginning to deliver at that point, I think."

"What time was that?"

Fingertips pressed against her mouth, she looked off. "About six fifteen at night, I think."

"All right. Go on."

"So I went back out. Started down the hallway, and then I heard a scream." She looked at Peter. "It wasn't the kind of sound you'd expect to hear in the clinic. It wasn't a series of cries, like you might hear during hard labor or anything. It was just . . . one loud scream."

"I stopped when I heard that scream, and then kept on down the hallway. I was going to get a Coke-Cola or something out of the fridge in the kitchen when I heard the bell ring again." She glanced at Mac, and he nodded. "So I went back into the room, the delivery room, and there was Glory Lynn and she was half off the table, trying to sit up and she was crying, just sobbing, and Eileen was struggling with her.

"Dr. Vicari was still on the stool at the end of the table, and I saw he was holding something in his hand. On the delivery towel in his left hand. And then I heard the cry." Her voice broke, and bending her head, she pressed her hand over her forehead. "I looked again, and then realized he was holding an infant, and that I'd heard it cry." She looked at Peter. "He'd cut the cord, but the baby, it was alive!"

An image of Rebecca's gently swelling belly rose in Peter's mind. And then, the autopsy photos rose and, swallowing, he forced those thoughts away; forced himself to concentrate only on Clara's words. This was critical. Clara was corroborating Glory Lynn Chasson's complaint.

He leaned forward, arms on the table. "You're certain that you heard a cry?"

Her shoulders heaved. "Yes. Yes!" A tear slipped down her cheeks and she brought the napkin to her eyes. "It was a boy—I found that out later. But after I heard that cry, Dr. Vicari told me to get over there, and when I came close, I could see that the fet . . . uh, the, the infant was breathing." Crumpling the napkin in her hands, she dropped them onto the table, looking at Peter.

"Glory Lynn was beside herself. She was crying and Doctor Vicari was telling Eileen to calm her down. He was worried about extracting the placenta, telling her to keep still."

Clara's eyes rolled toward the ceiling and then dropped back to Peter. "It was pandemonium in there, I'll tell you. Glory Lynn struggling with Eileen like she wanted off the bed. When I reached him, Dr. Vicari shoved it into my hands, towel and all. I looked down and . . . and, it was so small." Wide eyed, she looked at Peter, pausing, then she brushed the napkin over her face. "That's when I saw it was a little boy."

"And then what?"

"Well." She sucked in a shuddering breath. "I just stood there holding it, waiting. I didn't know what he wanted me to do."

"What was the doctor doing at that moment?"

"He'd turned back to Glory Lynn." She squeezed her eyes shut for an instant, then looked at him. "There was blood and he was telling Eileen to keep her still." She dropped the wadded napkin onto the table and brushed her hands over her eyes. "And I'm standing there holding the infant, watching him struggling to breathe, moving his legs, his arms, and not believing what I'm seeing." She shook her head. .

Peter steepled his hands beneath his chin, studying her. "You're certain of all of this?"

"Yes." Clara jutted out her jaw and looked at him. "I'm not a fool."

"I don't take you for one." He paused. "What happened next?"

"Well, Vicari finally noticed I was still there and he shouted at me, told me to take it away, take it away. He said to take it to the utility room. I thought maybe he hadn't realized it was alive. I thought maybe he didn't understand. So I said the baby was still breathing and I asked should I suction and call an ambulance?" She hesitated and lifted her shoulders. "I mean, it was alive!"

"And?"

"He said, no. He flew into a rage then. He turned around and took the baby from me. He wrapped the towel all around it, covering the face, too; like you've seen mummies wrapped? And then he handed it back to me. He'd covered him so I knew he couldn't breathe." She paused. "And then he turned back to Glory Lynn and said to get it out of there and put it in the utility room. Said I was upsetting his patient."

"What did he mean . . . take it to the utility room?"

"That's where medical waste is kept. There, or the freezer until it's picked up." She stared at him, as if deciding whether to go on.

He nodded.

"Well, I unwrapped the end of the towel from around the face and saw the baby still fighting to breathe. Dr. Vicari wasn't paying any attention to me right then. He was all focused on Glory Lynn."

She frowned and hunched forward, an intense look on her face. "I'd heard before, from a nurse at a clinic I worked in before coming to Alpha . . . I'd heard that sometimes when a fetus survives the abortion they'll just let it die."

"Was she talking about Vicari?"

"No. She just said that it happens." Clara straightened and shook her head. "The whole point of using the induction procedure that late is to keep the fetus intact, so I guess I should have thought of that before." She glanced at Mac. "It's safer for the woman. But I'd never believed that some could live through the trauma."

Peter fought the urge to close his eyes. He worked to keep his expression blank. "Did you ever hear anyone talking about that at the Alpha clinic?"

"No. But I hadn't been there long. A little over a month. And Eileen mostly worked with the doctor. I took care of clients before and after."

Peter took a deep breath.

Clara looked off.

Mac touched her arm. "Tell him the rest of it, Clara."

After a tick she turned back to him. "I didn't know what to do. I couldn't let the baby die alone. So I went into another procedure room, one way at the back of the clinic, where the lights were out. And I held him there in my arms until he died." She folded her arms on the table and dropped her head on top of them. Then she sat there, hunched, and very still.

Peter's throat seemed to close. An ache spread down his throat and into his chest. He put his hand on the aching spot, rubbing it as he looked at Clara Sonsten. To his left, Mac was writing. "What time did he pass away?"

"I don't know." She straightened. "Over an hour; maybe an hour and a half later. I can't remember exactly, I was upset."

Minutes passed. Then she added. "I quit the next morning."

Peter's eyes met Mac's. There were a lot of holes, but even so, he thought maybe they had a case.

18

ALICE HAMILTON'S APARTMENT WAS NOT FAR from Dr. Matlock's office; easy to get to on the streetcar. Her apartment was on the second floor of a wooden house on Oak Street, on the downriver side of the streetcar tracks and only one block off Carrolton Avenue. The house was built in the 1940s and had seen its best days years ago, but the rent was low and she liked the location. Right across the street on the opposite diagonal corner there was a small family grocery store.

The living room of Alice's apartment was spacious, and with two large windows, it got plenty of morning sunshine. She loved the light in this little place. The afternoon sun brightened up the kitchen, too, softened and shaded as it was by the elm tree in the yard. And there was one bedroom, with a small bath.

Alice was usually the last person to leave Dr. Matlock's office. Today had been an unusually hectic day and she was tired. She hadn't felt like cooking, so she'd stopped at Ciro's for fresh vegetables for a salad. Now she sat at the small square aluminum table in the corner of the kitchen drinking her first cup of hot tea, deciding whether to bother making a salad, after all. Her feet rested on a chair that she'd dragged over, and that felt fine. Sipping the tea, she looked down at the *Times-Picayune* newspaper lying on the table, and the article that she'd just read for the second time. She'd seen it in the paper this morning and it had worried her all day. Until this morning, she'd felt quite comfortable living in this city. Long ago, before she'd moved to Chicago, New Orleans was home. She'd grown up here. When she'd finally returned after working for over thirty years at New Hope Hospital in Chicago, she'd felt like she'd never left. Her friends were all gone; and most of her family. But everything else was familiar.

Why had she even left in the first place?

But she knew. It was because of Charlie Braxton of course. She couldn't stand it here, all alone, after he'd gone and died in the war. Couldn't stand day after day seeing the places where they'd had such good times. She shrugged to herself and put down the teacup. That was back in the days—the 1940s—just after the war when she was young and stupid.

She dropped her hands into her lap and looked again at the article that she'd just read. Just a paragraph on page eleven, but it had caught her eye. Police were investigating an incident at Alpha Women's Clinic in Metairie. The clinic was owned by Charles Vicari, a physician.

Turning her head, she gazed at the elm tree in the backyard. She'd thought of her job with Dr. Matlock as a kind of semi-retirement, really. Alice had saved a little, invested some. She'd had a choice whether to work or retire when she moved back to New Orleans. But she'd worked all her life and there wasn't anything else to do but sit around, so she'd decided not to give up and just molder away.

References were the problem, after what happened in Chicago. It hadn't been easy, but she'd thought maybe she could pull it off if she stayed away from hospitals, and applied only for nursing jobs in private practice. Even then, she'd worried until she'd thought of going back to her maiden name here in New Orleans.

After a week or two, she'd interviewed with Dr. Roger Matlock as Alice Hamilton. It felt great to use her own name again after all those years; she realized that she was sick of carrying Charlie Braxton's name and baggage around. She'd given New Hope Hospital in Chicago as a reference to the doctor, and figured if he came back and said they'd never heard of Alice Hamilton, she'd explain she'd used her married name, Braxton, up there. At least that would give her some breathing space. But, he hadn't even checked. She supposed he must have been desperate, because he'd hired her on the spot.

Her Louisiana license was still recorded under her married name, but she'd kept it current, and that's what really mattered. So . . . she tapped her fingers over the article on the table . . . she'd been shocked to see this article in the paper today. Chicago was supposed to have been left behind, and the name Alice Braxton, and all that had happened there.

Now what was she supposed to do?

19

SHE'D BEEN HOME FROM ITALY FOR almost a week, but it had taken a while to get in to see Dr. Matlock again. A smile lit his face as he walked into the examination room, followed by his nurse. Alice was her name, Rebecca recalled. He held her file in his hand.

"I'm glad to see you back, Mrs. Jacobs." Behind him, Alice also smiled.

"Thanks, Doctor. I'd have been here sooner, but we took a short vacation, and when we returned, as usual there was a backup of work."

He opened the file and ran his eyes down the page as he asked, "Where'd you go?"

"To Italy."

"Let's get started." He put his hand on her back and pressed the stethoscope to her chest, listening. Then, nodding, he stepped back and told her to lie down. Then he pressed the stethoscope to her belly, listening.

The examination didn't take long. She sat up, feeling relieved as he told her that she was healthy and the baby was growing.

"You're about ten weeks along," he said. "I'll want to see you again soon. You can make the appointment when you leave." He handed her a prescription for vitamins and a sample bottle, which she took, and said she should drink a lot of milk for the baby's bones and teeth. Remembering the Robert's Engineering meeting yesterday, she asked whether it would hurt if she traveled. She held her breath waiting for the answer, and in that instant decided she'd have to go if the client asked her, regardless of what he said.

"That's fine. It's still early," he said. "Just take care."

She let out her breath.

"Alice." He turned to the nurse. "Please bring Mrs. Jacobs a copy of the baby book." The nurse nodded and left the room.

"Great little book," Doctor Matlock said, heading for the door. "You'll enjoy looking at it. It's our baby guide, lots of detail, some medical artist renderings, and even some pictures taken with special lenses, endoscopes, and microscopes. Shows how baby's growing and changing during gestation. Sets out everything you need to watch for, and planning guides as you go along. And there are places for notes where you can put down changes you notice, like movement."

"When will I feel it move?"

"Not for a while yet. You'll feel some subtle movement any time now. But it will be a few months before you feel the real bouncing around."

"Thanks, Doctor."

Hand on the door, he turned back to her. "Remember, no alcohol. Take those vitamins. You don't smoke, do you?"

"No." The conference rooms were always filled with smoke. But that was only secondhand smoke, and she couldn't do anything about that anyway.

"Good. Alice will be with you in a minute. I'll see you soon."

Rebecca dressed and sat in the chair by the desk waiting.

The door opened and the nurse, Alice, reappeared. Rebecca looked up, smiling at the older woman. "You'll love looking at this," Alice said as she handed a large, hard-covered book to Rebecca. "You'll see the sonograms in here at each stage, like in the pamphlet we give out on the first visit. But this is much more detailed. It'll show you baby's growth almost week by week." She stepped back, standing near the end of the examination table. "The medical artist's pictures are wonderful. Someday maybe we'll see be able to see clear photographs."

Rebecca took the book and thanked her.

"Where did you go in Italy, on your trip?" Alice stood watching as Rebecca strapped her purse over her shoulder and tucked the book under her other arm, preparing to leave. Rebecca halted at the question.

"The Amalifi Coast. Have you ever been there?"

"No. Is it pretty?"

Rebecca perched on the edge of the desk, wrapping her arms around the large book. "I think it's the most beautiful place I've ever seen. It's a rocky coastline along the boot of Italy, near Naples, going south. Some of the villages there are thousands of years old; some, like Pompeii, were destroyed in the first century when Mt. Vesuvius erupted. And the island of Capri is there. You can get there by ferry."

Alice's eyes took on a far-off look. "Sounds wonderful," she said. "Someday, maybe."

Rebecca stood and opened the door for the older woman. "We stayed in a small old village, Positano, but everywhere there is so beautiful. If I had to choose some place in the world to live besides the U.S.A., that's where I'd want to end up."

Alice stopped in the hallway. "Don't forget to make your next appointment before you leave."

That evening Rebecca worked later than usual. Earlier Roberts Engineering had delivered several boxes of information on the Auriel mine. She was sitting at her desk, engrossed in trying to understand gold assay reports when Amalise walked in.

"You're still here."

Rebecca looked up. She'd been so busy she hadn't seen Amalise since returning from her trip to Italy.

"I saw Rose Marie on the elevator and she thought you'd gone." Amalise pulled out a chair as Rebecca rubbed her eyes and heaved a sigh. Amalise leaned back, crossed her legs and glanced at the file. "What are you working on?"

"The new client I mentioned. The company's considering a joint venture in a gold mine out in Nevada." Rebecca linked her hands and stretched her arms out over the desk. The stretch felt good, after sitting there reading for hours. "There's some litigation involved so I got Bill Brightfield to help, and guess what he did." Without waiting for Amalise to answer, she went on.

"In the blink of an eye he came into my office and tossed an assignment from his pile on my desk."

Amalise laughed. "You should have known. He does that."

"Yes, I should've. But it's too late now. He's got me writing an appellate brief on one of his cases."

"Good grief!"

"That's not quite what I was thinking, but"—she grimaced—"yeah." Then she shrugged. "Anyway, I'm stuck with that, but I'm thinking it's not too bad. It's an interesting issue. And this mining deal will be fun if it goes."

"How're things. How are you feeling?"

"I saw the doctor today. Guess I'll have to tell everyone the news soon." She patted her stomach. "I'm sure it's a girl. I'm calling her Daisy, in my mind."

Amalise smiled. "Did you tell Peter while you were in Italy?"

"He's thrilled. He's convinced he'll have a son." Rebecca pulled back her hair, twisted it at the nape of her neck, and let it fall. "How's Luke these days? I haven't seen him in a while. Tell him to come around next time he comes to the office with you."

"He'll be here Saturday. He's crazy about you." Amalise looked down as she picked a loose thread from her skirt. "You know, you're pretty good with kids, without realizing. You'll be a good mother. You let me know if there's anything at all that I can do to help." She glanced up. "Are you going to keep working after?"

"Of course."

Amalise laughed. "Why did I bother to ask?"

"I suppose the firm will offer maternity leave when I tell them. Three months." Rebecca picked up a pencil beside her and flipped it, catching it just before it landed on the desk. "I haven't decided whether I'll do that or not." She shrugged, looking at Amalise. "Maybe I'll take off a couple of weeks."

"Have you and Peter figured out how you're going to manage work time after?"

"Peter won't be any help. He'll want to, but that'll be impossible with his job—trial courts wait for no man, and all of that." She rolled the pencil on the desk with the flat of her fingers, giving this all of her attention. "I'll hire nannies, a live-in, or maybe several shifts."

Looking up, she caught Amalise's smile.

"No problem," Rebecca added irritably, wondering why Amalise had brought up the subject. Perhaps she thought this was her chance to get rid of the competition.

20

"SO WHAT DO YOU THINK?"

It was Saturday morning and Peter looked up to see Mac standing in the doorway, hands jammed in his pockets.

"I just finished reading your report on Clara Sonsten." Peter put the pages down and hooked one arm back over the chair. "It's good. Very good. I need to put something together that I can take to Ham." Hamilton Jadet, the district attorney, was only the first hurdle, he knew. "We need a time line. How many minutes passed between the infant's birth and death, and where did he spend each minute. You think you can get that out of Clara?"

"She's had trouble remembering exact times. I'll press her again, though. Once we can get a warrant for the records, that should fill in some of the blanks."

Peter shook his head. "Not yet."

Mac gazed at the wall behind Peter. "I ran a background on Clara Sonsten. There's nothing on record. She's clean and I think she'll be a good witness."

"What's the rest of the clinic staff look like?"

"It's a small group. Vicari owns the place. Real estate transfer was six months ago."

Peter nodded.

"Besides the doctor and his wife, there's the talkative receptionist. And a part-time nurse, and Clara—or at least, Clara was there until she quit." And a cleaning woman comes two times a week."

"Have any of the others been willing to talk?"

"The cleaning woman will talk all day, but she doesn't know anything. Says the utility room is where they keep the mop and buckets and cleaning materials. And there's a large plastic can in there with a top that's clamped on. She's not allowed to use that for trash, she says. She can't read. Says she doesn't know what's inside."

"Medical waste, probably. The search photographs should show that."

Mac nodded. "I talked to the local manager of the waste company they use, but he says we'll need a subpoena before he can talk, and he says no one checks that stuff anyway. It's incinerated." He linked his hands and jammed his elbows flat against the back of the chair as he spoke. "The part-time nurse wasn't at the clinic that night. Says she only does the intake exams and work-ups. Has no idea what's going on other than that."

He looked at Peter. "I'm working a couple other cases, but I'm going out to the clinic next week to talk to that receptionist."

"Good. We need more to convince Ham to go forward on a sensitive subject like this. Got to convince him we can carry the burden of proof."

"I ran some background checks yesterday on Broussard and Vicari. No malpractice claims on record for either of them, here or in Chicago. Licenses in order in Illinois, but neither one is licensed in this state."

"Follow up on the clinic licenses and permits, too, will you?"

"Sure."

"Keep looking, Mac. I've got a bad feeling about this. We can't let it go, not yet." He looked down, twisting the watch on his left wrist. "If Glory Lynn's story is true, I'd bet this isn't the first time this has happened."

"I'd like to take a trip to Chicago and poke around."

Peter thought about that a minute, then shook his head. "We need more, first. Let's get the time line from Clara and as much as we can from the rest of the clinic staff."

Mac nodded. He rose, jamming his hands into his pocket. "I'll get back to you."

Around noon on the same day, Rebecca glanced up to see Amalise's son, Luke, standing in the doorway of her office. Her brows shot up and she rose. "Luke. Come in. How's my favorite boy?"

Luke grinned, and gave a self-conscious shrug. "Mom says to tell you she'll be finished with her work in a while and we're going to lunch with Dad, and then the movies. Want to come? Dad's picking us up."

She laughed at the thought of abandoning the mountain of work on her desk for a movie, but waved him in. "Can't today, but come in. Sit down and visit a while." She walked to him and rested her hand on his shoulder, steering him toward the sofa and chairs in the corner. "How do you like my new office?"

He nodded. "Cool. It's really big. Mom's got one too."

"How about a Coca-Cola or 7Up or something?" she said. "The kitchen's right down the hall." She made a move as if to rise. "I'll show you."

"No thanks, Aunt Rebbe." With a crooked grin, his shoulders lifted around his ears. "Mom already said if you asked I had to say no. It'll spoil lunch." He made a face, then leaned forward and picked up a Lucite model of a Boeing 727 aircraft from the table between them. Northwest Airlines was written in script on the side, and the date, November 1977. "Mom's got one just like this."

"We worked on a transaction together back then, that's why." Luke turned it in his hand, studying it. "That's the one we were working on when you came into our lives, Luke." She narrowed her eyes, calculating. "Four and a half years ago, I think."

"Who was that mystery man?"

"Ask your mom." Rebecca kicked off her shoes and lifted her feet to the glass table. Luke's eyes followed her feet. "Don't tell anyone I do this," she said, smiling. And then she tucked her arms in, clasping her hands over the baby. "That deal was strange. But Raymond got the idea of having these souvenirs made, just for us. Sort of an inside joke."

"Yeah. I've heard about that." He set the Lucite memento back on the table. "When I was little I used to play with the one she keeps in her office." He looked at her, smiling. "I thought I might want to fly that kind of plane sometime. Maybe be an airline pilot someday."

Amalise thought that Luke had probably escaped Cambodia just before the fall of the country to the Khmer Rouge. That was in 1975, when Americans were evacuating Southeast Asia. Somehow Luke was one of the lucky children to make it onto Operation Babylift out of Saigon, those desperate flights in the last weeks of the Vietnam War. The planes were packed with young orphans as the Viet Cong advanced on the southern capital.

Rebecca watched him, thinking what a miracle it was that Luke had ended up with Amalise and Jude after traveling halfway across the globe.

"Hey, you two."

They both looked up as Amalise walked in. She halted in the middle of the room, smiling as she looked at Luke. "I thought I'd find you here." She tucked her hair behind one ear. "Dad's waiting downstairs. We'll have to hurry to make the show."

Luke slid off the sofa and gave his shirt a yank.

Amalise adjusted the purse hanging from her shoulder. "Come with us, Rebecca?"

Rebecca shook her head and stood, walking with them to the door. "Wish I could, but I'm working. Some other time."

She watched them walk together down the hallway and wondered again if she would ever be able to find the balance between work and family.

21

MAC OPENED THE DOOR AND WALKED into the clinic. Melanie, the receptionist, was reading a book. She looked up and frowned when she spotted him.

"Dr. Vicari says I can't talk to you," she said, pressing a pen against her lips, sealing them.

Mac knew better, but he leaned over and planted both hands on the desk. "I'm the law, Melanie, investigating a complaint." He pulled out his wallet, flipped it open, and showed his badge. "Remember?"

Her eyes flicked down, and then back to his eyes. "I can't talk to you about that."

"Do you have a lawyer?"

"Why. Am I a suspect or something?"

"Look, I just want to ask a few questions." Straightening, he gave her a slight smile as he shoved the wallet back in his pants. "If you don't want to talk here, we can go to the station over in Gretna."

She glared. The clinic was located in Metairie, a suburb west of New Orleans. Gretna was all the way across the city, and over the river.

"To the police station." She looked him up and down. "All the way to Gretna?"

"Unless it's been relocated in the last few hours." He patted the desktop with the palm of his hand. "Or we could just have a friendly talk right here. You choose."

Melanie put the pen down on the desk and glanced over her shoulder, to her right. The room there, a hallway, was empty. She twisted her lips into a scowl and her voice turned peevish. "Look. I don't know anything about Glory Lynn Chasson."

"How about you take a break and we'll go down the street for coffee."

"I can't do that. I'm alone here. I can't just leave."

"Where's the good doc?"

She crossed her arms and leaned back. "He's gone."

"Eileen Broussard?"

Her chin lifted a fraction of an inch. "Not here, either."

"So where is everybody?"

"We don't have any appointments for this afternoon."

Mac nodded. Good. He pulled a small spiral notebook from his pants pocket and a pen from the inside of his jacket. "Then let's you and me talk right here. Seems like the perfect time and place."

"I don't have anything to say."

"Fine. I'll ask the questions and you can answer if you want. Then we'll see." Dragging a nearby chair over to the desk, he sat and pulled out his notebook. Then he gave her a long look.

"First question. How long have you known Dr. Charles Vicari?"

She narrowed her eyes. "About six months, from when he took over the clinic. He came here from a hospital in Chicago. Said he was sick of the weather up there. Sick of the winters and the snow and ice."

Mac nodded. "And Nurse Broussard?"

Melanie dropped her hands onto the desk, entwining her fingers. She gave a slight shrug. "The same. She came with him. Six months ago."

"Did you ever hear either one mention why they moved down here?"

"To buy the clinic. They'd seen an advertisement. At least, that's what Eileen said."

"Is Charles Vicari the sole owner of Alpha Clinic, so far as you know?"

She shrugged. "As far as I know." She pursed her lips. "But listen, I don't know anything about their personal business, Mr. . . . ah . . ."

"Mac."

"I just know they arrived together and they're married."

"How many nurses are employed here?"

She gave him a peeved look. "I already told you that. Just Eileen, and Clara. Clara does interviews and some prep work, and helps Dr. Vicari with the physicals, and once in a while she's in the procedure room, when Eileen's not around." She looked off. "And there's the part-time, Anna Crane. She's here in the mornings for intake, mostly forms and interviews with the patients. Once in a while she helps with the physical examinations."

"She ever work with Vicari?"

"No. And that would be *Doctor* Vicari."

"But Miss Broussard and Dr. Vicari, they mostly work together on the procedures?"

She nodded. "And, like I said, once in a while Clara helps out."

"Who else works here?"

"Hmmm. Well, the cleaning lady, she's here twice a week, Tuesdays and Saturdays."

"Anyone else?"

She lifted one corner of her lips and arched a brow. "Just me."

Mac looked down at his notebook, writing. "Were you here on Tuesday, May 11, when Miss Chasson arrived at the clinic for the first time?"

She went silent, lips pressed together.

Mac hardened his tone. "Don't tell me you don't remember. Either you were here, or you weren't."

She nodded. "I was here."

"You two talk?"

"Not that I recall."

"She filled out some forms?"

"I'm sure she did."

"How about the next afternoon, when she came back. Did you talk to her then?"

"Clara took her back to the beds for prep. I had nothing to do with that. Don't know a thing."

Mac looked down at his notebook. "All right then. Let's move on to Thursday, May 13. Did you see Miss Chasson on that day, the day she went into labor?"

Melanie dipped her head and looked at Mac under lowered lids. "I don't remember."

Mac gave her a look. "What time did you leave?"

"About seven p.m., I guess. Miss Chasson was the last patient. I'd have left earlier, but . . ."

"But, what?"

She heaved a sigh, then enunciated each word clearly, as if he might be hard of hearing. "Miss Chasson was having some trouble, that night—that's why you're here, right?"

He nodded.

"She was still in one of the rooms. Dr. Vicari was still here, and Eileen doesn't like us to leave while he's still here. He's usually gone by five or so. And then, I'd heard a scream from back there; there was some commotion. So, I was sitting here, waiting."

"What time did you hear the scream?"

She shrugged. "I didn't check the time."

"Well, give me an estimate. How much time passed between when you heard that scream and when you left?"

She pursed her lips and looked up. "About forty minutes to an hour, I'd guess."

"Did you go into the procedure room?"

She shook her head. "No. I never do." She paused, and added, "Unless I'm cleaning up before we leave."

Mac gave her a quick look. Something in her voice told him she was holding back. "Were you cleaning up that night?"

"Yes." She hesitated.

"See anything unusual?"

Seconds passed. And then she looked down at her hands. "Umm, well, yes."

Mac's heart rate ticked up. "Tell me. Exactly."

Her head shot up and she glared at him. "Look, I've got work to do."

"So do I."

She looked off, tongue pushing against her bottom lip, thinking it over. When she looked back at him, he saw it in her face even before she spoke. "I saw Clara Sonsten in one of the procedure rooms that night. This was after all the commotion was over. The room in the back, all the way down the hall. I went in there to check if it was ready for the morning, and there she was, sitting on the stool and holding the, ah . . . Miss Chasson's baby."

Mac held her eyes, his expression a mask. If she was telling the truth, this was what he'd been looking for, corroboration of Clara's story. "What time was this?"

"About ten to seven."

"Was the baby alive then?"

She hesitated and then, dipped her chin, looking down at her hands again. "It was breathing then."

"How do you know that?"

She frowned and narrowed her eyes. "I leaned down and looked at him. How else?" With shake of her head, she added, "Look, I know what Glory Lynn's been saying, that the baby was born alive and Dr. Vicari killed it, but it's not like that, you know. Even if they breathe for a while, or cry once or twice, even if there's a little movement there, it doesn't mean anything." She spread her hands wide on the desk, pressing down. "I mean, they're *micro*-premies."

Mac's heart rate picked up. But his face was blank and his voice was casual as he asked the question he and Pete wanted to have answered. "So this has happened before?"

"I didn't say that. I . . . I've heard of this from other nurses, in other places, that's all."

Mac nodded. He chose his next words with care, watching her. "When a baby is born alive here during an abortion, what happens after it dies. I mean . . . is it sent on to the morgue?"

She shrugged and reached for the book she'd been reading, slipping her hand into the place where she'd left off. "That's not my job, sir. I'm not a nurse. I don't know what goes on back there. My job's to sit here and be nice to people like you when they walk in."

She looked up at him with a mocking smile. "I don't have anything else to say. Told you everything I know. So if you want to take me down to that station of yours, go ahead. Otherwise, leave me alone because if Dr. Vicari or Eileen come in and find you here, it'll be my job."

He closed his notebook. He was finished with her for now; but if they took the case forward, she'd be on the stand, that was certain. She'd told him plenty. "All right," he said. "Have it your way." He stuck the notebook in his pocket, and put the pen back in his jacket.

His hand was on the door, when she said, "Hey."

He turned his head.

"There's another side to it too, you know. It's the woman's right to choose."

Mac walked back to his car in the parking lot, opened the door, got in, and gazed through the windshield. Glory Lynn Chasson had told the truth. Then he banged his fist on the steering wheel. He'd learned to distance himself from cases long ago. And, he'd thought he'd seen and heard it all. But for a few minutes back there, it seemed to him that the world had just turned upside down. There should be cheers and congratulations when a child was born alive.

Shaking his head, he backed the car out of the parking spot, shifted the gear forward, and then suddenly hit the brakes. For a few minutes he sat there letting the engine idle, seeking a horizon. So he focused his eyes on the straight lines of the buildings across the street, anchoring himself with the dependable vertical and horizontal lines, and the solid walls.

"So it's true, then." Peter looked at Mac. Mac nodded.

Peter swiveled his chair toward the window. For an instant he closed his eyes, forcing the image away. "He told Clara Sonsten to take the baby to the utility room," he murmured, as if to himself.

Mac said nothing.

Peter gazed through the window, past the levee and out over the Mississippi River rolling south toward the Gulf thinking of Glory Lynn and that baby.

Mac was silent. The hour was late and typewriters and phones were quiet in the outer office. When, at last, Peter turned back to Mac, anger burned in his chest. The slow burn rose in the back of his throat, bringing with it the same choking sense of disbelief he'd felt when he'd first seen the autopsy photos. Glory Lynn's story was true.

"It's just hard to comprehend," he finally said.

Mac nodded, working a cuticle at the edge of his thumbnail. "I figure Vicari and Broussard have done this before." He lifted his eyes. "I figure they ran into some trouble up there, in Chicago."

"It's possible."

"I'd like to go up there and check things out, Pete. I'm thinking something might have happened that made them leave. I don't believe they left and came all this way just because the clinic was for sale. There's something more—some other reason for leaving. The hospital wouldn't give me much when I called, but I think I could do better in person."

Peter looked at the detective and their eyes met and held. He nodded. "I'll take care of the paperwork, and Ham." He leaned back, crossing his arms, and looking at Mac. If anyone could dig up information without a warrant, Fred McAndrews could. "You go on up there and see what you can find."

22

SHUFFLING FORWARD IN THE TAXI LINE at O'Hare Airport, Mac glanced at his watch. Four forty-five. Plenty of time to catch the night shift at the hospital. At the head of the line, he lifted his bag and swung it into the open trunk of the taxi. The driver slammed it shut, and Mac slid into the backseat.

The driver twisted his neck to look at Mac. "Where to?"

"New Hope Hospital." Mac read out the address.

The driver nodded and started the car.

"How long?"

"Little more than half-hour."

The hospital was located in Oak Lawn, a suburb of Chicago and south of O'Hare. It was a smaller place than he'd pictured in his mind. But still, it was a fully equipped hospital, not merely a clinic. Retrieving his bag from the driver he entered the revolving doors. At the reception desk, two ladies looked up. Both wore nametags identifying them as volunteers.

"My wife's having a baby," Mac said, sounding breathless.

They looked at the bag over his shoulder and his frantic expression and smiled. "The maternity ward is on the second floor," one of them said, pointing to an elevator bank to the left. "Take the elevator to the second floor and turn right. The waiting room's right down the hall. Just give the nurse your name."

"Thanks." Mac turned toward the elevators.

"Congratulations," she called after him.

He threw her a smile as he pressed the elevator button.

In the waiting room on the second floor, he set the bag down in a corner by a row of empty chairs. There was a family sitting in the far corner, a man, an older woman, and two children, waiting. He figured the bag was as safe here as anywhere for a while. Hands in his pockets, he strolled out into the hall and looked at the sign on the plaster wall facing him. *Obstetrics*, it read, with an arrow pointing to the right.

It was six o'clock and getting dark outside. Ahead he spotted a nurses' station, and there the hallway split in two along either side of the station. A sign to his right said *Pediatrics*, with an arrow underneath pointing to a doorway to the right. The top half of the door was opaque pebbled glass blocking his view. The door was closed.

He took a jog to the left, on past the nurses' station, his stride taking on a sense of purpose. On both sides of the hallway were patients' rooms. Most of the doors were shut. Ahead, where the hall ended, were two double doors, and the sign on those said *Hospital Personnel ONLY—O.R.*

Mac stood looking at the doors for a moment, considering. Then he turned and headed back toward the nurses' station. Behind the V-shaped counter a man in blue scrubs stood talking to one of the nurses. He held a cup of coffee in one hand and leaned against the wall while the nurse looked up at him, smiling.

Mac strolled on around the counter toward the other end where he saw a nurse sitting alone. He figured her for early to middle thirties. Her white-capped head was bent as she wrote. He stopped just before her and rested his hand on the countertop, waiting. She wore no wedding ring, he saw.

Just then she looked up. "Can I help you?"

With a tenuous smile, he ran his fingers back through his hair and shuffled his feet. "I'm looking for a friend," he said. "I haven't seen her in a while, and—well," he ducked his head and let her study him for a moment before looking up again. "I'm in town for a day or two and thought I'd look her up. Thought maybe I'd drop in and surprise her while I'm here."

The young nurse smiled. "What's her name?"

"Eileen Broussard? Is she, ah, is she around?"

The nurse put down the pen she'd been using and rested one hand atop the other on the desk. "I'm sorry, Mister . . ."

"Oooh, don't tell me." He shook his head. "She's not here." He slapped the counter, closed his eyes, and dipped his chin. "I knew it. I just knew it." From his lids he saw the pity forming, the wrinkled forehead, the eyes.

"Eileen quit six or seven months ago, sir."

He gave her a gloomy look. Seconds passed, and then somewhat awkwardly he reached across the counter, offering his hand. "Fred McAndrews," he said. With a worried look, she shook his hand."

"Broussard was her maiden name. I'm her husband."

The young nurse picked up the pen she'd been using and tapped it on the desktop. "Oh. Well, I'm sorry I couldn't help you."

"Do you know where I can find her?"

She shook her head, still tapping the pen, avoiding his eyes. "She's moved out of the city. I heard she went someplace down south."

Mac planted his elbows on the counter and rested his forehead in his hands.

The tapping stopped and she looked at him. "Are you all right?"

He lifted his head, staring at her. "No. Not really." Then he straightened. Dropped his hands to his sides. "I've been looking for her for a while."

He heard the chair squeak back on the tiled floor. "I'm so sorry," the nurse said in a tone of compassion. She stood. "How long has it been since you've seen her?"

Mac turned his eyes to her, releasing a long sigh. "She's been gone a while. Too long. I should'a come after her sooner." He drew out the words. "One day she just disappeared."

"Well, I never would have guessed that about Eileen Broussard." She came around the counter and he turned, looking down. She was a head shorter than him. "My name's Lucy Ringer," she said. She took his arm and he let her lead him down the hallway to the right, behind the counter and her desk. "We've got a kitchen back here. I'll take a break right now and fix you a cup of coffee, or a soda, or we have hot tea if you'd like that."

"I don't want to be a bother."

"No trouble at all."

"Well, that's nice of you. Thanks." She pulled him into a small kitchen, and she pulled a chair from underneath a table and motioned for him to sit.

"Coffee?"

Mac gave her a dazed look. "I guess so if you'll join me."

"Sure," she said. "You sit right there and just relax. I hated giving you bad news."

"Thank you, Miss Ringer."

"Lucy."

He nodded, watching as she bustled over to a counter near a sink and filled two cups with coffee from a machine there. "Cream and sugar?" she asked, looking over her shoulder.

"Just black."

She spooned sugar into her own, added cream, and stirred. Then she carried both cups to the table, placed one before him, and sat down. Reaching for the napkin dispenser on the table, she pulled out two and placed one near his cup.

"Thanks." Mac lifted the coffee, watching her over the rim. "What's her life been like, up here?" He glanced into the hallway and then back at her. "She was a nurse, at home. Is that . . ." His voice caught and his words hung in the air between them.

She rolled in her lips and reached across the table, patting the top of his hand. "She was in obstetrics and pediatrics here. She was a good nurse." Pulling back, she picked up her cup and sipped, holding his eyes. He knew enough not to break the silence.

At last she spoke. "I worked with Eileen, your wife, once in a while. I didn't know her well, though." She ducked her head and circled the cup with her hands, eyes focused on the coffee. "I wouldn't say we were really friends. She kind of kept to herself."

"She always was quiet."

He saw a flick of something in her eyes at that. Lucy gave the coffee cup a little shove with her finger tips and looked up, seeming to gather her thoughts. "Eileen worked mostly with Dr. Charles Vicari. He's Obstetrics and Pediatrics." She hesitated for a moment, pursing her lips, watching him. "Dr. Vicari left at the same time."

He jerked up his chin and let his voice trip up the scale. "They left together?"

She nodded. Glancing through the door to her right, she leaned forward, lowering her voice. "I don't want to upset you, Fred. But seems to me you're entitled to know the truth."

"They had something going?"

"Looked like it, I'm afraid."

He rubbed his eyes. Then, aware that she was studying him, he stretched his neck, stretching it to one shoulder, then the other, and then he straightened up and gazed at her. "I appreciate that. Truth can set a man free. But why'd they leave?"

"I don't know about that." She looked at him from under her lids.

He nodded.

Quickly, she dropped her eyes. Lifting the coffee to her lips, she took a sip, and set the cup back down. "There were rumors around the time they left, some problems."

He said nothing, watching as her brows drew together. The corners of her eyes turned down.

After a few seconds, she said, "I'll tell you what I know, but you've got to keep me out of this. You can't ever say that it came from me."

He said sure, but didn't promise. This was a murder investigation, after all. He'd use the power of the courts if he had too, but this way was better, for now.

"Lucy!"

Her head whipped around and she waved at someone passing by in the hallway. Then she hunched toward him and lowered her voice. "We can't talk about this here. I'm on shift. If anyone found out I told you . . ."

Mac felt a rush of adrenaline. Maybe he was getting somewhere. He glanced at his watch. "What time do you get off?"

She tipped her head to one side and gave him a look. "Half an hour. I'm off at seven."

"Can I buy you dinner?"

Seconds passed and then she nodded. "Sure. A frog's gotta eat."

She ordered grilled salmon with lemon butter sauce, and Mac had a steak, a good one, a filet cooked rare, and they both had salads. Might as well, he was on the dime and hadn't eaten all day.

"Dr. Vicari's a cold one," she said. "No one liked working with him, except Eileen."

"That doesn't sound like her. She's a hard case, herself. Usually, people like that, they look for someone more compliant, someone they can push around."

Lucy picked up her glass and pressed it close to her cheek, watching Mac. "That Vicari's a piece of work. You should try to forget her."

Mac looked about for the waiter. Caught his eye and signaled her that he'd like a cup of coffee. Then he turned back to Lucy. "Why do you say that—about Vicari?"

She leaned forward, lowering her voice. "Something happened one night. Eileen mostly worked with Vicari. But one night she wasn't around and I heard Vicari needed help and he pulled another nurse into the room. There was quite a row between the three of them the next day, between Dr. Vicari, your wife, and Alice."

Mac rested his elbows on the table and looked at her. "Alice?"

"Ummm." She picked up the fork and scrapped a bite of fish still left on the plate and ate it. "Alice Braxton was her name. Sometimes we called her Alice Jean." She smiled. "You know those Southern women like to use two names."

"What's your idea of what happened?"

"Vicari was a difficult man." She paused. "I never did hear all the details. But it had to do with a late-term abortion."

"My Eileen was doing that?"

"Yeah, she mostly worked with Vicari. But Alice had always refused to work with him. She'd filed a conscience objection. But somehow, that night, she'd been pulled in when Elieen was called down to work the emergency room. There was a pile up on the freeway, that's why I remember. It was just after that, next day that they argued." She glanced at Mac and he was careful not to react.

"They were shouting, and of course, Eileen took Vicari's side. Right after that, Alice transferred out to another department. Can't recall where. I heard he made a complaint. And then, few months later, three or four, I guess, I heard Alice left." She shrugged. "I heard it had something to do with Vicari. Or maybe your wife. Eileen really didn't like Alice; never did."

Mac took a chance. "Do you have any idea what made my wife so mad? Was it jealousy?"

She pursed her lips. Seconds passed. "It wasn't jealousy, that's for certain. Alice Jean was about twenty years older than Charles Vicari. Besides, she couldn't stand him. He does late-term abortions and she didn't want any part of that. Sometimes when the fetus lived for a little while afterward, Alice and some of the other nurses would want to hold them, until they—" Her eyes slid to the glass and she picked it up, gesturing. "—you know."

"Die?"

"Yeah, expire. They're supposed to be put in a warming pan until they expire naturally, until they stop breathing." She looked at him. "Dr. Vicari didn't know the nurses, like Alice, would sometimes decide to hold them instead."

The waiter put a cup of coffee, and cream and sugar on the table. Lucy's casual demeanor as she talked about the babies dying had hit him. He lifted the coffee and took a sip, buying time to sort through the issues, and his emotions. If what Lucy was saying was true, Alice Braxton might know something significant to the Chasson case. In the same causal tone, he said, looking over the cup, "How could he not know what they were doing, holding the babies?"

"Well he doesn't stick around afterward. Why should he? There're plenty of nurses around to finish things up." She shrugged. "Except that one night. But that was about two-and-a-half years ago."

"Maybe I could find Alice Braxton. Do you know where she is now?"

"Why would she know anything?"

He shrugged. "I've got nowhere else to go."

"That sounds a little futile to me, Fred." When he didn't answer, she sat back, thinking. "I don't know where she went," she finally said. "But she was always talking about Louisiana, down round where you live." She smiled and wrinkled her nose. "I remember because she talked about eating those crawfish that live in the mud down there."

"You think that was home?"

"It's the only place she ever talked about." She pushed her fingers across the table toward his until the tips of hers met his. "She complained about cold in Chicago, too. But why would you want to find Alice? Eileen is gone and Alice won't be one to have kept track of her."

"Maybe that argument between Alice and Charles Vicari had something to do with Eileen," he said. "I don't know what else to do. Maybe there's some kind of connection. You never know."

Lucy's eyes smiled at him. He'd taken this too far, he realized. Drawing back, he turned and lifted his hand for the waiter, signaling for the check. Lucy withdrew, sitting straight.

The waiter nodded. He turned back to Lucy and lowered his voice. "I can't think of anything else until I find my wife."

She touched the tip of earlobe. "Yes. Of course."

"But . . . I do thank you for your help, Lucy."

One corner of her lips quirked into a half-smile. "Just let me know if there's anything else I can do." She brushed a curl from her forehead, watching him.

"Could you get me a copy of the duty roster that night, when Alice Braxton worked with Vicari?"

"Lucy tossed her head and smiled. "There's nothing more focused than a jealous husband. Eileen Broussard doesn't deserve you. But I'll see what I can do. The duty rosters are in our records. I'll dig it up and make a copy."

Outside the wind from the lake was cool, a nice contrast to the heat and humidity he'd left back in New Orleans. He flagged down a taxi, and tucked Lucy Ringer into the backseat. He'd walk, he said. Needed the exercise, he said. And he needed to think.

She reached up and laid her hand on his cheek. "You're a good man, Charlie Brown," she said. "I'm on the same shift tomorrow. Stop by before you leave town, and I'll get you a copy of that roster."

23

THE FIRM TOOK THE NEWS WELL, Rebecca thought. Already the middle of June, the challenge of reorganizing the rest of her life could begin. Rebecca looked at Rose Marie who sat in front of her desk, taking notes.

They were talking nannies. "After you've made the list of agencies, we'll run through them and cull them down to two or three of the best. We need to find out how long each agency has been in business—ten years, minimum, I'd say. And then check out their references. Oh, and whether there've been any complaints."

Rose Marie puckered her lips. "All done already, Rebecca. I've talked to all of them. Even drove by their offices. The bad news is there're only three I think you'll want to consider. And one of those is fairly new. It's the only one without a waiting list."

Rebecca looked up, surprised.

Rose Marie tore a sheet from the notepad and handed it across the desk to Rebecca. "This is the last one. Their licenses are current, good references. I've set up folders for all three agencies for when you have time." She handed the folders across the desk to Rebecca. "There're brochures too; they've all got those. And I've jotted down what the referrals said."

Rebecca was already scanning the brochures and references for the one that had no waiting list. The brochure cover said *"British Nanny—Only the best for your child."* She closed the folder and set it on top of the others, looking at Rose Marie.

"All right. Let's start with British Nanny, but I want to talk to the others, too. You can go ahead and start scheduling interviews. We'll coordinate, and you can put them on my calendar." Smiling, she flipped the pencil in the air and caught it. "This will be easier than I thought."

Rose Marie's eyes slid to her thickening waist, and instantly Rebecca felt the waistband growing tighter. She was almost three months pregnant. She needed new clothes, but she didn't want to start wearing those shapeless billowing tops and dresses just yet. Especially not around clients. She'd tried one of those dresses on and thought she looked just like those old market women selling vegetables on the streets in Naples.

She'd scoured the shops on Canal—Gus Mayer, Godchaux's, Holmes, Maison Blanche—and Town and Country down on St. Charles, and found her only choice was to buy one dress size too large. A hopeless choice. With a sigh she pushed the agency folders aside.

∾〇)

An hour later in the eighteenth floor conference room, all thoughts of nannies vanished. It looked like the Roberts Engineering transaction was moving forward. Bill Brightfield's litigation report on Nevada Auriel was positive. The biggest problem was a personal injury claim. "But, my assessment is that the risk is minimal," he told Case Roberts and Warren Williams, handing each of them a copy of the memorandum he'd prepared. Rebecca had read it just before the meeting.

"I spoke with the insurer's counsel. Of course they wouldn't give me a number for settlement, but they're open, and the company's insurance will cover any potential loss."

"We can explain that in the documents," Rebecca interjected.

Roberts nodded.

"The other cases on record involve disputes with a few vendors, contractors—like that. Those will be a matter of negotiation, but again I don't see much liability there. You'll just have to quantify it on the financial statements and projections. Build it into your offer." He looked at Roberts, adding, "But, I'm sure you know all that."

"Of course." Case Roberts looked up from the memo. "We wanted fresh eyes on this, but you've confirmed what we were thinking." He put the memo down and glanced at Warren. Warren nodded.

"This all sounds good," Roberts said, turning back to Rebecca and Bill Brightfield. "Thanks for your good work, Bill." Looking at Rebecca, he held up both hands, smiling. "All right, then. It's a go. We're moving forward." Then he dropped his hands to Brightfield's memorandum lying before him on the table, smoothing the top page as if it were fine linen.

Warren leaned toward Rebecca. "Let's get started on the joint venture agreement. I'll touch base with the bank group doing the financing, but they're ready." He pulled some papers out of a folder before him and handed them across the table to Rebecca. "California Sun is the lead lender for the syndicate. I'll contact them this afternoon and they'll get their attorneys in touch with you right away."

Rebecca took the pages and glanced down at the terms of the transaction on the first page.

Case Roberts nodded. "We'll want a group of your young lawyers out there by next week for the due diligence. We've got to move fast, Rebecca. The company's sitting on the news while we get this done, but it'll leak sooner or later, and if that happens before we've got things tied up, we'll lose our deal."

"We'll get started today." She'd put Sydney in charge of the initial due diligence. As Case and Warren talked on about the transaction, Rebecca took notes, creating a mental list of things to be done and who'd be in charge of what. She'd manage the joint venture negotiations and agreements herself, with Sydney as the point person for the financing, under her supervision. And they'd hire local counsel in Nevada, where the mine was located, and for real estate and environmental issues.

"We'll want to close the transaction no later than a month from now," she heard Warren saying. "We'll close at Auriel's headquarters in Bakersfield, California."

She gripped her pen as she looked up, suddenly realizing she'd be over four months along and then some. Some companies she knew, not this law firm, still required a woman to stop working at five months pregnancy. One woman she'd met at a party last week had been required to provide a letter from her doctor confirming that date of termination. And not maternity leave—it was termination. So she had no idea whether flying out to Bakersfield would be a problem with Dr. Matlock or—given the baby—with Peter.

"Right." Case looked at Rebecca. "We've got an option; but the closing date for our offer is firm. After that, all bets are off. They'll keep it quiet until then, but once word of the strike gets out, if we don't have this tied up we'll find ourselves in an auction."

Bakersfield, California in one month!

To her left, Brightfield coughed and she saw him glance at her from the corners of his eyes. Worried about the deadline on his appellate brief, she supposed.

"So what do you think?"

Swallowing, Rebecca turned to Case Roberts, her new client, and managed a smile. "If the banks can do it, we can too. No problem."

Good." Roberts slapped both hands down on the tabletop and stood, turning to Warren Williams. "Let's get back to the office, Warren. We'll get Auriel on the line—give them the good news."

Rebecca tucked Brightfield's report between the pages of her legal pad, preparing to rise. Beside her Bill shot up and reached across the table to shake Case Roberts's hand. "Congratulations," he said in a hearty man-to-man tone.

"Oh, by the way," Roberts said, turning to Rebecca. "I understand congratulations are in order."

"Thanks." She wondered how he'd already heard.

As Case and Warren packed up their briefcases and prepared to leave, Brightfield turned toward her. "Don't forget the brief's due in six weeks. Now's the time to let me know if there's any chance you can't meet the filing deadline."

"I'll meet it." Hugging the notepad to her chest, she gave him a carefree smile. "You'll have a first draft to review in a few weeks." She didn't know how she'd get the brief completed and Auriel closed on such a schedule. But she'd do it.

He smiled and slapped his hand on her shoulder as he walked by. "Attagirl."

24

DOCTOR STEPHANIE KAND HAD FINALIZED THE forensics pathology report, analyzing the results of the autopsy of Baby Chasson in a medical legal context. Peter read this methodically, walling off all emotions that might contaminate his judgment. He'd resolved to keep his mind clear in order to make an objective decision about the merits of this case.

Stephanie Kand had performed thousands of autopsies over the years for the Jefferson Parish District Attorney's office. She would be a good witness, he knew; she always was. He'd worked with her in many cases. Her *curriculum vitae* read like an introduction to a textbook.

Peter had intended to review the photographs again before reading the report, but after the first one, he put the rest aside. That could wait, he told himself. It was Dr. Kand's final analysis and conclusions he was after now. So instead, he'd just begun to read. She had autopsied the entire body, as well as the placenta—to make certain there was no infection between the mother and the infant.

Kand reported that the body appeared to be in a good state of preservation. The infant had been found wrapped in a small blue birthing towel; the same one described by Clara Sonsten. Kand had noted that the soft cloth was made of special fibers that generated almost no lint and fuzz, and leaving behind little debris.

The blood type of the infant matched that of the mother, Glory Lynn Chasson. The infant was male. The body measured 11.8 inches from crown to heel, and weighed one pound, eight ounces, 680.4 grams. Based upon those facts and the autopsy, gestational age of the infant was estimated to be twenty-four weeks.

Six months. He looked off. So Glory Lynn Chasson's initial calculation had been off by two weeks. The defense would use that uncertainty to confuse the jury, he knew.

He went back to the report. The infant's skin was loose and wrinkled and covered with a cheesy protective substance. His ears, eyes, nose, and lids were formed and would have been functional for the age, Kand concluded. The eyes had developed to a point able to sense light in the womb when alive, the ears able to detect sounds outside the womb. The still delicate skeleton was fully assembled. The circulatory system was fully formed and was functional. Visceral organs, like the liver and heart and lungs, appeared normal for the premature age.

Microscopic study of the lungs confirmed that the baby had breathed on his own for some period of time after birth and before death, conclusive that this was indeed a live birth. Glory Lynn Chasson had been right that she'd heard her baby cry. More important, air was also found in the stomach, further proof that the infant had been breathing for a while. He read this section over twice. Swallowing, he set the report aside.

His diploma from Loyola Law School hung on the wall before his desk, near the door. Peter gazed at it now, thinking of Dr. Kand's conclusions, and of the scene in that procedure room that night, how it must have been with the infant crying and Glory Lynn struggling with the nurse to get to her child when, instinctively, she'd realized that the unthinkable had happened and everything suddenly flipped upside down.

And then he thought of all the hours he'd spent in classrooms in law school, taking lecture notes and reading and outlining cases, tearing them apart to understand the issues, the facts, the court's rationale and verdict— now realizing that none of that had prepared him for a case like this one.

Once again he picked up the report.

The skull was normal, the smooth plates connected by thin membranes providing helmet-like protection for the brain, as expected for the infant's age. Dissection of the brain showed no abnormalities. He read through the entire report of Stephanie Kand's forensic analysis, and then read it through again, absorbing the details, evaluating the weight of each detail for himself, and also in light of how a jury would see it.

At last, Peter put down the report and rubbed his eyes, thinking of the implications of Dr. Kand's conclusions. There were no major congenital abnormalities found in the autopsy. The forensic pathology report was thorough. Slowly the conclusion formed in his mind—chances were Baby Chasson would be alive today if he'd been given adequate medical assistance.

At the very least, with neonatal intensive care in a hospital, he'd have had a chance.

The feeling of despair turned to anger, then to a rage that began roaring through him. He would prosecute this case if Ham would let him. Not only because a crime had been committed, but also because the world outside seemed oblivious that such things were happening. But this was an explosive set of facts, and Ham would resist at first, he thought, because of the political sensitivity. The district attorney was an elected office.

Somehow he had to convince Ham to let him take the case forward. He had to convince the DA that they had the evidence to carry the burden of proof, and that the jury would be with them all the way. He'd go on home and try the State's case out on Rebecca, he decided, as if she was a juror. He would lay out the evidence and catch her reaction. She'd always been good at spotting the weak points.

But he'd have to do this carefully, with sensitivity, he knew. Rebecca was tough. But the sorrow they both felt for Baby Chasson already cast a shadow over their joy for their own coming birth.

Two infants, each eliciting opposite emotions. It was growing more complicated by the moment.

At seven thirty that night Peter stopped the car in his driveway and got out to pick up the newspaper. Rebecca wasn't home yet, he supposed, and he was relieved. He had a lot of thinking to do. Newspaper in hand, he got back into the car and pulled into the garage, then turned off the engine. Sure enough, her car was gone. Slowly he edged out of his own.

Entering the kitchen from the garage, he set the paper down on the kitchen table and strolled through the living room, into the study, closing the door behind him. There he sank into an overstuffed chair near the bookcase and, with a long sigh, leaned back against the cushion.

He closed his eyes and he prayed for the infant Chasson; for the baby in God's grace. And for Glory Lynn Chasson, too; a young woman now in despair, filled with remorse. And he gave thanks for his own child and prayed for guidance, and for Rebecca's faith to grow. He'd seen some hints along that line, little things she'd said that told him she was thinking things over as the child inside her womb was growing. Since they'd returned from Italy, week after week he'd seen her looking at pictures in the book that Dr. Matlock had given to her weeks ago, pictures of the miracle of life.

Thinking of their child, Peter smiled, wondering if they'd have a son or a daughter and what it would be like to be a father. For a while he let his thoughts jump from one thing to another. As he relaxed with his eyes closed, soon he began drifting in that space in between sleep and awareness.

Rebecca parked in the driveway and came in through the front door. As she headed toward the kitchen all she could think about right now between Brightfield's deadline for the brief and Roberts Engineering's deadline for the closing in Bakersfield, and the baby growing every day, was that she felt like a balloon filled to capacity and ready to explode.

She reached into the refrigerator for a carton of milk. Then she retrieved a glass from the cabinet above. Then, glass of milk in hand, she headed once again for the living room, and toward the stairs. The study door was closed, as she'd left it this morning. She wished that Peter was home, but decided she was too exhausted to wait up for him. She hadn't been feeling that well today and thought that maybe she'd call Dr. Matlock's office in the morning.

Holding the glass in her right hand, she pulled herself up the steps with her left, thinking of the soft mattress on the bed, and of the pile of pillows waiting for her, and the cool fluffy white quilt. She'd reached the fourth step when a sound below startled her. The sound of a door opening and closing below, in the empty house.

Gripping the bannister, Rebecca turned, peering over her shoulder, looking down in confusion, and in the instant her right foot slipped from the edge of the next step, shifting her weight as it went airborne. As she turned, twisting, losing balance, her mind screamed no, and then she felt herself falling forward with one arm flung across her midsection protecting the baby, the other flailing for the railing that she could not see, and screaming—*thebaby-thebaby—ohthebaby* . . .

And then, just as suddenly it was over.

Strong arms caught her, and a body was there absorbing her weight, stopping the fall. Strong arms wrapped around her as she trembled, sobbing.

Peter held her, steadying her as she sank onto the steps, his voice soothing. Soothing as he knelt with her, whispering in her ear—"I've got you, Rebbe."

She collapsed then, curling into a ball, as images of Elise's bike sailing into the street flashed through her mind. Elise, oh how she'd let down Elise, and now what had she done to her own child! She buried her face in her arms forcing away those memories, the car's screaming breaks, the sounds of metal crushing . . . and Peter tightened his grip on her, his voice thick now and choked as he cried how he loved her and that everything would be all right. That she was fine. That the baby was fine.

Minutes passed right there, with Peter holding her, with his head bent so their foreheads touched and he told her just to rest, not to move and her throat feeling tight, closing, and her heart beating fast. But slowly, slowly as Peter held her and she pressed both hands over the baby, feeling nothing out of the ordinary, in the stream of his comforting words, she grew calm.

At last, standing on the lower step just before her with his hands under her arms, Peter helped her up. And, that's when she saw the blood. And when she looked up at Peter once again, she saw her terror reflected in his eyes.

"We're going to the hospital, Rebee. Stay calm." He moved back, bracing himself, and then he slipped his arms beneath her under her back, under her knees, and lifted her up.

"My guess is a partial previa," Dr. Matlock said after she'd dressed and Peter had come back into the room. She sat on the edge of the bed. "The ultrasound didn't confirm one way or the other. It's too early to tell." They were in the emergency room of Baptist Hospital.

Rebecca flinched, and he added quickly, "Look, the baby's fine. Your placenta's lying low in the uterus is my guess. We'll have to watch things and take it easy."

"What's that all mean, Doctor?" Peter stood beside her with his hand on her shoulder.

He fingered the stethoscope. "It's not unusual. As the uterus grows during pregnancy the placenta grows too, stretching. Right now I suspect it's near the cervix, causing that sudden bleeding, but gradually it should stretch, moving clear allowing the cervix to open for birth. I'd expect that to happen by the third trimester."

"You used the word *should*, Doc. What's that mean?" Peter's voice had taken on his trial tone, Rebecca realized. Dr. Matlock took a step back.

"If it interferes with the cervix and complicates delivery," he looked at Rebecca, "then, you might need a C-section. We'll have to wait and see."

Peter's hand tightened on Rebecca's shoulder as she recoiled. The thought of any danger to the baby, anything at all, turned to panic. "But the baby . . . the baby will be all right either way?"

"We're not even certain that's what caused the bleeding, yet. Let's not get ahead of ourselves." He rubbed his eyes. "It seems to have stopped, for now. Let's keep it that way." Matlock took a couple steps back, so that he stood in the doorway as he fingered the stethoscope. "If we're lucky you'll just have to miss a little work. Avoid stress. Take things easy."

Rebecca started. Avoid stress. The new woman partner must avoid stress? Impossible. She fixed her eyes on a chart of the human body on the wall before her, thinking that over.

Matlock seemed to read her thoughts. "This isn't a suggestion. It's an order. You're going to have to stay in bed. Only for a few days, if the bleeding doesn't resume."

There was the Auriel deal. There was Brightfield's brief. Peter squeezed her shoulder.

Her voice ripped up the scale when she was able to speak. "For how long, exactly? How long in bed?"

"We'll just have to see. If there's no more bleeding, I'd say you could try getting up and around after a few days."

"But . . ."

"But none of those long hours I know you're used to working. No stress. No heavy lifting, or long walks or exercise."

"I can't . . ."

"And," he went on, ignoring Rebecca's protests, moving his eyes to Peter. "Romance will have to wait awhile."

"Listen, Dr. Matlock. I've got work to do. I can't just go to bed for a few days."

"Yes, you can." His voice was casual. He took the stethoscope from around his neck, and turned around, looking for his black bag. The bag was on an aluminum table, painted white, just under the chart on the wall. "You'll do it because that's what you need to do for your baby." He opened the bag, stuck the stethoscope inside, snapped it closed, picked it up, and turned back to Rebecca.

The Auriel closing was in a month. And it would take place in Bakersfield, California. "Will I be able to travel after that, after I'm up and about again?"

He gave her a long look. "I doubt it."

Peter spoke up: "Tell us; what's the worst that could happen?"

Matlock paused. Worked his tongue around in his cheek. At last he said, "Miscarriage, possibly."

Rebecca bowed her head. Matlock quickly added, "But that's unlikely if you're careful."

She nodded.

"I want to see you once a week from now on. And we'll schedule another ultra-sound in about a month." He picked up the hat he'd worn and put it on his head, looking at them both.

"We're going to watch this carefully and take every precaution. Baby's going to be fine. Just fine."

Alice was resting in bed, her feet propped up on a pillow she kept just for that purpose.

When the telephone rang, she decided to ignore it. And then it rang again. Once. Twice. She struggled to her feet. Hurrying into the kitchen she picked up the receiver. "Hello?" She could hear the hint of worry in her voice.

"Alice. I'm so glad you're there."

She slumped against the wall. Chicago. Not again. "I'm here. What's wrong?"

"Nothing's wrong. At least, I don't think so. But a detective came by our office today. A man named Fred McAndrews. From New Orleans, he said. He was looking for you, Alice. Asked for you by name, Alice Braxton."

"Did you tell him anything?"

"Of course not. You know how New Hope is. I just wanted you to know. Like you asked."

25

A FEW DAYS LATER, MAC SAT in Peter's office, legs crossed, notebook open and resting on his knee. An accordion file folder was on the floor beside him, standing upright against the leg of his chair. He was describing the conversation he'd had with Lucy Ringer in Chicago. When he got to the part about Alice Jean Braxton, Peter felt it—there was something here.

"Vicari routinely performed late-term abortions, Lucy says."

He nodded, not wanting to interrupt.

"The blow up between Alice Braxton and Charles Vicari made a big impression on the staff, according to Lucy. Apparently it's unusual for a nurse to go to war with a physician. Lucy was able to pin down a range of dates from the other nurses' recollections and then she checked the duty rosters. Only one date around then showed Alice Braxton working with Vicari." He reached down and heaved the file to his knees and looked through it until he came to the page he wanted and pulled it out.

"Here's a copy of the roster for that day. Alice Braxton worked with Vicari on December 3, 1979, about two and a half years ago." He handed the page over to Peter. Bending over the desk Mac pointed upside-down to an entry on the sheet that Peter held, a notation at 5:30 p.m. "It looks like Eileen Broussard was originally scheduled to work with Vicari, and then her name was crossed off and Alice Braxton's is scribbled above that. According to Lucy, the next day they had that argument."

Backing into the chair again, he leaned back. "Ordinarily Alice refused to work with Vicari, Lucy said. He performed abortions and Braxton had filed a conscience objection with the hospital, Lucy says. So this particular substitution was unusual."

"The nurse you talked to, did she know if there was an investigation on what happened, afterwards?"

"She didn't know of anything and I couldn't push that far." He gave Peter a wry smile. "I was supposed to be looking for my missing wife."

"Missing wife?"

"Yes. Eileen Broussard."

Peter frowned. This was more than he wanted to know.

"I tried getting information from personnel about Alice's whereabouts and got nowhere. The lady in PR picked up the phone and called house counsel the minute I asked the question. He must've told her to clam up because she had a sour look when she hung up the phone. Bottom line—they don't give out information on former employees without a local subpoena."

"Do they know you talked to Lucy?"

"I didn't mention that."

No one spoke for a moment. Mac broke the silence. "So. What do you think?"

Peter pushed out his bottom lip, studying the detective. He swung his hands onto the desk before him. "You think you could get a sworn statement from Miss Ringer?"

"Once we've got a case filed I think she might cooperate."

"All right. Even without her, I think we've got a case. I'd sure like to talk to this other nurse, this Alice Braxton." He looked off for a moment, then turned his eyes to Mac. "But, I'll talk to Ham this afternoon anyway. We've bypassed the usual screening process here, but with the forensic report and Clara Sonsten's statement backing up the complaint and the receptionist Melanie Wright supporting Sonsten, I think we've got enough to take to the grand jury."

"Good. I want another look at that clinic."

"Hold off on the warrant until I talk to Ham. I'll give you a call soon as that happens." Leaning back, Peter clasped his hands behind his head. "We need to find Alice Braxton though. Something happened up there in Chicago, and if it's anything like this, we'd be able to show he's done this before. To show prior knowledge of such a thing happening, and intent."

"Lucy Ringer thinks Alice Braxton was from Louisiana so she may have had a nursing license here. I'll start in Baton Rouge. That's not much to go on. But if her license is current in this state, I'll find her." Mac slapped his hands on the tops of his thighs. He stuck the notebook into his jacket pocket and picked up the file from his side of Peter's desk, then stood.

"What are you thinking for Vicari? Manslaughter? Homicide?"

Ham would want to go for manslaughter which required a showing of real negligence, but wouldn't have to prove intent—the intentional killing of a human being. Homicide laws in Louisiana were divided into first and second degree murder, manslaughter, negligent homicide, and vehicular homicide.

Peter met Mac's eyes. "As far as I know, a baby born alive in this state has a constitutional right to life; some sort of medical assessment, and then appropriate medical care. I'm tempted to go for second degree murder, but we'd have to prove that Vicari specifically intended to kill this child."

Mac didn't say anything.

Peter shook his head, looking off. "I don't know. Maybe Alice Braxton can shed some light on that issue. But I'm guessing, if we go forward, Ham will want manslaughter."

"That's too bad."

"Yeah. Well, we'll see." He'd fight for second degree murder, but that was between him and Ham. "Either way, though, if we take this case forward, we've got to win."

Mac gave him a nod and headed for the door. Peter watched him go, but as he reached the door, Peter called to him.

Mac halted and turned.

"We need to keep this low-key, Mac. No media. If anyone from the press contacts you, refer them to public relations."

"You got it."

Peter picked up the phone and began to dial the district attorney's office.

"Abortion is established law, Peter. The Supreme Court in *Roe v. Wade* established that nine years ago. And that decision wiped out the State of Louisiana's abortion laws." Ham stood at the window, hands clasped behind his back as he looked out over the river toward New Orleans. He'd finally gotten Ham's attention on the Chasson case. They'd spent an hour going through the evidence.

"This isn't about abortion," Peter replied, yet again.

Ham turned. He studied Peter for a moment. Peter held steady, but he could almost see the wheels turning in the district attorney's head, evaluating the chances for success, and failure. This case was sure to attract the press. He was stepping down in two years and the last thing he wanted was a big loss on his record at the end of the road.

Peter sat on the corner of Ham's desk with one foot on the floor and the other dangling. When Ham walked back to the chair behind his desk, Peter stood and took his place at the window, looking out over the river.

"Tell me again why you think you can prove second degree murder."

"The Chasson complaint says it loud and clear," Peter said, turning around. He crossed his arms and began pacing back and forth before Ham's desk, speaking in a reflective tone as if this was the first time he'd run through the argument. "Look at the facts. We have a living human being, outside the womb and completely separated from the mother. Breathing. Crying. Moving. The abortion's over." He stopped and looked at Ham. "What could be more clear?"

"Nothing in this area's clear."

"The facts are there. Dr. Kand's report is clear." He continued pacing back and forth. "Stephanie concludes that the infant lived for some period of time after birth, breathing voluntarily on his own." He halted and wheeled toward Ham. "Time to get to a hospital."

The DA held up his hands. "I'm the devil's advocate for a minute." He paused, worked his tongue around in his cheek, and then looked at Peter. "The mother chooses to have an abortion. Roe v. Wade gives her that choice. She does not want to be a mother. So when the infant accidently survives the procedure and the doctor renders medical assistance and the child lives, what's happened to her choice?"

"Her right to choose ends at birth."

"Have you got a case on point that says that, a case that's been tried?"

"There are a couple manslaughter cases, but different facts. None where the infant was completely separated from the mother and continued breathing."

"No second degree murder?"

"No." Peter let a beat go by. "Like I said, none with these facts."

Ham looked at him in silence.

Peter dropped into a chair before the DA's desk. "Listen. We've got a live birth here." He raised fingers one at a time to tick off his points. "One: The autopsy concludes the child was alive for a period of time, and yet no medical assessment was performed. Two: The autopsy and the forensic analysis determined that the infant was well formed, premature, of course, but well formed. And, three: We have intent. According to the witness staements, there was plenty of time to get that baby to a hospital. Plenty of time to try to save his life. And according to one witness, Charles Vicari said no. He refused to let the nurse clear the infant's air passages, or to call an ambulance."

Ham shifted his eyes to the door behind Peter. Minutes passed. Peter sat before the DA's desk stiff and silent, almost holding his breath.

"We'd do better with negligent homicide," Ham said at last. He picked up a pen on the desk beside him and focused all of his attention on rolling it back and forth between his fingers.

Peter shook his head. "This was deliberate, Ham. I want to go for second degree murder."

Ham looked up. "How will you prove intent?"

"We'll get there." Once again he summarized Clara Sonsten's testimony. And Melanie Wright's. He went through the autopsy report and the pathology conclusions again. Ham reviewed the autopsy photos as he talked, his eyes narrowing as he replaced each one with the next. Peter considered telling Ham about Lucy Ringer's statement that this circumstance wasn't unique, but didn't want the DA's answer to depend on that. The Chicago nurse's cooperation wasn't assured.

"And this nurse Sonsten, and Miss Wright, they'll both testify?"

He hesitated. Melanie Wright might be a hostile witness, but Mac thought she would tell the truth. And Clara Sonsten was reliable. "Yes," he said.

Ham pushed the pencil back and forth. "Second degree, you say?"

"A line's been crossed here, Ham."

The DA grew still. He held Peter's eyes. "I'm retiring soon, you know."

Peter nodded.

"I'd like you to be my replacement, you know." He looked off, pushing out his bottom lip, then back at Peter. "But, if you take this case, you'd better win, Peter. Because if not . . . you won't stand a chance, politics being what they are. This one's explosive."

"We can win it."

"All right, then," Ham said, tapping the stack of photographs on his desk to square them. He set them down beside him and looked at Peter. His brows met, forming slashing lines between his eyes. "Last time I looked at the Code, any infant born alive in this state is a 'person' with all the rights that entails, including the right to live, to fight for his life. We'll go for second degree murder."

Peter nodded. He stood, feeling the flutter in his stomach. Ham handed the file back to him.

"Take it to the grand jury, Peter." The grand jury would give the DA some cover with the voters, Peter knew.

"Let's move forward."

26

OVER THE NEXT WEEK REBECCA FELT Peter's growing tension, but she didn't ask what was wrong and he didn't volunteer. Preparation for the grand jury on the Chasson case absorbed all his time and attention. She'd returned to work five days after the incident that had landed her in the hospital, but since then problems at work were mounting.

The meeting with Case Roberts and Warren Williams to inform them of her doctor's orders not to travel had not gone well. She'd tried her best to convince them that with Sydney Martin handling things in Bakersfield at the closing, and with Rebecca available at all times on the phone, the closing would go smoothly.

Case had worn a pained look as he listened. When she'd finished arguing her case, there'd been a long silence in the room and then, clasping his hands on the table, he'd looked down at them and said, "This is disappointing, of course, Rebecca." He'd glanced at Warren and back at her. "I understand your problem. Doctor's orders are final. That's that."

She'd just begun to relax when he added, "But I'm not comfortable not having a partner present at the closing." He turned to Warren. "What do you think?"

Avoiding her eyes, Warren clasped his hands together, exactly as Case had done, and studied them in the same melancholy manner. "Things come up, you know. Eye to eye is best. Sometimes those are the most controversial, most important discussions."

He turned his eyes to her. "Problems often come up at the last minute; you've got to be in the same room."

Case interrupted. "Warren's right, I'm afraid. Faxes and telephones are fine, and I'm sure Sydney Martin's a capable lawyer, but we need a partner that can make decisions right there in Bakersfield." He sat back and crossed his arms, his brows lowering, his eyes sorrowful.

Rebecca felt her throat close. His meaning was plain and if she didn't take charge quickly and give them what they wanted, they would go someplace else. To some other law firm. She'd break a record—the firm's first partner to bring in a client and lose him before the first transaction.

"I understand. And certainly no one here at Mangen & Morris wants Roberts Engineering to be unhappy," Rebecca said, elbows and arms on the table, as she leaned forward, smiling. Her tone was casual, cheerful. "That's not a problem. I've got someone in mind, Amalise Catoir. She's one of our best and she could step right in."

Oh please, please, let Amalise have the time.

Case and Warren glanced at each other.

"All right. That's fine," Warren said. "You'll get her up to speed quickly?"

"Yes, right away." She pushed a strand of hair back from her forehead, talking a deep breath as she added, "And since this is our problem, not yours, we'll bill Roberts Engineering only for her time on this project from now on."

Case frowned. "But, you'll stay involved?"

"Sure. I'll be here, in the background. This is just a little lagniappe." A little something extra that meant she'd be working for free on what had just become Amalise's deal. Acid burned in the back of her throat. She was having to turn over her first big client to Amalise.

Back in her office, Rebecca called Amalise and explained the situation. Amalise said that she'd be glad to help. Rebecca didn't mention the billing arrangement. Amalise would report all of her billable hours on the deal, and there'd be plenty. But she'd have been uncomfortable knowing that Rebecca was donating her own time. Still, she was doing what was necessary to hold on to the client.

When they'd finished talking and hung up, she asked Rose Marie to have someone duplicate all of the Roberts Engineering files and have the originals sent to Amalise, and the copies returned to her. Rose Marie stared, and then nodded, wearing a disconcerted look as she went off.

She ate lunch in her office alone, absorbing the damage from the morning meeting with Roberts Engineering. When she'd finished, she brushed her hands together and told herself to stay positive. Brightfield's brief would keep her busy for a few weeks at least. And there was plenty to do to get ready for the baby. Rose Marie had set up two interviews with prospective nannies this afternoon. And she was looking forward to planning the nursery.

No billable hours there, though.

At three o'clock she returned to her office for the first of the interviews. The second was set for four thirty. Once she was able to hire help with the baby, she could make plans, she told herself. She'd be moving forward again, and she'd have something to build on, freedom to plan her new schedule. And after the baby was born, there'd be no problem traveling then, not with good help. She'd work all this out she knew—she was the It Girl. She could handle a child at home and a career at work; like walking and chewing gum, or something.

Her telephone buzzed. "Your three o'clock appointment is here," Rose Marie said. "She's in the reception area."

"Fine. Bring her in, please."

Five minutes later Rose Marie appeared in her office with Cassandra Mayfield. Rebecca looked up. As they were introduced, Rebecca's first thought was that this was a stern-looking woman. Rebecca tried to picture her rocking Daisy, and couldn't.

Miss Mayfield's hair, streaked with gray, was pulled back into a tight bun. She stood beside Rose Marie just inside the doorway with her feet apart, weight evenly distributed, and a slight stoop of her shoulders. Her shoes were brown oxfords. She wore a plain brown suit with a boxy jacket, a white blouse buttoned to her neck, and a skirt that hung three inches below her knees. She looked years older than her résumé had promised, which was forty-three.

Rebecca stood and motioned Miss Mayfield toward the sofa and chairs in the corner. "Thanks for coming. Let's sit over there to talk."

Cassandra Mayfield's smile was flat, as were her eyes, as she thanked Rebecca and moved toward the corner area. Once there, tucking her skirt under, she sat and planted her purse beside her, pressing her shoes together on the floor as she looked about. Rose Marie asked if she would like coffee, or tea, or a Coke, but Miss Mayfield shook her head. No thanks.

Rebecca stifled a sigh and stood.

Picking up Cassandra's résumé from her desk, she walked to one of the chairs near the sofa and took a seat, putting the résumé down on her lap. She didn't really need it, she practically had it memorized. On paper, Cassandra

Mayfield looked good. She came with high recommendations from the service, and her last job had been with an uptown matron who Rebecca did not recall ever having met, but who'd once been queen of the Krewe of Athenians at Carnival, which provided a certain reference.

Rebecca settled back, resting one hand over the baby, struggling to picture this stern woman in the nursery. She smiled, and lifted a corner of the résumé, looking at it. "Your references are good." She glanced up. "I see you were with your last employer for three years. Why did you leave?"

The woman placed her hands atop her knees and looked at the wall, just past Rebecca's shoulder. "There was a family problem, of sorts. I don't feel comfortable talking about it, really. Nothing to do with me." She glanced at Rebecca. "I don't mind your calling the references though."

That sounded good. She respected family privacy. "Was it your choice to leave?"

She gave Rebecca a cool look. "Yes. Of course."

"All right, then. How many children were in your care?"

"Only one. I had him until he was two, almost two."

"And according to the agency, you lived with the family?'

"That's right. I had my own room. And private bath." She pursed her lips. "That's a requirement for me. I must have a private bath."

Rebecca nodded. The bedroom she had in mind had a private bath.

"And a car, of course, to get around with baby."

Uh oh. It wasn't the money. But she didn't know this woman well enough to let her drive Daisy around. And, besides, there was potential liability. "That won't be necessary where we live," she said in what she thought was a pleasant tone. "I think you'll agree. We're half a block from the streetcar on St. Charles. There's a playground right across the street. And we don't mind paying for taxis."

Miss Mayfield shook her head. "Having a car is one of my conditions."

"I see." Rebecca crossed her legs and folded her arms. "Perhaps we should go straight to your terms. What else do you require?"

"I have Sundays off."

That could be a problem.

"And baby will need quiet in the home. I run a tight ship in the nursery, Mrs. Jacobs. I'll be training baby from the start. That's how you keep them from being spoiled. Have to set a schedule, let them cry until they learn who's boss. So I need to know that Mom and Dad won't come running in at the wrong time, if you know what I mean. The worst thing that can happen to an infant, in my view, is to overreact."

"Overreact?"

She shrugged. "Too much coddling. Picking baby up every time he whines or cries, giving them too much attention." Her mouth creased into a thin smile. "It's difficult for a new mother at first, I realize. But that's how baby learns to respect the rest of the family's boundaries." She dipped her chin. "And mine, of course."

Rebecca looked at her for a long moment. Then she glanced at her watch. Miss Mayfield was out of her office before the second hand made another round. And the next interview didn't go much better. She went home with a pounding headache.

27

THE GRAND JURY ISSUED AN INDICTMENT charging that Charles Frank Vicari committed the offense of Murder in the Second Degree against a human being, the infant born of Glory Lynn Chasson, contrary to laws of the State of Louisiana. The essential allegations and evidence in the case were set forth by the prosecution for the jurors—Infant Chasson was born alive during an abortion procedure. Charles Frank Vicari delivered the infant, and was the physician in charge. The defendant knowingly withheld medical assistance from Infant Chasson, with an intent to kill. The infant lived for over an hour, struggling to breathe before his death.

A warrant for Vicari's arrest was issued immediately, to be executed by the sheriff's department. The charges were second degree murder, with lesser included offenses. The case was assigned to Senior Assistant District Attorney Peter Jacobs, as requested.

Vince McConnell, Vicari's lawyer, was among the best of the defense bar in New Orleans and the metro area, and his clients paid him well. McConnell called Peter to advise that Vicari would come in voluntarily. They agreed that Vince would drive him in, and that he would arrive at the station house in Gretna at four o'clock that afternoon, where he'd be taken into custody. The press would not be notified.

The deal was fine with Peter. Publicity was the last thing he sought. The facts in this case were unique and inflammatory and the prosecution and the defense had a mutual interest in keeping things quiet for as long as possible. From Vicari's point of view, Peter judged, his desire to keep out of the media spotlight was personal.

Keeping things low-key was the goal. Mac laughed off the possibility. But Peter thought the strategy might work since *Roe v. Wade* was old news now from the media's point of view. And, he reminded Mac, the city of Gretna was a ferry and a bridge and a world away from the city of New Orleans.

⟨6∼9⟩

The next morning Peter sat at the prosecution table in the courtroom, wait-ing for Vicari's first appearance. The other half of the prosecution team sat beside him. Dorothea St. Pierre, known as Dooney, was a young assistant district attorney who'd recently graduated from LSU Law School. She was seven years Peter's junior. Dooney would sit as second chair. She was quick, precise, and driven, glossy and slick on the outside, but soft inside, reminding him of Rebecca in that way. They'd worked together before.

Dooney was very good with juries, and that was the main reason that he'd picked her to assist him on this case. As a woman prosecutor she related well to both men and women on juries; she was professional and efficient with a feminine touch, and she was smart. He would take the lead in the courtroom; she was too fresh out of law school to question material witnesses.

He'd pulled Dooney into this case while preparing for the grand jury. Now, as they waited for court to convene, she leaned over and said that Mac had called just before she'd left her desk. He'd phoned from Baton Rouge where he was looking for that nurse, Alice Jean Braxton. Lucy Ringer had guessed right. Alice Braxton's nursing license was on record, since 1945.

Peter nodded. Good. Maybe they were getting somewhere.

The docket was heavy this morning, and *State of Louisiana v. Charles Frank Vicari* was next up. But the judge, an interim judge from Houma named Rafael Plaissard, had just called a short recess and turned away to confer with his clerk. The clerk's desk was located to the right of the bench, between the witness stand and the jury box, but back against the wall so as not to disrupt the jury's view of any witness.

A few minutes passed while the judge and his clerk spoke, and then His Honor stood and disappeared through the door behind the bench. Peter tapped the tabletop with his pen, his eyes roaming over the well of the court-room while they waited. Dooney began reading something she'd pulled from her briefcase.

Between the prosecution table where he sat, and the bench, the court reporter sat, winding tape into her machine. To his left was the defense table, currently occupied by three lawyers, stragglers from earlier hearings, talking and laughing while they stuffed papers into their briefcases. They walked off, and then Vince McConnell tapped him on the shoulder as he made his way to the defense table where he took a seat. He sat alone. His client would be brought into the courtroom by the sheriffs when called.

Just then several lawyers pushed through the gate in the rail behind Peter, and to his left. The rail separated the well of the courtroom from spectators. The group stormed toward the clerk's desk, all hunched, charging like bulls.

Opening the briefcase on the table before him, Peter pulled out a yellow legal pad. The first page was covered with scribbled notes. He set the tablet down on the table, snapped the briefcase shut, and pushed it out of his way. Behind him he could hear the melancholy hum of mothers, fathers, wives and girlfriends, children—the families and friends of defendants waiting in the holding cell outside the courtroom, most gathered to catch a glimpse of their loved ones when they appeared one by one before the judge at some time during the day. For the most part they were impatient, bored, irritable, unhappy, and uncomfortable on the wooden benches, but there was nothing for them but to wait because you never knew when, or who, would shuffle through that door.

To the right of the prosecution table where he sat was the empty jury box. As in every courtroom in the building, twelve chairs in the box were welded to the floor of a slightly raised platform, with two movable chairs at the end for the alternates. A railing separated the jurors from the well.

Suddenly, like a flurry of small fish sensing the presence of a shark, stragglers in the space between the railing and the judge's bench, including the three lawyers surrounding the clerk, all scattered. The door behind the bench opened and Judge Plaissard appeared. The bailiff announced that court was back in session and called the case, *State of Louisiana v. Charles Frank Vicari.*

The judge took his seat and looked at McConnell and then at Peter. "Are counsel present?"

"Yes, Your Honor." Peter and Dooney stood and gave their names as counsel for the State. McConnell did the same, announcing for the defendant.

Judge Plaissard instructed the bailiff to notify the deputies to bring in the defendant. Peter and Dooney sat down and turned, watching as the door to the hallway at the back of the courtroom opened. Charles Vicari had been in custody now for twenty-three hours. The defendant's looks and demeanor after time spent in a jail cell would telegraph clues to his attitude and resolution.

Surrounded by deputies, Charles Vicari walked into the courtroom with his chin high and his expression blank. His hands were cuffed before him, but his legs weren't shackled. His hair was brown and neatly slicked back from a receding hairline, as if he'd just come from a barber shop. He was tall, about six feet. His forehead was high and smooth, although lines between his eyes were deeply furrowed, more with anger than fear, Peter judged. The doctor's fine arched brows formed a perfect V over his dark eyes. And despite the night in lockup, his tailored gray suit was unwrinkled. His shoes shone. His white collar was pressed. Vince must have gotten the clothes to him right before the appearance.

When they reached the defense table, one of the deputies pulled out a chair and stood aside. Vince McConnell greeted the doctor like they were old friends, shaking one hand and pressing his other on the defendant's shoulder as he sat. The doctor did not respond. The deputies moved to one side, standing near the wall. Peter watched with curiosity as McConnell sat back down and bent his head toward the defendant. They were in this together, he was probably whispering. They would run this race together, and they would win.

Charles Vicari listened and then nodded and sat back. He adjusted his jacket collar, yanked down his sleeves, and turned, letting his eyes roam over the courtroom, over the spectators behind him, his gaze drifting with studied disinterest past Peter and Dooney and on to the judge.

The arraignment was brief, as expected. Judge Plaissard read the State's charges against the defendant: Second Degree Murder, with lesser charges included.

Defendant entered his plea. Not guilty.

The judge then looked at McConnell. "I understand we have some motions?"

McConnell stood. "Yes, Judge."

The clerk handed some papers to the judge, which he scanned, frowning. And then the clerk walked over to the prosecution table and handed copies to Peter and Dooney. Peter looked down, read, flipping through them one at a time, and then he rose. He objected that he'd not seen these motions before, and he'd been given no notice that they were coming. Vince argued that they were routine, and that they'd only just been completed a few minutes before he'd left his office for this hearing. He'd been working on them through the night. After some back and forth, Judge Plaissard overruled the State's objection.

Peter began reading the paperwork as the judge turned to McConnell. Plaissard spread his hand, palm up. "These are your motions, Counsel."

McConnell nodded and stood. Holding the pages in one hand, he spoke without looking at them. "In the first motion, Your Honor, Defendant moves for release on bond, pending trial. In the second . . ."

"Let's take the first one, first," replied Judge Plaissard.

"Yes, Judge. Defense is requesting release on recognizance, or alternatively, on bond, pending trial."

Peter rose, fingers pressed down, arched against the table as he looked at the judge. "The Defendant is on trial for murder, Your Honor. The State objects to his release pending trial. Given the nature and seriousness of the charge, the State believes the Defendant is a danger to the community."

Vince's tone was weighted with sarcasm as he replied. "Given the situation, Your Honor, it's clear the Defendant won't be practicing medicine between now and the trial. Doctor Vicari owns property here; he is the sole owner of a business in Jefferson Parish. He's a respected physician, practicing fourteen years." He spread his hands. "He's a danger to no one."

Peter walked around the table toward the bench. "The Defendant is a flight risk, Judge. He moved to New Orleans six months ago and rents an apartment. He does own property here, the Alpha Women's Clinic in Metairie. But he has no family in the area other than his wife, who came here with him. He has no established connections to this community. And, we ask the Court to take into consideration the fact that the Defendant, as a medical doctor, is charged with committing a particularly onerous breach of public trust."

"We object to the State's inflammatory characterization." McConnell threw Peter a heated look. "Perhaps the State thinks a trial is unnecessary?"

The judge scowled and the gavel banged. "That's enough. Bail is set at five hundred thousand dollars."

Five hundred thousand dollars was high, but given the fact that the first Republican governor of the State of Louisiana was in office, Vicari could count himself lucky it wasn't more. With a bondsman and the clinic for collateral, he'd be out in a couple of hours. No surprise. As Peter returned to his seat, he glanced at the defendant. McConnell was still standing.

Charles Vicari sat looking ahead, stiff and straight-backed, his chin still lifted, his face cold and filled with disdain, and arrogance. But his shoulders were relaxed, like a man who wasn't worried. And his cuffed hands were loosely clasped before him on the table. Peter had observed many successful defendants sitting in that seat over the years, and overall he'd found that each one's demeanor at this first hearing generally painted a true picture of their character. Some radiated charisma, despite their crimes. Charles Vicari was not one of those. Vince had his work cut out for him with a jury, he mused, feeling good. This defendant was not a sympathetic client.

Vince was explaining the second motion. Under the Speedy Trial Act, defense had the right to demand trial within one hundred and twenty days. In the usual course of events, with bail granted, a defendant would want to stall. This motion caught Peter by surprise. They were putting the pressure on and turning up the gauge.

"Is the state ready to proceed to trial?"

Peter rose. "Yes, Your Honor." To stall, to argue that the State needed more time to prepare the case was a losing battle. The right to a speedy trial was the defendant's to demand. "The People are ready to proceed," he said. But he knew what this meant. Life outside this case would stop for him, and for Dooney, for the next six months.

The judge nodded. "Defendant's motion for speedy trial is granted. Trial to be set within one hundred and twenty days." This was June 15. Trial would be set around December 15, he guessed, just around the time of Rebecca's due date. Inside, Peter groaned.

O'Connell stood with the defendant as the deputies stepped forward. He remained standing while his client walked from the courtroom back to lockup to wait until bail had been arranged. After the door closed, the judge's clerk called the next case on the docket.

Peter gathered up his files and stuck them in his briefcase. Dooney did the same.

"Peter."

He looked up and stuck out his hand. "Vincent." They shook. "Haven't seen you around in a while."

"We want this thing set as early as possible. I'll call you tomorrow; see if we can agree on a date."

Peter thought quickly. The earlier the better, given Rebecca's due date. "That's fine. I'll check my calendar."

"We need to talk about discovery."

"I'll give you what we have." Peter, still jolted by this turn of events, was curt. He'd have to rearrange his trial schedule for the next six months. Eying Vince, he knew he'd give Vince everything the defense was entitled to under the law—anything he discovered that would benefit the defendant's case— but that didn't include Mac's ongoing search for Alice Braxton, or his discussions with Lucy Ringer in Chicago. All of that was still mere speculation.

Vincent nodded. "Talk to you soon."

As Vince walked through the gate, Peter swung his briefcase from the table, and turning, stepped aside for Dooney. He followed her down the aisle just behind McConnell. When they reached the hallway, however, they stopped and stood near a window until Vince boarded an elevator.

Dooney turned to Peter. "Do you think he'll want to bargain?"

"A plea?" He shook his head. "No. Not Vince. And we won't make an offer." Another elevator arrived within the minute. This one was empty. Dooney stepped on and he followed. He pressed the button for the tenth floor and looked at the closed metal doors.

"My guess is the defendant doesn't think he's done anything wrong," Dooney said as they ascended in the green glass tower. "My guess is he's going to hold us to the fast track so Doctor Vicari can get back to business as usual."

"He won't get back to business if we can help it." Facts swam through his head, and images flowed into his mind, weighing him down. Glory Lynn struggling to reach her child in that room. Clara Sonsten holding the dying baby in her arms. The body found in the freezer. Dr. Kand's autopsy photos—the tiny body intact. The baby.

And his own child, on the way. He pressed his hand to his forehead, suddenly overwhelmed. Then the elevator stopped and they both stepped out.

The next day the trial was set to begin on Tuesday, November 30.

28

REBECCA STOOD IN THE DOOR WATCHING as the photographer and reporter moved furniture around. The firm had spread the word that one of their new female partners was pregnant—an almost irresistible lifestyle story in the city of New Orleans in 1982. This interview was with *Women in Law*, a national magazine with good circulation.

When she'd first told Doug Bastion that she was pregnant, his immediate response, just after the congratulations, was to ask if she would mind this kind of publicity—good for the firm, he'd added, casually as he'd looked off, shooting his cuffs. This interview was the result.

And she admitted to herself as she stood waiting to get started, since Amalise had joined the Auriel team, she'd begun feeling slightly irrelevant. Roberts Engineering had warmed to Amalise a tad too quickly. Rebecca couldn't travel, Dr. Matlock still said. And she was to avoid stress, he repeated every time she saw him. So, for now all she had was Brightfield's brief to work on, and the publicity the pregnancy was generating. She smoothed her hands down over the new silk suit, an Armani she'd just purchased and had altered. Still in the first trimester, the magic of the designer hid her thickening waist very well.

"Rebecca, come over here, will you." The photographer motioned.

She walked to him and he placed his hands on her shoulders, positioning her so that she stood before the windows, looking out over the city.

"Now. Turn your face this way, please," he said, tipping her chin to the right. "That's good, that's good." The camera flashed, once. Twice. They'd been at it a while. Then he pulled the camera from the tripod and knelt, sitting on his heels. "Give me that smile one more time, please."

She complied. The camera clicked.

Amity Jones, the reporter, sat on the sofa in the corner, waiting. She looked at the photographer now. "All through?"

"I think so." He turned to Rebecca. "The camera loves you, lady."

"We all love her." Doug Bastion stepped in. Rebecca introduced the firm's managing partner to the photographer and reporter.

She looked at Doug, lifted her hair, twisting it, then let it fall around her shoulders. "We're just starting the interview. Do you need me?" She heard the hopeful note in her voice and blushed.

Doug took three steps back, hands up. "No. I was passing by and saw the lights. Thought I'd stop in and say hello to these folks."

"Would you like to add something for the story?" the reporter asked.

Doug smiled at her and said, "Sure thing."

He crossed his arms, looking down at Amity Jones, ready with his quote. "From the day she joined us, Rebecca has blazed her way through this firm like a shooting star. Just tell your readers that times have changed and with education and hard work, any woman can do the same and have a family too." He nodded toward Rebecca. "She'll soon be a mother, a wife, a success-ful lawyer." He shook his head, smiling. "It's 1982. Women today can have it all, if that's what they choose."

Rebecca looked at him. *So easy for you to say.*

As he left, Rebecca moved to the sofa and Amity Jones. The interview would take about one hour Amity had said. Rebecca already knew the questions; she'd seen them in all the magazines lately. How do you do it all? And now, a baby, too?

What's your plan?

The answer, she'd thought, was good help. But, smiling at Amity Jones, she gritted her teeth at the thought of the nannies she'd interviewed. The women who'd be taking her place with her daughter.

Amity asked if she was ready and Rebecca glittered. For the next forty minutes she focused on the questions and her answers. As they were wrapping up, she placed her hand over the baby spot, and that brought a smile.

"That's it!" Amity Jones looked at her. "That smile lights your face, Rebecca. That's what I came to capture in this interview—the utter joy for the girl who's got life all figured out."

29

ABOUT A MONTH AND A HALF before the trial date, which was November 30, Vince McConnell filed a motion that threw Peter's entire trial strategy into a spin. When the envelope arrived by messenger, he opened it, began to read, and then stopped and held it out before him, looking at it in disbelief.

There would be no jury at this trial. Charles Vicari, M.D., had elected to fight this battle for his life and reputation before one man, and one man only. He was waiving his right to trial by jury. He was demanding a trial to the bench, meaning the most Honorable Calvin Morrow, the judge who'd been appointed to hear the case. Attached to the motion was a notation from Molly. A hearing on the defense motion had been set for two o'clock on the following afternoon.

Now, at 2:15 on the following afternoon, Peter and Dooney waited in Judge Morrow's courtroom on the fourth floor of the courthouse. As usual, lawyers from the last hearing were still gathered around the defense table nearby, shoving papers in their briefcases, joking, arguing.

This was the same courtroom in which the actual trial would be heard. Beside him at the prosecution table, Dooney was humming a song under her breath, too low to be recognizable. Peter beat an erratic rhythm on the table with the tip of his pen, watching the judge up on the bench, still studying the paperwork.

McConnell walked in, preceded by his client. The other lawyers vacated the defense table, pushing through the railing gate. Peter barely gave them a glance.

His thoughts still roiled at this last-minute trick nullifying all the work he'd put into his strategy, a large part of which concentrated on the psychology of juries. His opening statement; the closing argument. Consideration of the evidence—how to present it in the way that would most impact the men and women sitting in those twelve chairs. The judge's instructions to the jury.

Everything.

But, the right to waive the jury was the defendant's.

So now, Peter's focus was on the judge, the man who would determine the verdict. Peter had tried several cases before Calvin Morrow, and each time he'd found the man to be unpredictable, an enigma. Socially, he wasn't the person you'd seek out at a party, and he never attended them anyway; not even birthday parties for his own staff. Not even retirement celebrations.

Juries were easier to read than Calvin Morrow. During the process of *voir dire* when prospective jurors are questioned, you could find out a lot about a man or woman: what books they were reading while they waited to be called, their education, work history. From bumper stickers on their cars, you'd learn their political affiliations and the organizations they support.

But Judge Calvin Morrow was a complete unknown.

Still, Peter mused. The defendant was rolling the dice by putting his life in the hands of one man, rather than twelve good men and women. Unless he knew something about the judge that Peter didn't know. That sent a chill up his spine.

And, knowing McConnell, that idea wasn't too fantastical.

Irked at the thought, he glanced at Vince, seeking clues. But counsel for the defense radiated confidence while he spoke in low tones with his client, leaning back, his arm resting over the back of the defendant's chair.

Peter fixed his eyes on the Louisiana flag hanging at one side behind the bench. The American flag was on the other. There was always the chance that Morrow would refuse to take this case on his shoulders. The law did not require a judge to accept a trial to the bench. If he refused, it would be reassigned. A bench trial in a criminal case was a huge responsibility and a political nightmare. Morrow was elected to his position, as were all other state judges in Louisiana. And juries provided political cover in sensitive cases like this one with explosive issues.

Suddenly he recalled that Morrow was up for reelection in two years. Peter began to allow himself the shred of hope that Morrow might transfer the case to another judge. Any other judge in the district would be better than Calvin Morrow, with a case like this—*sui generis*—one of a kind, without precedent. Dooney had been unable to find any other case on record involving an infant born alive, completely separated from the mother, and then allowed to die with zero medical attention.

If what Lucy Ringer had said to Mac was true, that this happened all the time, then the practice was the best-kept secret in the country.

When Peter heard Morrow mutter, "All right," he blinked, straightened, and looked up. The bailiff announced that court was back in session and called the case. Michelene, the court reporter, arched her fingers over the stenography machine. Morrow pointed to Vince, who stood.

"State your case for the record, please, Mr. McConnell."

"Yes, Your Honor." Vince quickly summed up the defendant's motion waiving his right to trial by jury. The defense was convinced that the inflammatory nature of the charges and the religious demographics of this state would combine to deny due process to Charles Vicari anywhere in the state of Louisiana. Even a change of venue would not solve the problem. But, he added, the defendant had full confidence in Judge Morrow's ability to remain objective.

Peter rose. Morrow pumped his hands, "Sit, sit, sit, Counsel. This is between the Court and the Defendant." Beside him, Dooney clicked her tongue. Peter sat. The judge was right—the defendant could make this choice. The prosecution really held no marbles in this game.

Now Morrow peered down at Charles Vicari. "Do you understand what's happening here, Dr. Vicari?"

Charles Vicari pushed back his chair and stood. "Yes, Your Honor," he said.

"Is it your desire to waive your right to a jury of your peers?"

"Yes, Your Honor."

Judge Morrow leaned forward, squinting down at Vicari as if he were looking into the blinding light of his own future. "If I grant this request, do you understand that I will be the only person determining your guilt or innocence? There will be no jurors. Is that what you want?"

"Yes, Your Honor."

Peter groaned. The judge was going to take it.

Calvin Morrow nodded and leaned back in his chair, folding his hands together before him. "You may be seated."

Charles Vicari sat, along with McConnell.

Minutes passed while Judge Morrow considered the request. Fleeting expressions crossed the judge's face as he deliberated. Peter's hope rose again. Perhaps he'd take a pass.

At last he looked up. "Counsel, I'll see you in my chambers." He looked at the court reporter. "You too, Michelene."

Peter, Dooney, and McConnell—leaving Vicari at the defense table— filed out through the side door, located behind the jury box. Michelene followed with her machine. When they arrived in chambers, the judge, still wearing his robe, was already seated behind his desk.

The room was dark. The walls, the interior frames of the windows, the bookcases behind the desk, and the desk itself, were all custom-built mahogany, gleaming in the artificial light. Again, the American and Louisiana flags hung behind the desk. The long rectangular conference table took up most of the left side of the room. The table was set against the inner wall of the judge's chambers, the side which had no windows.

Michelene pulled a chair over to one side of the desk and set up her machine. Peter and Dooney leaned against the conference table, arms folded, waiting. McConnell stood before the judge, arms at his sides.

"This is off the record," Morrow said, glancing at Michelene. She nodded and rested her hands in her lap. Judge Morrow leaned back in his chair, elbows braced on the armrests and hands folded over his chest as he looked at the three lawyers.

"I'm inclined to accept trial to the bench," he said, fixing his eyes on Peter and McConnell. "But let's get one thing straight. I'm setting some limits here. I'm telling you now what we will not hear in this courtroom. Not once."

He leaned forward and banged his fist on the desk, his eyes shifting between the lawyers. "I will not under any circumstances allow either side to challenge the right to abortion already established under *Roe v. Wade.*" Then he leaned back and fixed his eyes on Peter. "The State has the burden to prove that the infant was fully separated from the mother, and was born alive. Then, and only then, will we reach issues governing the defendant's culpability. Understood?"

The sanctity of life prior to birth could not be addressed in Calvin Morrow's courtroom.

Peter leaned forward. "Your Honor, the Supreme Court acknowledged the State has an interest in protecting the potential life of the unborn child under, *at least,* some circumstances. And that may be an element of proof in establishing the Defendant's intentions prior to Infant Chasson's birth."

Morrow looked at Vince.

"The defense is prepared to prove that Doctor Vicari was justified in believing that Miss Chasson's pregnancy had not progressed to viability, Your Honor."

The judge frowned. "My point is that I will accept no arguments from counsel in this room that are inconsistent with the holding in *Roe v. Wade*." He looked at Michelene. "We're going on record now." Shifting forward, Morrow flattened his hands on the desk before him and stated the limitation for the record.

"Based upon that condition, I will accept trial to the bench."

Peter was in the office when he got the call from Rose Marie, Rebecca's secretary downtown. His hand tightened into a fist as he held the phone and listened.

"Amalise Catoir has taken Rebecca to the hospital, Mr. Jacobs. They went to Baptist Hospital and Rebecca asked me to call you. To meet her there."

"What happened?"

"She, um, was having cramps all morning and . . ."

"Why didn't she call me! When did she leave?"

"Uh, they left about five minutes ago. She was having those cramps and then she began bleeding. I've called her doctor, Dr. Matlock, and told the nurse there what was going on. She said he would meet her at the hospital right away." Rose Marie paused. "They're going to the emergency room."

"Thanks," Peter said as he stood and slammed down the telephone. "Molly? Molly."

Molly appeared within seconds in the doorway of his office. "Yes, Peter?"

"Call Judge Bridey, will you? Tell him an emergency has come up and we'll need to reschedule the Cleary hearing this afternoon." He glanced at his watch. "It's in a half-hour, at three, and if Bridey won't—"

"Is Rebecca all right?"

"—reschedule, send Russell down there. Just give him the file and tell him if he can't convince defense counsel to move the hearing, he'll have to do the best he can. And no, Rebecca's not all right."

He grabbed his jacket from the back of the chair and began forcing his arms into the sleeves. "Rebecca's on her way to the hospital. Say a prayer this isn't a miscarriage."

Molly stepped aside. "I will. I certainly will," she said as he flew by. "Thanks, Molly."

With the traffic at the toll bridge and the lights, driving took thirty minutes from the courthouse in Gretna. Peter wheeled around Lee Circle and down St. Charles Avenue, hanging a right on Napoleon, praying all the way. And still, parking took another seven minutes, and counting five more to get into the building and three or four to find out where to go, Peter arrived in the emergency room only about twenty minutes after Amalise and Rebecca arrived.

He found Amalise standing in the emergency room hallway by herself, outside a closed door. When she spotted Peter, she lifted her hand. He hurried toward her and they hugged. There were tears in Amalise's eyes.

Seeing her tears, a wave of sheer panic rose. "What's happening?" he said, struggling for control. He moved toward the door, and Amalise put her hand out to stop him.

"She's in there with the doctor," she said. "She's frightened, Peter. I know she wants you in there, but the doctor's probably examining her and you should probably just wait right here for now."

He hesitated, and then nodded, letting his arms fall to his sides as he stared at the door. "What do you think happened, Amalise?"

She shook her head. "I don't know. But Rebecca says the doctor's a good man; he knows what he's doing."

He didn't hear anything. Just closed his eyes and sank back against the wall, feeling limp. Amalise stood silently beside him. Peter's chin dropped to his chest and he was quiet.

Please, let the baby live. And let Rebecca be all right.

He would be Rebecca's strength if she fell apart, he resolved. Remembering all the discussions they'd had over the years about never having a child, he almost shook his head. A knot of fear in his chest tightened at the thought of what might now be happening on the other side of that door. He couldn't bring himself to think any further and there came a hammering in his chest. All the tricks that he'd learned over the years about remaining cool under fire failed him now. He tossed prayers to heaven wildly, hoping they'd create a blanket that could cover Rebecca and the child.

Seconds turned to minutes. Minutes seemed to turn to hours.

At last the door opened. The doctor came out and through the open door he could see Rebecca lying on a table with a white sheet pulled up to her neck. Her knees were up, her arms folded over her chest, her head was turned toward the wall and he could see her shoulders shaking. As he started toward the door, the doctor stepped aside and he walked in. He heard the door close and he could hear the doctor moving around behind him. Walking over to Rebecca, he pulled up a chair and sat down beside her.

"Rebbe, I'm here."

She turned her head to him and he saw that she was crying. Then she reached out and he leaned down and she wrapped her arms around his neck. He cupped her face in both hands, holding her eyes, struggling to read her thoughts, wanting to know, and not wanting to know.

"It's going to be all right, Peter," she said.

He froze, afraid to hope. What then?

But she released him and looked over his shoulders, and so he turned, watching the doctor's face.

Dr. Matlock nodded. "The bleeding has stopped, for now. She'll need bed rest for the next few weeks; and then she'll take it easy for the remainder of her term." He gave Rebecca a look. "No going down to the office, nothing like that."

Peter took a deep breath and let it out.

Rebecca nodded.

"We'll do an ultrasound and keep her here tonight," Matlock said to Peter. "But I'm fairly certain that what we've got here is what I suspected before, placenta previa. The test will confirm how much of the cervix is covered."

All right. Rebecca and the baby would be all right.

Those were the only words he heard at first. Holding onto Rebecca, Peter dropped his head, pressing his face into the soft curve in her neck and squeezing his eyes together. Rebecca rubbed circles over his back with one hand,

and her other hand stroked his hair. Her touch was soothing. He closed his eyes, blinking back the tears.

He heard things in bits and pieces after that. Not unusual. Bed rest again. Should be all right. Caesarean. He sat up and turned to Dr. Matlock at that last part.

"We'll just have to see; might not be necessary. It's too early to know." Matlock bent and stretched his fingers, one hand, then the other. "As the baby grows, the uterus stretches. So it's possible the previa could be out of the way by the time of delivery, or if it's just marginal, we could still have a natural birth." He spoke in a smooth, practiced way as he added, not to worry—that either way, both mother and child would be safe and healthy if she followed his instructions.

Peter and Amalise waited in the room while Rebecca was taken off for the ultrasound test. Relief had lightened both their moods.

"Your real problem, Peter," Amalise said "is how in the world you're going to keep Rebecca in bed for the next few weeks, and at home until the birth."

30

THE ROOM WAS DARK. SHE'D ASKED Peter to leave the curtains closed when he left for work. That fit her mood. The dark room matched the gloomy feeling inside.

Then she turned over, hugging the pillow and closing her eyes, hoping that she could go back to sleep because the thought of facing yet another day with the clock slowly ticking backward was driving her mad. It was a good metaphor, she thought. Her life was moving counterclockwise now. She'd made partner, and then everything had suddenly changed.

She'd been lying in this bed for almost a week now. This was only the middle of October and she couldn't imagine how she'd survive the next six weeks, with Amalise downtown bonding day by day with Roberts Engineering. Images of the bustle continuing without her at Mangen & Morris rose. Her new office was going to waste. She could see Amalise and Preston and Raymond and Doug all moving forward, while she moved backward. They'd be laughing with friends, their telephones ringing, people coming and going, arguing in conference rooms, or maybe off to Bailey's for lunch. But they were there, and she was here, and life as she had known it had suddenly stopped.

She pounded the pillow with her fist. Then, gently, so as not to disturb Daisy, she rolled onto her back and flung her arms out to the sides, hitting the bed with both fists. Then she stared at the ceiling, feeling hopeless. Because, there was nothing else that she could do.

Beside her, on the bedside table, the telephone rang. She turned her head and looked at it. Her first impulse was to let it ring. So she let it ring three times, and then couldn't stand it anymore and picked it up.

Rose Marie was on the other end. The files that Rebecca had said she needed to work on Brightfield's brief would be delivered to her in a little while. Amalise would drop them off. Rebecca told her secretary where the key was hidden in the garage, and then she hung up.

Pushing herself up, slowly she crawled out of bed. She would take a shower. She would brush her hair and put on a bit of lipstick. Perhaps that would cheer her up. Besides, there was no way in the world she'd let anyone see her looking like this. Not even Amalise.

A half-hour later, Rebecca heard the door open downstairs. Amalise called out, and Rebecca yelled to come on up.

"Hey," Amalise said when she breezed in, hugging a stack of file folders to her chest. "This room's too dark," she said, setting the files down on the bed beside Rebecca. There was a book on top of the files, she saw.

"It's good to see you."

"You're just glad to see a living human being. This place is a morgue."

Amalise walked to the windows on the far side of the room. "I can't stay," she said over her shoulders as she yanked a curtain aside. Sunlight streamed in. "I'm late. I've got to meet Jude. We've got a parent-teacher conference at Luke's school this afternoon."

Rebecca watched in silence as Amalise pulled each curtain aside and the room turned from dark to light. When she'd finished this, she did the same with the windows on each side of the bed. Then she rushed to Rebecca's side, leaned down, planted a kiss on her forehead, and said that she was sorry that she had to leave. That she'd be back tomorrow for a long visit. And then she was gone.

Rebecca stared after her for a moment, wondering if she'd just seen a mirage.

Then she reached for the files that Amalise had left beside her, and the book slid off onto the bed. Picking it up, she turned it to the front cover. It was a Bible.

She smiled. First the curtains and the light; then a Bible. That was just like Amalise. She put the Bible down on the bed and lifted a file from the top of the stack. She'd asked Brightfield to send transcripts of the trial in the lower court for her work on his appellate brief. Reading the transcripts would take a while, but she certainly had the time. Flipping through the pages, she scanned several. Then with a sigh, she closed the file again.

Maybe later. She put the file on top of the others and looked down at the Bible beside her.

A slip of paper was stuck between the pages. Amalise again. Curiosity won. Pursing her lips, Rebecca picked up the book and opened it to the page marked by the first slip. There, in bold red ink, Amalise had circled a passage. The marked words read:

"Therefore don't worry about tomorrow, because tomorrow will worry about itself. Each day has enough trouble of its own."

Amalise was incorrigible. She let out a laugh, and glanced at the top of the page. Matthew: Chapter Six. This was verse 34. Then she lifted her eyes to read the verses above, from the beginning of the poetic wisdom. At the end of chapter six Amalise had written: "Rebecca, also see John 19:35."

She pressed her lips together, irritated that she was so predictable. Amalise had known she'd read on.

It took a few minutes to find. She wasn't used to the organizing system. But after she found the passage, and read it, she rested her head back on the pillows and pondered the words. "He who saw this has testified so that you also may believe. His testimony is true, and he knows he is telling the truth." From the book of John, chapter 19, verse 35. They were the words that any lawyer would want to hear from a witness. They were words that touched the heart of a woman who wanted to seek answers.

She set the book down on her lap, thinking of the baby growing inside of her. If anything was evidence of a miracle, it was the very existence of Daisy.

And then she picked up Amalise's Bible again and found the beginning of the book of John, the witness. And she began to read.

Part Two

~✦~

The Trial

31

TUESDAY, NOVEMBER 30, 1982. *First day of the trial.*

Alice Hamilton had read about it in the paper yesterday. Just a short article on page seven of the *Times-Picayune* about the trial of Dr. Charles Vicari. The article wasn't terribly clear, it mentioned an abortion that had gone wrong and that the infant had died, and then the reporter outlined the Supreme Court decision in *Roe v. Wade* in 1973 and that was all.

But that name had gripped her. Doctor Charles Vicari had been indicted for murder. The name had jumped off the page as if the three words were written for Alice Hamilton, or perhaps since he'd emerged from her past, for Alice Braxton. It had taken a minute for the information to travel across the synapses in her brain and rise to the conscious level. *Look here, Alice! This is for you.* It was a name she'd been praying she'd forget for over two years. The phone call a few months ago should have alerted her, she realized. But she'd forgotten all about it. Until now.

Luckily she'd been sitting down when she came across the story. It had transformed an ordinary day into a nightmare. There she was in her own home, minding her own business—relaxing, reading the paper, and eating breakfast—and then . . . the invasion.

But even more shocking, another name had startled her, too. The prosecutor for the district attorney's office was Peter Jacobs. She recognized Rebecca's husband's name immediately from her file. This was too close—way too close. Someone could be searching for her now.

So, here she sat at her kitchen table with yesterday's paper folded to that article and a decision to make. She sat gazing through the window at the elm tree, thinking about what should come next. She'd had a difficult time maintaining composure yesterday at work. Alice decided she had to find out exactly what was going on in the trial.

So she'd called in sick today—and now sat in her kitchen fighting off a tension headache and wringing her hands. She'd never thought she would cross Charles Vicari's path again, and she really did not want to see him now.

She read the article over again once more, and then called for directions to the courthouse. Hanging up the phone, she went into the bedroom, looked into her closet, and pulled out her best dress.

Leaning toward the mirror, she powdered her face and added some lipstick, and then dressed. When she was ready, she called a taxicab. Then she picked up her black straw hat from the dressing table, a small hat that she'd clung to for thirty-seven years. The hat had net veiling, a half-veil that she could lower over her eyes, or push back, up over the brim, according to her mood. She'd noticed that when she pulled down the veil, people seemed to leave her alone. As if she'd suddenly become invisible. She didn't care that the hat was out of style, old-fashioned. She'd long ago decided that she'd earned the right not to care.

Standing before the window while she waited for the taxi, she watched people across the street entering and leaving Ciro's. When the taxi arrived she put on the hat, and pulled on her short white gloves, picked up her pocketbook and left the apartment, locking the door behind her. There was nothing for it but to do it.

She told the driver that she was going to the courthouse in Gretna, across the river from downtown, and he shook his head, but then said all right. Then she leaned back and closed her eyes for a moment. At the courthouse she'd find a place to sit in the back of the room and find out what was going on. And whether this trial would change her life. Again.

Her head ached and her stomach churned as they rode from Oak Street to Carrolton, Carrolton to St. Charles Avenue, then a few miles down, around and up the ramp onto the freeway and across the Greater New Orleans Bridge to the courthouse in Gretna. Exiting the highway, they turned right on Huey Long Boulevard and eventually drove through a pretty area of creole cottages and shotgun houses. This was a wide street separated by a broad neutral ground; plenty of green grass and a tunnel of old oaks.

Close to the levee guarding the city of Gretna from the Mississippi River, past a small town square situated between an old post office building and a one-room red train station, she could see the courthouse. The front of the building was made of green glass, as described to her by the woman on the phone who'd given her directions. Just behind the tower was the hulking Parish Prison. The driver hooked a U-turn and stopped.

She paid and thanked the taxi driver, even though he failed to come around and open the door for a lady. Then, standing on the sidewalk, she halted and took measure of the place. At last, clutching her pocketbook in one hand, she walked up the steps, opened a door and went inside. There, again she halted, and looked about. Crowds of people dressed in business suits rushed past, peeling off right and left, moving fast. Ahead she saw a bank of elevators, with people pushing toward them.

Pulling the net down over her eyes, she moved forward. To her right she spotted a desk with a sign that said *Information*. A gentleman in uniform sat behind it.

He looked up. "May I help you, ma'am?"

"I'm here for the trial of Dr. Charles Vicari," she said. "The paper said it's starting this morning."

He ran his finger down a list then looked up. "That would be courtroom 404, Judge Calvin Morrow." He stood, pointing as he gave her directions.

She thanked him and headed off. She would locate a seat in the back of the room, in a corner away from the light, but close to the door. And she would make certain not to stare at Charles Vicari or Eileen Broussard, because she believed that it is true that people can feel your eyes on them when you look too long.

There was a crowd in front of the elevators, but when she walked up, a kind young man stepped aside, allowing her to enter. As they ascended she told herself that no one ever had to know that she'd come here, and that even if the doctor or Eileen spotted her in the courtroom, there wasn't much chance they'd recognize her after almost three years.

Entering the courtroom, she realized she was early. The seats were only half-filled, and most people had crowded toward the front. She spotted Vicari immediately, sitting at a table with someone else on the other side of a railing. His lawyer, she guessed. She looked about, but didn't see Eileen Broussard.

Then, holding her pocketbook tight against her chest, Alice Jean Hamilton slipped into the last bench in the rows running down toward that railing. She sidled down to the end, beside the wall, in the corner. She put the purse down beside her. Lifted the veil. Removed her gloves. And then she began to wait.

᠍ೞ᠍

At the front of the courtroom, sitting at the prosecution table, Peter and Dooney were settled in and, along with everyone else, waiting for the judge to arrive. To his right Peter could feel Dooney's tension building, the same simmering cauldron of fear and excitement inside that still hit him on the first day of every big trial. He glanced down at the evidence boxes on the floor. Those were Dooney's responsibility. Still, he always checked. And all was well.

His own briefcase, slim and sleek, made of the finest leather with gold fixtures, was on the table before him. It was a birthday gift from Rebecca a few years ago. He smoothed his hand over the leather, and the worry that shadowed his thoughts lately rose again. He forced it away. She'd begun working at home, writing that brief for her partner, Bill Brightfield, and that seemed to have pulled her out of the angst that had first taken hold when the doctor ordered bed rest. Rebecca and the baby were fine, the doctor had said. They'd be okay.

Suddenly the door behind the bench opened. Peter glanced up, his heart racing. But only the bailiff appeared. So he settled back again and dropped his eyes to the court reporter, Michelene, sitting before her machine with her hands on her lap. She glanced up and Peter caught her eye and winked. She smiled. Michelene had worked in the courthouse as long as Peter could remember, long before he'd ever arrived, he supposed. She'd seen almost everything, he knew. But he bet himself that this case would be something new even to her.

To Peter's left, Vince McConnell conferred with his client. He wore a suit that Peter recognized as a custom fit, not off the rack. Rebecca had taught him how you could tell. Beside him, Charles Vicari also looked dapper in a neat dark gray suit. He also wore a crisp white shirt. And a silver and black striped tie. If a jury were impaneled, Peter guessed that Vicari would have toned down the sartorial effect.

He turned and saw that behind him, on the other side of the railing, the courtroom was filling up. The *Times-Picayune* had run a brief story about the start of the trial on page three yesterday, but it hadn't contained many details. Even so, he was surprised not to see more press in court this morning, particularly the local press. He turned back again, knowing that his hope that most of the media would stay away through the entire week was probably futile.

With a sigh, Peter folded his arms over his chest and closed his eyes, running through his opening argument again. Beside him Dooney began weeding through files in the big briefcase on the floor beside her. The courtroom was well insulated from outside noise, but behind him the ambient hum of the gallery rose and fell. Minutes passed, five, then ten.

Suddenly the door behind the bench clicked open. Peter jumped and opened his eyes just as the bailiff's voice rang out.

"All rise. The Twenty-Fourth Judicial District, Jefferson Parish, Louisiana, is now in session. The Honorable Judge Calvin Morrow, presiding."

Everyone stood when the judge entered in his long black robe. The clerk of court announced commencement of the case, *State of Louisiana v. Charles Frank Vicari*, and Alice saw the stir of excitement at the two long tables on the other side of the railing.

When everyone around her sat down, she sat too, thinking of that phone call from Chicago, and then, yesterday, the article in the paper. Her first instinct when she'd read it had been to give notice to Dr. Matlock and flee. But now she was glad that common sense had prevailed. No one here had even glanced her way. She had a nice job, even if it was a little boring, and a nice apartment too, a place that felt like home. Too much to lose to panic yet, she told herself.

Not yet.

And then those doubts that had nagged her since the last phone call rose again. The State's investigator had been in Chicago asking about her. She told herself there was no reason to worry—unless Rebecca Downer Jacobs somehow made the connection between Alice in Chicago and Dr. Matlock's Alice. The irony of Rebecca's pregnancy and her husband's prosecution of this case at the same time struck her and a thought popped into her mind. Rebecca had been ordered by the doctor to stay at home. Still, she turned and looked about, craning her neck. That was one independent young lady, she'd realized during Rebecca's first visit to the office. Scanning the other spectators in the gallery, she was relieved to find her absent. Then she settled back against the hard wooden bench to watch what was happening up front.

On the other side of the rail, two men and a woman were clustered around the judge's high desk, to his right—her left—speaking in tones too low to hear. Once in a while one of the lawyers would dart over to the clerk's desk, or back to the long tables, and then would return with papers that the judge would read for a moment and hand back.

Then suddenly things changed. As if they'd all heard the same dog whistle, all three lawyers about-faced and headed for the two tables, two to the right, and one on her left, where Vicari waited. The one on the right must be the prosecution, she realized. And the man was Peter Jacobs. The judge pounded the gavel and the murmuring in the galley diminished as he demanded order in the courtroom. When everyone was quiet, the judge announced that opening statements would now commence.

She watched as Rebecca's husband stood, straightening some papers on the table with a kind of last-minute urgency. He was handsome, she thought. A little under six feet tall, well dressed. He strode to the lectern in the center, before the judge. Peter walked in a confident manner, head up, shoulders back. And then he gripped the sides of the lectern and looked up at Judge Morrow.

The courtroom was silent.

"Your Honor," he said, in a firm, steady voice. "I'll make this brief. Under your instructions, both the State and the Defense have stipulated that the issue in this case is not abortion. We are here today because of the murder of an infant born alive during an abortion procedure. The abortion was performed by the Defendant." Here he turned, angling his body toward Charles Vicari. Vicari appeared to be looking straight ahead.

"The State will prove beyond a reasonable doubt that after the live birth of Glory Lynn Chasson's infant son, the Defendant's actions knowingly and intentionally caused the death of that child."

He waited a beat, turned back to face the judge, dropped both arms to his sides, and added, "Your Honor, this is a case of an *accidental* life."

Alice shivered. Peter Jacobs continued for ten more minutes about the things the State intended to prove during this trial, but her vision blurred and she couldn't think. Instead, memories rose of that night in Chicago. She closed her eyes, willing them to go away, with Peter Jacob's words reverberating in her brain—over and over again came the words: an accidental life.

When at last she could focus on what was happening, the prosecuting attorney seemed to be wrapping up.

"In summary," Peter was saying. "The State will prove that the Defendant's actions harmed two people, Your Honor. There are two victims in this case—Miss Glory Lynn Chasson, and her child—Infant Chasson."

With a dramatic pause, Peter stepped back from the lectern. Alice studied the judge's face, looking for some hint of what he might be thinking. But his expression was blank. He seemed almost bored.

She watched as Vicari tilted his head back, observing the prosecutor as he walked back to the table as though he were a specimen on a slide back in his medical school days. That was the same righteous and uncompromising look the physician had given her and every other nurse at New Hope every day.

Fierce tears rose and anger swept her—fury for giving in to these emotions and fury toward Vicari. She'd promised herself that she'd not let this happen if she came here today. Yanking a Kleenex from her purse, Alice dabbed the corners of her eyes. She'd thought that by now the deepest parts of the wounds had healed. But she was wrong.

Judge Morrow was speaking. "Mr. McConnell, are you ready for your opening statement?"

McConnell stood up. "Defense will present an opening statement at the close of the State's case, Your Honor."

"Very well." The judge glanced at the clock hanging on the wall over the jury box. It was twelve fifteen. "We'll recess for lunch, now, and return at two o'clock. He turned to Peter. "Be prepared to call your first witness then, Counsel."

"All rise," the bailiff called.

32

AS JUDGE MORROW DISAPPEARED THROUGH THE door, the hum of the voices behind him rose. Peter picked up his briefcase and looked at Dooney. "Who's with Glory Lynn?"

"Shauna's got her. They'll be here at one thirty."

"Good." If anyone could keep the witness calm, Shauna Rameri could. The paralegal was a star, every lawyer in the DA's office fought to have her on their team. Shauna was organized and efficient, with a warm, easy-going personality.

"Let's grab some lunch," he said, picking up his briefcase. "I told Mac we'd be at Lockdown Brown's and to join us if he has time. I want to talk to Mac, see if he's made progress finding that Chicago nurse."

Dooney nodded. She glanced down at the boxes and briefcase. "They'll be all right in here," Peter said. Then she put on her coat and slung her purse over her shoulder.

Dry heat and the smell of hamburgers hit them as they walked into Lockdown Brown's. The restaurant was empty, except for an elderly man hunched over his plate at a table in the corner, and a woman wearing blue scrubs sitting at the counter. She didn't look up from her paper when they entered. Peter gestured toward an empty booth by a window. Dooney slid in on one side, and Peter on the other. Dooney reached for the menu.

"You ordering the same thing?"

"Sure." He opened the briefcase and pulled out a yellow legal pad. "You should have that menu memorized by now," he said. He put the tablet down on the table and slipped sideways out of the seat. "Be right back. I need to call Mac."

He went to the pay phone booth in the corner and slipped in a dime. Then he dialed the number for Mac's office and waited.

Mac answered at once. "How'd it go?"

Peter leaned a shoulder against the wall of the booth, looking through the glass door. "All right, I guess. I'd have rather been talking to a jury." He watched the woman at the counter folding her newspaper. She put it on the counter beside her and picked up her purse. "Have you been able to get Lucy Ringer on board yet?" '

"She's furious about that story I told her. Says she can't remember what we talked about when I was up there, and she's positive it won't come back to her anytime soon. I told her the long arm of the law could reach that far, but she didn't blink. Says she'll lose her job if she testifies." He paused. "And she's probably right."

Peter turned, studying the wall. He'd known it was a long shot, but couldn't vanquish the disappointment.

"So now we've got to find that nurse, Alice Braxton. Any luck yet?"

"A little. She's activated her Louisiana license."

"So she's practicing somewhere in the state. That's good news."

"Easy as finding a goldfish in the Gulf."

"We're recessed 'til two. Dooney and I are at Lockdown's. We're putting Glory Lynn on this afternoon. Everything set for tomorrow?"

"Yeah. We worked with the out-of-town witnesses on the phone all last week. They're set. Listen, I'm on my way, order me something, will you? A hamburger's good. Dressed. Ice tea."

"You got it." He hung up and pushed the door open. The woman at the counter was digging through her purse. She pulled out a wallet and looked around. Spotting the waitress, she held up a couple dollar bills. The waitress nodded and left the cloth on the table that she'd been wiping down.

Dooney lounged back against the burgundy vinyl seat, watching people passing by on the sidewalk. "Mac says Alice Braxton's in Louisiana. She reactivated her license."

"That's good news."

Peter pulled a pen from his pocket and looked down at the tablet containing notes for the first witness, Glory Lynn Chasson. He ran his eyes down the page, mentally checking off the points he would need to make. Glory Lynn would set the scene. She'd tell her story—paint a dramatic picture that he hoped would stick with the judge throughout trial. Going first was one of the benefits of prosecution.

"How's Rebecca holding up?" Dooney said.

Peter made a small dot at the end of each paragraph as he ran his eyes down the pages. "She's doing fine. She was bored for a few days, and then one of her partners in the Mangen & Morris trial section asked her to write another appellate brief." He glanced up. "She's getting some good experience on those things. She thinks Brightfield—that's her partner—might be angling to set up a new appellate section in the firm."

"How's she doing the research?"

"She'd been giving her secretary lists of cases, then the firm sent photocopies to her. But a couple weeks ago I bought her a computer." He smiled. "It was a surprise, an IBM. It's one of those new personal computers. It's small; not like the big ones, the mainframes. You've probably seen them before; some libraries have them now. They've got databases in various areas. And some news reports are available, like the AP wires."

"We learned a little about that in law school. They're amazing. But everyone's still using books." With a wry smile, she added, "No surprise."

His eyes were on his notes, but he thought of Rebecca's expression when he'd wheeled the computer into the bedroom. Without explaining, first he'd brought in a small table, placing it next to the one that held her nightlight and phone and other things. Then he'd wheeled in a rolling desk, one with a top that would slide over her legs in bed, like hospitals use, but the sliding part was wider. He'd bought it at a medical supply store on Claiborne Avenue.

But her eyes had grown wide and her mouth had dropped open when he'd brought in the computer, monitor, and keyboard. He'd put the computer on the new table, and the monitor and keyboard on the rolling desk. Then he'd hooked them all up according to the directions.

"Just look at this," he'd said, holding his hands up like a magician when he'd finished. He slid the desktop with the monitor and keyboard over her legs so that she could reach it. The monitor, with the curved screen and the workings behind it in a large, rounded case resembled a television set, he thought.

"I don't know how to use it," she'd said, looking up at him. But her eyes shone.

"Someone's coming over tomorrow to teach you." Sitting beside her on the edge of the bed, together they'd looked at this pile of technology. "You'll be a one-man band with this equipment, Rebbe. This is everything you'll need for research. There's data storage capability in this machine, and that new legal system that organizes all the cases."

Peter smiled to himself and focused again on his notes.

Dooney watched him in silence for a while. Then she asked, "Why do you think Glory Lynn agreed to testify? Her name will be splashed all over the papers."

Peter looked up. Dooney's brows drew together.

He shook his head. "It was the cry she heard. That's what she says. Until then she'd just thought of what was inside as tissue, but the cry took her by surprise, made everything real." He pushed the legal pad aside and folded his arms on the table, gazing through the dirty windowpane to his right.

"Now, she's a mother who's lost a child, and she's angry. She talks a lot about that struggle she had with Eileen Broussard and realizes how different things would be today if she could have just gotten out of that bed."

"From the autopsy report, it looks like she's right."

"I imagine she blames herself." Peter picked up his menu. "Let's order. Mac's on the way."

The waitress arrived and they told her someone else was joining them, and ordered. Immediately she returned with three glasses of iced tea and set them down on the table.

When she'd left again, Dooney said, "I got to know Glory Lynn some in the past few weeks. I sure hope you can keep her calm on the stand, Peter. She's fragile; just can't let go of the fact that she gave her consent in the first place. Even with all our preparation, I don't think she really understands what McConnell's going to do to her on the witness stand."

"I'll do my best." He lifted a shoulder. "But you know, it doesn't hurt for the judge to see her remorse, the real emotion." He glanced at his watch. Mac had better hurry. "She likes you. That'll help, seeing you sitting there in front of her will help. But it's not going to be easy."

Dooney lifted her arm, waving to someone outside, and he turned just as Mac entered the shop. Raking his hand back through his hair, Mac walked to the booth. Dooney scooted toward the wall to make room.

"Where do we stand right now on finding Alice Braxton?" Peter looked up from reading his notes.

Mac crossed his arms on the table and leaned forward. "I've scoured Baton Rouge—hospitals, private offices, agencies. Nothing."

Mac spooned sugar into his iced tea and stirred, looking across the table at Peter. "I'm looking here now, in the Parish. And also New Orleans."

Peter nodded. The waitress arrived with their food and set the plates before them. They were silent until she'd left.

Mac picked up his burger. "My idea is to check all the hospitals in both places first. If she's working here, most likely she's in a hospital. If not, then I'll backtrack to the private offices. But that's where the real problem is. There could be thousands." Shaking his head, he bit into the hamburger and chewed.

Peter picked up his sandwich. "How old did Lucy Ringer say she was?"

"Around sixty."

Dooney pushed lettuce around her plate. Peter bit into the sandwich and looked at Mac. "We don't have much more time. I figure we'll take two days, maybe three, before we rest our case."

"We could be on a wild goose chase, Peter."

"Keep trying." Peter swallowed some tea and picked the sandwich up again. It tasted like crumpled cardboard. "I'm putting you on the stand tomorrow, Mac." As lead detective in the case, Mac would testify as to evidence from the clinic searches. "We'll be dealing with motions first, so plan on being there at ten."

He turned to Dooney. "Make sure we've got copies of all the search photos and records. We'll need them for Mac's testimony. Triplicate copies."

"Already done."

"Double check. Make certain, will you?"

"Yes."

Mac scowled. "How long do you think I'll be on tomorrow? I need all the time I can get looking for that nurse."

Peter shrugged. "It's not a complicated crime scene. A couple of hours at most." Absently he moved the fork beside him one inch to the right, and then one inch to the left. "We're putting Clara Sonsten on tomorrow afternoon." He looked at Dooney. "Who's babysitting?"

"Shauna, again." Dooney stabbed a piece of tomato with her fork and looked across the table. "She'll get Clara to the courthouse at twelve forty-five. We can join them during the break."

He nodded. "Good. I want you to talk to Clara this evening. Make sure she's sticking to her statement." He watched absently as Dooney chewed the tomato. Clara Sonsten was on edge, he knew. But Dooney was good with this witness. She had the right mix of compassion and determination needed to keep up Clara Sonsten's spirits.

Dooney nodded and swallowed. "I'll do that."

He looked at his notes and then at Mac. "What about Dr. Stern?" Mortimer Stern, M.D. would be a formidable expert witness for the prosecution. Ham had recommended him; he'd remembered Stern from a conference last year where the doctor was the keynote speaker. His credentials were not only in the field of obstetrics—he also held a law degree from Stanford University.

"His flight gets in around two tomorrow afternoon and I'll pick him up. We're putting him up at the Royal Orleans."

"Get someone else to pick up Stern. I need you looking for Alice, Mac. Find someone to meet him and take him to the hotel. Let him know that we'll want to go over his testimony tomorrow night, though. Tell him Dooney and I will meet him there around six thirty." He glanced at his watch, then Dooney. "You ready?"

She stuck her fork into a hunk of lettuce and snatched a last bite, nodding as she pushed the plate away.

Mac put his burger down on the plate and slid from the booth to let Dooney slide out. "I'll stay and finish lunch," he said.

Peter shoved his notepad into his briefcase, and stood. "Get word to us if you have any information on Alice Braxton. The clock's ticking, Mac. We need to find her fast."

33

"THE STATE CALLS GLORY LYNN CHASSON to the stand."

Alice felt her heart pumping in her chest. She turned her head as the bailiff opened the courtroom door and the young woman lawyer, the assistant DA who'd been sitting at the prosecution table with Peter Jacobs all morning, entered along with another woman, someone much younger. They started down the aisle together, the lawyer steering the young woman toward the gate.

So. This was Glory Lynn Chasson, the mother who'd made the complaint. Alice leaned forward for a better look. It couldn't have been easy to step up to the altar of public opinion the way she had. Glory Lynn clung to Peter's assistant as they walked past. Alice guessed her age at nineteen or twenty. Her face was pale. Her expression was set, her lips pressed together into a thin line and shadows deepened her eyes. She wore a soft green dress with long sleeves. The skirt billowed around her knees. About a decade out of date, Alice figured. As they reached the rail-gate, she stumbled and the lawyer caught her. Nerves.

Peter Jacobs was waiting for her. He reached out and Glory Lynn took his hand, while the woman lawyer hurried back to her seat at the table. Peter walked the witness toward the stand where the clerk was waiting. He watched while she put her hand on the Bible, looked at the clerk, and swore to tell the truth, the whole truth, and nothing but the truth.

Peter waited until Glory Lynn was settled in the chair behind the wooden partition. Then he turned to her and asked her to state her name for the record. For about ten minutes they wandered through some questions about her life—her age, Alice had been right, she was young, twenty. Occupation: secretary. He asked a little about her job and her life, and what schools she'd attended. Even from the back of the courtroom, Alice could see the girl slowly starting to relax.

And then, like a sudden shift in weather, everything changed.

"Miss Chasson." Peter turned toward the witness, leaning one arm on the lectern as he looked at her. "You could have chosen to remain anonymous. You could have chosen to give your testimony in camera, or in a closed court. Why didn't you?"

Glory Lynn looked out over the spectators. Her voice now was clear and firm. "I want to take responsibility for what I've done. I want other women to know that . . . that when they chose to have an abortion with induced labor there's a chance the baby may be born alive." She paused, shivered. "I don't think people realize that. And, now I know that even as premature as my baby was, it's possible that he could have lived a normal life. I . . ."

"Objection!" Vince McConnell shouted.

"I'd just never thought of that." Glory Lynn's eyes darted toward the witness table.

"Objection."

"So I want them to know, to hear what can happen from someone who's gone through it, from a real person just like them."

Vince was on his feet. "The witness is testifying without any foundation, Your Honor. Miss Chasson is not an expert on the life expectancy of a fetus."

Peter looked at Judge Morrow. "The witness is merely stating her belief, Your Honor. And we'll be presenting autopsy evidence later to support her statement, so far as it addresses her belief."

Morrow swept his eyes over both lawyers. "The objection is overruled, pending prosecution's submission of evidence supporting the witness's statement." He glanced at Vince. "There's no jury here to be confused, Counsel."

Peter turned and walked to the witness stand, standing just to one side. "Miss Chasson, have you sought counseling since the night of the abortion?" Her remorse was deep and he wanted the judge to understand her state of mind. But he'd warned her that this would open the door for the defense on cross-examination to probe what had happened in those sessions.

She'd readily agreed.

"Yes," she said. She dropped her eyes. When she looked back up, her eyes glistened. "After it all happened, I couldn't sleep. Couldn't eat." She shook her head back and forth slowly. "So, I made an appointment with Dr. Maxwell Tombe two days after . . . after I left the clinic. He's a psychiatrist my parents recommended."

Peter looked down at his notes. "And how many times did you see him?"

"Twice a week, for three months." Glory Lynn put her hand on her forehead, and then it slid down the side of her face and dropped into her lap.

"Tell the court, please. How many times did you see Dr. Tombe altogether?"

"Twenty-four."

"And did you talk with him about the fact that you would testify in court? That your name would be revealed?"

"Yes." Her voice rose. "I don't want any questions left unanswered after this trial is over."

Peter nodded. He folded his arms and took a step back, looking across the well of the courtroom at the Defendant. "Did anyone at the Alpha Women's Clinic ever mention to you that with an induced labor abortion there was a risk that the infant could be born alive?"

"No."

"No such warning is required under the law, Your Honor," Vince said, waving his arm dismissively toward the witness box."

"Is that an objection, Mr. O'Connell?" the judge asked.

Vince stood, hands braced on the table, leaning forward. "Yes, Your Honor."

"Does Louisiana law require such information be given to the patient prior to the procedure, Counsel?" Judge Morrow looked from one to the other of the lawyers.

"No, Your Honor."

"I'll sustain the objection."

"Miss Chasson," Peter turned to Glory Lynn. "Did you have a personal physician, an OB/GYN before you became a patient at the Defendant's clinic?"

"No." She looked down. "I was afraid. I didn't want to know, I guess. And I'm . . . ah . . . a little overweight anyway so I was able to hide it." She glanced up at the judge. "I was waiting to see what my boyfriend would do. I was hoping, ah . . ." She turned back to Peter. "We'd been going together for so long. I was hoping we'd get married."

"What caused you to go to the clinic?"

She hesitated. Coughed. Asked for a glass of water. When the bailiff handed the glass to her she drank, then resting the glass on the partition, still holding onto it, she looked at Peter.

"I, um, didn't know what to do. I kept going back and forth in my mind about an abortion. My boyfriend . . . wanted me to do that."

"And for some time you waivered?"

"Yes." She lifted the glass and took another sip of water. "Like I said, I wanted to get married." She looked down. "And then, Christmas came, and then the weeks seemed to fly by so fast."

"What finally got you to the clinic?"

She hesitated, looking up at Peter, she took a breath and lifted her chin. "He did. The father—my boyfriend. He that said he just didn't want it. And then, he told me that he didn't want to get married, either. He's in school, in college." Her tone was bitter. "He'd have to quit school, he said, if his parents found out. They wouldn't pay for school if he got married and had a kid. He'd have to quit and get a job."

"So, the relationship was finished?" Peter leaned against the jury box, arms crossed.

"Yes."

"And after that?"

Glory Lynn glanced over at Dr. Vicari. Her voice broke. "And then, it was just my problem. That's when I made the choice. Blake . . . He wouldn't go with me. So, I went alone."

"And how did you choose this particular clinic, Alpha Women's Clinic?"

"I heard about it from a friend. And they do some advertising too." She paused and looked at the empty jury seats behind Peter. "And I'd heard about them from others who'd been there."

"And what had you heard?"

"I'd heard that it was easy."

"Objection." Vince McConnell stood. "The question calls for hearsay."

"Sustained." Morrow looked at Michelene. "Strike the last answer."

Peter straightened and stood and stuck his hands in his pockets, looking at Glory Lynn. "The first time you went to the clinic, you said you were alone?"

"Yes."

"And you filled out some forms. Were there a lot of them?"

"Yes. There were plenty."

Peter dipped his chin. "Please describe the procedure required to become a patient of the clinic."

Glory Lynn described the process. She described the forms that she'd filled out to her best recollection. And she described the initial interview in a separate room, and then the physical examination.

"And the interview and examination occurred on your first visit?"

"Yes."

"And that was, on May 11 of this year?"

"Yes."

Peter walked to the table and Dooney handed him a sheaf of paper. He looked at Judge Morrow. "May I approach the witness?"

Judge Morrow nodded. "Yes."

Studying the top of the first page, Peter walked back toward the witness and handed her the forms. She identified the date and her signature on each one. He had her read specific parts out loud. One by one they went through the forms that she'd signed, consents to the abortion, statements of her medical history, prescribed medicines.

Peter handed them to the clerk, to be admitted as State's evidence. He returned them to Peter. Holding onto the forms, he returned to Glory Lynn.

"Who performed your initial physical examination, Miss Chasson?"

Her eyes slid toward the defendant's table. "Dr. Vicari."

"The Defendant, Charles Vicari?"

"Yes."

"And is that the first time that you'd seen or met Charles Vicari?"

"Yes. It was."

"Was there anyone in the room with you during the examination?"

"A nurse named Clara Sonsten."

Peter nodded. He stepped back, leaning against the railing before the jury box. "In all this time at the clinic, while you were filling out forms and being interviewed and during the examination, at any time did you discuss the gestational age of the unborn child?"

"I wrote it down on several of the forms that I filled out."

He handed one of the forms to her. "Is this your signature?"

She took the page, glanced at it, and looked up. "Yes, it is."

He leaned toward her and indicated a space on the page. "Will you read this to the court, please—the gestational stage of your pregnancy, as you gave it to the clinic?"

"Approximately, twenty-two weeks." She looked up, eyes wide. "I know it's a long time to have waited, but . . . the pregnancy was unexpected."

Peter nodded. "And how did you calculate that information, the number of weeks?"

Glory Lynn looked to her left at the empty jury box, then her eyes fluttered over the galley, and back to Peter. "I figured it from the first time I remembered missing my period."

"And were you certain of that date?"

"No. I told Miss Sonsten that was the best I could remember. We talked about it for a while. After the examination, Dr. Vicari said he thought maybe I was a little further along. He asked if I'd seen another doctor yet, and I told him no." Her voice turned defensive. "I mean, I kept thinking we'd get married and then I'd go to a doctor and everything would be all right."

"And so, gestation was calculated based upon your best memory?"

"It was my best guess."

"After the physical examination, did the Defendant agree?"

"He said afterward he thought I was twenty-three weeks along." Peter saw her face close. They were getting close—tiptoeing up to the heart of the case and she was losing courage.

She lifted her chin and said with a sudden note of defiance, "My pregnancy was still within the second trimester."

With his back to the gallery, he gave her an encouraging smile. "What happened after the physical?" This part would be difficult for her, he knew. They'd worked on this testimony, on keeping it concise, and yet correct.

Glory Lynn took a deep breath and knotted her hands together on top of the wooden partition, her eyes riveted to his. "Well, Dr. Vicari explained that induced labor would be the best procedure to use, the safest, he said—for late term. It would take about twenty-four hours, in all, he said. And then he left and I got dressed and made an appointment to come back the next day when they would . . . um, get things started."

"Was Nurse Clara Sonsten present during that conversation?"

"Not all the time." Glory Lynn seemed to shrink back, knowing what was coming.

"Miss Chasson. Can you tell this court what happened on the following day when you returned to the Alpha Women's Clinic?"

Seconds passed as she looked at him, and in her eyes he saw sorrow morphing to a deadening acceptance, as if all of the emotion that she'd stored inside for the past months had suddenly burst through a new level of awareness. He'd heard about iced-fog in northern winters and her expression reminded him of that; the sudden, all-encompassing recognition of consequences freezing into place.

But she kept going. Glory Lynn told how she'd returned to the clinic the next day, again alone. "I was nervous that day. Crying. There was a different nurse this time. Nurse Broussard. She told me there wouldn't be much pain."

"And, what happened then?"

"Nurse Broussard inserted lamanaria to start the procedure. She said it would all be over in about twenty-four hours or so."

"Lamanaria?"

She flushed. "Small pieces of kelp that induce labor. She looked down. "That first part didn't take long at all."

"And what happened next?"

"I was told to go home. That I shouldn't feel much pain, maybe mild cramps or something. And to take a Tylenol if I needed that. I was to come back the next afternoon. My appointment was for four o'clock on the next day. They said I'd be there for a few hours afterward."

"And did you have any problems after going home that evening?"

"Not at first. I woke early in the morning feeling mild cramps. About six o'clock in the morning. So I took a couple Tylenol and went back to sleep." She clasped her hands together, twisting them. "But later on, about ten, I began feeling more pain."

"Did you call the clinic then?"

"No. I waited as long as I could. Took some more Tylenol. But finally, I couldn't stand it anymore." She looked into Peter's eyes. "They'd said the pain wouldn't be that bad. I thought maybe something was wrong."

"So what did you do then?"

"I took a cab to the clinic."

"And tell the court what happened when you arrived."

"I went into a room. There were other girls there, most of them younger than me. We all sat in a row. No one was talking. Some had brought books to read. Some of the girls were called while I waited, and I remember . . . I was very frightened."

"And how long did you have to wait?"

"A couple hours, maybe more. The cramps had grown worse and I asked the nurse for another Tylenol and she gave me one, and I was shaking so she gave me a valium."

"Which nurse gave you the valium?"

She straightened and looked at him. "Nurse Sonsten."

"Do you know how many milligrams?"

"Five." She hesitated. "And then the pain got worse, and Nurse Sonsten called Miss Broussard—Nurse Broussard—and she removed the laminaria. Then they gave me another valium . . ."

"Please tell the court, how much valium you received this time."

"Five milligrams again."

"And then what happened?"

"The nurses helped me out of the bed and took me into another room and helped me up onto that table." She twisted her hands, looking at Peter now. "Nurse Broussard seemed worried and kept asking where the doctor was, and Nurse Sonsten went out to look for him."

"Nurse Broussard seemed worried?" He asked the question in a tone of surprise, and turned so that he could see both the defense table and the galley.

"She sounded worried, or maybe surprised. She said things were moving fast. And when Dr. Vicari arrived, she told him to hurry."

"Do you know what time that was?"

"No. I'd lost track. Couldn't think." Tears ran down her cheeks now. He wished that he could reach out and hold onto her hand, but all he could do was turn to the bailiff and ask for Kleenex. She wiped her cheeks with the heel of her hand, and when the bailiff brought the box over, she pulled out a tissue and patted her face.

"Please continue. What happened then?"

"It all happened so fast," she said. Wringing the tissue in her hands, she looked up at the judge, then back to Peter. "I, I . . ." Her eyes swung to the Defendant and she lifted her arms, flailing as her voice rose. "I could see that things weren't right, that things were happening too fast. Everything seemed so far away and I could hear the nurse talking to him, and—"

Peter broke in, moving toward her. "By him, do you mean Dr. Vicari?"

"Yes, yes. Dr. Vicari." Her eyes darted to the defendant and away. Then she looked out over the courtroom, and he knew that she saw no one in the gallery. She was watching herself on that long afternoon. "Suddenly, I felt it . . . the baby . . . I felt it slip through me and out . . ." Her voice broke.

"Just like that," she cried, swinging her eyes from one side of the room to the other. "There wasn't any pain then, not really. It just slid out." And she lifted her hands, cupping them, as if she could feel it. "I could tell that something was wrong . . . I could tell from the nurse's voice, and then Dr. Vicari pushed her aside, and then I heard the cry!"

Peter walked to her side. Stuck his hands in his pockets and looked across at the defendant. "You heard the infant's cry?"

"Yes. Yes!"

The room was silent as a stone as Glory Lynn bent forward, sobbing.

Peter looked at the judge. "May we take a break, Your Honor?"

The judge's face was creased, strained. He gave a brief nod and looked out at the spectators. "Court will recess for fifteen minutes."

Dooney took Glory Lynn to the ladies room down the hallway and waited for her there. Peter returned to his seat at the prosecution table. He wished that there was some way he could help Glory Lynn with the guilt and remorse that she'd bottled up inside. Anger tightened in his chest as he thought of what Vince McConnell would likely do on cross-examination. *Please God, help her take some of the steam out of Vince McConnell's engine. Please protect this child.*

34

GLORY LYNN CHASSON WAS BACK ON the witness stand. Peter stood at the prosecution table. Judge Morrow leaned back in his chair, hands crossed and resting on his stomach as he stared up at the ceiling.

"Read the witness's last two answers back, please," Peter said to Michelene.

Michelene looked down at the tape and read, her voice devoid of emotion:

Answer: "There wasn't any pain then, not really. It just slid out. I could tell that something was wrong . . . I could tell from the nurse's voice, and then Dr. Vicari pushed her aside, and then I heard the cry!"

Question: "You heard the infant's cry?"

Answer: "Yes. Yes!"

Michelene looked up.

"Thank you," Peter said. He strolled around the table toward the jury box, stopping about ten feet before reaching Glory Lynn.

"Now, Miss Chasson."

Glory Lynn stared at him, eyes wide, hands settled on her lap.

"You say you heard the infant cry?"

"Yes." She pushed back her hair. "Twice."

"You've just testified about the first time. When did you hear the second cry?"

"Well, the first time took a few seconds, maybe half a minute, to register, I guess. And then, when I realized what I'd heard I think I screamed . . . I screamed, and all I could think of then was to get to my baby, to hold my baby, and Nurse Broussard was holding me down, pushing me back down, and Dr. Vicari was saying something, and someone else came in, Nurse Sonsten came in, and that's when I heard the second cry and it just cut right through my . . . heart."

She choked on the last words, ducking her head. "All I could think of was getting to my baby."

"And tell us, then what happened?"

"It's all so confusing and hard to remember." She hesitated, looking at Peter, hanging onto his eyes, and he felt that if he moved one fraction of an inch, Glory Lynn Chasson would collapse.

"I . . . I was trying to tell Nurse Broussard that I wanted my baby, trying to make her *understand* . . ." She curled her hands into fists, pressing them together as she lifted them, pumping them with the cadence of her words. "I was fighting her, trying to make her understand, trying to make Dr. Vicari understand, and she was telling me to lie back down, to lie back down."

The courtroom was silent. Glory Lynn slowly dropped her hands, and leaned forward gripping the partition.

This was the moment. Peter worked to keep his voice steady, and soothing. "What was it that you wanted Dr. Vicari and Miss Broussard to understand?" He held her eyes and prayed that Judge Morrow would take this in and sympathize with Glory Lynn.

"I wanted my baby." Her tone was fierce as she looked at Peter. "I didn't want anyone to hurt my baby."

"But hadn't you come to the clinic especially for an abortion?"

"Yes. But everything changed when I heard him cry! That made everything different. My baby was alive, and I wanted him to live."

Seconds passed. Glory Lynn slumped in the chair and looked out over the courtroom.

Peter's voice turned gentle. "What do you remember next?"

Slowly she shook her head from side to side. Glory Lynn's voice dropped a key. "I was fighting and no one would pay attention. I remember the nurse pushing me down on the bed, and . . . and then . . . the lights overhead seemed to spin and I just felt so tired, and I think I must have closed my eyes, because that's all I can remember." She choked back a sob. "Just those lights."

She looked at Dooney, then at Peter. "And then I woke up in a different room and everything was over. They told me that I'd done fine; that I could go home."

"Who told you that?"

"Miss Broussard."

"Did you see Nurse Sonstein after that?"

"No." She hesitated. "Miss Broussard, Nurse Broussard drove me home."

"All right. Just a few more questions." Peter moved closer.

She looked up.

"When you first went to the clinic and signed forms consenting to the abortion procedure, was it ever your understanding that if the infant was born alive that medical assistance would be withheld from the child because of that consent?"

"No. Of course not. I never thought of—"

"Objection, Your Honor." Vince was on his feet. "The question assumes evidence not of record, that the infant was viable, and that medical assistance was necessary and withheld."

Peter walked to the bench. "Respectfully, Your Honor—"

Judge Morrow threw up his hands. "Objection sustained."

"I'll rephrase the question," Peter said.

Peter walked back to the center of the well and looked at Glory Lynn. "Miss Chasson, let me put the question this way." He folded his arms and looked up, searching for words. "When you signed the consent forms at Alpha Women's Medical Clinic prior to the abortion procedure, was it your understanding that there was any possibility that the infant could be born alive in any manner of speaking?"

"No."

"Thank you."

"And I will never forget the sound of that cry. Never."

"Objection."

"The witness will answer only questions asked," Judge Morrow said. He looked at Michelene. "Strike the witness's last statement from the record."

But Peter knew that Calvin Morrow would remember the sound of those agonizing words. He turned to the bench, and said, "No more questions for this witness, Your Honor."

Morrow nodded and beckoned to his clerk. "We'll take a fifteen-minute break, Counsel." He looked at Vince McConnell. "You'll take the witness on cross when we return."

"All rise," the bailiff called. Judge Morrow rose, and disappeared through the door behind the bench.

Dooney asked Glory Lynn if she'd like to go to a private witness room to wait during the short recess. Glory Lynn said no, she just wanted to be left alone for a while. She would wait in the chair on the witness stand.

When Doony returned, Peter glanced up at her. "Clara Sonsten's on next. Make certain Shauna and Clara are here, please."

"Sure." Dooney rose and headed toward the room where the prosecution witnesses would wait prior to being called.

A few minutes later, Dooney pushed through the gate to his right.

"They're not here." She sounded breathless

Peter looked up, frowning. "Shauna and Clara?"

"Right." Dooney brushed hair back from her forehead. "They're not here, Peter. I phoned the office. Molly says she hasn't heard from them."

"Great," Peter muttered. He blew out his cheeks, thinking. Behind Dooney he saw Vince McConnell coming down the aisle.

Glancing at his watch, Peter gazed over the courtroom, lowering his voice. "I don't know how long Vince will take on cross with Glory Lynn, but we've got to have a stand-in, someone else for the rest of the afternoon. Calvin Morrow will go ballistic if we're not ready. See if you can find Mac, will you? If he's not in his office, have him paged. And find out how long it'll take him to get here." He glanced back at the empty bench.

"And hurry. If we don't have someone lined up when Vince is finished, Morrow will eat us alive."

35

COURT WAS BACK IN SESSION. JUDGE Morrow held up his pen and pointed it toward Vince McConnell.

"Counsel," he said. "Your witness."

Vince picked up a manila file folder, stood and walked to the lectern, Without looking at the witness, he opened the file—taking his time—running his eyes down the first page before closing it again. Then he strode toward the witness stand where he stood ten feet away, arms behind his back, hands clasped, looking at Glory Lynn.

"Miss Chasson. My name is Vince O'Connell, and as you know, I'm counsel for Dr. Charles Vicari."

Glory Lynn looked at him and nodded. "I know."

"Something's been puzzling me since I heard your testimony earlier." He paused, studying Glory Lynn. "You came to the Alpha Women's Clinic of your own accord, did you not?"

"Yes."

Vince nodded. "It was your own choice. No one dragged you there?"

Glory Lynn shook her head.

"Answer for the record, please."

"No. It was my own choice." Peter saw Glory Lynn's anger rising, exactly what Vince was after. Vince raised his voice and half-turned toward the gallery, with a bemused look on his face. "So no one dragged you to the Alpha Women's Clinic. You went there on your own and asked them to take you as a patient, do I have that right?"

Peter rose. "Objection. Asked and answered."

"Sustained."

Peter and Dooney had spent hours preparing Glory Lynn for this cross-examination. They'd shown her a few tricks, how not to show when she was angry, but to let the energy out by wiggling her toes or feet behind the wooden partition where no one could see. He'd warned her to sit up straight, and to press her hands together in her lap to keep them still. No fidgeting to signal that she was nervous. And volunteer nothing.

Yet, two minutes into the cross-examination, there she sat with her hands gripping the top of the partition, knuckles turning white.

Vince stood beside the witness box, looming over her. "You testified there were several forms you filled out when you first entered the clinic, did you not?"

"Yes."

"And did you bother to read those forms, Miss Chasson?" His voice dripped with sarcasm.

She hesitated. "Yes. Ah, some of them. Not all."

O'Connell walked back to the lectern and pulled several pages from the folder on the lectern, holding them up, like grenades. They were copies of the forms that Peter had introduced into evidence earlier. He turned and waved them toward Peter. Peter nodded.

Vince looked at Judge Morrow. "Permission to approach the witness, Your Honor?"

"Permission granted."

Vince handed one of the forms to Glory Lynn and stood beside her, pointing. "Is this your signature on the bottom of the page?"

She glanced down. "Yes, it is."

He nodded. "Then, please read for the court what is written across the top of this form."

Glory Lynn read out the name of the clinic, and then "Consent for Medical Procedures."

Vince nodded and tipped his head toward the page. "And below that, two lines, down. Please read that part also. What medical procedure is described on this consent form?"

"Induction abortion."

Vince nodded. "And now, a little further down to the middle of the page, where it says "Gestation." Do you see that?"

Glory Lynn nodded.

"You must answer out loud, please."

"Yes. I see it."

"And what is written on that line, underneath, beside the word *gestation*?" He stepped aside, allowing spectators full view of the witness.

Glory Lynn jutted out her chin, looking down at the page. "Twenty-two weeks."

"And is that your handwriting?"

She looked at Peter, then Dooney. "Yes," she said.

Vince clasped his hands behind his back and looked at Glory Lynn. "And based upon that information, and a physical examination performed by the Dr. Vicari at the clinic, Dr. Vicari estimated the gestational age of the fetus you carried as twenty-three weeks. Is that not correct?"

"So far as I recall."

"Yet, thereafter the autopsy report indicated gestation at twenty-four weeks." He paused. "That's quite a difference from your original guess. Half a month, in fact."

Peter lifted his hand. "Objection. I didn't hear a question there."

The judge gave him a look. "Sustained." He turned to Vince. "Rephrase the question, Counsel."

Vince turned to Glory Lynn. "Isn't it true that you lied about your period of gestation to obtain an abortion, Miss Chasson? Isn't it true that you knew if you told the truth, that your pregnancy was more advanced, the clinic might have been reluctant to admit you?"

Her eyes grew wide. "How dare you!"

"Objection!" Peter was on his feet. "Counsel is badgering the witness."

Morrow frowned. "Overruled; this is cross, Mr. Jacobs. I'm giving the defense some leeway here." He looked down at Glory Lynn. "Answer the question, please."

Glory Lynn flushed. "I didn't lie. I—"

"But that is your handwriting?" Vince pointed to the line on the page again. "Here, where you wrote twenty-two weeks?"

"Yes." Her eyes darted to Peter. Peter couldn't help her. He knew that Vince was setting the groundwork for a defense. Later he would argue that Glory Lynn's misdirection had caused the defendant to underestimate the age of the unborn child, "I was mistaken," Glory Lynn said.

Vince nodded. Hands clasped behind his back, he turned, angling his body toward the spectators, He let a beat go by, emphasizing this self-indictment.

"Did it occur to you that if Dr. Vicari believed the fetus was a week or two younger, that he would also believe that it was impossible for it to be viable?"

Peter had explained this reasoning to Glory Lynn in their sessions preparing for trial. If Vicari could claim that he'd had no way of suspecting that her unborn child was viable, able to survive outside the mother's womb at the time of the abortion, he was on his way to a possible defense to the charges—complete and utter surprise at the live birth. Confusion.

"My guess of twenty-two weeks wasn't a lie. It was a mistake." Glory Lynn's glared at Vince McConnell. "I was confused, that's all."

Vince pressed his hand to one side of his forehead and stepped back. "That's all? That's all?"

"Objection." Peter stood. "Harassing the witness."

"Sustained." Morrow turned to McConnell. "If you have a question, Counsel, ask it."

Vince changed the subject abruptly. "Miss Chasson, you testified that on the day you arrived at the clinic for the abortion you were given five milligrams of valium while waiting to go into the delivery room. And again you were given five milligrams right before you went into the procedure room. Is that correct?"

"Yes."

"Had you ever taken valium before?"

"No."

Peter braced his elbows on the table and his chin on his knuckles, holding his breath, watching Vince spring the trap.

Vince turned back toward the lectern and Glory Lynn frowned. "Did you drink any alcohol on that day, the day of the procedure?"

Glory Lynn tossed her head. "Of course not."

"Is it fair to say that you were experiencing a high level of stress by the time you arrived at the clinic that day?"

"Yes, I was in pain."

"Ah, yes. The pain." He turned on his heels, facing Peter and Dooney, tapping a finger to his lips. "Were you anxious about the procedure?"

She lifted her chin. "No. Not then. It was the pain that bothered me."

His brows arched high and he turned back to her. "So your only concern before the procedure was the pain?"

"Yes."

Peter managed to keep himself from closing his eyes.

"No second-guessing at that point? Just concern about the pain; so please tell the court how it was that in the procedure room, after taking a strong drug that you'd never taken before to settle you down, you suddenly became so concerned about the fetus that you'd decided to abort?"

"It was the cry—I heard my baby cry!"

"Then why didn't you just say so? Whether such a cry was your imagination or not isn't the question. If you thought you heard an infant's cry and you could see that the Defendant hadn't, why didn't you just tell him? Why the incoherent screaming; fighting with the nurse, the confusion?"

"I don't know," she said, shaking her head. She looked at the floor. "I don't know what I was thinking. Everything was such a mess. And they'd told me there wouldn't be much pain, and then I was in the labor room and it all happened so fast." She pressed her hand to her forehead. "Like I said before, I don't remember much after I heard that cry."

Hold on, Glory Lynn. Hold on.

"Isn't it true that you were confused by the large dose of valium that you'd taken before the procedure?"

"No."

"Isn't it possible that you imagined that cry?"

"No!"

"Isn't it true, in fact, that it wasn't until you woke up the next morning that you had second thoughts? Isn't that when the remorse struck, Miss Chasson, after it was too late? Isn't that why you've sought help in counseling, and this . . . this . . ." he turned and arched his hand over the courtroom, "this public flagellation? You need someone to blame and that someone is the Defendant!"

"Objection, Your Honor! This is outrageous." Peter was already halfway to the bench. From the corners of his eyes he saw Glory Lynn hunch over and drop her face into her hands, sobbing.

The gavel slammed down. "Objection sustained." Calvin Morrow looked at Vince McConnell. "Let's move on, Mr. McConnell."

Peter halted near the lectern.

"Any redirect Mr. Jacobs?"

Peter looked up at the Judge. Glory Lynn had done well, but she couldn't handle any more. "No, your honor," he said. With a long deep breath he nodded to Glory Lynn and she rose. He waited for her, then slipped his arm around her shoulder and walked her to the gate in the railing.

Glory Lynn's father and mother stood as she came through the gate. Her mother put her arm around her daughter's shoulders. Her father followed them up the aisle, fury stiffening his neck and back.

Peter returned to the table, and stood behind it, arms dangling, looking up at Calvin Morrow. He drew in his breath as Judge Morrow's voice rang out.

"Call your next witness, Counsel."

Turning, he scanned the gallery futilely for Mac. "The State calls Clara Sonsten," he said.

The bailiff opened the door and peered into the hallway and Peter looked at Dooney. She shook her head—I don't know. The bailiff turned his head from left to right, scanning the hallway as he held the door. "Miss Clara Sonsten? Sonsten. Clara Sonsten?" After a moment he shook his head and turned back toward the front of the courtroom, "No one out here answering to that name, Mr. Jacobs."

Dooney rose. "I'll check the witness room again." Peter stood as Dooney brushed past him and he heard her hurrying up the aisle toward the door. Too late for that, he knew. They wouldn't be there.

"The State's witness has not arrived yet, Your Honor. If you'll give us a moment . . ."

"What's going on here, Mr. Jacobs?" Morrow's voice was ice. "We don't waste time in my courtroom."

"I understand, Judge. Miss St. Pierre's going to find out what's happened, and if we could have a short break, perhaps ten minutes, I'm certain we can straighten things out."

Vince McConnell stood. "The defense objects to a recess at this point, Your Honor. It's late in the day and counsel's wasting time. Every minute passing in this courtroom further damages an innocent man's reputation, and his business. Let the prosecution call another witness."

Peter opened his mouth and then caught Morrow's glance at the clock. Seconds passed as Morrow frowned and looked down at something on his desk. Peter turned his head, still hoping to see Dooney come through the door with Clara Sonsten.

"It's four o'clock," Morrow said at last. "We'll recess for the day."

With a deep exhale, Peter felt the tension leaving his shoulders. "Court will reconvene at nine sharp in the morning."

In the general melee, Alice rose and hurried out following the crowd from the elevator, through the lobby and out onto the sidewalk. The weather had changed and there was a new chill in the air. She buttoned her sweater as she scanned the traffic for a taxicab.

Leaning her head back against the seat she looked blindly through the window thinking about what she'd seen in the courtroom that day. Vicari hadn't changed a bit. The thing that worried her the most was that she'd detected a slight sympathy in the judge's attitude toward the defendant, and she'd sensed that growing throughout the day. That could make her decision more difficult, she mused. But, the day in court had confirmed her worst fears, regardless. She had a decision to make right now.

36

REBECCA WAS STRONG ENOUGH THESE DAYS to walk down the stairs and wander around the house. She smiled to herself, thinking that only two weeks were left until the baby's arrival. There was so much to be accomplished before that event; there were only a few days left before Brightfield needed the new brief that she was working on. She wanted to hire someone to paint the nursery; had finally picked out the color. White.

When she'd told Peter that, he'd laughed. Weeks of agonizing over paint, and she'd decided on white?

And then, there was still the nanny problem.

Last week Rose Marie called to say that she'd found several good possibilities. Rose Marie had interviewed them herself, this time, and said she'd found one woman that she really liked. Rebecca had asked her to hold off for a week or two, until she finished Brightfield's brief, and—although she didn't mention this—until a verdict was rendered in Peter's case.

The baby moved then and she rested her hand over the spot, feeling the sharp little jabs, reminding her again that soon she'd have to make a decision on a nanny, or two, or three. Frowning, she pressed a protective hand over Daisy.

She heard Peter coming down the stairs and through the living room. She put a smile on her face and turned just as he entered. The last thing he needed this morning was to worry about his wife. Clara Sonsten hadn't shown up in court the day before, she knew. Illness, she'd said.

A case of nerves, Shauna, Peter's legal assistant had said. Shauna was certain that Clara would revive after a good night's sleep. If not, a subpoena would be issued, and a sheriff would deliver her to the courtroom. But Clara Sonsten as a hostile witness was not a happy thought.

When he walked into the kitchen, Peter looked tense. With a quick peck on her cheek and a little pat for the baby, he went straight to the coffeepot.

Rebecca leaned against the counter while he poured coffee into a mug and then turned to her, gulping it down. The lines around the corners of his eyes and mouth were deeper today, she noticed. He said he didn't think he'd be home until late again, and her heart sank.

The newspaper article about day one of the trial had generated some commotion. There were a few protestors gathering at the doors of the courthouse when Peter arrived on Wednesday, but, for the most part the crowd was polite, quieter than he'd expected.

Some of them were in the courtroom now, the bailiff told him. He saw signs piled against the wall in the hallway.

Judge Morrow was already present, sitting at the bench, dealing with a motion from another case. Peter took his place at the table and opened his briefcase, pulling out the notepad. He saw that Dooney had been here; the evidence boxes were on the floor near her chair. A third chair had been placed beside the boxes.

Shauna was here today, talking to the bailiff. They stood near a small table with a slide projector set up near the jury box, just in front of the witness stand.

Dooney arrived just before nine o'clock, when court was convened. Shauna took a seat in the chair beside Dooney, waiting.

At a nod from the judge, Peter stood.

"The State calls Fred McAndrews to the stand."

Peter turned his head, watching as the bailiff stuck his head out into the hallway and called to Mac. Peter, Dooney, and Shauna watched Mac walk toward them carrying a large brown paper bag, folded and clamped shut at the top. Mac was wearing his court suit today, Peter saw. The same old dark blue suit that he insisted on wearing for good luck every time he testified as the lead investigator in a case.

He turned to Dooney. "Go find out if Clara's been rounded up for this afternoon, will you? By the time I've finished with Mac, we need to know. If we need to stall, call Stephanie Kand. I've got her on standby."

Dooney nodded.

Peter greeted Mac, and watched as he walked to the table where Shauna had been standing with the bailiff, and set the brown bag on it. After the swearing in, Peter ran quickly through the preliminary questions. Then he moved on and asked the detective to describe what had happened the morning that Glory Lynn Chasson and her father had appeared at the station house to file the initial complaint.

Mac described his interview with the accuser and her father.

"Did you advise her of her rights at that time?"

"No. It wasn't necessary. She was not a suspect." He described in detail the process of the interview, then the filing of the complaint, and later obtaining a warrant to search the Alpha Women's Clinic for the body of Baby Chasson.

"So you executed the warrant immediately after receiving the complaint?"

"That's right." Mac established that the warrant was signed by a judicial officer in Jefferson Parish, and executed on the same day, and this was entered into State's evidence for the record.

Then Peter returned to the witness stand and looked at Mac. "Why the hurry in obtaining the warrant, Detective?"

Mac looked out over the spectators. "Miss Chasson was concerned that the clinic would dispose of the infant's body right away. These were extenuating circumstances."

The testimony was clear as Mac explained step by step how he'd developed the case leading up to the defendant's arrest. He'd attempted to talk to both Charles Vicari and Eileen Broussard, Vicari's wife, during this process, he said. But both, through their lawyers, had refused.

"Who else was there conducting the search, beside yourself?" Peter asked. As he asked the question, he glanced at the place where Dooney usually sat. She had not yet returned. His heart raced as he turned back to face his witness.

Mac named several officers from the sheriff's department, Dr. Stephanie Kand—the forensic pathologist from the coroner's office—her assistant, and others who were present at the time of the search. Peter then turned toward Shauna and she rose and carrying a box of slides, took a seat at the table holding the projector. During the search of the clinic, the team had taken pictures. They waited while the bailiff set up a viewing screen in front of the projector at an angle visible to everyone—including the judge, the defense, spectators, and the press.

The photographs, selected in pre-trial hearings and reluctantly approved by the defense were admitted as State's evidence. The judge then told Peter to proceed.

And so they began. Shauna stood behind the projector, turned it on, and as Peter introduced each photograph taken by the search team, Shauna slid the matching slide into the projector so that the same photo showed on the screen. With Mac's testimony, Peter's plan was to give the judge and the spectators in the gallery a clear picture of the scene that would stay with them throughout the trial. He wanted to burn into their minds that the clinic was a crime scene.

To set the first scene he showed a picture of the procedure room used by Glory Lynn Chason on the night that Infant Chasson was delivered. Mac identified the room. The slide showed a stark room with fluorescent lights overhead casting sharp-edged shadows of a wide, six-foot long metal table onto a white tiled floor. Metal stirrups were attached to the bed at the end nearest the camera.

Peter paused, letting a few seconds go by, giving everyone time to visualize Glory Lynn lying on the big table. Then he asked Mac to describe each item found in the room. The room was designed for precision and efficiency, not warmth and comfort. A table on the left side of the slide held several gleaming instruments, bottles, a glass jar of swabs and cotton, and a stack of folded gauze. Underneath the table were shelves storing sheets, thin blankets, and disposable blue padding and towels.

Moving on to the reception room at the entrance of the clinic, Peter led Mac room by room through the Alpha Women's Medical Clinic, a tour for the court. With each photograph Mac described the area and if it was searched, and if so, what was found and taken as evidence.

Beyond the reception room, there was another waiting room for patients scheduled for physical examinations, and for those waiting to go into the procedure rooms. This room contained rows of metal folding chairs lined up against a wall. There were lockers for clothing and a dressing area with benches and long mirrors, and a restroom, which was large and appeared clean.

At one end of the hallway leading from the interior waiting room was a storage closet which Mac referred to as the utility room. The camera view from the doorway, from right to left, showed it to be about twenty feet by ten, with a narrow cabinet running the length of the wall facing the doorway. Above the cabinet were rows of somewhat narrower steel shelves reaching to the ceiling. Folded sheets and towels and other such items were stacked along the shelves. To the left of the doorway, in the interior of this room, the camera swung to a large, round metal container with a top held closed with clamps. A large label on the side said Medical Waste.

At a signal from Peter, Shauna then showed a picture of a large square freezer. The room housing the freezer looked like a garage with boxes and large cans and tools scattered around.

Peter took a deep breath. "Please tell the court what we're looking at in this photograph, Detective McAndrews."

"This is a photograph of a storage room at the back of the clinic." He pointed, looking at the screen. "And over to the side, there, that is a large storage freezer."

"Was this area included in the search warrant?"

"Yes, it was."

Peter nodded to Shauna and then turned, looking directly at the defendant. Shauna clicked on the next slide. On the screen the photo loomed. Behind him, Peter heard the gasps. He waited for the gavel, but Judge Morrow was staring from the matching photograph in his hand to the enhanced one on the screen. On the screen, he could clearly see the frozen body in the slide.

"Please identify this photograph for the court, Detective McAndrew."

"This is a picture taken inside the freezer." He leaned forward, peering at the screen. "You can see, there on a shelf to the right side, wrapped in that blue towel, you can make out the body of a premature infant."

"Oh." Someone in the gallery cried out. "Oh, no. No!" Judge Morrow banged the gavel. "Order in the court. If there's another outburst, I'll clear the courtroom."

Turning to Mac, Peter took a step back. "Please continue."

Mac nodded, leaning now toward the screen. "The infant in this photo has been matched by blood type to Glory Lynn Chasson. It . . . he . . ." Mac paused, glancing at Peter. "The infant is a male, approximately a foot long, and as described in the autopsy report, weighing one pound, eight ounces.

"The body in this photograph is frozen. As you can see, it's partially wrapped in a blue towel, similar to the ones stacked on a shelf of the small table in earlier photographs of Miss Chasson's procedure room."

In pre-trial hearings, McConnell had fought hard to keep this picture out, arguing that it was inflammatory. Peter had wanted to show several photos from different angles, but Judge Morrow had allowed only this one from the initial search, and two others from the autopsy which Dr. Kand would later introduce in her testimony.

"Who was the forensic pathologist at the scene?"

"Dr. Stephanie Kand, from the coroner's office."

Mac described the procedures used by Dr. Kand to bag and preserve the body, three fibers, and the blue towel. Shauna clicked the slides to a photo of the fibers.

"At this time the State would like to introduce into evidence the blue towel you saw in the slides and fibers seized under warrant." Peter looked at the judge.

Morrow nodded. "Go ahead."

Mac stood and walked to the table. From an inside pocket of his jacket he pulled two gloves and slipped them onto his hands. Opening the brown bag, he lifted two plastic bags from inside, one large, one small. These he placed on the table. He identified the large bag as containing the towel; the smaller bag as containing three fibers.

Carefully he picked up the larger plastic bag, unsealed it and pulled out a small blue towel. He held this up by the top two corners, turning, so that everyone could see.

The towel was wrinkled, with dark stains, and worn around the edges. Mac turned the display once more to the judge and the defense before returning it to the plastic bag. He then placed the plastic bag inside the large brown bag and after resealing it, handed it to Peter. Peter had the clerk admit the evidence into record for the State, than took it back for later use if necessary.

The process was repeated for the smaller bag containing the fibers. Here, Shauna clicked a new slide onto the screen, showing magnification of the fibers.

When Mac returned to the stand, Peter stood beside him and asked him to describe the fiber evidence. The fibers were identified as coming from the blue towel, Mac testified. When the defense objected, Peter assured Judge Morrow that Dr. Stephanie Kand's testimony would support this conclusion.

Two of the fibers were found in the freezer in the storage room in the location of the body, Mac testified. Peter turned slightly so that he could see Vicari's reaction to his next question.

"Please tell the court, Detective McAndrews, where the third fiber introduced as evidence was located."

"The third fiber was found in an empty procedure room at the end of the hallway," Mac said.

Neither Vince nor Charles Vicari showed any emotion; even though Clara Sonsten had refused to talk to them prior to trial, as was her right. He turned back to Mac, and they followed the same procedure to introduce the fibers into evidence.

"Detective, was another warrant issued to search the clinic?"

"Yes," Mac said. "Subsequent to discovering the body, we obtained a warrant to search the clinic records, with specific limitations."

Because of health privacy restrictions, the warrant limited the State's search of records to particular entries evidencing only Glory Lynn Chasson's visits to the clinic. Peter took Mac through a description of copies of pages from the clinic appointment book, redacted to show only Miss Chasson's name, confirming her three visits to the clinic as described in her testimony, as well as the brief records of her procedure, but with no notation of a birth.

Peter, standing before the witness stand, fixed his eyes on Mac. "Just to clarify, Detective. There was no mention of a live birth on the Alpha Women's Clinic records of Miss Chasson's abortion procedure on May 13 of this year?"

"None at all."

Peter nodded. "Thank you, Detective." He turned toward the bench. "That's all for now, Your Honor. The State may want to recall this witness later."

Judge Morrow glanced at the clock on the wall. Mac's testimony had taken almost three hours. "Now's as good a time as any to break for lunch," he announced. "We'll reconvene at one thirty, and at that time"—he glanced at Vince—"you may take Detective McAndrews on cross-examination."

Judge Morrow looked at Mac. "I remind you that you're still under oath, Detective."

Peter turned, looking for Dooney. She was there, and she nodded. Relief flooded him—Clara was back on board. His heart rate slowed as he turned back to Mac.

"Yes, Your Honor." Mac stood, adjusted his tie, and stepped from the jury box. With a smile for Dooney as he passed by, he hurried through the gate.

At twenty minutes 'til two that afternoon, Vince McConnell stood at the lectern before the bench looking down at the notepad he'd just placed there. Time stretched as he adjusted his tie, his sleeves, and then turned toward Mac. Vince had his own assistant working the projector and slides during the cross.

But Mac's testimony was factual and he was a strong witness. Peter wasn't worried. Vince would get nothing new from Mac. Still, once again he regretted the loss of the jury. Smart move on McConnell's part, he admitted, watching Vince pace up and down the well of the court, beginning to poke at Mac.

37

AT THREE O'CLOCK MAC ESCAPED THE witness stand, and, at Peter's request, the bailiff called Clara Sonsten. Peter watched as Clara appeared. She wore high spike heels, a tight red skirt that ended some inches above her knees, and a long-sleeved black sweater that showed her curves. The sweater had red and green and white Christmas designs knit around the neck and sleeves. Well. You do what you can.

With a sideways glance at Peter, Clara walked to the witness stand. Reaching the box, she fixed her eyes on the clerk's, seeming to freeze him with a long slow smile. And then she swore to tell the truth, the whole truth, and nothing but the truth in a low drawl. A flush ran up the young clerk's cheeks. Then he returned to his desk, and Clara entered the jury box and sat.

Peter stood and walked to the lectern. "Please state your name for the court," he said, looking at the witness.

"My name is Clara Sonsten. I am a Registered Nurse."

A series of personal questions followed, her background, her education, the places she had worked, her experience at the clinic. She testified that she'd been on duty when Glory Lynn Chasson had first come in to register as a patient at the clinic, and on the night that she'd delivered.

And then she'd quit her job.

"And where are you employed now, Miss Sonsten?" Peter moved a few steps back from the lectern, facing her, hands loose in his pockets.

Miss Sonsten said that she now worked in the Obstetrics Department of a large hospital in the city. Returning to the lectern, Peter braced his fingers on the edge of the stand and began a general line of questions on her new employment. And then, he began walking toward the witness box, halting halfway between the lectern and Clara.

Jamming one hand into a pocket, he looked at Clara. "On the night that Glory Lynn Chasson was in labor at the Alpha Women's Clinic, were you assigned to assist the Defendant at the birth?"

"No. My job was to look after two patients who'd had procedures earlier that day. I was to give them follow-up instructions. Watch them for a couple hours. Give them some medicines for pain, if they needed it. That sort of thing."

"But at some time that evening you ended up in the procedure room with Dr. Vicari?"

"Yes. Both patients had just left when Miss Broussard called for me. There's a bell in the room, and she rang the bell. And then I heard a scream."

"Where did you think the scream came from?"

"It came from the procedure room, where Dr. Vicari was with Glory Lynn . . . uhm, Miss Chasson."

Peter moved toward her. "And what time was that?"

"It was about fifteen minutes after six, in the evening."

"How can you be so precise?"

"I'd just heard the bell when I was headed to the kitchen to get a Coca-Cola. I was scheduled to work overtime that night, and there's a big clock there on the wall and I was looking at it wishing I were home when I heard the bell ring."

Peter raised his brows as if this was new information to him. "What did you think was happening when you heard that bell?"

Her eyes darted to the defendant, and away. "It was the call bell. I knew Eileen Broussard was in there with Dr. Vicari. The call bell meant she needed help."

"And what did you do then?"

She cocked her head. "Well I went immediately to the procedure room."

"And what did you see when you entered?"

Clara's eyes faded again toward Vicari as she described what she'd seen upon entering the room, just as she'd described it to Peter and Mac at the pizza place over six months before, and many times since. The facts as she gave them had never changed, and her voice was steady, almost monotone as she spoke. Vince McConnell, eager to break the rhythm of Peter's examination, interrupted with frequent objections.

When Clara described entering the procedure room, Peter turned aside in order to watch the defendant while he questioned Clara. He'd waited for this moment for six months, struggling to understand.

"Dr. Vicari was sitting on the stool at the foot of the bed," Clara said. "The sheet was up, and I saw that he was holding the infant in the blue delivery towel in his hand. Of course it was so small. I saw some blood, but not so much. He'd cut the cord, but he was struggling, holding that baby and trying to help Glory Lynn expel the placenta, and like I said, there was some blood. And Miss Broussard was over by the patient, over at the side of the bed, pushing her back down. It looked like Miss Chasson was trying to get out of the bed; she was fighting some, pushing Eileen away, and crying and struggling to sit up." She hesitated, took a breath.

"And then I heard the baby cry."

Peter paused long enough to let her words sink in. Behind them there was the hum again, but muted. "Are you certain, Miss Sonsten?"

"Yes. I know what I heard."

"And then what happened?"

"Dr. Vicari shouted to me to get over there."

"And at that time, was Dr. Vicari still holding the infant?"

"Yes. So I walked over there and when I looked down I saw it move, its legs and arms . . . and it was breathing on its own." The corners of her eyes and mouth turned down. "I was startled, you know, that it was . . . that it was alive."

"Objection, Your Honor!" Vince didn't rise; he gave Clara a look of distaste as he went on. "Move to strike the witness's answer. The term *alive* has no relevance in this case. Under *Roe v. Wade*, the question is whether the fetus is viable—at a minimum, able to sustain life independently for a period of time—after separation from the mother."

"I don't think we need to thread that needle, Judge," Peter said. "Moving voluntary muscles and breathing are obvious signs of *life*." Peter had expected Vince's objection. Life, to Vince McConnell, was a subjective judgment. But Clara's testimony here was critical to establish a fact, that Glory Lynn Chasson's infant was born alive.

Still, Vince battled on. "The movement the witness claims to have observed could have been purely mechanical, Your Honor. Instinctive movements, and the witness is not an expert on that question. It's well known that mechanical movement like breathing, muscle movement, sounds, can occur when the unformed brain is dead."

"Overruled," Morrow said in a dry tone.

Peter turned to Clara. "Miss Sonsten. You say you saw the infant moving?"

"Yes. The arms and legs were moving."

"And what happened then?"

"I held out my arms and Dr. Vicari handed me the towel and the infant, and I held him." She paused. "It was a boy."

"And what was Nurse Broussard doing at this time?"

"She was still trying to get Miss Chasson to lie down. And Miss Chasson was all upset, crying, but I couldn't understand what she was saying. By the time I was holding the infant, Nurse Broussard had got her down on that bed and she seemed to be calming down."

It was the valium that calmed down Glory Lynn Chasson, Peter knew. He paused for a moment because the next line of questions and answers would help establish Vicari's intentions that night. He gave Clara a hard look, hoping she'd remember his warning to be precise in her answers.

"Did the Defendant say anything to you at the time he gave you the infant?"

"Yes." She looked down at her hands. "He told me to take it out of there, to the utility room. That it was upsetting the patient."

Peter turned so that the gallery could clearly see and hear. "And what did you take those instructions to mean, Miss Sonsten?"

"I took that to mean I should take the baby to the utility room." She paused and lifted one shoulder. "What else? I was to leave it there to die, I suppose."

A collective gasp rose from the spectators. Peter dropped his head and passed his hand over his eyes. As the hum continued, Judge Morrow banged the gavel. "Quiet, or I'll clear the courtroom."

Peter waited until the room behind him was silent. And then he looked at Clara. "To your knowledge, has that ever happened before at the clinic? Leaving an infant to die in the utility room?"

"I've never seen it, but I've heard that's what happens sometimes, when the fetus survives the abortion."

"Objection." Vince was on his feet. "Hearsay. Your Honor, please. The Defendant can't defend against wild speculation and rumors!"

"Sustained."

Peter had expected this. Clara's testimony about prior live births was clear hearsay, something she'd heard from someone else. But Judge Morrow had heard her words and Peter hoped that they were burned in his mind.

Now he folded his arms across his chest and turned, looking at Charles Vicari. "Let's get this straight. Dr. Vicari has handed the infant to you, in the towel, and while you're holding it the Defendant instructs you to take it out of the room, to take him to the utility room?"

She nodded, and followed it with, "Yes."

"And what was your response?"

"I asked Dr. Vicari if I should suction and then call an ambulance for help."

"Can you explain to the court what you mean by that?"

She shrugged. "Sure." Turning, she spoke to the judge. "You use a little suction bulb to clear the throat, try to clear the air passages for the baby to help him breathe. Sometimes you can clear the throat with your fingers if you have to. Premature babies have immature lungs, and this could give us time to get him to a ventilator."

"A ventilator, respirator, monitors. To your knowledge does the Alpha Women's Clinic maintain that type of equipment?"

"No." With a glance at the defendant, she frowned. "But I was thinking that might give us time to call an ambulance, get him to a hospital."

Peter nodded. "Your thought was to get the infant to a hospital neonatal intensive care unit?"

"Yes." Again, she glanced at the defendant.

Peter followed her eyes. He'd expected more reaction from the defense table during Clara's testimony. But Vicari sat casually back, one elbow planted on the arm of his chair, his cheek resting in his hand. His look was one of disdain.

He looked back at Clara. "And Dr. Vicari said, no?"

"That's right." She looked down. "He was furious. He took the baby back from me. Then he wrapped that towel all around, kind of tight, so it covered the baby's face. Like a mummy, you know? And then he handed it back to me and told me to get out, to take it to the utility room. He said I was upsetting Glory Lynn."

Peter turned, angling his body toward the spectators. "So what did you do then?"

"He went back to working on Glory Lynn and I unwrapped the towel from the infant's face. He was still struggling to breathe."

"Did Dr. Vicari see that?"

"No. He was focused on his patient."

"What did you do next?"

"I left the procedure room, with the baby. I kept the towel around him best I could to keep him warm. He looked to me to be a perfectly formed little boy." In the silence, she began to cry.

"Objection." Vince McConnell lifted his hand without rising. "Strike the last sentence. Beyond the witness's expertise."

"Sustained." Morrow looked at the court reporter. "Strike the last sentence from the record, Michelene."

Peter signaled the bailiff. The Kleenex box appeared. He pulled out two tissues and handed them to Clara, then placed the box on the wooden partition beside her. She took the tissues from him without looking up. Wiped her eyes. Blew her nose.

"So you left the delivery room with the towel wrapped around the baby. What did you do then?"

Minutes passed. She sniffled. Blew her nose again, then looked up at Peter. "I took him into an empty room, down the hallway, near the back." She ducked her head and dabbed at the corners of her eyes. "Lights were still on in there." She looked at Peter from under her lids. "And then . . . then I sat down on the stool and held him. I cleared out his mouth and throat with my fingers, best I could to help him breathe. Then, I just cradled him in my arms."

Spectators erupted. Judge Morrow banged the gavel. "One more outburst and I'll have the bailiff clear the courtroom." He glared out over the courtroom, the gavel hovering midair.

Peter turned back to Clara. He didn't want to lose this momentum.

"Why did you do that, Miss Sonsten?"

"I didn't want him to be alone. Or cold." She leaned forward, clenching her hands on top of the partition. "He was alive . . ." She put her fingers over her mouth and looked at the judge, then back to Peter.

"He was breathing, shallow little breathes, he was fighting for air. I could see his heart beating through his chest wall. When I put my hand on his chest, I . . . I could feel his heart beating." Her voice broke. She straightened and turned her face aside, toward the jury box.

Peter understood. The vision haunted him, too, and he hadn't even been there. He couldn't imagine how Clara Sonsten lived with that memory.

"How long did you hold him?"

"Until he died. At first," she went on in a low voice. "He was struggling to breathe. At first . . . at first he moved his arms and legs, and for a while he made some little sounds. He was about a foot long. I guessed he weighed about a pound and a half or so. He looked all right to me. I didn't see anything wrong."

"Objection."

Peter turned to Vince.

"Again. Miss Sonsten is not a physician. She's not qualified to offer opinions as to the fetal condition or possible disabilities."

Peter turned to Judge Morrow. "Again, Your Honor. The witness is merely stating what she saw. And Miss Sonsten is a Registered Nurse and has worked in the profession for three years. She is stating her opinion based upon her experience as a trained nurse."

"I'll allow the testimony. Objection overruled." Morrow looked at Vince. "But Counsel, you are of course entitled to cross-examine the witness's credentials."

Peter turned back to Clara. "How long did you hold the infant?"

Clara looked up at the ceiling and then gave Peter a resigned look. "Over an hour. Maybe an hour and a half. I lost track of time, so it could have been more." Seconds passed. "After a time I would hold him up to the light to see if his heart was still beating. His skin was almost translucent. And the last time, I could see it wasn't beating any more. His heart had stopped."

Peter swallowed, imagining the scene. Behind him there was not a sound in the courtroom. Clara pulled another Kleenex from the box and dabbed at her eyes. Then she crumpled it in her fist and looked up at him.

"And after he died—what did you do then?"

"I followed Dr. Vicari's instructions. I put him on the shelf in the utility room."

Peter closed his eyes for an instant, forcing the images aside, struggling not to think of his own unborn child and Rebecca. Behind him Peter heard the scrape of chairs at the defense table. He stepped to the side of the jury box and saw Charles Vicari, hunched toward his lawyer, whispering in his ear as he gestured toward the witness.

Clara stared at Peter without moving, hugging herself. Holding her eyes, Peter nodded, fighting, yet failing to give Clara an encouraging smile. There was no sense of victory. Despite his greatest efforts, images of Clara holding Baby Chasson in the empty room that night flooded his mind, tangling with pictures of Rebecca glowing with health as she carried their child.

Turning, Peter walked back to the prosecution table almost bowed under the weight of Clara Sonsten's words. Reaching the chair at last, slowly he sat.

"Are you finished with the witness, Counsel?" Judge Morrow's voice broke through his fog.

Shaking his head, he quickly rose. Knuckles pressed against the table, he looked up at the judge. "Yes, Your Honor. That's all I have for the witness." He looked back at Clara. "Thank you, Miss Sonsten."

Judge Morrow turned his eyes to Vince. "Your turn, Mr. McConnell."

Vince picked up a few pages of notes, stood, and walked to the lectern. He looked at the notes for a moment, then at Clara Sonsten. Slowly he shook his head.

"Miss Sonsten. Were you promised anything before you agreed to give this testimony?"

"Yes."

"And what was that?"

"A grant of immunity."

"Immunity from what?"

Her eyes darted to Peter. "Ah, from aiding and abetting I think . . . just in case."

"I see." Vince raked his fingers back through his hair. "So it's in your best interest to make your testimony as dramatic as you can, isn't that right?"

Clara lifted her chin and held his eyes. "No. I wanted to testify. Facts are facts, sir. I'd have been here either way after what I saw that night."

Vince's tone dripped with sarcasm as he slapped the notes back down on the lectern. "Let's go back to the beginning. Miss Sonsten. Let's go back to the moment when you first entered Miss Chasson's procedure room after Nurse Broussard rang the call bell."

Without looking at him, she shrugged. "All right."

"You testified that you answered the call bell at 6:15, is that right?"

"Yes."

"Now." Vince moved toward her. "When you were talking to Mr. Jacobs, you described several events in the procedure room all occurring at once when you entered. It must have been a confusing scene, all that going on at once. So, I'm asking now for a little clarification. Please tell the court, how long were you in that room altogether that evening?"

She turned her head and looked at him. "I didn't time it."

Vince flipped his wrist. "Take a guess. An estimate—how many minutes total would you say you spent in that room after you responded to the call bell."

She pushed out her bottom lip and looked up, as if at an invisible clock. Then she turned her eyes back to Vince. "Altogether? I'd say two, maybe three minutes."

Vince stood arms at his sides and held her gaze. "All right. Let's say three. We'll give you the benefit of having been in that room for three full minutes. Does that sound about right?"

Clara arched a brow. "I suppose."

Vince strolled back to the lectern, picked up a piece of paper, and scanned it. "And in those three minutes in the delivery room you testified that you saw all of these things happening at once . . ." Without raising his eyes, he held up his fist and lifted a finger. "One: You saw the patient, Miss Chasson struggling with Nurse Broussard and crying . . . sobbing is the way you put it, I believe?"

"Yes. She was very upset."

Vince continued, his voice building to a steady, gradual beat. He raised his fist and held up two fingers, eyes still on Glory Lynn. "Two. At the same time that Miss Broussard, that is, Nurse Eileen Broussard, was occupied . . . was fighting, to keep the patient still and to lie back down . . ." He paused. "You said that she was pushing Miss Chasson down on the bed with both hands, is that correct?"

Clara said yes.

He nodded. "So the patient, who has just screamed, is now sobbing and fighting with Nurse Broussard." His tone took on a drawl. "That must have been some commotion. And a lot of noise." Vince shook his head and moved a step closer to the witness box.

Glory Lynn gave him an annoyed look.

Vince held up three fingers. "And third." He swung his arms behind his back and leaned toward Glory Lynn, weight rocking from heel to toe. "Doctor Charles Vicari is occupied with attempting to complete the procedure, with—as you mentioned—only one hand. Tell us again, please, Miss Sonsten, about Doctor Vicari—what you saw at that moment when you walked in, just before you say you heard a cry."

"He was sitting on the stool at the end of the bed holding the baby . . . the ah, fetus . . . in one hand, and I couldn't see very well what he was doing with the other. Like I said before, there was some blood."

"Go on. Then what did Dr. Vicari do?"

"Well he said, take it—meaning, the baby—out of there, to take it to the utility room."

Vince planted his hands on his hips and looked at Clara. "And you are telling this court that in the midst of all this noise and confusion, the turmoil, that you heard a cry from a premature human fetus with underdeveloped lungs?"

She looked at him for a minute. He waited. Then she said, "That's right. I heard it cry." She hesitated and looked past Vince, avoiding Peter's eyes. He sucked in his breath. "And when I got close, I saw the arms and legs move too."

Vince paused, hands in his pockets, and turned toward the gallery in a slow stroll past the prosecution table. "Did it ever occur to you that perhaps what you saw was a manipulation of the fetus caused by the Defendant's own movements, since he was also attempting to render medical aid to his patient at the same time?"

Clara began shaking her head. Her eyes darted to Peter and back. "I don't think so. I saw the baby move his arms and legs, I'm sure. I saw those tiny arms and legs moving."

Vince held up both hands and turned half-circle back to her again. "I am asking you to consider whether the *possibility* exists that the fetal body movement that you thought you saw could have resulted from something other than voluntary muscle movement." He tilted his head, watching her. "Is there room for that possibility in your mind?"

Seconds passed, and then to Peter's chagrin, Clara shrugged. "Like you said before, I'm not a doctor. I guess anything's possible." She tilted her head and looked at him. "But whatever caused it, I saw that baby move, and then I heard the cry."

"Ah yes. We'll get to that." Vince turned on his heels, and leaned back against the partition before the jury box. "But for now, since I'm asking the questions and you're here to answer them, let's go back to where we were." He paused for a beat.

"In the delivery room, you are now testifying that you saw movement, but there's a *possibility* the fetal movement you thought you saw could have been caused by the Defendant's own moving around and not necessarily by *voluntary* muscle movement of the fetus. Isn't that what you just said?"

Clara blinked. "You've changed the words all around. But I guess so."

"Would you like to rephrase your testimony?"

"No."

"Alright." Vince glanced at Peter with a slight, almost imperceptible smile. Then he turned to Clara. "And then I believe you testified that the Defendant took the fetus from your hands, wrapped the towel around it, covering the face, and returned it to you. Is that correct?"

"Well, first I asked if I could suction the baby, and call an ambulance for help."

"And after that, what happened?"

"He became angry. He took the baby from me, and that's when he wrapped it all up in the towel."

Vince's tone was strident. "And you ask us to believe that in the middle of all that was going on in that room at the moment, that the Defendant turned away from his patient, Miss Chasson, and took the fetus from your hands only to wrap the blanket around its face?"

"That's what happened, sir."

He whipped around to face Clara. "And you would have this court believe that this Defendant would spend precious time on that for what reason?"

"Because he did not want the baby to breathe. He wanted it to die."

"And yet, assuming the facts are as you state them, isn't it just as possible that he wrapped the fetus in that blanket as you described because Dr. Vicari believed that it was not alive, that it was nothing more than expelled tissue?" He stalked closer. "Isn't that just possible?"

"No. I'd told him the baby was alive."

"But you'd also talked about the noise in the room. Isn't it possible that he hadn't heard you?"

"No."

McConnell hestitated and touched his forefinger to his lip. "Tell us, Miss Sonsten, if you believed that you were holding a live infant in your arms, when the Defendant—as you say—handed the infant back to you to hold, why didn't you pull a clean blanket from the table right there to wrap around the baby? Why leave it in a soiled delivery towel?"

Clara stared at him.

"Please answer the question."

"I guess I didn't think of that."

"What usually happens to a delivery towel after it's used?"

"They're put in medical waste."

Peter stifled a groan.

"Yes. Like any other tissue." He moved a little closer toward Clara.

McConnell's voice turned acid. "Let me ask this question. In all the time you were in that room, did it ever occur to you that Miss Chasson had come to the clinic specifically in order to terminate her pregnancy? To be specific, that she'd chosen not to have a child?"

"Yes."

"And you've testified that the scene in that room was confusing, and you did not understand what Miss Chasson was saying over there with Nurse Broussard, isn't that right?"

"Yes."

"So are you telling this court that in the midst of all that confusion you suddenly took it upon yourself to overrule not only the judgment of the physician in charge, but also Miss Chasson's constitutionally protected choice?"

"But she'd already given birth and the infant was still alive!"

He wagged his finger. "There's that word again."

Clara flushed.

But Vince went on. "Do you agree that the decision to use an induction abortion procedure—that is, to induce labor, is a judgment call to be made solely by the doctor and his patient?"

Clara frowned. "Yes, of course."

"Are you aware that with an advanced stage fetus, say beginning at twenty, twenty-one weeks and after—late term—other methods of abortion carry increased health risks to the woman, damage such as perforation of the uterus, parts left behind, hemorrhage, even death?"

"Sure. I've heard of that."

"So, are you telling this court that because the Defendant chose to use an induction procedure for the abortion, which results in an intact fetus and is therefore the safest—that when you walked into that room and saw the intact fetus in the Defendant's hand, in the midst of all that confusion you somehow determined in a split-second that the Defendant's considerable judgment and work, and Miss Chasson's clear decision not to have a child— all of those decisions should be reversed so that you, Miss Sonsten, could call an ambulance?"

Clara dropped her arms to her sides, uncrossed her legs, and glanced at Peter. He saw the growing confusion in her face. She turned to Vince. "Yes. I wasn't thinking of any of that. What else could I do? The baby was alive!"

"I'm asking the questions, Miss Sonsten." Vince stepped close. His voice dropped, sounding low and ominous. "Should a woman choosing to have an abortion during late term be required to accept the risk of a far more danger-ous procedure than induced labor, just to make absolutely certain that the fetus will expire in-utero—before it's expelled?"

"No, of course not."

"Do you believe that you have the right to interfere with the physician's judgment?"

"No."

"Do you believe that you have the right to interfere with the woman's decision not to be a mother, based upon a snap judgment you've made in the midst of confusion?"

"Ah. No. But . . ."

Clara began shaking her head, but before she could answer, Vince stepped back, away and turning to the gallery, said, "Let me put it this way: If you'd been in Miss Chasson's position, if that had been you, would you have wanted to use the safest procedure for an abortion, induced labor, even though there may be some slight, very slight risk that the intact fetus might take a few breaths after being expelled?"

Peter shot up. "Objection, Your Honor. The witness is not here to answer hypothetical questions."

Judge Morrow's expression as he gazed at Peter was cold. "I'd like to hear the witness's answer. Overruled."

Vince turned and looked at Clara.

"Well, I don't know. I don't know what procedure I'd choose!" Her eyes shot to Peter, then to Dooney. She put her hands to the sides of her face, turning to Vince. "All I know is that I held that infant and there was time to get it to a hospital, time to save his life."

"Objection," Vince said, turning toward the judge. "Move to strike the last sentence of the witness's answer."

"Sustained." Morrow waved his hand toward Michelene.

Vince looked at Clara. "Your answer is that you don't know?"

Clara's eyes were wide. "Yes."

Before she could say anything more, Vince turned toward his client and held out his arm, looking over his shoulder at Clara. "But you see, Miss Sonsten, Dr. Charles Vicari did not have the luxury of musing over that question on the day that Miss Chasson came to him for help. He had to make a decision. Miss Chasson wanted an abortion. The doctor, the Defendant, offered her the procedure that he, using his best medical judgment, believed to be the safest one for his patient." He turned back to face her.

"So, again I want to ask. When you asked the Defendant's permission to clear the fetal air passages and call an ambulance, did it cross your mind at all that you were interfering with Miss Chasson's constitutional right to choose under the laws of this nation?"

"But he lived," Clara cried. "I held him in my arms for over an hour."

"So you say. But, then what happened?"

"He died."

He gave her a long look. "Exactly."

"He could have lived longer. With help he could have lived."

Vince angled himself toward the gallery, smirking. His tone dripped with sarcasm. "You'd been working in the clinic for a while, hadn't you?"

"Yes."

"So you had no illusions about what happens in an abortion clinic. Are you now telling this court that on the night of Miss Chasson's procedure, it suddenly occurred to you that the location of a fetus is what made the difference in your mind?" He turned back to her, holding up his hands.

"If the fetus had died one second earlier, Miss Sonsten—say, two inches back inside Miss Chasson's body, that would have been all right with you?"

She looked at him and seconds passed. Then she said in a trembling voice, "It's a question, isn't it? I'd never thought of it that way before, but it's really all the same, isn't it?"

"Move to strike the witness's last answer as unresponsive," Vince said.

"Overruled."

"I'm finished with this witness." Vince's tone was thick with sarcasm.

Peter exhaled and only then did he realize that he'd been holding his breath. But inside he almost smiled. Because with his last question and Clara's answer, Vince had made a point that he didn't even understand.

38

IN THE GLOOM THAT EVENING PETER sat in his office, thinking. One element of Vince's strategy was coming clear: Vince intended to convince Judge Calvin Morrow that Infant Chasson's live birth had been a complete surprise to the defendant, and given the confusion in the room and Glory Lynn's needs, there'd been no time to make any other decision. And Morrow would probably fall for it, he thought. That was the easy way out for the judge. Unless he, Peter Jacobs, could come up with something more.

Ham had warned him that if he took this case he had to win—you don't charge a physician with murder without clear legal precedent to stand on—as here—unless you're certain you've got the proof. He dropped his face in his hands and took a deep breath. He needed to be able to show that Charles Vicari was well aware of the risk of live birth during late-term abortions, and that he'd done this before. Lucy Ringer would have been a trump card if she'd been willing to come down and testify. But she'd made clear to Mac that was out of the question.

"Is this a bat cave, or the office of Peter Jacob's, chief prosecutor?"

He looked up to see Mac standing in the doorway, backlit by the light behind him in the hallway. "Come on in. And switch on the light."

The room flooded with electric light and Mac pulled up a chair before the desk, facing Peter.

"Tell me you've found Alice Braxton."

"Nope."

"Any leads?"

"None. It's been pretty futile; she could be anywhere, but I'm still looking. The health care industry is paranoid about patients, their procedures, their employees. Everything. It's like trying to get information out of East Berlin."

Desperation made Peter push. "Call Lucy Ringer again, Mac."

The detective gave him a look. "She's not going to help. And worse, she'd lie on the stand if we try to force her."

"Then, we've got to find Alice."

"Every hospital I've visited so far has called their lawyers the minute I opened my mouth." He shook his head and stretched his legs. "And every lawyer requires a subpoena. And every subpoena gives them plenty time to pull the stuff together." He shook his head. "Two, three, four days."

Peter clicked his tongue. "We're working a criminal case here. A murder charge. You'd think they'd cooperate. And we don't have much time left."

Mac shook his head. "Beyond privacy rights, we're dealing with bureaucrats protecting territorial imperatives, my friend. Every department head demands to review the records before they'll even send the request for information on to their lawyers.

"Private practitioners move a little faster, but there are hundreds of doctors' offices in the city and in the Parish where this nurse could be working."

"We've got to find her, Mac."

He held up one hand. "I know. I've pulled in two other guys to work on this. We're moving fast as we can." And with that he headed for the door.

When Mac was gone, Peter looked down at the notes he'd been making for tomorrow. Dooney had called earlier from the Royal Orleans, where she was with Dr. Stern. They planned to review his testimony again, later on tonight.

He thought of Rebecca and he thought how much he'd like a break from it all right now and he made up his mind. Home was out of the way, but he longed for a little down time, an hour or two with Rebecca, talking about the baby, planning. Just laughing together like they'd used to do before this case took over his life. He glanced at his watch. It was six-thirty. Half an hour to get to home, an hour for dinner, and half an hour to drive down to the Quarter and find a parking spot.

First he phoned Rebecca and said he'd be there in half an hour, just for a break, and that he'd be bringing dinner with him. Then he left a message for Dooney at the front desk of the hotel that he'd meet Dr. Stern and Dooney in the lobby at eight thirty, at the latest.

He stopped for Popeye's fried chicken and mashed potatoes. "It's all low-cal and heart-healthy," he told Rebecca when she recoiled. They were sitting at the table in the kitchen.

"So, tell me what happened in court today."

"Not now." He watched the candle she lit flickering. "Later, Rebbe. I need a break." He needed a respite from the darkness. He picked up a piece of chicken and held it with the tips of his fingers, studying her in the candle-light. She was beautiful. "Tell me what you did today."

She smiled. "Well, for one thing, I finished the brief for Bill." Her eyes shone. "I never would have thought I'd like doing this so much, the research for an appeal, putting it all together." She began gesturing, telling him about the key issues and the cases she'd found, and the new way she'd thought of to use the reasoning from two cases to make a point.

"The computer is amazing. It saves hours of time in research." Cutting a piece from the chicken breast on her plate, she brought it to her mouth. "I got the brief off to Brightfield this afternoon. He was thrilled. Says he'll have another one coming up soon."

"Sounds like you're keeping the messenger room busy."

She smiled. "They're here several times a day."

"How're the interviews with nannies going?"

"Hmm." She hesitated. "Well. Rose Marie's got a couple lined up. But, I've put that on hold for a while. Just for a few weeks." She smiled at him. "I've decided to take the maternity leave the firm offered after all. Three months."

"That's good. I'm glad." Nodding, he watched Rebecca as he chewed. A change had come over her lately that he couldn't quite figure. She picked up a fork and pricked the mashed potatoes a couple time. He took another bite. The chicken was crisp and spicy, and still hot.

"How's this going to work with these nannies after the leave? What's the plan?"

Rebecca gave a little shrug. "Either we hire someone to live with us, or we've got to hire a couple to work in shifts." Her expression went blank as she sliced another bite of chicken and ate it.

"Shifts." Peter ate and thought about that for a minute. Then he looked at Rebecca. "How many shifts of nannies would we need to hire, do you think?"

She lifted the iced tea and took a sip. "With our work hours? Unless we find a live-in, I guess we'll need three shifts, eight hours each through the first year at least. After that maybe we'll cut down to two." She lifted a brow, watching him. "I don't really know, Peter. It'll be trial and error, I suppose."

He reached across the table and gave her arm a pat. "We'll figure this out." He forced a hearty sound into his voice. Their house was turning into a hotel. But Rebecca loved her work as much as he loved his, and he would honor any choice she made.

He leaned forward. "How's Gatsby?"

She lifted her eyes with a slight smile. "Are you referring to Daisy?"

Peter's spread his hands. "It's a million to one," he said. "The odds were always against you. It's the great race."

"Men. Listen, mothers know. Women are intuitive. She's a girl." Sipping the water, she studied him. "You look tired, Peter."

He massaged his temples. "I am."

As they talked on, avoiding discussing the trial, he felt Rebecca's strength and love, a bond vibrating between them that gave him new energy. The painter had come at last; he was almost finished in the nursery. And Amalise and she had picked out curtains—Rebecca had described what she wanted and Amalise had brought her samples. The baby's chest of drawers was filling up too. Amalise again—she was enchanted with the idea of a daughter for Rebecca.

Peter snorted. "She'll be surprised when a son arrives."

"I'd like to ask Amalise and Jude to be the baby's godparents, Peter."

His fork stopped halfway to his mouth.

She continued eating as if nothing she'd said should surprise him.

"Well of course. That's a great idea," he finally said.

"And I want her baptized at Rayne Memorial, too."

He nodded. "Another good one," he said. Something had changed. Rebecca—an agnostic as long as he'd known her—was talking about godparents and baptism. As she went on detailing everything that she and Amalise had accomplished with the nursery in the last few days, he found her mood infectious and began feeling better. For the moment, all thoughts of the trial slipped away.

When they'd finished eating, he glanced at his watch and saw the respite was over. He had to meet with Dr. Stern and prepare him for his testimony scheduled for tomorrow afternoon. As he stood and Rebecca walked with him to the door, he felt rejuvenated, committed again as he'd felt at first. The case was solid. He could do this.

39

THE NEXT MORNING IN THE COURTROOM on Thursday, Peter called the receptionist Melanie Wright to the stand. She'd refused to cooperate, refused to give a sworn statement, so Peter had her subpoenaed. She was frightened, she'd said. Didn't want to lose her job. Things would be different when she was on the stand, though, he knew, unless she chose to take the Fifth.

He glanced at Charles Vicari when the bailiff called Melanie's name and caught his reaction, the startled look just before Vicari twisted around to watch the witness arrive. When the door opened and she came in with the bailiff, he grabbed Vince McConnell's coat sleeve and they began a *soto voce* conference.

Melanie gave Peter a furious look as she swung through the railing gate and past the prosecution table, heading for the witness stand. He'd have to work for every answer he could pull from her, he knew.

Across the aisle Vince shook loose his client, and stood. "Permission to approach the bench, Your Honor?"

"Come on up."

Peter and Dooney joined him. They all huddled around the side of the bench opposite the witness stand. Vince spoke first.

He jerked his chin toward the witness. "This young woman is an employee of the Alpha Women's Clinic, Your Honor. The defense objects; we received no notice that she'd be taking the stand."

Peter turned from Vince to Morrow. "The witness has been on the list for months, Judge."

Vince: "We've got nothing, Your Honor. No statement, or suggestion that Miss Wright would testify has ever been turned over to us in discovery. This is outrageous." Vince crossed his arms over his chest. "Whatever happened to full disclosure?"

"We've got nothing to turn over," Peter said, spreading his hands.

"Miss Wright has refused to provide a formal statement." Mac had only one conversation with Melanie Wright. He'd tried to get her to talk a few more times, but each time she'd refused. No cooperation.

Morrow turned to Vince. His tone was dry. "If she's been on the list all along, Counsel, you've no one to blame but yourself for the hubris."

Vince leaned in toward the judge, lowering his voice. Peter and Dooney did the same. "There must . . . I repeat, must . . . be some boundaries placed on this witness's testimony, Your Honor. Our concern is patient privacy rights. As the clinic receptionist, Miss Wright is the first person anyone meets when they walk in for help. And in the course of her employment, she has access to every patient's file."

Frowning, Judge Morrow glanced over the galley and rose. "Let's continue this in chambers." He stood, signaled Michelene, and announced that court would take a brief recess. A low, collective groan rose from the gallery.

In chambers, Judge Morrow motioned for them to take a seat at the conference table.

Seconds passed, and then Vince glanced at Peter. "I'll take a continuing objection on this one, Peter. And you can be sure we'll check this out."

"Go right ahead."

"I don't imagine she'll be employed by the clinic much longer."

"You may object for the record, but the defense will not retaliate against a witness who's been subpoenaed and is required to testify under oath in my court," the judge snapped, walking over to the table and sitting down. He sat at the end, facing Peter. Holding up one hand, Morrow looked at Michelene. "We're off the record here."

She nodded.

Peter chewed his bottom lip, pondering the situation. What was the defense so worried about? He decided that if there was time, he might rethink some of his questions for the witness.

The judge leaned back and stretched one arm flat on the table before him, looking at Vince. "Am I making myself clear? No retaliation; not against any witness in my courtroom. Not without cause separate and apart from giving testimony in this case. Is that understood?"

"Yes, Your Honor."

This must have happened before. It had to be that the receptionist could testify that this had happened before at the clinic.

Morrow's narrowed eyes roved over Peter and he snapped to. The judge's eyes moved on to Dooney, and then again back to Peter. "You're aware of course of the State's legal duty to turn over to Mr. McConnell here any exculpatory evidence in your possession, information you may have that could benefit or assist the defense in any way."

"Yes, Your Honor, and there is none. For one thing, Miss Wright is a hostile witness for the State. We had to subpoena her to testify, and she's refused all along to give any statement." And there was certainly nothing in what she'd told Mac that would *help* the defense.

The judge nodded and turned to Vince. "You mentioned placing limits on this testimony? What do you have in mind?" Morrow's heavy lids dropped like shades pulled halfway down as he looked at Vince, waiting.

Vince straightened under the scrutiny. "We're concerned about patient privacy rights, Your Honor." He placed his hands flat before him on the table, spreading his fingers, studying them.

Peter spoke up. "We're aware of the privacy concerns, Your Honor. But the defense has the opportunity to object at any time, and they have not objected on that basis during Miss Sonsten's testimony, nor with respect to any of the other employees on the witness list that may be called—the part-time nurse, the cleaning woman."

Vince interrupted. "Miss Wright is different. Miss Wright sits in the reception room all day long chatting with patients while they're waiting. She knows their names. She knows more about most patients than are kept in their records—private confidences—and those women are entitled to their privacy. As you know, Judge, patients' privacy rights are protected by state and federal law and even the slightest invasion will subject the clinic to liability. Not to mention frightening away the very young women the clinic supports."

Morrow nodded, as Peter had expected.

"And in addition, we've got the press out there."

"Why wasn't this issue addressed pre-trial?"

Vince opened his mouth and closed it again. He'd had a copy of the potential witnesses for many months and Melanie Wright's name had been on it, along with all other employees in the clinic, with the exception of Eileen Broussard.

"There were one hundred, twenty-five names on the State's list, Your Honor," Vince said. "This particular employee is never involved in cases—and she wasn't involved in this one. We had no reason to believe that she'd be called."

Morrow turned to Peter, reinforcing the point. "You understand the gravity of the situation, Counsel—patient privacy rights?"

"Yes, Judge." But while he had the receptionist on the stand he hoped to pry from her any information she might have on past born-alive infants at the clinic. She'd been unwilling to go that far with Mac, but he'd sensed that she wasn't surprised by what had happened to Glory Lynn Chasson's infant. She knew something more, he was convinced.

Judge Morrow turned his eyes to Vince. "I'm inclined to let the witness testify and address problems if and when they arise." Then he swung his eyes to Peter. "But I don't like tricks in my courtroom, either, Mr. Jacobs. You will not ask the witness to discuss or otherwise identify any patient at the clinic, at any time, other than Miss Chasson."

"Yes, Judge."

Before Peter could say anything, Morrow held up his hand. "If I hear one question from you or Miss Dorothea in breach of my order"—his eyes strayed to Dooney, then back to Peter and his hand cut through the air like a knife—"then I will hold you both in contempt."

The room was silent as he looked from Peter to Dooney. "Is that clear?"

"Clear, Your Honor," Peter said. Dooney echoed him.

"Good." With a huff, he turned to Michelene. "We're going on record now." Peter, Dooney, and Vince sat in silence as he stated for the record the limitations he'd placed on the State's questions and the witness's testimony in the case. And, he added the warning of contempt charges against both Peter and Dooney if the warning was violated.

Back in the courtroom, Peter heard Vince arguing with Charles Vicari over the results of the meeting in chambers. Vince and his client continued arguing even after the judge arrived and was seated. Melanie was sworn in and sat in the witness chair looking bored. Morrow slammed down the gavel and told McConnell and the defendant to quiet down.

Once they got started, Melanie Wright was clear and concise in her answers. Peter led her through the initial questions about her position in the clinic, what she'd been doing on the afternoon of Glory Lynn Chasson's procedure, letting her set the pace. And then, at last, as they came to her testimony about that night, he led her into it slowly, gradually pulling from her the corroboration he needed for Clara Sonsten's testimony.

In a strong, clear voice, she told how she'd come into the procedure room in the back of the clinic, planning to set it up for use in the morning. This was her routine before she left the office at night, she testified. And then she told of finding Clara Sonsten, sitting in the room, holding the infant.

"She had the fetus wrapped in one of the blue towels. She was sitting on a chair near the bed, holding it in her arms." Her eyes slid to the defendant and quickly away. "The light was off when I went in there. I saw them when I turned it on."

From the corners of his eyes, Peter saw Charles Vicari grab his lawyer's arm, pulling. Vince pushed him away.

"Did the infant show signs of life when you saw him in Miss Sonsten's arms?"

"It was difficult to see. She had the towel wrapped around him." Her eyes faded to the left, toward the jury box. "Like I said, it was all covered up, and she held it down, like this . . ." She demonstrated, cradling her arms and lowering them, holding them toward her chest. "So I really couldn't see."

"Did you see movement?" She hesitated and he jumped on that. "Any movement of the arms, the legs."

"Well. I thought I saw the legs moving a little while I talked to her."

Peter moved close, looking down at her. "Did you or did you not see the infant move?"

She linked her hands in her lap and studied them. Peter waited, letting time impress its weight.

When she looked up, he saw it in her eyes. "Yes. I saw the fetus moving under the towel she'd used for a blanket. I bent down once and looked at him." She shrugged. "Just curious, you know?"

Peter said nothing.

"His arms and legs moved a little bit. I could see that he was breathing. And his mouth, his lips would press together and push out, like they do. He did that a couple of times."

"How did you know the infant was a boy?"

"Clara told me."

"And you're certain of what you're telling this court. You're certain the infant that Clara Sonsten held in that room was still breathing."

Her eyes darted to the defendant, and away. "Yes. I'm certain."

"Did you notice the time?"

"Yes. I was getting ready to leave, to go home, so I was aware of the time. It was a little past six forty-five when I left that night. And I left right after I saw Clara in the empty labor room."

He looked at Melanie and it took every bit of control he had developed over the years not to push further with direct questions about other times, other infants. Melanie knew of other live-birth cases at the clinic, he was certain. But remembering the judge's threat, he knew that if he went in that direction it would have to be subtle, with a hope that somehow she'd slip up and reveal what she knew.

"Miss Wright, tell us what happened the next morning, when you arrived at work. Did you run into Nurse Broussard that morning?"

"Yes."

"What time was that?"

"Uhm . . . about nine thirty or so. I was getting some coffee in the break room and she walked in."

"And did you tell her that you'd seen Clara with the infant in that labor room?"

"No." She hesitated. "I didn't tell her that."

"Why not?"

She shrugged. "It wasn't a big deal. Sometimes they live awhile . . ."

"Objection!" Peter turned to find Vince flying toward the bench. He stretched his hand toward the judge. "Your Honor . . ."

"Objection sustained." Judge Morrow's eyes narrowed as he turned to Peter. With a glance at Melanie he said, "Watch yourself, Counsel."

"Sorry, Your Honor." Inside, he smiled.

As Peter watched Michelene erasing the statement he'd prayed for from the record, he also prayed the judge wouldn't forget what he'd just heard . . . and the implications.

He walked back to the table. "Your witness," he said to Vince.

Vince waved him away. With a look of disdain toward Melanie Wright, he said, "No questions for this witness."

40

AFTER LUNCH PETER CALLED DR. MORTIMER Stern to the stand.

Peter took him through the bona fides to establish the doctor's expertise. Mortimer Stern was a licensed medical physician certified in the state of Louisiana, board certified in neonatology and pediatrics. He'd been practicing for thirty-seven years in New Orleans and named the hospitals in which he was currently admitted to practice in Jefferson and Orleans Parish, which included most of them. He also held a law degree from Tulane University. He'd never practiced law, nor had he ever taken the bar exam. But the degree qualified him to testify regarding the impact of law on medicine.

At the end of all of this the defense conceded that the witness qualified as a medical-legal expert.

"Dr. Stern," Peter said after they'd finished the preliminaries. "You are familiar with Louisiana law and federal laws governing abortion?"

"Yes, I am."

"For purposes of clarity, would you please state for this court your understanding of the meaning of a live birth?"

"That is a birth in which a child after being expelled from the mother shows such signs of life as breathing, a heartbeat, pulsation of the umbilical cord, or movement of voluntary muscles." He tipped back his head and gazed at Peter. "In other words, one or more of these things happens after the child is entirely outside and independent of the mother. My definition is consistent with that used by the World Health Organization."

"Does it matter whether the umbilical cord is cut?"

"No. Not for purposes of the definition."

"Thank you. And now, can you state your understanding of the meaning of the term, viability?"

"Viability is the stage of development of the fetus when the physician, in light of information available to him . . . or her, judges that there is a reasonable likelihood of sustained survival for the unborn child outside the body of the mother, with or without artificial support."

From the corners of his eyes, as he'd expected, he saw Vince McConnell stand. "Your Honor, for the record the defense disagrees with Dr. Stern's definition of viability. We'd like a continuing objection."

"Duly noted." The judge turned to Peter. "Please proceed."

Peter turned back to his witness. "And how is the time at which viability is expected to occur usually determined, Dr. Stern?"

"During the interim between conception and live birth, the Supreme Court in *Roe v. Wade* held that the point of viability—the recognition of potential life—is usually placed at about twenty-eight weeks gestation, but that it may also occur as early as twenty-four weeks.

"'That said'"—he went on—"'nine years have passed since *Roe v. Wade*, and the question of whether an unborn child has a possibility of surviving outside the body of the mother at earlier gestation has improved as medicine has advanced. And that will continue to be the case." He paused and turned, making eye contact with Judge Morrow, as Peter had suggested. This was a critical point.

"With the neonatal intensive care available in hospitals today, an infant born alive has a much better chance of surviving outside the mother than, say, in 1973. So, we're back to this—a determination of viability is always somewhat subjective."

Peter nodded. "Now. Please tell the court how a physician determines gestational age."

"Fetal gestational age is determined in three ways." Stern held up one hand and begin ticking off his fingers as he spoke. "First, by the patient's calculation of the number of days since her last menstrual period, beginning with the first day. Second, through physical examination of the patient. And third, through sonogram, although those are not often used, not available. Not yet." He frowned. "But we're working on that."

Peter crossed his arms. "Based upon your experience, in your expert opinion what would you say is the earliest gestational age given medical knowledge today, in 1982, at which an unborn child has a chance of survival outside the womb?"

Stern looked out over the gallery. "First, understand that reporting information on live-birth abortion is almost—but not completely—nonexistent.

The CDC, Centers for Disease Control, has recently admitted as much. Having said that, we know that live births sometimes occur with late-term induction since the purpose of that procedure is to allow the fetus to arrive intact. Which, in my opinion, is necessary for the woman's health in a late-term abortion."

"Can you give this court an idea of the expected survival rates for prematurely born infants today?"

Mortimer Stern adjusted his glasses and nodded. "Chances of earlier survival in premature births have vastly improved in the last nine years since *Roe*. One neonatal mortality study completed just last year, in 1981, concluded that infants born alive at less than twenty-five weeks, with birth weight between 500 and 1,249 grams, have a 20 percent rate of survival. Another comparative study in 1978 found that infants born in one hospital with a weight of 1,000 grams, and some less, had a 42 percent rate of survival."

He took off his glasses and leaned slightly forward. "And recently a hospital in Los Angeles reported that an infant, gestational age twenty-two weeks at birth was still thriving, with a 95 percent chance of survival."

"Can you explain the conversion between metric weight and pounds and ounces to the court?"

"Of course." He looked out over the gallery. "One pound equals 453.6 grams." He took off his glasses and looked at Peter. "These are not necessarily abortion statistics, you understand. These are prematurely born infants."

"Thank you, Doctor." He handed Stephanie Kand's autopsy report to Dr. Stern and asked him to identify it. After the report was admitted into evidence, he asked the witness to look at the first page and read the weight of Infant Chasson.

"Infant Chasson was determined to weigh twenty-four ounces at the time of birth. One pound, eight ounces." He looked up. "That is 680.4 grams."

"Objection. Judge, no foundation has been set for this testimony." Peter turned to see Vince McConnell standing at the defense table, spreading his hands. "Where are those studies?"

"We've got copies of the studies to enter into evidence, Your Honor." Peter walked to Dooney and she handed him the copies. He heard McConnell exclaim under his breath as he sat down.

"Defense objection is overruled," Morrow said in a lazy tone.

Approaching Dr. Stern again, Peter handed the witness a set of copies and Stern identified each study. They worked their way through the details then, the background and credentials of the participants, while Morrow and McConnell followed along.

When they'd finished, he clasped his hands behind his back and walked toward the lectern. "Dr. Stern," he said, halting and turning around. "Can you give us an idea of your own experience with what we've been talking about here today?"

Stern shifted his position so that he could look at Judge Morrow. "I am currently participating in a Japanese study on the mortality and morbidity rates of infants less than 600 grams at birth. These are micro preemies, you understand."

"And what is the purpose of this study?"

"The Japanese government recognizes that survival rates are increasing as medical knowledge advances. The government is considering an amendment to their Eugenic Protection Act to reflect that." He gestured to the study in Peter's hands. "I've included my own journal records as well. The survey, still in progress, examines the mortality and morbidity rates of infant subjects less than 600 grams, less than infant Chasson."

Peter nodded. "And what has the Japanese study shown so far?"

Stern went on. "Indications so far are that survival rates of infants over six hundred grams weight, at twenty-three and twenty-four weeks are approximately twenty-one percent and thirty-four percent, respectively. It's too early yet to state numbers definitively, but this is certainly a study worth following."

"But the study has not concluded yet?

"No."

"Thank you, Dr. Stern." Peter walked to the witness stand and stood, facing the judge. "Did this study also examine the cause of death in these infants born-alive, the ones that did not survive?"

"Yes." Stern took off his glasses and looked at Peter. "The primary cause of death in the studies was found to be acute respiratory failure." He looked up. "That is also consistent with my own experience."

"And given your opinion, what medical treatment would you advise in the case of a twenty-two to twenty-four-week infant born alive during an induced abortion?"

The witness took a deep breath. "Well the physician should do an immediate medical assessment at birth, looking for tone, color, temperature, heart rate, respiration, his or her response to stimuli. Then, if there is a reasonable possibility for sustained survival, you'd place the baby in neonatal intensive care. He'd be placed under a warmer in an incubator, and because of the prematurity of the lungs he would likely be hooked up to a ventilator for breathing assistance. Blood gas, glucose, calcium, and bilirubin levels, would be monitored."

"And if the facility does not have the necessary intensive care on location?"

Seconds passed. Stern lifted one shoulder and said, "In that case, the only practical alternative would be to attempt to clear the air passages best you can, place the baby in a warming pan . . ." His eyes faded toward the defense table. "Call an ambulance, and pray."

Peter paused, letting the words sink in. Then he turned toward the judge. "Pass the witness, Your Honor."

Dr. Matlock was called to the hospital for a delivery that afternoon, and patient appointments were cancelled and rescheduled. Alice left work at three o'clock. She'd been thinking about the trial all day, wondering what was going on. She couldn't go back to the courthouse; couldn't take that much time off and this was driving her crazy—wondering if Charles Vicari would get away this time, as he always had before.

When the streetcar stopped at Oak Street, she climbed down the steps and headed toward Ciro's. She'd buy the morning paper before going on home. Surely there'd be something about the trial in the paper.

A bell rang over the door when she opened it and stepping in, Alice saw Ciro's oldest daughter sitting on a stool behind the counter. "You're early today," she called.

"Not so much," Alice said. She pulled a *Times-Picayune* from the rack and took it over to the counter to pay.

"Anything else??" Franchesca asked.

"Not today, thank you."

She was in no mood for conversation this afternoon, not with the trial going on. Once she was home, Alice dropped onto the sofa in the living room and looked down at the newspaper. The article was on page one, above the fold. It took only a few minutes to read, but the point was clear. So far, the reporter wrote, the State's case was floundering.

She read through the story again, then dropped the paper onto her lap and gazed through the living room windows, thinking about that night, about Charles Vicari and Eileen Broussard and Chicago. She thought of all that she remembered, almost every minute. Across the street she saw Franchesca come out onto the sidewalk in front of Ciro's with a broom. As the young woman began sweeping, Alice pressed her head on her hand and closed her eyes. The prosecution of Charles Vicari was in trouble.

And now she realized that, at last, she'd run out of time. If she didn't make the call, Charles Vicari would probably walk away without a second look.

Vincent McConnell stood beside the defense table and Peter saw that Charles Vicari now had a legal pad before him. He held a pen in his hand as he stared at Stern, poised to take notes. McConnell looked up and greeted Mortimer Stern.

"Dr. Stern, in your earlier testimony you stated a definition of the term 'viability.' In your mind, when a fetus is viable, that changes everything, doesn't it?"

"Yes. At the point a fetus is viable, courts hold that the state has an interest in protecting potential life."

"So, the concept of viability draws a line for a physician, is that what you're saying?"

"Of course, legally . . . and, in my opinion, morally."

"And it closes some of the woman's options, too. Isn't that right?"

Stern gave a thoughtful nod. "There are exceptions for the woman's health after viability. But, yes, I suppose you're right."

Vince tipped his head and casually strolled toward the witness stand. "Yet you have testified earlier today that premature infants have a greatly improved chance of survival at an earlier stage of development these days because of medical advances since the decision of *Roe v. Wade* nine years ago." He halted and looked at the floor. "And in fact, you said that each year the point of viability moves to an earlier point in time as medical knowledge advances. Is that right?"

"Yes."

"So, for clarity; please give us once again your definition of viability."

"The Supreme Court has defined viability as the point at which the fetus is potentially able to live outside the mother's womb, albeit with artificial aid."

"Not quite, Doctor." Vince shook his head. "Isn't it true that in fact, the Supreme Court went a little further in *Roe v. Wade*, stating that viability is presumed to also include the capability of *meaningful life* outside the mother's womb." He paused then asked the question. "What do you think the Court meant by inserting that idea, the idea of sustaining a *meaningful* life . . . as opposed to merely existing."

"I can't answer that." He frowned at Vince. "But what is meaningful to one person, may not be to another."

"Perhaps it means quality of life?"

Peter fixed his eyes on Stern, willing him to stick with his first answer. It didn't work.

"Yes," Stern said. "I suppose so."

"Thank you." Vince then walked toward the jury box and turned, angling himself so that he faced the judge. "Now then, please tell this court, Doctor, since we have established that the question of whether a fetus is viable is subjective, would you agree that when the Defendant concluded prior to the abortion that the fetus wasn't viable, that his *subjective* conclusion was reasonable under the circumstances, and within the standard of good medical practices?"

"His disregard for the infant born alive certainly was not."

"That wasn't my question." Vince turned his face to the judge. "Move to strike the last answer as nonresponsive."

The judge concurred. Vince turned back to Stern, moving toward the witness. "Let me rephrase. In your opinion, given the circumstances, was there any way for the Defendant to know with certainty that the fetus carried by Miss Chasson was viable at the time he began the abortion procedure?"

Mortimer Stern was silent. Seconds passed.

Judge Morrow leaned toward the witness. "You must answer the question, Dr. Stern."

Stern looked up, shook his head, and with a glance at Peter, said, "Given the circumstances, no." He cocked his head, looking at Vince. "But, it is not for me to judge, sitting here today whether or not the Defendant's judgment was reasonable."

Vince had gotten what he wanted. "Thank you," he said, his voice turning cheerful again. Peter set the pencil down on the table and braced himself.

"And in fact, if you are correct that as the years pass and medicine advances, the point of fetal viability—as you have defined it—moves closer and closer to conception, in your opinion is it possible that a time will come, perhaps years from now, when a fetus in an extremely early stage of development might be considered viable?"

Peter rose, knowing where this was going, and knowing that Calvin Morrow would allow the question. "The State objects, Your Honor. The witness is an expert in his field, not here to answer hypothetical questions."

The judge's answer was quick. "Overruled. On cross-examination I'll allow it." He looked at Stern. "Answer the question."

Stern shrugged. "Yes, I believe a time will come when early fetal life will be sustained outside of the womb and develop to full term with assistance as medicine advances."

"And when that happens, what will that do to the woman's right to choose to terminate her pregnancy? Are we coming to the day when the woman is limited to making her decision within a few weeks of conception?"

Stern adjusted his glasses and peered over the rims at McConnell. "I beg your pardon?"

"Let me put it this way. Will the time come when it is possible to sustain the life of say, a ten-week-old fetus in the first trimester using all our medical technology?"

"Possibly."

"And what then happens to the woman's constitutional right to choose an abortion? Is she then going to be limited because *by your standard* the child is possibly viable in the first trimester?

"Objection," Peter said. "Argumentative, and again, hypothetical."

"Sustained. Rephrase the question, Mr. McConnell."

McConnell turned back to Mortimer Stern. "When speaking about viability in *Roe*, the Supreme Court said this was the compelling point when a state is justified in protecting a potential life because"—he lifted a finger—"and here I quote: 'Because the fetus then presumably has the capability of meaningful life outside the mother's womb.'

"In your opinion, Doctor, is it possible that the Court inserted that word *meaningful* when speaking of viability in order to *expand the concept of life beyond mere existence*—an existence dependent entirely upon tubes and ventilators and monitors—and instead was requiring something more—a certain quality of life?"

"I have no way of answering your question, sir."

Peter rose. "Your Honor, we're getting far afield here."

Morrow turned to McConnell. "You're allowed some slack on cross-examination, Counsel. But I'm starting to agree with Mr. Jacobs. Get to your point, or move on."

"Yes, Judge." McConnell walked back to the lectern, taking his time. Then he turned back to face the witness. "Dr. Stern, given that we're in agreement that the concept of viability is subjective, if a physician concludes that the fetus is not yet viable, would you agree that a live birth would be quite a surprise?"

Dooney scribbled a note and slid it over to Peter. "What is he getting at?"

"Intent," Peter wrote. If the defendant was caught by surprise, he could argue that he couldn't have had either a specific or a general intent.

Stern began shaking his head before the defense lawyer finished. "No," he said immediately. "Any physician understands the risk with this procedure. And given Miss Chasson's indecision, and the absence of a sonogram, any physician would understand there was room for error in determining the gestational age. In my opinion a physician or any other abortion provider should anticipate the possibility of a live birth with an induction procedure, as with Miss Chasson."

"Good answer," Dooney whispered. But Peter was silent, knowing they'd lost some ground in this cross-examination.

"No further questions for this witness, Your Honor," Vince said, taking a seat.

41

ON FRIDAY MORNING, IN THE GREEN glass courthouse, Judge Calvin Morrow sat on high looking out over his domain. Court had just convened for the day. He gestured to Peter that he was ready to begin.

Peter stood. "The people call Dr. Stephanie Kand to the stand."

Stephanie Kand was an experienced witness, always professional, thorough, and her cool demeanor made her effective. She had the ability to translate complicated medical ideas for people who would otherwise not understand a word she was saying. She'd worked at the Parish coroner's office as a forensic pathologist for twelve years, and Peter had worked with her on many cases.

Once again Shauna had set up the projector on a table near the witness stand. The bailiff had prepared the screen. Photographs were always taken at every stage of an autopsy, beginning at the scene of the location of the crime. On the table next to the projector was the container of Dr. Kand's slides. With a click of a button, Shauna would move from one photograph to the other on the screen as Stephanie Kand testified.

Qualifying Dr. Kand as an expert went quickly. Peter began with the question he asked of her in each trial. "How many autopsies have you performed in the state coroner's office, Dr. Kand?"

She looked off as if recalling the information to her mind for the first time. "Thousands—six or seven thousand," she said as she turned back to him. "I keep a book with dates on that." She looked out at the gallery. "There are two systems of death investigations in the United States. A forensic pathologist in the coroner's office in this state is the equivalent of a medical examiner in other states.

"Here, in this parish in Louisiana, I'm the forensic pathologist in the coroner's office. When there's a suspicious death I attend the scene of violence just like the medical examiner would in another state, working with the crime team. I'll direct the crime lab as to what evidence is important. The crime lab then collects the evidence, photographs it, and starts the chain of custody, and they write up a report. My forensic analysis begins with that report. So, we're correlating the investigation with the autopsy."

Peter nodded, and turned toward the gallery so she could look out over the courtroom. "And can you explain the purpose of your work as a forensic pathologist?"

Again Peter felt the loss of the jury. If a jury were impaneled, Stephanie Kand would have them mesmerized right now. She would look into the eyes of each person on that jury while she testified, creating a bond. Without a jury, she trained her eyes on Peter, or let her gaze rove over the spectators behind him as she spoke.

"We're looking for a specific thing in forensic pathology. We're looking for the cause and manner of death, so I conduct the autopsy in that medical-legal context, although I don't form purely legal conclusions. I'll perform an internal and external examination of the entire body. We want to look at everything."

"And what do you mean when you speak of the *cause* and *manner* of death, Doctor?"

"The cause of a death is the process or injury that initiated the death. The manner of death is how that cause of death came about." She shifted her position. "For example, homicide in Louisiana is death by the act or omission of another person."

"Did you perform the autopsy of the infant, Baby Chasson?"

"Yes. That autopsy was performed on May 14 of this year."

"How did the body appear when it first arrived at the forensic center?" As he asked this question, Peter walked to the prosecution table and picked up the stack of autopsy photographs. Handing copies to Vince and the judge, he offered them as State's evidence.

"No objection," Vince said, looking up. The judge then accepted the photographs as evidence, and they were given to the clerk to mark before returning them to Peter.

Holding the photographs in his hand, Peter walked back to the witness. Peter handed the first photograph to Dr. Kand, and the slide appeared on the screen. Dr. Kand pulled a pair of glasses from her purse and put them on as she turned toward the screen.

"Dr. Kand, does this photograph accurately reflect the body as it was received in the morgue?"

She glanced at the photograph in her hand, and then leaned forward peering at the slide on the screen. "Yes. As you can see in this picture, the body was bagged to preserve the evidence."

He handed her the next photo. "And can you describe this one for us?"

There was a low hum in the gallery as a slide photograph of the infant's full body appeared on the screen. A ruler was placed beside the infant in the picture.

"This was taken after the body was cleaned up, before the autopsy." Shauna left the photograph on the screen as Peter turned back to her.

"Where was the body found?"

"In a freezer at the clinic."

"Does the fact the body was frozen complicate the autopsy?"

"No, not at all." Taking off the glasses, she folded them and pointed them toward the screen. "In fact it helped. As you can see from the slide, there's almost no decomposition, meaning that the body was placed in the freezer very soon after death. Infant Chasson was well preserved."

"Based upon your examination were you able to determine a time of death?"

"With adults, lividity is a starting point for determining time of death, but with a newborn baby, all bets are off."

"Can you explain that?"

"Lividity occurs postmortem in an adult. When the heart stops pumping, blood settles in the part of the adult body that is dependent—meaning what they're lying on. Gravity pulls the body's blood to that place. But even with an adult, time of death can only be set within a range between minutes and hours, say between six and twenty-four hours. And an analysis of the state of rigor mortis also helps.

"But with a newborn, the circulatory system is still immature—you can see it here." She pointed with the glasses again. "That's why the newborn infant appears red all over. A newborn doesn't present the same changes after death as an adult." She looked out at the gallery. "Because of the immature circulatory system in a newborn, gravity doesn't force the blood to the lowest point—it's not dependent upon what they're lying on."

"During an autopsy, are you able to determine whether an infant was alive at birth?"

She nodded. "Yes. We're able to determine whether the death was intra-uterine fetal demise or whether the baby was alive at birth through micro-scopic examination of the air sacs in the lungs."

"Can you explain that for the court?"

"We do microscopic sections of the lungs to see if the air sacs—the alveoli—and airways have expanded, which occurs when the child is taking breaths. If the baby took breaths, the air sacs won't be collapsed; there will be some extensions." She paused.

"And what was your conclusion after examining the Chasson infant?"

"We concluded that the child was alive at the time of birth, and for some period after. In addition to examination of the alveoli, we tested the lungs in a fixative solution to see if they would float. They did—evidence that there was air in the lungs. Additionally, we found air in the stomach."

"You concluded that the child was alive and breathing for some period of time after birth. Are you able to give the court a range of time during which the child was breathing?"

"From the expansion of the air sacs combined with our finding of the presence of air in the stomach, the child was breathing for several minutes after birth at least, and perhaps longer. But there's no way that I could give you a clear range, for example an hour, or two hours, as opposed to only minutes. It could have been either."

Peter turned toward the defendant. "It could have been minutes, or perhaps hours?"

"Yes."

"Enough time to call an ambulance, to get the infant to intensive care?" He caught Vicari's eye and the defendant stared back.

"Possibly."

Charles Vicari's face revealed nothing. His expression was blank. His eyes were flat and cold. After a beat, Peter turned back to the witness.

"Did you autopsy the entire body?"

"Yes, that's standard to determine whether any major congenital abnor-malities existed. We found none."

"Were you able to determine the gestation age of the infant during the autopsy, Dr. Kand?"

"Yes." She gave a firm nod. "The body measured 11.8 inches, crown to heel. Weight was one pound, eight ounces, 680.4 grams to be precise, consistent with gestation age twenty-four weeks. Growth appeared average for that age."

"Twenty-four weeks." He nodded. "I'd like to go over your conclusions in the autopsy report now, please." He presented copies to the defense and the judge.

Right now his goal was to make the life of this baby real to the judge. He wanted Morrow to feel something deep, sorrow for the loss of this life, for the human potential this little body represented. It wasn't often a prosecutor was called to prove that a life had existed before it was extinguished.

"During your examination," Peter went on, looking now at Dr. Kand, "—did you find anything unusual in the formation of the body, any abnormality in the organs—the heart, lungs, brain, kidneys?"

She turned her head toward Judge Morrow, as she spoke, as she and Peter had discussed, struggling to make the personal connection that usually softened her words with a jury.

"The visceral organs, including the heart and liver showed the stage of development expected for the age. Some of the intestines were already fully retracted into the pelvic basin, as would be expected. The lungs showed normal development. The circulation system was functional. The skeletal system, including the spine appeared normal for the age."

A quick smile crossed her face. "Toenails were visible," she added. But Judge Morrow was looking off over the courtroom now. Peter wished the judge had caught Dr. Kand's spontaneous reaction.

Turning back to Peter again, Dr. Kand continued. "No abnormalities were found in the formation of the skull—the partially calcified plates were knit with fontanels, the thin membranes covering the brain. The brain itself appeared normal, the surface was smooth. The eyes were structurally complete, eyelids formed."

And then, suddenly she turned again toward Judge Morrow. Catching the motion, the judge looked at her.

In a tone of wonder, she said, "The eyes at this age are already beginning to sense changes in light and dark." The courtroom grew hushed.

Judge Morrow's brows lifted slightly. He blinked, and when she turned back to Peter, he saw the judge's eyes remained fixed on the witness. Morrow was listening now.

"Please tell us what this picture shows, Dr. Kand."

She put on her glasses and turned toward the screen.

"That is a photograph of the infant's brain during autopsy," she said. "We remove the brain during the autopsy and fix it in a container of embalming fluid for two weeks. This is a photograph taken after the two weeks, and before we began the sectioning."

Consciousness. He wanted to show the potential was there.

Shauna handed Peter a pointer and he handed it to the witness. "Can you show us what you were looking for?"

"Certainly." Dr. Kand stood and stepped down from the witness stand. With the pointer in hand, she walked up to the screen and stood to one side, pointing to various parts of the brain as she spoke. "We were looking for any evidence of abnormal formation. Here . . ." She began moving the pointer across the photograph.

"Here you can see the folds in the brain appear normal for the age. We looked at the shape of the brain stem, here. We looked at the mid-brain. Here and here, we ruled out defects and immature formation of the lobes of the brain." She looked at the judge. "Those are evident if they're present." She dropped her hands to her sides and turned to Peter.

"Thank you, Dr. Kand."

Walking back to the witness stand, Dr. Kand handed the pointer back to Peter.

"As a result of your examination, would you say that the brain of the Chasson infant had matured normally for the gestational age of the child?"

"Yes."

"And in your expert opinion, if the infant had been immediately placed on a ventilator, and had been given pediatric intensive care treatment, would the brain have continued to grow and mature in a normal manner, as the other organs?"

"Under the right medical conditions this infant could have grown to full term. So, yes. All evidence points to a healthy baby."

Vince leaped from his seat, his voice booming. "Objection. Objection! This is nothing more than speculation."

Peter turned. "Your Honor, Dr. Kand is giving her opinion as an expert in forensic pathology after full examination of the victim's body and brain."

Judge Morrow looked at the slide on the screen. Seconds passed. At last he turned to Vince. "The witness is stating her opinion. I'm going to overrule the motion, as I would assume I would do, should the defense call an expert on the subject."

Peter met Stephanie Kand's eyes for an instant and saw the flicker of hope. Now he drew in his breath. This was the big question. "As a result of your autopsy and examination, are you now able to come to a conclusion as to the cause and manner of death?"

"The manner of death was poor temperature regulation resulting in hypothermia, and inability to continue breathing."

"In your expert opinion, could the child have continued breathing with medical assistance?"

"Yes. If the air passages were cleared and the child was placed on a ventilator, with temperature regulation."

"Thank you." He swallowed. "And as to the cause of death?"

He knew what she was going to say, and wished he could change her words. But she'd been adamant that since there was no obvious wound in this case, the cause of death was a legal conclusion that she could not address.

"That's strictly a legal question in this case," she said. "I'll have to leave that to the lawyers and the court."

Peter smiled at his witness. "Thank you, Dr. Kand." He glanced over at Vince. "Please answer Mr. McConnell's questions now."

Judge Morrow glanced at the clock and looked at Vince. "This looks like a good time to break for lunch. You can take the witness on cross when we reconvene at 1:30."

"We're ready, Your Honor," Vince said, smiling.

At lunchtime Alice waited until everyone had left the office, and then she locked the door, as usual. Dr. Matlock liked to go out for lunch, to get away from the place for a while. She didn't blame him. Often he was up all night with a patient in labor.

Walking into the file room, she sat down at the desk and picked up the phone. She had made her decision. She didn't hesitate. Once Alice made up her mind about a thing, she carried through. She dialed zero and gave the long-distance operator the number in Cincinnati.

The phone rang and only then did the first shiver run through her. Her call was answered on the third ring.

"Hello?" a voice said.

She'd forgotten how sweet the voice was.

"This is Alice," she said. "Alice Braxton."

There was silence on the other end.

"I'm sorry to intrude. I'd . . . I'd never thought I'd be speaking to you again. But, this is important. Do you have a few minutes to talk?"

The words came out a sigh. "Yes, of course. Hello, Alice."

On Octavia Street, Rebecca sat in a rocking chair in the nursery, thinking of Peter's trial. He'd tossed and moaned all night in his sleep as he'd done for months now. The Chasson case had taken over Peter's life, she knew; he was obsessed with making people understand what he had learned—that babies born alive during induced abortion were being allowed to die.

She looked at the crib that Peter had set up. She thought of Daisy—or Gatsby—whichever arrived she would love. Day by day she'd felt her baby grow. Week by week she'd studied the pictures in the book that Dr. Matlock had given to her. And she'd begun to understand that life cannot be explained in human terms. That the creator exists, just as the witness John had written thousands of years ago, and that he listens and loves every little life on earth.

She hadn't spoken about these thoughts yet to Peter. They were too private, still. Too deep; too vulnerable, as yet. But she thought of Glory Lynn Chasson's baby and how he'd grown unloved, in contrast to her own. She spread her hands across the pages of Amalise's Bible, open on her lap.

It was open to these words: "Life was in Him, and that life was the light of men. That light shines in the darkness, yet the darkness did not overcome it." The Gospel of John, again—chapter one, verses four and five.

Darkness could not be conquered without hope, without revelation.

And then, once again she began to pray for something good to happen. She prayed for the power of God to flow through Peter, so that he could help to shine that light.

When court reconvened, Vince bypassed the lectern and headed straight for Dr. Kand. Peter wasn't worried; McConnell wouldn't have much to work with on the autopsy and pathology reports and he would most likely call his own experts to rebut Stephanie Kand's testimony.

"Now," he said. "After concluding the autopsy, you stated that you were unable to establish a finite range of time that the fetus might have lived without medical assistance after birth, isn't that correct?"

"Yes, that's correct."

"And yet your answer in fact did state a range of time, did it not?"

She arched one brow. "I don't think that's right."

Vince turned toward Michelene and asked her to find the answer he referred to, and read it back. He stood, hands folded before him while he waited.

Michelene found the passage and read from the transcript: "From the expansion of the air sacs combined with our finding of the presence of air in the stomach, the child was breathing for several minutes at least, and perhaps longer. But there's no way that I could give you a range, for example an hour, or two hours as opposed to minutes. It could have been either."

"Thank you," Vince said, turning back to Stephanie Kand. "In that answer you stated that there was no way that you could state a range for the amount of time the fetus breathed, and yet immediately after making that statement, you suggested a range between minutes up to two hours." He looked at his shoes and walked to the jury box and back.

"So which is it, Doctor?"

"I'm standing by that statement, Counsel. From the expansion of the air sacs, and the fact that there was air in the stomach, we know the fetus was alive at the least for several minutes. We know the time of birth, according to Dr. Vicari's notes, and from the preservation of the body prior to freezing we know it was placed in the freezer within a few hours of death." She shrugged. "I can't be more specific than that."

"You are correct. There's not much to work with in coming to that conclusion. You will admit, won't you, that you had much more information at hand when you came to your conclusion as to the gestational age of the fetus than the Defendant did at the time of birth?" He turned and extended his hand toward Charles Vicari.

"Yes, of course."

"Are you aware of the conditions in the labor room at the moment the Chasson fetus was born?"

Stephanie Kern cocked her head to one side. "Conditions?"

"Yes. The fact that the patient was struggling to get up from the birth table, that she needed medical attention and that Dr. Vicari was left on his own, holding the just-born fetus in one hand, and attempting to attend to the patient with the other, while the assisting nurse fought to control the patient's hysteria?

"Given all that was going on in the labor room at the moment of birth, the turmoil and screaming and coming and going—do you agree that under those circumstances that it was not unreasonable for Dr. Vicari to focus all of his thoughts on Miss Chasson, rather than a fetus that he thought had expired?"

"I'm not an expert on whether that's reasonable or not, Counsel. It's my understanding that several witnesses have testified to hearing the infant cry out, and seeing some movement."

"In your opinion would a premature infant be able to cry out and be heard?"

"Yes. Of course."

Peter watched as Judge Morrow looked down and made a note in the book. Dooney kicked him under the table, and he gave her a nod.

Vince turned his back on the witness and walked to the defense table. "I'm through with this witness, Your Honor." Reaching the table he threw down his notes. Charles Vicari grabbed his forearm as he sat and Vince looked down at the table while the Defendant whispered into his ear.

Judge Morrow looked at the clock and then he looked at Peter.

"No more questions, Your Honor."

Morrow waved the lawyers up to the bench. Dooney went with Peter.

"What do your schedules look like?" he asked.

"We've got three more witnesses this afternoon. I don't anticipate any of them taking more than ten or fifteen minutes under the State's examination." Besides the ambulance driver, who'd testify the drive to the nearest hospital would have taken twenty minutes, he would call the clinic's cleaning woman, and the part-time nurse. The latter two wouldn't add much to the prosecution's case, but this would cover every clinic employee, other than Eileen Broussard and the defendant. "After that, we'll rest our case this afternoon."

He hated speaking those words. There was something in Charles Vicari's past, he felt it; and he needed evidence to show the doctor was completely aware that live-birth was a risk, in order to prove the specific intent required under Louisiana law for second degree murder. He needed to show that Vicari wasn't taken by surprise when the infant was born alive, that he'd known that when he'd wrapped the infant's head in the towel, and that his instructions to Clara Sonsten were clear orders to let the infant suffocate.

Judge Morrow looked at Vince.

"We're ready."

"Will you have an opening argument?"

"A brief one."

"All right. We'll adjourn for the weekend after your next three witnesses, Mr. Jacobs. The defense will move forward on Monday. I'll review the exhibits and testimony in the case over the weekend, and defense will do the same. Then absent any complications, we'll proceed on Monday morning at nine a.m. sharp."

42

DOONEY AND PETER PUSHED THE ELEVATOR button and stood, looking at the closed doors in silence. When the elevator arrived they stepped on. Peter pressed the button for the tenth floor.

"It seems to me that we've proven Baby Chasson was alive when he was born," Dooney said. "And between Clara Sonsten and Dr. Kand's testimony, we've established the possibility that he survived independent of his mother for at least an hour. If they'd called an ambulance, he'd be alive." She gave Peter a sideways look. "What do you think the defense strategy will be?"

He pursed his lips, thinking he knew exactly what they'd do, but he was tired and didn't want to speculate right now. His tone was laconic when he replied. "They'll bring in their own experts, try to pull apart Kand's testimony. They'll attack Clara Sonsten's credibility, argue that she lied, that at most the infant only lived a few minutes after birth."

The elevator stopped. The doors opened. He shook his head as he followed Dooney down the hallway toward the office. "They'll argue surprise; that there was no credible reason for Vicari to have anticipated the situation, and under the circumstances, without more evidence . . ." His voice trailed off. He'd seen the verdict hidden in the judge's eyes.

They pushed through the doors to the big outer room where Dooney had her desk. Peter's office was on the other side. Dooney nodded. "I wouldn't be surprised if they also argued that every woman's right to choose would be diminished if we set a precedent here. A woman exercising her right to choose an abortion isn't expecting to leave the clinic a mom."

Both of them were silent.

Dooney headed for her desk, then halted. Turning, she looked at Peter. "I'll be working for a while. Brought a ham sandwich for dinner; plenty for two. Want some?"

Peter shook his head. "Molly said she'd leave one on my desk. I'll be working on our closing argument tonight. And I'm hoping Mac will stop by later. I told him I'd be here."

"You think they'll put Vicari on the stand?"

"No. Not a chance."

"What about Eileen Broussard?"

"She's protected by privilege as Vicari's wife. Vicari won't waive that; and she won't help us out." As he headed into his office, he glanced at the clock on the wall. Time was running out. The defense wouldn't take more than a day or two, he predicted.

He needed something more.

43

REBECCA AND PETER LIVED JUST OFF St. Charles Avenue on Octavia Street. Alice pulled the cord and when the streetcar slowed to a stop, she got off. It was Saturday morning. She'd skipped her usual leisurely Saturday morning breakfast in order to get here early.

She glanced at her watch. It was still only nine o'clock. But this was urgent, and she suspected that Rebecca was a woman who got moving early in the day, even on a weekend. Alice was glad Rebecca was housebound on Dr. Matlock's orders. Otherwise she'd have probably been long gone.

So now she stood looking at the large, white house, wondering what to do next. The newspaper still lay on the sidewalk, she noticed. Should she ring the doorbell, or wait here until someone ventured out? Perhaps the paper meant that her husband was still here. That thought almost drove her away.

Minutes ticked by while she stood there gathering her courage. Streetcars came and went down St. Charles Avenue. The morning was cold and she blew on her hands, looking at Rebecca's front door, forcing herself to remember the importance of why it was she'd come. Whether the prosecutor was still home or not, she finally decided, there was too much at stake to let this go. And so, sticking her hands inside her pockets, she stepped down the curb and headed across the street. This wasn't about Alice, she reminded herself. This was about Charles Vicari. Then she marched up the sidewalk toward the front door.

Her heart pounded while she waited. Turning, she watched the children playing in the park across the street, and remembering that Rebecca's child was soon due, she smiled, thinking of what a nice home the baby would have.

She was still smiling when the door opened a crack and Rebecca peeked out. Rebecca looked at her, frowning, and then she opened the door a bit wider and Alice saw the recognition dawn. Rebecca's hand flew to her midsection, over the baby. "Is that you, Alice? Is something wrong with the baby?" The words rushed out all mashed together as she gripped the door. "Did Dr. Matlock send you?"

She swayed and quickly Alice reached out, afraid that she would fall.

"I'm not here about the baby. There's nothing wrong. But . . . but this is important, or I wouldn't have disturbed you."

But, it was necessary. "May I come in?" she asked. "Please? I have information that might help your husband's case."

Rebecca's face closed. She looked at Alice and said, "I really cannot discuss my husband's work, not with anyone. And he's not here; he left about an hour ago. So if you want to talk to him, I could give you his office number over in Gretna."

Alice fingered her purse, determined. "I came to talk to you, Mrs. Jacobs. I heard that your husband was looking for me. I heard from a friend; someone named Fred McAndrews was in Chicago a few months ago . . . looking for me."

Rebecca's eyes lit. "You're Alice."

She nodded. "Used to be Alice Braxton. That was my married name. Now, I'm Alice Hamilton."

Rebecca stared. Seconds passed, then she opened the door wide, and moved aside. "I'm sorry," she said. "I'm being rude. Please come in."

Alice ducked past her, apologizing for the intrusion. As she walked through the door she felt her courage draining. But, Rebecca would know what to do.

"I've got coffee made," Rebecca said over her shoulder. "Or would you prefer tea?"

"Coffee's fine."

They walked down the hall and through a living room into a bright, cheerful kitchen with a large window with sunshine streaming through. Rebecca took her coat and hung it by a door, and invited her to take a seat.

At eleven thirty in the morning Mac and Peter were eating what Mac called brunch at Common Ground near the courthouse in Gretna. The restaurant was a big, sprawling place with indoor and outdoor tables and plate glass windows on three sides. It was Saturday morning, and cold outside, by Louisiana standards. They went inside and took a table by one of the windows near the empty shoeshine stand.

The waitress came. She set down two cups and poured coffee without asking; chicory for Mac. She'd been around the courthouse area longer than Peter had been practicing law. Peter ordered tuna on toast, dressed, and a Coca-Cola. Mac ordered breakfast: two eggs sunny-side up, four pieces of toast, four links of hot sausage, and grits. When the waitress walked away with their orders, Mac lifted his cup toward Peter and sipped the steaming black coffee.

"I don't know how you can drink chicory," Peter said, picking up his own cup.

"It sus-*tains* me."

They talked for a while about yesterday's testimony. "We need more," Peter said. "The problem's proving Vicari intended to let the infant die, and for that we have to show he knew a live birth was a possibility and had an established way of dealing with that."

"Lucy Ringer hinted that he was dirty."

"Well we've got to prove that. Maybe they'll give us an opening on rebuttal." Absently he unwrapped the napkin on his right and freed the knife and fork, placing them beside him on the table. "You certain Miss Ringer won't testify?"

Mac shook his head. "I've called her three times. Not a chance. She says she'd lose her job."

"Well, we need proof that Vicari knew . . . *he knew* . . . the infant might have survived if he'd done something." He placed the napkin across his lap.

The waitress brought the food and set it down on the table.

"It's too bad we couldn't find that nurse. Alice Braxton." Peter pushed the remaining half of the sandwich around on his plate.

"We're done looking through the hospitals," Mac said, glancing up at Peter. "Got through about a third of the private practice offices, so far. But we'll keep looking." He hesitated and lay his fork down on the edge of the plate, looking at Peter. His eyes reflected his thoughts: It would be too late.

"You know, Alice Braxton might not be here at all, Pete. The trail's pretty cold. And we don't really know if she'll help the case. We've really got nothing to go on except what Lucy said." He picked up his fork and scooped up some eggs. "On top of that, you know as well as I that even if we find her, at this late date it's going to be impossible to get Morrow to let her testify. He's a stickler for procedure."

"You find her and I'll get her on that stand."

Back at the office, Peter sat at his desk staring off. Mac was right—it would be difficult to get that Chicago nurse's testimony on record even if they found her now. The only chance he'd have was through rebuttal of the case put on by the defense, starting on Monday. The prosecution had the advantage in trial of having both the first word and the last.

Still, in order to introduce new evidence at this point, the defense would have to raise some new issue—a new issue that he could use new evidence to rebut. Just then the telephone rang. He picked it up.

"Peter?" Rebecca sounded tense, strung tight.

One hand flew to his chest and his pulse began to race. He glanced at his watch. "I can be there in fifteen minutes. Is it time?"

"No. It's not that. But you need to come home. There's someone here that needs to talk to you."

Peter was silent.

"Dr. Matlock's nurse. She's the nurse you've been looking for from Chicago."

"Alice?" Peter was stunned.

"Yes," she said. "She came to me because she knows me. She wanted to talk to me first. But now she's ready, Peter. She's ready to tell you the whole story of what happened three years ago in Chicago with Charles Vicari."

44

PETER, REBECCA, MAC, AND DOONEY ALL watched Alice as she began, again, to tell the story. She'd been right to come to Rebecca, she realized. Rebecca had listened without interrupting when she'd told what happened that day in Chicago, and then she'd folded Alice into her arms as if she were Rebecca's own mother. Alice had felt the warm comfort flowing from this young pregnant woman and for the first time in three years, she'd known that everything would be all right.

Now, looking at the faces around the table she also knew that she could never have done this any other way.

"It happened at New Hope Hospital in Chicago. It was three years ago, December 1979, about six o'clock in the evening. I was on duty, but I wasn't supposed to be working with Dr. Vicari on that night," she began. "Not on any night, actually."

Alice Hamilton, a.k.a. Alice Braxton, had turned out to be older than Mac had imagined. He'd assumed that she was Eileen Broussard's age, or Lucy Ringer's. Mac studied her face, the fine, striated lines that would deepen in the next few years, the gray strands woven through her hair. But there was a grace about this woman that softened the lines, and she had good features—high cheekbones, a firm chin, a good smile. He figured Alice was in her midsixties, and she looked good for her age.

He settled back and crossed his arms as she got started. He thought her eyes were pretty; they were blue, bright and alert as she looked around at all of them. She was what he sometimes thought of as a woman of the forties, that generation of young men and women that had been through the war, so bright and ready to rebuild everything back when the battles were over.

During the war women like Alice had taken their men's places in the factories and shipyards. They'd struggled hard through those years and when it was all over in 1945, they'd been ready to dance and laugh and have a little fun.

He glanced over at Peter, still feeling elated. Peter's eyes were riveted to Alice while she talked. Mac smiled. He figured once Alice told her story, she'd turn this case around.

Alice's eyes dropped to her hands which were planted firmly before her on the kitchen table. "The hospital had a policy that anyone working in obstetrics and pediatrics could abstain from working on abortions if we stated on record that our conscience prohibited that. But that night we were in a crisis mode. There'd been a horrible accident on the freeway involving an overturned tanker and explosions and fire and cars skidding into the fire."

She hesitated and her eyes landed on Peter. "So the emergency room was a disaster zone." He nodded that he understood. Alice was nervous he saw, but still she was able to maintain a calm, self-confident demeanor. She'd be a good witness if she had something to say.

Alice swallowed and looked at her hands again. "Dr. Vicari's patient that night was a late termination. She was twenty-four weeks, as I recall, so he'd used induction and she was already in hard labor when Vicari found me in the hallway. Eileen Broussard, the nurse he usually worked with, wasn't around. I'd just arrived on shift and no one was around. Everyone else was down in the emergency room, pitching in. And . . . so, Charles Vicari grabbed me by the arm and pulled me into the labor room and just took for granted that I would help him."

"Even though he knew that you were exempt?" Peter asked.

She nodded. "I'd probably have left anyway, but when I saw that young girl, I felt sorry for her."

She pressed the back of her hand against her cheek as if she could see that room right now before her. No one said a word, and she went on, her voice turning flat. "I don't want to go through all the details, now. Just let me say that the baby was born alive. You could see the little heart beating in her chest while the doctor clamped the cord and cut it. Then he wrapped her up in the towel and handed her straight to me.

"I stood there holding the baby, not knowing what to do. She was breathing, struggling for breath, but breathing. I knew that when live births survived an abortion on that floor they usually died within a few minutes in the operating room—"

Her eyes flicked up to Peter's and away. "Or they were taken to the utility room off the hallway and left in a bedpan to die. Let them die a natural death; that was Vicari's protocol. And the hospital permitted it. Looked the other way. Sometimes if a nurse had the time, she'd ask Eileen Broussard if she could hold the baby 'til it died."

Alice lifted her head, her face contorting as she said, "Expired, was how some of the nurses would say it. Until the fetus expired."

She stopped talking and looked off. "So I was standing there holding the newborn, and he"—she gestured with distaste—"Vicari, suddenly looked around and asked me what I was doing still standing there. He needed assistance, he said. He said to get rid of it and come right back."

"I suppose I gave him a stupid look, because he started shouting that I was to take the fetus out of there, to get rid of it and get back in a hurry. So, I fled, holding onto the baby." She looked up and Peter saw tears in her eyes, and her voice grew husky. Her hands tightened their grip on each other and her knuckles turned white.

"I could feel the little heart beating as I held it, and I fled and I just didn't know what to do. I couldn't bring the baby to that utility room, I knew that. I just could not. And I wasn't going back into that operating room with Dr. Vicari. So I sat behind the station, holding her for a few minutes, trying to figure out what to do."

She banged both hands down on the top of table, now, looking down. Everyone was quiet, waiting for her to continue.

Seconds passed, and then a minute. Then she looked up, at Peter. "I don't remember how long it was that I sat there, holding that newborn. A few minutes, maybe. Not long. I was afraid Dr. Vicari would come looking for me. And then without really making any kind of decision, I took her on down to the NICU, the neonatal intensive care unit." She sat back and dropped her hands into her lap as if exhausted.

Rebecca reached over and rested her hand on Alice's. "Tell them what happened next. Tell them everything you can remember, Alice."

She nodded and looked back at Peter. "A friend of mine was on duty in NICU that night, another nurse. We'd been friends for a long time." She paused.

"Lucy Ringer?" Mac asked.

She gave him a surprised look. "No. But I know Lucy. She told Nan, my friend, that you were looking for me."

Mac nodded. "Sorry to interrupt. Go on."

"Well, I knew Nan was on duty that night, so I went into NICU and called her over. I'd worked intensive care rotations myself many times. We both knew what to do. She called a resident on duty and we suctioned her throat and lungs, her air passages." She looked off. "It wasn't easy; they're so tiny."

Alice gave a shuddering sigh. "Then we put her in a warm incubator to get her body temperature up, and put her on a ventilator. Hooked her up to the monitors."

She shivered, breathed in and out, and went on. "Then I started a chart for her. I wrote that I'd found her abandoned in a bathroom on the second floor, a public restroom not far from the cafeteria. When Nan went off shift she signed the chart, verifying what I'd written. All night I sat beside that little girl. And the next day I went through the paperwork with intake."

Peter leaned forward. "She lived through the night?"

Alice looked at him. Her face lit with a smile. "She lived, Mr. Jacobs." Her voice trembled as she spoke.

"How long?"

"She's still alive."

Peter stared. As Alice continued, her voice seemed to him to separate from her body and come from a long way away, disembodied, strange. "She's adopted now," he heard her say. He heard a name.

"Abigail. She's three years old." Alice smiled at him. "Her parents, the Gordys, call her Abby, I understand. I talked to them yesterday. Asked if they would testify in this trial." She hesitated. "If you need that."

Peter sucked in his breath, and slowly nodded.

"Good. Well." She folded her hands on the table before her. "When they heard it was Charles Vicari on trial, of course they said, yes."

Fireworks exploded in Peter's mind—how to get this new evidence before the court, trying everything together, making arrangements for Abby's parents, the arguments he'd present to Calvin Morrow. But he could do this. This was truth.

Mac reached over and slapped his back, and Dooney burst into tears. From across the table, Rebecca looked at him and smiled.

Suddenly a thought struck Peter. He looked at Alice. "Does Charles Vicari know that Abby survived?"

She shook her head. "He thinks I did what he told me to do, so far as it went. I just never went back into that operating room. He was furious about that. We had an enormous argument the next day, but I was able to get a transfer to NICU, and after Abby was healthy and her family took her home to Cincinnati, well, I left. Came home. Here."

"So far as New Hope Hospital knows, the baby was abandoned and I found her and then she was adopted."

45

ALICE WAS RESTING IN THE GUEST room. The morning's stress had exhausted her.

Peter, Dooney, and Mac sat together at the kitchen table, planning the weekend. It was already five o'clock on Saturday afternoon. They had forty hours to prepare before court resumed at nine o'clock on Monday morning, when the defense would begin presenting their case. To get Alice admitted as a witness, and hopefully, now, Abby's adopted parents, they had to move fast.

"Call Shauna at home and tell her what's going on," Peter said to Dooney. The paralegal was quick and efficient enough to coordinate an army. "Tell her we'll need her to set up travel and hotel arrangements for the adopted parents, and then ask her to go on up to their home in Cincinnati and travel back with them. Put them up in the Royal Orleans. Take them out to dinner. Stay with them. We can't take any chances on losing them now."

Dooney nodded and he turned to Mac. "When Alice feels better we'll call the Gordys together. I'll ask them to provide a formal consent to New Hope Hospital for release of Abby's medical records. We'll need to link Abby to Alice, and Alice to Vicari. Go on up to Chicago, Mac, so when the consent arrives you can walk it through the procedures and get those medical records back here pronto."

"I'll leave this afternoon," Mac said.

"You'll need to work fast. My feeling is that McConnell's pretty confident right now. Morrow seems to be leaning his way, so he won't chance stringing things out too long. He'll put on a few witnesses to counter ours and get that on record, and he'll call a character witness or two—"

"If he can find any." Dooney rolled her eyes.

"And he'll rest the case sometime on Monday night or Tuesday. Monday afternoon's our working deadline. Morrow holds to a tight schedule, and if we're going to put on a rebuttal we'll need Abby's hospital records here by Tuesday morning at the latest."

"What about the adoption records?" Dooney asked. "They'll be sealed."

"Alice says the Gordys have certified copies of those. She'll ask them to bring them along." He lifted his eyes and breathed a silent prayer. "Assuming they're still willing to do this."

All three stood, Dooney slung her purse over her shoulder. Mac helped her with her coat, and then picked up his own, and his hat and they walked to the front door.

"I'll be going over Alice's story again after she's had a rest and then we'll get in touch with the Gordys," Peter said, putting his hand on Mac's shoulder. "But call me if anything comes up, or if you need help getting any of this done."

"And Dooney?"

She'd reached the porch just outside the door. He dropped his hand and turned to her, holding the door open behind him as Mac passed through. "Have you got the defense experts publications in medical journals or anywhere else, anything on pediatric care, obstectrics, bioethics, or medical-legal subjects?"

"I have copies for you. Thought you'd need them this weekend to prepare for cross-examination."

He nodded. "I'm going to be tied up with Alice most of the weekend. Take another look at those, will you? Just highlight anything that sheds light on how they're thinking about this issue of live birth. Look for anything I can use in cross that might open the door for rebuttal, anything in Vicari's practice in Chicago—anything that shows knowledge. Anything that might help us get Alice and the Gordys on the stand for rebuttal."

He watched as they walked to their separate cars and then glanced at his watch, wishing that he could stop time, wishing that he could wake up Alice. As he went back inside he could almost hear the clock ticking.

46

AFTER LEAVING THE JACOBS' HOUSE, DOONEY drove to the office in Gretna. There she contacted Shauna and asked her to come into the office, filling her in, giving her the names, addresses, and phone number for the Gordys. Shauna would have to wait until Alice and Peter talked to them before she called. But then she'd need to move fast to get the parents in New Orleans no later than Monday, noon.

She told Shauna about Mac's trip to Chicago, and that Shauna would have to locate the correct form of consent and draft it and get it to the Gordys in person. Then Abby's parents would sign the consent for release of their adopted daughter's medical records before witnesses and a notary, after which Shauna would send copies to Peter's office and to New Hope Hospital. Mac would need a copy too.

"Oh," she added. "And don't forget. When you escort the Gordys to New Orleans, be certain they've got the original of the hospital consent they signed with them. And the adoption records, and anything else certified by the family court."

Assuming that Peter could get the evidence in at all, the Chicago records were critical. Morrow would require absolute proof that Abby was the same child that Vicari had delivered during the abortion procedure as Alice described.

Pushing that worry aside, she pulled the files she'd created on likely witnesses that the defense would call on Monday. She'd culled these down to seven, and knew that of those Vince McConnell would probably call only two or three. From the various files, she pulled the probable witnesses' publications. With a sigh, she stuck them in her briefcase. She would work on them at home. This would be a long night.

Mac's flight landed at ten o'clock that Saturday night at Midway Airport in Chicago. There were only three people in the taxi line, so he walked over and stood behind them in the cold, shuffling forward with his bag until he reached the cab.

"Wainwright," he said, naming a downtown hotel the cabbie would recognize.

The cabbie nodded and set the meter as they rolled forward.

Mac leaned his head back and closed his eyes. He would call Dooney as soon as he reached the hotel to get the number for local counsel. By the time he reached the hotel though, it would be too late to get anything started today. Briefly he thought about calling Lucy Ringer again. But he dismissed the idea almost as soon as it popped up. There was too much to get done on this trip, and not enough time. He'd stick to the plan.

As the unending vertical streaks of colored lights in downtown Chicago appeared ahead, he did something he hadn't done in years. Eyes still closed, head resting on the back of the taxi seat, he said a prayer. Maybe God would be glad to hear from him after all this time.

47

"ALL RISE. THE TWENTY-FOURTH JUDICIAL DISTRICT, Jefferson Parish, Louisiana, is now in session. Judge Calvin Morrow, presiding."

Monday morning and the clock was ticking. Peter looked up and rose along with Dooney. They watched as Judge Morrow swept through the door. Over the weekend Mac, Dooney, and Shauna had arranged between them to obtain duplicate originals of the necessary consents for release of Abby's medical records. One would be delivered to New Hope Hospital in Chicago this morning by Federal Express. The other would arrive in New Orleans with Shauna and the Gordys this afternoon. Peter glanced at his watch, realizing suddenly that on Central Standard Time, New Hope should have the consent right now, and Mac would be there to shepherd it through the system.

Time was the problem. He needed Mac on a plane by late this afternoon so they could look over the records before tomorrow morning's session began. Meanwhile, he had his job cut out for him here: How to get Alice and the Gordys on the stand in the State's rebuttal tomorrow.

Someone tapped him on the shoulder and he turned to see Stephanie Kand on the other side of the railing. "Just letting you know I'm here," she said. "Traffic tied me up."

"Thanks," he said. "Let's get together at lunch to compare notes."

She nodded and took a seat

Watching Vince McConnell from the corners of his eyes, Peter pulled the yellow legal pad toward him. Dooney's work on the witnesses' publications had been invaluable in preparing for the cross-examinations today. He shook his head just thinking of the ideas contained in some of those articles. But, whether he'd be allowed to use any of this information depended upon the direction Vince McConnell took in his examination of the witnesses today.

Judge Morrow's voice roused him.

"Are you going to make an opening statement, Mr. McConnell?"

"A brief one, Your Honor." Vince rose and walked to the lectern without any notes. Peter saw the tension in his back. For a moment Vince McConnell stood there, hands on the lectern, looking down. Then, with a slight heave of his shoulders, he looked up at Calvin Morrow.

"When Miss Chasson first appeared at the Alpha Women's Clinic on May 11, she was seeking help in asserting her constitutional right to terminate her pregnancy. She was in a fragile state, as we've heard from the testimony of her behavior in the procedure room two days later. She'd been abandoned by the prospective father and she arrived at our clinic alone, anxious, frightened." He turned and stretched his arm toward the defendant. "The clinic was her refuge and the Defendant took her in."

Briefly Vince ran through the facts from the perspective of the defense. As he spoke, he paced back and forth in the well of the courtroom, fixing his eyes on individual spectators from time to time. A good reaction from the gallery and the press could set a tone that Peter knew might have an effect on the judge.

"The defense will prove that the State, even with hindsight, has failed to prove that the Defendant had any reason whatsoever to anticipate the birth of a viable fetus in this case.

"As we move on, I ask this court to keep in mind that we must distinguish between fetal ability to breathe for a short period of time outside the mother, and the ability to sustain a meaningful life separate and apart from the mother."

Vince halted behind the lectern where he'd started and gripped each side, looking at the judge. "In summary, the defense will prove to this court not only that the State has failed to prove the elements of the charge of second degree murder. But that the State has also failed to prove even negligence on the part of Doctor Charles Vicari."

"Is the defense ready to call the first witness?"

Vince turned toward the gallery, looking at the hallway door. "Yes, Your Honor. The defense calls Dr. George Barnett to the stand."

Peter took notes, although George Barnett had so far said nothing unexpected. Barnett was there to give his views on Stephanie Kand's testimony and her conclusions in the autopsy report. Stephanie, sitting behind him, would be taking notes that would help him on cross-examination, and if necessary, in rebuttal.

He gave his watch a nervous glance. Hopefully, if everything went just right, the Gordys and Alice would be all he'd need for the rebuttal. So Peter sat back and watched the testimony unfold.

Dr. Barnett was certified in anatomic clinical and forensic pathology. He'd studied Dr. Kand's pathology report and the autopsy photographs, copies of which Peter and the judge had before them. Step by step Vince took him through Dr. Kand's report and the classifications of death, in which Dr. Barnett also concurred. He reviewed the physical aspects of the body prior to autopsy without using the slides. The witness agreed that the body had appeared to be in a good state of preservation.

"Does anything in the autopsy report indicate to you that the fetus was viable?"

"No. The alveoli, the air sacs, were somewhat extended, but in my opinion the pathology report was more than optimistic. In my opinion the autopsy shows only that the fetus breathed for minutes—more than that is only a guess. A few minutes of breathing does not indicate viability." He shook his head. "The lungs, of course, were not fully developed."

"In your opinion, was the fetus viable?"

"Not in my opinion."

"Thank you. Now. Dr. Kand testified that she found no congenital abnormality in the brain. You studied the autopsy report on the brain?"

"Yes, I did."

"Do you agree with Dr. Kand's conclusions?"

Barnett pushed out his lip, with a slight movement of his head as he looked at Vince McConnell. "Dr. Kand's conclusion was premature. In my opinion it is not possible to conclude with a twenty-four-week-old brain whether congenital abnormality exists. We just have no experience with that."

"Would your conclusion be the same if the subject of this autopsy had been put on life support in intensive care?"

"My conclusion stays the same. Without evidence to the contrary, I have no reason to believe that the infant's brain would have developed normally through term by artificial means and outside the mother's womb, as Dr. Kand testified. And twenty-four weeks is just too premature to speculate."

"Thank you, Dr. Barnett." Vince pulled on his lip and looked off. "And have you come to a conclusion as to the cause and manner of death in this case?"

The witness lifted one shoulder slightly, an almost an imperceptible shrug. "As one would expect given the gestational age, in my opinion death was caused by several events, all complications due to extreme prematurity." He spread his hands. "Inadequate oxygen. Low body temperature."

"And the manner of death?"

He dropped his hands into his lap and his voice rose. "In my opinion, this was a natural death due to premature development."

Peter stood before the witness and had Michelene read Dr. George Barnett's last question and answer aloud. When she'd finished, he said, "You've stated it's your opinion that Baby Chasson died a natural death."

Barnett gave him a cold look. "Caused by the prematurity of the, ah, human fetus."

Peter nodded. "In your opinion would an infant born prematurely not due to abortion and an infant of the same age born during an abortion have the same chance of survival with intensive care, neonatal intensive care— ventilation, temperature regulation?" He heard Vince's chair pushing back.

"Objection. That's inflammatory, Your Honor."

The witness took his cue. "I don't have any basis for an opinion on that."

"Sustained."

Peter went on. "Are you familiar with Dr. Mortimer Stern's testimony on premature infant morbidity rates?"

"Yes. Of course. But the Japanese study that he relied upon is incomplete and therefore, in my opinion, provides no basis for an opinion on the ability of a twenty-four-week fetus to survive after separation from the mother. The others?" He shrugged. "I wasn't impressed with the controls. But, as you are well aware, my profession forces me to deal with facts, on what *is*, not on that type of research."

Peter turned, watching the defendant. "Have you ever autopsied a prematurely born infant?"

Barnett's response was quick. "Yes, of course."

"And were any of those infants survivors of an abortion?"

"I really couldn't say."

"Can't?" Peter cocked his head. "Or won't? When a body arrives, doesn't it arrive with records making that distinction?"

"Objection!" Vince stood and Peter turned. "Arguing with the witness."

Morrow straightened and looked at Michelene. "Objection sustained," he said.

Peter went through Stephanie Kand's autopsy conclusions and the path report step by step with the witness to no avail. An hour passed and Barnett stuck to his opinion throughout. Even without opposing Kand's conclusion that Baby Chasson was twenty-four weeks, Dr. George Barnett stated unequivocally that the autopsy was inconclusive as to what the future would have held for the infant. Peter was unable to move the witness from that position.

"There's just no evidence to support optimism," Barnett added.

By the end of the cross-examination Peter's earlier spirits had faded. He looked at the witness for a long moment before turning away. "Those are all the questions I have," he said heading back to the prosecution table.

Behind him, Morrow said. "This is a good time for a break."

Stephanie Kand caught his eyes and shook her head.

"All rise . . ." the bailiff called.

Peter stood behind the table and, as Dooney rose, he leaned toward her. "Call the office, will you? See if anyone's heard from Mac yet. And get in touch with Shauna and let me know when the Gordys' plane will arrive."

"You think you'll be able to get them on the stand?"

"Don't know yet." He glanced at Vince. He needed to buy more time somehow. If he were McConnell, he'd be tempted to rest his case right now.

During the break Peter sat at the table once again reading Dooney's notes on the articles she'd located.

He saw the judge's clerk entering the courtroom just then; he stood near his desk, talking to the bailiff. Behind him he could hear the bailiff warning people in the hallway. Dooney had not reappeared by the time the bailiff announced the court back into session.

His stomach churned. He figured there was about a fifty-fifty chance that McConnell would allow any defense witness on the stand to open the door for the State to present new evidence in rebuttal. Not to mention the odds on Mac and the Gordys all arriving on time even if he got the chance.

48

DAISY WAS RESTLESS THIS MORNING. REBECCA stood in the nursery looking around, thinking that at last, everything was ready. With the white walls and furniture, the room looked as fresh and pure as new snow on the runs at Christmastime on Ajax Mountain in Aspen, where she and Peter loved to ski, although she thought that type of vacation might have to wait awhile.

She sat down in the rocking chair, imagining holding the baby in her arms. She'd come to love this room—more than she loved her office downtown, she realized. But of course, the two places really could not be compared. And she had three months at home before she had to go back to Mangen & Morris. Three whole months at home with Daisy.

Hands over the baby, slowly Rebecca rocked back and forth in the nursery. There was plenty of contrasting color, she thought, enough to keep Daisy from boredom. She loved the way the light streamed through the two big windows overlooking Octavia Park. In the springtime when the windows were open, Daisy would hear the children's laughter across the street, and then she pictured Daisy as a toddler, gripping the windowpanes a year from now, standing on her tiptoes and looking out.

The room was like a picture come to life from her imagination. White curtains splashed with pictures of animals and toys in those bright, primary colors. The curtains were pulled back with ties so the sun would come in, and trees and flowers across the street seemed a part of the room itself.

Glancing through the window at her side, she saw a child, just about Elise's age skating down the sidewalk across the street, her mother tagging along behind. The mother was watching the children playing in the park, and the little girl rolled on ahead of her. And then, suddenly she noticed, a half-block ahead, a driveway sloping down into the street.

Images of Elise on her bicycle that day flashed through her mind, as she watched the child, now far ahead of the mother, now close to the driveway.

In a shot she rose from the rocking chair, twisting toward the window as the girl glided forward on her skates. She could hear it all from years ago as she reached down for the locks on the window and clicked them open—the screaming brakes of the car, the sound of the bicycle under the wheels, the hopeless wailing of the driver—she could hear it all as, helpless, she fought to lift the window.

And then the little girl on the skates rolled on. Past the sloping drive. She saw the mother, realizing now, hurrying her pace as she called out to the little girl. The child rolled to a stop in the grass, and turned, waiting for Mom to catch up.

The girl was safe. She'd passed the driveway and she was safe.

Rebecca's hands slipped from the window as she stood watching. The little girl looking up at her mother; the mother's finger wagging.

All was well.

Slowly she walked back to the rocking chair, where she sat down and closed her eyes. But, instead of the usual reel of devastation that a reminder of Elise would bring—the loss, the funeral, her mother—she saw nothing in her mind. The images had vanished. The child across the street was safe, unlike Elise. It all happened in an instant. Now. One child now lived; one child had died.

For a long time she sat in the nursery rocking, looking at the crib. She would be a good mother, she knew. And then she put her hand over Daisy and took a long, deep breath, as she leaned her head back and prayed a thanksgiving, releasing the last remnants of those years and years of guilt.

Peter watched as the next witness for the defense strode down the aisle swinging his arms, his back straight, and his chin high. He'd bet this witness had practiced that walk. As he came through the gate, Vince was waiting. They shook hands and then he pressed on toward the witness stand. There he was sworn in.

Dr. Paul Strickner was a pediatrician practicing in the obstetrics department of a teaching hospital in a medical center in Houston, Texas. As Vince walked toward the witness stand, Dooney reappeared and sat down beside Peter. She shook her head. No word yet.

On the stand, under Vince's careful guidance, Paul Strickner was now agreeing with the previous witness's conclusion that it was impossible to ascertain from an autopsy whether the Chasson infant would have lived if he'd been given intensive care, and even if that had happened, whether his functions would be normal. At the gestation age twenty-four weeks there was just no way to come to that conclusion, he said.

And then Peter detected a slight change in the defense lawyer's voice. He looked up.

"In your opinion, Dr. Strickner, given the age of the fetus, do you believe that the Defendant's choice of induced abortion was the safest procedure available to terminate Miss Chasson's pregnancy?" Vince was standing at the lectern, arm resting on it while he looked at Strickner.

"Yes. Induction abortion is well known to provide the least risk to the woman after twenty weeks where the fetus is more advanced. There are many reasons for this." He went on to describe them all again.

"Under those circumstances, was there any reason for the Defendant to suspect that Miss Chasson's fetus was viable?"

"Not in my opinion."

He glanced at Peter. "I would certainly agree that Dr. Vicari's decision was well within medically recommended standards."

"So," Vince said. "In your opinion, Dr. Strickner, would it have been possible for the Defendant to have anticipated a live birth in Miss Chasson's case?"

The witness frowned. "It depends on what you mean by the phrase, live birth."

"Let's say it's this: heartbeat, breathing—in each case for one or two minutes."

Strickner looked down for a moment. "Occasionally that could be a possibility, but it would be rare. I've never encountered that in my practice." He straightened and looked over the gallery. "I'd say that live birth is a slight risk that the physician must weigh against the woman's safety. And as you know, the courts have said that the woman's health and safety are her doctor's primary concerns.

"You want what's best for the woman. In my opinion a twenty-three-week gestation, as Dr. Vicari *believed*, could not produce a fetus that was viable. With a glare at Peter, he added, "And given *Roe v. Wade*, I find it almost inconceivable that a physician is charged with murder on these facts today."

Vince wandered back to the lectern. "You just used the term *viable*, Doctor. Please explain to the court what you mean by that term."

"My understanding of the law is that in order to be viable the fetus must be capable of sustaining a meaningful life separate and apart from the mother."

Vince looked at his witness. "In other words, there must be some potential for a certain basic threshold of quality in the ongoing life?"

"That is correct."

Peter saw the judge glance at him, waiting for an objection. Vince was clearly leading his witness. But Peter had no intention of interfering. He planned to handle the quality of life issue in his own way

"Your witness."

Judge Morrow nodded. He glanced at the clock over the jury box and said, "We'll recess for lunch now and reconvene at one thirty for the State's cross-examination of this witness."

"All rise," the bailiff called.

Peter smiled to himself as he and Dooney stood.

In his office during the lunch break, Peter sorted again through the stack of publications that Dooney had found. He was looking for one that he particularly remembered; the title had caught his eye. *The Line Drawn at Birth—New Ethics for a New Age,* a publication in a prestigious medical journal by Dr. Paul Strickner, the defense witness that he would take on cross after lunch. Picking up the sandwich, he began to eat while he read through the publication, looking for the paragraphs that he remembered.

He was still engrossed fifteen minutes later when the phone on his desk began to ring. Without waiting for Molly to pick it up, he answered, hoping this was Mac.

"Chicago's cold. And it's a fight, Pete." Mac's voice, a combination of irritation and resignation, came through.

Peter looked down at the article he'd been reading. The fight was worth it, he thought. "What's happening?"

"The consents have arrived. I've spent the morning cooling my heels in the hospital's lawyers' offices. Local counsel's with me, and that helps. They're not happy, but they'll do it. The problem is, when? They've been picking through the records, going page by page, redacting things . . . I guess we'll have to fight about that later if we can, about what's missing, what they strike out. Because, if I start that argument, I'll never make the plane."

"Just get what you can, Mac, and get back here. I think I've found what we need to get the Gordys on the stand during rebuttal." He picked up the sandwich and held it mid-air as he said, "I don't trust Vince. I think he'll rest today, and if he does we'll be on tomorrow, and I've got to fill the time until you arrive."

He bit into the sandwich after he hung up, and chewing, looked at the door. Then he picked up the telephone and buzzed Molly. "Find Stephanie Kand, please," he said when she answered. "She was in court this morning, but I need to make certain she's there this afternoon as well. Have her paged if she's not in her office, or down at the morgue. Tell her I might have to put her on for rebuttal as early as this afternoon." He might have to fill some time, to stall.

"I'll find her."

He hung up the phone and glanced at his watch. Thirty minutes left. Sandwich in one hand, article in the other, he went back to Dr. Paul Strickner's theory of life.

49

ALICE WENT TO WORK ON MONDAY morning, but she asked for the afternoon and all day Tuesday off. Dr. Matlock had grudgingly granted her request. She called the agency for temporary help, and now, as she followed the doctor from one examination room to the other, from patient to patient that morning, she felt she had to preserve her energy for all that was going to happen.

At noon the office closed for lunch. Alice called a taxi to pick her up at one fifteen. The agency nurse arrived on time and Alice introduced her to Dr. Matlock. She'd stacked the afternoon patients' files in order on the fileroom desk and now she handed those to Miss Ruston, explaining how things worked.

A rush of anxiety overtook Alice when she caught sight of the clock and realized it was already one fifteen. Quickly she changed from her uniform to a dress that she'd brought along. She put on her hat and pulled on her gloves.

The taxi ride was uneventful and she arrived at the airport with plenty of time for lunch. She checked the schedule for incoming flights and saw the Gordys' flight from Cincinnati would arrive on Concourse B. Walking down the concourse, still holding herself together, she spotted the Lucky Dog cart.

Despite the gloves she ordered one Lucky Dog with mustard and chili, and a 7 Up. These she took to a chair in a nearby vacant gate area. The sign above the check-in counter said the next flight would leave for Dallas at 2:10. She'd never been to Dallas—wondered what it was like.

She managed to set the purse down on the chair beside her and the drink on the floor near her feet, and then slid back in the hard chair with a sigh. Pulling off her gloves, she set them aside and clutched the hot dog with both hands. She ate the hot dog slowly, enjoying the taste as she looked about thinking how strange it was that she was sitting here right now, waiting for the Gordys to arrive; pondering how much her life had changed in the past few weeks.

When she'd finished eating she headed further down the concourse until she found Gate 22 where she would wait for Shauna Rameri and the Gordys. She thought about how it must have been for Kenneth and Suzanne Gordy to watch that little baby grow, and that made her think about the old days, and Charlie—the days when she'd still had hope for her own.

At Gate 22 she found a comfortable place to wait. Then she pulled a book from her purse and concentrated on reading, struggling not to think about what might happen at the courthouse tomorrow.

The thought crossed her mind that perhaps when this was all over, she'd take a vacation some place nice, someplace serene and relaxing. Like that little town in Italy that Rebecca had talked about so much. Some place like that.

Court was back in session. Peter walked to the lectern, turned toward the witness stand, and introduced himself. In his hand he held the article he'd reread during the lunch break.

"Dr. Strickner," he began in a reflective tone. "Earlier you also stated that induced labor abortions have been known to result in a live birth, did you not?"

"I believe I said that is rare."

"But, the risk is there?"

Strickner tilted his head to one side watching Peter. He wore a half-smile and a puzzled look. His tone when he answered was cautious. "Yes, if by live birth you mean the rare presence of a fetal heartbeat after the fetus is expelled, a heartbeat for a short period, perhaps some involuntary muscle movement, and breathing for a minute or perhaps several minutes, culminating in a natural death. Then,"—he lifted his chin—"that is correct."

Peter clasped his hands before him and leaned slightly forward. "If the risk of live birth, *however slight*, exists, then wouldn't best medical practice require a physician to plan ahead for that contingency?"

Silence rang in the courtroom. The witness's expression did not change. Still wearing that same half-smile, he shook his head sadly.

"The Chasson fetus was twenty-four weeks gestation, according to the official autopsy. The Defendant believed that it was twenty-three weeks when he began the procedure. Neither the brain nor the other major organs of the fetus could possibly have been developed to the point of consciousness awareness at that stage."

Peter picked up the article from the lectern. Dooney had made copies, and as he offered the publication into evidence, she gave copies to defense counsel and to the judge.

Vince objected on the spot, arguing that he'd not seen these before. But the fact that his own defense witness was the author was inconsistent and defeated the argument. At least for the moment, Morrow allowed the evidence.

Holding the article in his hand, he glanced at Judge Morrow. "Permission to approach the witness, Your Honor?"

Morrow flapped his hand toward the witness stand. "Go ahead."

Peter walked to the witness stand and stood five feet from Paul Strickner. He handed the article to the witness. Strickner took the pages from him and looked down at them.

"Are you the author of this article?"

The witness put the pages down on his lap. "I am."

"And will you read the name and date of the publication aloud, please?" He did so.

"That is a peer-reviewed journal?"

"It is." Strickner's voice was haughty.

"Thank you." Peter stood, half-turned toward the gallery. "Would you please read aloud for the court the paragraph that I've marked on the third page?" As he spoke, Vince and the judge turned pages.

Strickner began to read aloud. "There is currently no evidence to suggest that a newborn infant is capable of conscious self-awareness, premature or otherwise. Even a full-term newborn infant cannot conceive itself as an individual, nor can it conceive of ongoing life. Even a healthy newborn infant at the beginning lives in the moment, from moment to moment. But what makes human beings different from animals is rational thought—that is what establishes the value of human life."

He paused and looked up. Peter rolled his hand. "Please continue."

"The undeveloped brain of a human fetus even at twenty-eight weeks, the point established by *Roe v. Wade* for viability, is certainly not capable of rational thought," Strickner went on. "Nor does it have a conscious awareness. Therefore, the actual separation of the premature fetus from the woman who has chosen to terminate her pregnancy at twenty-eight weeks, even if it thereafter breathes or moves or makes a sound, should not be viewed as an artificial line called 'birth,' automatically bestowing 'personhood' on the undeveloped fetus.

"We must understand that life without conscious awareness has no value, and we must balance that fact against the predictable poor quality of life that the fetus would endure using medical heroics, as well as the wishes of the person who will be most affected by forcing it to continue breathing, forcing the heart to continue beating—that is, the woman who made the choice in the first place. A fetus at or under twenty-eight weeks is not capable of sustaining an ongoing meaningful life."

"Thank you, Doctor. Do you stand by those statements?"

"Your Honor, the defense objects to this line of questioning!"

Peter turned toward Vince, then to the judge, spreading his hands. "The witness is merely reading his own words, Your Honor."

With an aggrieved look, Vince stalked toward the bench. "May we have a moment, Judge?"

Judge Morrow raised his brows and motioned Peter over to the side of the bench away from the witness where Vince now stood. "Now, what's this all about Mr. McConnell? This is your witness as I recall."

"Yes, Your Honor, but this line of questioning is inflammatory and irrelevant. It's outrageously far afield. Move to strike the last two questions and the answers from this witness. The witness cannot speak for the Defendant on the question of infant personhood—"

Peter broke in. "This goes to intent, Your Honor. I assume Dr. Strickner's beliefs are consistent with the Defendant's on these questions. The defense called this witness; are they now repudiating him?"

Morrow looked at Vince McConnell. His look said it all: The defendant could speak for himself anytime he wished. "I'm going to allow this," he said. Before Vince could reply, Morrow looked at Michelene. "The defense motion is denied. The record stands."

Peter took a deep breath as Vince pushed past him, hurrying back to the defense table. He walked to the witness box, and stood before the witness. "Dr. Strickner, in your testimony this afternoon, even though evidence presented in this case establishes that Infant Chasson did in fact breathe after separation from his mother, even if only for a few minutes, are you telling this court that child after birth was never a 'person' in any sense of the word?"

The witness glanced at Judge Morrow.

"Answer the question," the judge said.

With a quick look at the defense table, Paul Strickner crossed his arms, leaned back, and said, "No prematurely born infant is a person with conscious awareness, or a separate identity. It cannot experience a meaningful life. But, do not attempt to put words in my mouth, Mr. Jacobs. In my opinion, the Defendant was correct in first and foremost focusing upon his patient, Miss Chasson, and that fact takes precedence over everything else at the time.

"I am saying," Strickner continued, "that in the case of an infant that has not yet developed conscious awareness, there is no life to save. There is no 'personhood.' To believe otherwise is to diminish the woman's right to make the choice in the first place."

Peter gazed at the witness while seconds passed. Behind him, not a sound came from the courtroom. And then he turned to Judge Morrow and said that he was through with the witness.

Judge Morrow nodded, expressionless. He glanced at Vince McConnell and then said, "The witness is excused."

Vince's face was flushed as he slowly stood. He placed his hands flat on the table and looked at Calvin Morrow. He glanced at Vicari and the defendant nodded.

"The defense rests, Your Honor."

Dooney leaned toward Peter as he sat down. "Was that the sound of a door creaking open that I just heard?"

"Yep."

Judge Morrow looked at Peter. "Will the State have a rebuttal?"

Beside him he sensed Dooney's excitement. The clock over the jury box read three thirty—the Gordys would have arrived by now.

He stood. "Yes, Your Honor. The state calls Dr. Stephanie Kand." He'd use up the rest of the afternoon with Dr. Kand's defense of her earlier testimony. Hopefully, by the end of the day the Gordys would have arrived from Cincinnati, and Mac from Chicago.

"We'll take a ten-minute recess," the judge said. He glanced at the clock. "We'll resume at three thirty."

50

DURING THE RECESS, PETER AND STEPHANIE Kand waited in the witness room down the hall from the courtroom. Stephanie grabbed a glass and filled it with ice and water, then threw herself into a chair. "How long do you think this will take?" She looked at Peter over the glass.

Peter raked his hand through his hair and perched on the edge of the sideboard. "Not long. About forty-five minutes." And then, he'd have to face Morrow's wrath when he told him of the witnesses he intended to call tomorrow.

"Let's go over your earlier testimony and George Barnett's and see what we need to cover. We've still got a few minutes."

Stephanie nodded and moved her chair closer to Peter's chair. "Right. Let's start with Barnett's finding of the cause of death, accidental death." She pursed her lips. "Natural death, my eye. And after that, I'd like to go over his conclusions about the development of the baby's brain. He's confusing what is, with what could be."

Stephanie Kand was effective in her rebuttal of the conclusions of the defense witness, George Barnett, Peter thought, although Morrow had showed no sign of particular interest. During Dr. Kand's testimony the judge had stretched back in his chair with his hands clasped behind his neck and stared at the ceiling.

Could be, he was bored.

Or, could be he'd already made up his mind.

But the judge hadn't heard the story of Abby Gordy yet, either, Peter reminded himself. He stood by the prosecution table watching Stephanie Kand as she walked back through the railing gate and up the aisle to the exit door. It was four forty-five. Now was the time to confront Morrow.

Morrow roved over the courtroom. "This is as good a time as any to stop for the day." His eyes stopped on Peter. "What's our schedule look like for tomorrow, Counsel?"

"Here we go," he muttered to Dooney. "May we approach the bench, Your Honor?" he said.

Morrow eyes roved over the courtroom. "That was a simple question."

"We need to discuss it, Judge."

"Come on up."

Peter rose along with Dooney, and Vince McConnell, and the three of them walked toward Judge Morrow.

"The State will call two witnesses in rebuttal tomorrow morning, Your Honor." Alice and one of the Gordys. He'd have to meet the parents before he decided which one.

Morrow's eyes narrowed.

"New witnesses?" Vince turned to Peter. "Are they on your list, or were you saving them for a surprise?"

"They're not on the list." Ignoring Vince, Peter kept his eyes on Morrow. "We've been looking for one of them for months, not knowing if she was even relevant. Just found her. We only learned about the existence of the other one two days ago."

"Two days would have been better than no notice at all, Mr. Jacobs." Judge Morrow crossed his arms over his chest, the billowing sleeves flowing into a waterfall of black cloth.

"This is rebuttal, Your Honor. The evidence was speculative until the defense presented its case." Peter cut in. That was a stretch, but it would have to do for now. "One is from out of town."

"Your Honor, this is outrageous," Vince said, his voice rising, his face turning red. He shot Peter a look. "The defense knows nothing about these witnesses. We'll have no time to prepare."

"Pipe down," Morrow snapped.

"My client is under great stress, Your Honor. His business has been closed for months, his reputation ruined. No new issues were raised by the defense. Nothing to justify these tactics."

"I'm inclined to agree with Mr. McConnell." Morrow nailed Peter with his eyes. "We've got a schedule to keep—I've got a full docket to consider."

"Excuse me." All heads turned toward Dooney.

Peter hid his surprise.

She looked up at Judge Morrow. "Your Honor, I find it hard to believe defense counsel's statement that the witness testimony this morning presented nothing new when his own witness suggested that there is no possible way for a twenty-four-week-old infant born alive after an induced labor abortion to survive in any ongoing, meaningful way, and that therefore the infant is not a person . . ." She paused, took a breath, and spread her hands, "*Ergo* . . . killing the living breathing infant is not the same as killing a person. That is a new claim that the State must rebut."

Morrow looked at her and then looked off. He shook out his sleeves and flopped his arms down on the desktop and looked at Dooney again. "You do make a point, Miss Dorothea."

Dooney flushed. It was unusual for Morrow to remember a young ADA's name at all, even if only her first. The judge picked up a pen and rolled it between his hands, looking down. After a beat he put down the pen and turned to Peter.

"We'll reconvene tomorrow morning at nine sharp, Mr. Jacobs, at which time you may call your witnesses." His eyes narrowed and the corners of his lips turned down. "If the evidence addresses new issues raised by the defense in rebuttal, we'll hear it before deciding whether it's admissible."

Vince exclaimed and Morrow turned to him. "If the evidence turns out to be inadmissible, Mr. McConnell, the court will not consider it when rendering the verdict." He spread his hands. "You'll have your cross-examination. And, no jury—no prejudice."

Vince muttered something under his breath.

Morrow put his hand behind his ear, and leaned slightly toward Vicari's lawyer. "What did you say?" His tone was malevolent.

Vince's response was quick. "Nothing, Your Honor."

Morrow gave him a long look. Then he turned to Peter. "But I don't like tricks in my courtroom. New witnesses brought in at the last minute had better be addressing testimony that hasn't been worked over in this courtroom for the past week." He lowered his brows. "Or you'll regret it. I'll be on the bench in this courtroom for a long time, Counsel, as long as you're around."

"Yes, sir."

51

THE DOORBELL RANG AND HEAVING A long sigh, Peter put down
the pen and rose. He glanced at his watch and saw it was eleven thirty p.m.
This must be Mac. The Gordys' flight had been delayed. Shauna had just
called to say they were now ensconced at the hotel and exhausted. He would
meet them at the hotel in the morning. They were cutting things close.

As he passed the study, heading for the front door, he stuck his head
in and Rebecca looked up. They'd moved the computer from the bedroom
down to the study two weeks ago. Now she sat there surrounded by case-
books and paper. Rebecca had volunteered to write the brief that Judge
Morrow had demanded from the prosecution and defense at the end of the
trial. He would use it when considering his verdict.

"Mac?" she said.

"Yeah. We'll be working for a while."

"I will too."

"How's it coming?"

"Great. I'm finally getting somewhere."

"That's good." With a smile he said to remember that Gatsby needed his
sleep, and withdrew.

The bell rang again. Peter opened the door, greeted Mac, and stepped
aside.

"The flight was late, but we got what we need." He hustled past Peter and
turned, setting down the briefcase he carried. He slipped off the raincoat and
glanced around. "Snow in Chicago. Rain here. Cold both places. Where to?"

"The kitchen. Are you hungry?" Mac picked up the briefcase and they
walked through the living room. "We've got some cold chicken and potato
salad. Or I could fix sandwiches."

Mac shook his head. "Ate on the plane. Let's get through this so I can
go on home. I'm bushed."

Mac threw his coat over the back of a chair and set the briefcase on the table. Peter went to the counter and poured two cups of coffee.

"Did the Gordys arrive?" Mac asked.

"They just got in. Dooney and I are going over there early in the morning, before court. Shauna was taking them to get something to eat. Alice Braxton, ah, Hamilton, is with them. Then they'll go on to the hotel. Shauna says they're exhausted."

He brought the two cups of coffee to the table and set one down before Mac. He stood, sipping from the cup looking over Mac's shoulder as Mac pulled two thick brown envelopes from his briefcase. "This is the treasure," he said, holding up the envelopes.

Peter nodded and sat beside him. Mac tossed down one down on the table and opened the other. He drew out the papers, and set them before Peter. "The baby's medical records. Four months intensive care. Certified."

He picked up the coffee and took a swallow, then set it down and picked up the second envelope.

Peter was already scanning the medical records.

"There's an affidavit in there from Nan Allan, that nurse in NICU, Alice's friend. The one she mentioned. If the defense challenges Alice's testimony that she brought Baby Doe into intensive care that night, we can use this. Then, to link them up, Baby Doe's blood has been matched to Vicari's patient that night, the mother. And we've got the duty roster, certified, showing Alice was the nurse."

"Good. That's just what we need."

Peter glanced over as Mac began shuffling through the second set of documents. Mac pulled out some papers and held them up. "The adoption records and Abigail Gordy's birth certificate—the one created after the infant was placed in NICU."

"Good. All good." Peter swallowed some more hot coffee. "Let's go through these one by one. I've got to take notes for tomorrow. I'll introduce the certified records into evidence, then ask you to read them aloud on the stand. We've got to show an unbroken line of identification between the child the Gordys adopted, and the infant delivered by Charles Vicari that night, and we'll do that through Alice."

"I've spent the last four hours going over this stuff on the plane," Mac said. "It's solid." He began spreading the documents in order.

Rebecca heard Mac come in. She tapped her pencil against her bottom lip, looking across the room. She could hear rain hitting the windows and the bushes outside scraping against the glass. The fire was lit and she watched the flickering flames. Putting one hand over Daisy, she bent her head and closed her eyes. She wanted to ask God's help for Peter in court tomorrow, and for comfort for Alice and the Gordy family. Prayers did not come easily to her. They never had.

This was all so new.

But feeling the baby under her hand stirred something. And Peter's passion for this case, the almost desperate feeling she sensed building in him day after day as the trial progressed, brought the prayer. Day by day since she'd begun reading the four Gospels of Matthew, Mark, Luke, and John in Amalise's Bible—the four witnesses to an event that spoke for itself—she became more certain that someone was listening. That he was there, and that he'd been there all along.

And she asked him also to protect her child, and to help her as she learned to be a mother, because she didn't know a thing about it, not even how to change a diaper or how to bathe a baby, or anything else that a baby would need. The months seemed to have flown by and she'd always meant to dig into these things, but she'd been so busy, she explained, and then, the thought struck her out of the blue—the sudden realization that the only thing she knew for certain about motherhood right now was that she couldn't stand the idea of leaving Daisy with a stranger.

As the rain beat against the windows outside and thunder cracked, she settled back in the big leather chair beside the fireplace with her eyes still closed, feeling something new, a settling feeling, like the great white egrets in the swamps fluffing their wings before they tuck down for the night.

"Just take it all to the Lord," Amalise had said. And for the first time, Rebecca understood those words.

In her apartment on Oak Street, Alice lay in her bed under a thick quilt on this December night, listening to the thunder rolling across the city. Seeing

Kenneth and Suzanne Gordy tonight had brought back memories of the old days, her days as the wife of Charlie Braxton—brief as that time was—and of the child she'd once dreamed they'd make. Through the window by the bed she watched a flash of lightning light up the sky for an instant; just a flash, a moment in time, like the love she'd felt for Charlie that had burned up of its own accord when she'd finally realized he wasn't coming back from the war.

It wasn't that she still cared for him. But thinking of all those years, she realized what was missing, what had always been missing. Another human being that cares how you feel, who celebrates when things are good, and comforts you when things are bad. Someone to count on, who loves you always no matter what. Like a parent loves a child. Like a man should love a woman.

Through the window she could see the Christmas lights strung along the edge of Ciro's roof—red, yellow, green, and blue—flashing on and off in the darkness. They were the big, old-fashioned kind. She thought perhaps she might put up a little tree this year. She could find one small enough to string the lights on her own. She'd never had a tree of her own before, but she could buy one down in the French Market, she thought, and she could carry it home on the streetcar. Woolworths on Magazine Street would have ornaments, or maybe the hardware store on Oak near the river.

Then Alice smiled to herself, thinking of Rebecca's description of that village they'd stayed in, in Italy. She thought of Rebecca and Peter there on the narrow curved beach, picturing it all. The name of the town was Positano, she remembered, and it was on the Amalfi Coast. She'd written everything down just for fun and then had looked it up. She'd seen pictures, so she could dream with some precision.

Smiling, she thought of those pictures; the blue sky and the white houses climbing the cliffs, the green vines shading the winding walkways, the sea spread wide before the mountains, rippling water sparkling in the sunshine. And she imagined the small green islands just offshore, seeming to float on top of the magical sea, the magazine had said.

Laying warm under the blanket and the quilt on the soft mattress on a rainy night, Alice spread her arms and imagined herself floating, floating in that sea. One by one her muscles seemed to melt. Minutes later, to the sound of the thunder outside—*out there*—she drifted off to sleep, still envisioning the islands and the gloss of gold that falls over the water at dusk in that Italian light.

52

THE AIR WAS CLEAR AND FRESH after last night's storm. The sun was just rising as Peter parked his car in the lot across from the Royal Orleans Hotel in the center of the Quarter. Grabbing his briefcase from the passenger seat, he slid out of the car. It was six thirty in the morning and the parking lot was almost empty. The attendant walked up and Peter paid him, adding a couple of extra bucks because it was going to be that kind of day. He had a feeling that even the tough old judge might crack, once he heard Abby Gordy's story from Alice and her parents.

He stopped at the corner of Chartres and St. Louis to let an empty mule drawn carriage move slowly down the still deserted street. The driver, hunched under his wide-brimmed straw hat and barely holding the reins that were draped across his fingers, looked at him. "Mornin'," he said.

"Good morning," Peter replied as wagon, man, and mule rolled on toward Jackson Square to wait for tourists. He crossed Chartres and headed toward the main entrance to the Royal Orleans in the middle of the block. Across Toulouse the beautiful, but vacant, Wildlife and Fisheries Building loomed with Victorian majesty. The magnolia trees around it had been planted in 1908 when the white marble mansion was a courthouse.

The tall doorman saw him coming and opened the door with a tip of his hat. Peter nodded in an absent manner, scanning the block-long lobby for Dooney and the Gordys as he walked up the inner steps. Immediately he saw them seated in the spacious parlor area on the rise to his left.

Dooney waited in a chair beside a deep-cushioned sofa, upon which sat a man and woman. And then, suddenly, he stopped and caught his breath. Between them stood a small child, a little girl with two brown ponytails tied up with yellow ribbons over her ears. She stood with one hand planted on each parent's knee as she looked about. Seconds passed, and then he tore his eyes from Abby. He needed to focus this morning, to make a decision quickly about which parent would make the best witness.

The man nearest Dooney was Kenneth Gordy, he supposed. As Peter studied the group he judged the father to be around forty years, or so. He exuded self-confidence as he sat quietly, arms spread over the back of the sofa watching his wife, Suzanne, while she talked to Dooney.

Suzanne kept one hand on Abby's shoulder. She appeared younger than her husband. She wore a floral print skirt and a white blouse. But it was the child that pulled his eyes. The toddler's head tilted back as she looked upside down at her mother, then, laughing, she reached up to touch her mother's chin with her finger. Suzanne looked down at her and laughed.

He was stunned that they'd brought Abby with them.

Dooney looked up and, spotting him, lifted her hand. He smiled and waved and walked over to the group, still watching Abby from the corners of his eyes. She backed into her mother's skirt as he grew closer, one finger now hooked in the corner of her mouth. Her skin was the color of butterscotch and her eyes were wide as he approached. Kenneth Gordy stood. He shook Peter's hand and introduced his family.

Suzanne remained seated, but she watched Peter carefully, assessing. She nodded when they were introduced and said hello. Her voice was soft and low—not the best voice for the witness stand. Abby ducked her chin and looked at him from under her lashes. She had inquisitive eyes, as bright as a little bird's. Her cheeks were pink, like the summer roses growing wild in the backyard on Octavia.

As he took a seat in a chair nearby, Dooney said that Alice would be here soon. She suggested they all have breakfast in the hotel restaurant on the Royal Street side of the lobby. It was quiet there this time of day and they could talk.

Suzanne bent and told Abby to say hello to Mr. Jacobs, that he was the man they'd come all this way to see. After a few stubborn shakes of her head, and urging by her mother, Abby obeyed in a small, tentative voice. Kenneth picked her up by her waist, surprising her as he lifted her high and plopped her down on his knee. His daughter laughed then, a bubbling giggle that ran up and down the high scales. Then she flung one arm around her father's neck and leaned back against him, watching Peter.

Dooney's eyes met his. *Can we put her on the stand?*

He shook his head. Calvin Morrow would view that as theatrics. They were already pushing their luck; there wasn't a chance.

Alice arrived just then. She sat on the sofa beside Suzanne and Suzanne put her hand in Alice's while they talked. Peter noticed that Alice's eyes seemed almost glued to Abby. Everyone agreed that they could get to know each just as well other over eggs and toast, crispy bacon, hot buttered biscuits, and pancakes for Abby.

As Dooney herded them all toward the restaurant at the end of the lobby, Peter glanced at his watch. It was seven a.m. In two hours court would convene.

෬ᄋ

Rebecca had decided that she would take a taxi to the courthouse in Gretna and watch this day unfold in Judge Calvin Morrow's court. After Mac had left at two thirty in the morning, she'd informed Peter of this decision. There was no way that she would miss this, she told him. Not with Alice on the stand, and the Gordy family coming all this way to testify.

And Peter hadn't attempted to argue. In fact, he'd looked a little pleased. After the last ultrasound, Dr. Matlock had said that she and the baby were doing fine, the previa was marginal, and she just needed to take things easy. And as Rebecca had pointed out, sitting in a courtroom for a few hours wasn't exactly hard work.

She'd woken after Peter left to meet the Gordy's and Alice. She brushed her teeth, and showered and dressed, slipping on a dark blue skirt and a loose white blouse that hung to her hips. Sitting before the mirror she put on a little makeup, a swish of blush, a swipe of neutral lipstick. Then she called a Yellow Cab, and went downstairs to wait.

She would sit in the back row, on the aisle, she decided. Close enough to the door that when nature called, as happened frequently these days, she could answer.

෬ᄋ

After watching Kenneth and Suzanne Gordy all through breakfast, Peter decided that, of the two parents, Kenneth would be the most effective witness. The father and child had a special relationship; she'd sat in his lap most of the time and they'd talked constantly, long conversations during which sometimes her eyes would go wide and she'd burst into paroxysms of laughter.

She reminded him that he would soon be a father. Gatsby or Daisy? He smiled. Maybe a daughter would be all right.

Abby, Suzanne, and Alice rode in Dooney's car from the hotel to the courthouse in Gretna, and Kenneth rode with Peter so that Peter could prepare him for what was ahead. He went over the chain of proof they would establish to show that Abby was the infant that Alice had brought to the NICU. From there they would move quickly through the months when Abby was in the incubator, recovering and growing, until the day the Gordys had taken their new child home. Abby had been in NICU for four months— she'd fought every minute for her life, Kenneth Gordy said. And despite living in Cincinnati, little Abby had had her parents with her every minute of that fight—sometimes one, sometimes both.

He warned Kenneth that he would see Charles Vicari in the courtroom, and noted the tight flex at the corners of the father's mouth at the mention of the name. Kenneth's thoughts were reflected in the narrowing of his eyes, the tense muscles, the deepening of the two vertical lines between his brows while they talked. During the silence that followed this warning, Peter wondered if Kenneth would have the strength to face Charles Vicari in that courtroom, knowing that the man would have let their daughter die.

They'd discussed this discreetly at breakfast, but now, as they drove through the Quarter, then down St. Charles Avenue to the interstate and over the Greater New Orleans Bridge, Peter pounded his point home in as gentle a way as possible. Kenneth should not look at the defendant. He should keep his eyes on Peter.

Peter and Kenneth met the others in the witness room. Mac was already there and the door was closed. Dooney had called Shauna from the hotel, and said that the legal assistant was on her way, that she would take care of Abby in the witness room while her parents were in the courtroom. Suzanne expressed some doubt at this plan. Perhaps she should stay with Abby?

But Peter wanted Suzanne sitting front and center in the courtroom. If Kenneth Gordy's testimony left any room for doubt, he was determined that Calvin Morrow would be aware of the child's mother sitting right before him. He'd considered bringing Abby into the courtroom too. But thinking of his own child, he'd decided against it. Protect Abby from eyes in the courtroom, and the press, and from any possibility of confusion for a toddler who'd already been through so much. Who knew how events play out in our minds over a lifetime.

Still. The prosecutor in him grumbled; he'd have loved to have the child sitting alongside her mother in the courtroom. As a poor substitute, he asked Kenneth to stop and give his wife a hug on his way down the aisle when he was called so that Judge Morrow would realize who she was. Mother-love radiated through Suzanne's entire being, and he wanted Morrow to see that, a constant reminder to the judge of the crime committed against her daughter by the defendant, and that—as with Baby Chasson—what had happened was no accident.

Dooney had worked with Alice last night on the questions that Peter would ask this morning. She only had to tell her story. Alice, in the way of efficient nurses everywhere, had remained calm and unemotional during the session and said that everything would be all right. Dooney was certain that Alice would be a good witness.

But Alice, too, was warned not to look at the defendant.

53

"ALL RISE."

Peter stood, sensing the full fury of the occupants of the defense table this morning.

Looking over his shoulder, he saw Rebecca taking the seat that had been saved for her in the back row, near the door. Molly had said that she would sit with Rebecca, just in case. As she sat down, she spotted him and waved. He waved, and turned back, facing the empty bench.

Dooney reached across the table and squeezed his arm. He shot her a smile.

Over his shoulder, Peter saw the courtroom quickly filling. The press was here in full force today—the *Picayune*, the *Baton Rouge Advocate*, the *Houston Chronicle*, and a reporter he recognized from the AP. Word had gotten out, he supposed. He met the *Times-Picayune* reporter's eyes and nodded. The man had covered every day of the trial, and if he was honest, he'd be the one to put it all together and write the real story today.

Peter turned his eyes back to Judge Morrow, still conferring with his clerk. Across the aisle, he could hear Vicari arguing in a low tone with his lawyer. Michelene was preparing her machine for transcription, and the bailiff wandered back to his post at the door behind the jury box and clasped his hands behind his back. Peter studied Calvin Morrow. His eyes had met Peter's the instant he'd walked through that door.

Judge Morrow finally straightened, turned toward the prosecution and defense and the gallery, and clasped his hands before him. His expression was cold as he looked at Peter. "We're not going to waste any more time today, Mr. Jacobs, are we? Are your witnesses present and accounted for?"

Peter stood. "Yes, they're here, Your Honor."

Morrow flipped his hand. His tone was piqued. "Call your first witness for rebuttal."

Peter turned. "The State calls Fred McAndrews."

The bailiff opened the door to the hallway and called out, "Lieutenant? We're ready."

Judge Morrow reminded Mac that he was still under oath. Mac said he understood and took the stand. Under questioning, Mac described his recent hurried trip to Chicago to obtain various records from New Hope Hospital.

Peter handed Mac the duty roster, showing that Alice had worked with Charles Vicari in operating room number three at New Hope Hospital on the night of December 3, 1979. Mac identified the record. Peter handed Mac the medical chart with the name of Vicari's patient when Alice was on duty redacted, her blood type, the time of the procedure, and a few sketchy details. The medical records of the abortion procedure, an induction, further recorded that gestation was twenty-three weeks. No birth or death was recorded.

"What's this got to do with anything? This is a travesty!" The shouting startled Peter and he turned to see the defendant rising even as his lawyer shot up, standing over him, hissing in undertone as he pressed his hands on Charles Vicari's shoulders, pushing him back down.

Morrow's gavel pounded once, twice—loud cracking sounds that reverberated through the room even as a hum rose in the galley. The judge half rose as he motioned toward the bailiff standing near the jury box calling, "Bailiff! Order, order in the court."

The bailiff called out into the hallway. Two sheriff's officers appeared, hurrying down the aisle one behind the other. By the time they'd reached Vicari, Vince had him back down in the chair, his hand firmly clamped upon his client's arm. As the officers reached for Vicari, Morrow called out and stopped them. They halted, handcuffs dangling midair.

Half-standing, Judge Morrow glared down at Vince McConnell: "Counsel, be warned! You'll have one more chance, given the situation. But one more outburst and the Defendant will be handcuffed, shackled, and gagged." He glared at Vicari as he lowered back into his chair. "We will tape his mouth if that's the only way to keep it shut. Is that clear?"

"Yes, Your Honor."

Peter glanced over his shoulder at Suzanne Gordy. As the sheriffs moved to the wall nearest the defendant, hands braced behind them, eyes forward, Peter saw her eyes brimming with tears, and her hands gripping the ends of the armrests as she stared at Charles Vicari.

Seconds passed and no one moved. Then, "Proceed," Morrow said.

As Mac and Peter continued, going through the records from New Hope, Mac described the contents of each one for the court. When they came to medical records of the baby in NICU, Peter handed the first one to Mac and Mac identified the date and time of the first entry, and identified it as belonging to Baby Doe. Alice Braxton's signature was on the page, along with the signature of another nurse, the nurse on duty that night, Nan Allen.

"We're wasting time on irrelevant matters, Your Honor. The defense objects to this delay." Vince flung his hand toward Peter.

"This won't take long," Peter said. "Bear with me, Judge. Just a few more minutes."

Morrow pursed his lips and studied Peter. Peter held his breath.

The judge made up his mind and nodded. "Objection overruled, for now," he said. "But get on with it, Mr. Jacobs. And I'd better start understanding the connection to this case very soon."

"Yes, Your Honor."

Mac and Peter sped through the remaining records. The infant's medical records recording her struggles under intensive care were introduced and entered as evidence. The last date recorded in NICU was April 15, 1979, four months after admission.

Peter avoided mention of the adoption at this time. He would save that for Kenneth Gordy's testimony, he'd decided.

At the end of Mac's testimony, Vince McConnell registered his standing objection to the new witnesses, arguing that he saw no connection between the testimony that he'd just heard and the present case.

Without a break, Morrow instructed Peter to call his next witness to the stand. There'd be no more time wasted in his courtroom, he announced.

Alice had been on the stand for an hour. She'd told her story, beginning with how she'd been conscripted to work with Charles Vicari that night at New Hope Hospital, and ending with her decision to bring Abby to the NICU, and how she and Nan had worked to keep the child, Baby Doe, alive on those first few nights. As he stood beside Alice, Peter could almost feel Charles Vicari's hatred for the nurse.

Vince had objected immediately to Alice's entire testimony.

"It goes to intent, Your Honor," Peter had said. "Miss Hamilton's testimony is offered to prove that the defense could not have been taken by surprise by a live birth, since he'd experienced this before."

After several minutes of back and forth, with fierce arguments from Vince, Calvin Morrow had allowed the State to move forward.

Peter showed Alice the medical records for induction abortion performed by Charles Vicari that night; the certified records that Mac had obtained from New Hope Hospital. She identified the records. He pointed out the lack of any notation of a live birth.

"That is Dr. Vicari's handwriting," she said in a cool tone. "He recorded the procedure as he saw it."

"And this signature at the bottom of the page?"

"That is Dr. Vicari's signature."

Vince didn't interrupt with an objection. He couldn't, really. The defendant would not testify under oath. From the legal perspective, his plea of not guilty said it all.

But the remainder of Alice's testimony was interrupted continually by Vince McConnell's objections. And occasionally Vicari would break out with an exclamation, *soto voce,* but loud enough to make himself heard in the well of the courtroom. Each time that happened, Morrow's head would whip around and then Vince would get his client to calm down again. Peter was surprised at the judge's restraint. Maybe Morrow, at last, was allowing himself to dip beneath the surface of the law, into an unfamiliar realm of compassion and emotion. Just for a short time.

Through it all, Alice maintained her composure. She wore the same little black hat she'd worn to the hotel that morning, white gloves that reached just above her wrists. She wore a dark blue jacket and skirt that brought out the unusual cobalt color of her eyes. She was an excellent witness, Peter thought as they moved though the time line of that night in New Hope, linking the baby in NICU brought in by Alice, with the infant born alive and delivered by Charles Vicari. Through it all, Alice sat with her back straight, hands folded in her lap, answering each of Peter's questions in a clear, confident tone without once looking toward the defendant.

"To your knowledge was Baby Doe the only live birth infant delivered by the Defendant while you were at New Hope?"

"No."

"Were you present on those other occasions?"

"It happened many times on my shift, but I was not working with those doctors. There were several."

"Objection." Vince rose. "Hearsay."

Peter turned to Morrow. "Give me a minute, Your Honor."

Morrow nodded. "Overruled."

"If you weren't present at the live births, Miss Hamilton, how did you know that they'd occurred?"

Peter saw that Alice's eyes were fixed on someone behind him as she began to answer. Suzanne, he realized. "I'd been at New Hope for years before I became aware that this was happening. That was several years before I left. Around 1975, '76. But once I knew, well, like some of the other nurses on the floor, I would hold an infant . . . until it died."

"How many times did that happen?"

She shook her head. "I don't know, sir. I didn't count."

"Every night?"

"Oh no. Once in a while. If the mother didn't want it, or didn't realize, then sometimes the infant would be put in a warming pan, and then I'd pick it up. Sometimes the nurse on duty would know to find me or one of the other nurses that did this, and then we'd hold it." Her voice dropped. "Occasionally, this happened, but it wasn't considered unusual and it wasn't hidden."

He'd thought long and hard about going further, about asking whether some of the infants she'd held over the years had been delivered by Charles Vicari. But there lay dragons: because, if so, he'd never been charged. In the end, he'd decided to end things here, rather than to risk a mistrial.

But now, cross-examination loomed.

"Thank you, Miss Hamilton," Peter said at the end. "The defense lawyer, Mr. McConnell, will ask you some questions now," he said to her. She nodded. He turned to the judge. "Tender the witness, Your Honor."

He'd prepared Alice for this over the weekend—knowing that Vince, good lawyer that he was, would channel his defendant's disdain and rage toward Alice. But she was a woman of grace, a woman telling the truth.

McConnell struck right away. Halting ten feet from the witness stand, he posed, arms crossed as he stood silently observing Alice. Peter, sitting at the table now watched the standoff as Alice peered back at him, unblinking.

Resting his elbow on his forearm, Vince pressed his knuckles against his chin, his finger bracketing the corner of his mouth and said, "If you are so opposed to abortion, Miss Hamilton, why didn't you merely leave New Hope Hospital and find other employment? Why did you allow yourself to stay in that department, on that floor, with full knowledge of what you are now telling this court was going on?"

It was a good question. Peter already knew the answer.

"I'm a nurse. I love my work. There were other doctors in pediatrics that I liked working with."

"So you just looked the other way?"

Peter flinched, but he'd expected that. And Alice had lived with those memories long enough to have absorbed the pain, deep down inside, where she kept it private. "I wanted to do what I could. I would hold those infants when they lived, when I was there."

"But nurses are in demand everywhere. You could have gotten another job in another hospital, couldn't you?"

She gazed at him for a moment. "This happens in other hospitals, too. There's no way to know when you're looking for a job. No one talks about failed abortions out loud. And, I'd been at New Hope for years, long before Dr. Vicari arrived."

Good answer. Peter put his elbows on the table, clasped his hands, and rested his chin on his knuckles. *Keep going, Alice.*

Vince stuck his hands in his pockets and let a beat go by. "How old was the fetus that you took from the room that evening, Miss Hamilton?"

Alice drew back. "She was twenty-three weeks gestation."

"How did you know that at the time? You didn't work with the Defendant on a regular basis. And by your testimony, you hadn't time to look at the records."

"As a pediatric nurse I had a good idea of the infant's age. But, of course,

I couldn't be exact. I just knew she ought to have a chance to try to survive, at least."

"Without giving any consideration to the mother's wishes, you took the infant down to NICU. Did that make you feel heroic, Miss Hamilton?"

"I wasn't thinking that way, Mr. McConnell. I was merely trying to save that baby's life."

"You ignored the physician's judgment."

"Yes."

"And upon what expertise did you base that decision?"

Alice frowned. "I'd worked with micro preemies for years in NICU."

"But," Vince leaned forward, raising his voice, jutting his finger toward Alice. "Did it ever, even once cross your mind that by substituting your judgment for the physician's, you had also stolen from the patient that night her peace of mind, not to mention her constitutional right to choose not to have that child?"

Alice studied him, and then said, "No. I wasn't thinking of any of that. I was thinking of the baby's life."

"Did you have any reason to think that the . . . baby, as you call it . . . could possibly sustain life after that in a meaningful way?"

"I thought it could, yes. I'd seen . . ."

Vince's voice was harsh. "Just stick to my questions, please."

"Then, my answer's yes. I've seen many preemies develop to full term."

"Not from twenty-three weeks, I'd guess, and you're not able to say for certain, are you."

"No. In general? No, I cannot say for certain what would happen with each case."

Vince slowly turned around to face the gallery. "So please tell the court this, Miss Hamilton. How long did the infant survive that night?"

Peter drew in his breath, unable to believe Vince had crossed into the minefield. He could feel Dooney's tension as they both sat very still. Vince had just violated trial procedure 101: never ask a question of a witness unless you're pretty sure you know the answer.

He let out his breath as the first mine exploded.

"She's still alive," Alice said. "She was adopted."

54

VICARI ROSE TO HIS FULL HEIGHT and shouted that Alice was a liar. In the courtroom, pandemonium ensued. The gavel banged—Morrow threatened to clear the courtroom. Vicari shouted liar twice more before the officers got to him. He twisted and turned, struggling as they fought to snap the handcuffs on. Then, Vince was able to convince him that it was in his interest to quiet down.

Judge Morrow's threats to clear the courtroom quieted the gallery too, but still he called a short break in the proceedings, motioning all three lawyers to a sidebar. The sheriffs now stood behind the defendant, hands clasped behind their backs, while Vince walked up to join Peter and Dooney at the bench.

Morrow leaned down and hissed that he was inclined to send all three lawyers to lockup overnight. "If we'd had a jury I'd have probably had to call a mistrial," he said. Then he looked at Peter. "I told you, no tricks."

"That wasn't a trick, Judge," Peter said. "The witness answered defense counsel's questions."

Morrow turned to Vince. "And you. One more outburst from your client and I'll revoke his bond and he'll sit in jail for the rest of the trial, and during the time I've got the verdict under consideration." He narrowed his eyes. "Understand?"

"Yes, Your Honor."

"And that could be a long time."

"I understand, Judge."

"Well see that your client gets it too."

"Are you finished with this witness?" He nodded to Alice, still on the stand.

"Yes, Your Honor."

The judge then called for a brief recess, just long enough to hear a quick motion on another case.

Peter went to the witness stand, took Alice's hand, and helped her out.

He told her she'd done a fine, fine job. As he turned, he saw Suzanne rising from her chair behind the railing. Alice took the lead, and he followed her up the aisle. They would spend the recess time in the witness room. He looked at Dooney, but she shook her head and said she'd wait right there.

Rebecca caught his eye from her back row seat. He was relieved to see her smiling; she was a tough judge herself. If Rebecca was smiling, he knew they'd made some progress.

Molly sat beside her. He stopped, greeted Molly, and leaning across his secretary, brushed a kiss on Rebecca's cheek. "How's Gatsby doing today?"

"Daisy's fine."

Straightening up, he asked if they'd like to go to the witness room. He needed to make certain that Kenneth Gordy was ready to testify next. Both declined. They were comfortable now. They'd stay where they were.

Suzanne and Alice were waiting just outside the door when he came through, and together they headed for the witness room. He warned Kenneth that cross-examination would take place after he'd finished with his questions. Kenneth just said, "Bring it on." Suzanne was anxious about Abby, but the quick peek on her daughter turned out to be a mistake. Abby wailed when, a few minutes later, the bailiff called down the hallway that time was up, trial was resuming. Peter, Alice, and Suzanne turned to leave. Kenneth took Abby's hand.

"No!" the child cried, turning away from her father. She began tugging on her mother's skirt.

Shauna, smiling at Suzanne, pulled a doll from her briefcase. "I brought this with me for just this occasion," she said, with a wink.

Suzanne turned Abby around so that she could see the doll dangling from Shauna's fingers. Abby's mouth closed and she stared at the doll for a moment. Then slowly she reached out with one hand, and Shauna knelt beside her, handing her the doll. Abby released her grip on Suzanne's skirt and held onto the doll, gripping it with both hands as Shauna began telling her the doll's name, and where she lived, and . . .

And they slipped out.

Still, Peter's backward glance caught Abby's baleful look, just before the door closed.

"It's kind of you to join us, Counsel," Judge Morrow snapped when they returned. Suzanne took her seat behind him.

"Call your next witness, please," he said, writing something on his notepad. Then he looked up again. "Is this your last one?"

"Yes, Your Honor." When the judge remained silent, with a glance at Suzanne, Peter called Kenneth Gordy to the stand.

The bailiff went into the hallway, and a moment later Kenneth appeared in the doorway. He watched as Abby's father marched down the aisle with a determined stride, like a soldier going to war. Kenneth stopped at Suzanne's side and touched her shoulder before pushing through the railing. As he greeted Kenneth and showed him to the witness stand, Peter tried to imagine the emotion this man must be struggling to contain as he stood in the same room with Charles Vicari.

Kenneth was sworn in and entered the witness stand. When he sat, he sat upright, both hands gripping the wooden partition, locking eyes with Peter and studiously avoiding Charles Vicari's.

Peter walked to the witness stand. "Good morning, Mr. Gordy. Please state your name for the court."

"Kenneth Chase Gordy."

They went through his place of residence, his marital status. Peter caught the judge's glance at Suzanne Gordy once again. Kenneth stated his profession, schoolteacher, math, ninth grade.

"Any children?" Peter asked.

"One. Abby is her name. Abigail Suzanne Gordy." He looked at Peter. "As you know, she's adopted."

Suddenly it seemed to Peter that the entire gallery behind him drew breath and held it, everyone at once.

Peter handed Kenneth the court records of his and Suzanne's adoption of their daughter and asked him to identify each document. Then he gave copies to Vince McConnell and the judge, and entered the originals into evidence. The clerk stamped and recorded them, and returned them to Peter.

With the remaining records in hand, Peter walked to the open space between the prosecution table and Kenneth Gordy and looked at his witness. "Mr. Gordy, how old is your daughter?"

"She is three years old."

"Please tell the court the circumstances of your daughter's adoption."

Kenneth shifted back in the chair and his hands slipped to his knees. Eyes on his wife in the gallery, he began. "My wife was in New Hope Hospital.

She'd had a hysterectomy, and was extremely upset over this because we so desperately wanted a child." He looked down for an instant, then back at Peter. "I can't put into words the disappointment we were feeling."

His voice grew husky as he went on. "Well anyway, to cut through it all, one of the nurses on the floor told us about Abby, how she'd been abandoned, how she was in neonatal intensive care, struggling for her life."

"Can you tell us the date you first saw Abby?"

"I'll never forget it. It was December 17, 1979. Just before Christmas."

When he paused, Peter said, "Please continue."

Kenneth leaned back and cleared his throat. "My wife asked if we could see her, the little girl—pediatrics was just down the hallway, and Suzanne was feeling low. The nurse said, sure, and took us down to see her, and there she was . . ." His eyes strayed to his wife again. ". . . all hooked up to those machines, and fighting for her life."

"Do you know how long she'd been there when you saw her that day?"

"They said a couple of weeks." He glanced at Suzanne. "I don't remember exactly."

"Objection, hearsay."

Kenneth turned his eyes to Vince, and then quickly back to Peter.

"Sustained," Judge Morrow said.

"I'll withdraw the question," Peter said. The New Hope medical files on Abby's time in NICU were a matter of record. He could link the facts in his closing argument.

"Please go on, Mr. Gordy."

Kenneth held his eyes on Peter's like a lost sailor spotting a lighthouse, his way of fighting the urge to look at Charles Vicari, Peter supposed. "Well we fell in love with her right away. She was ours from the moment we saw her." He shrugged. "The rest of it, we had lawyers to handle the paperwork and the court and all that. When Suzanne—that's my wife—when Suzanne was released from the hospital, we took an apartment in Chicago, one of those temporary ones you can rent near hospitals with furniture in them and all, just until Abby could come home. We ended up being there almost four months. I took a leave of absence for the first few weeks."

He looked down, wiped his brow, then looked back at Peter. "After that, I'd go back to Cincinnati for work, and return on the weekends. Suzanne stayed the whole time. She was with Abby in the nursery all day every day, and many nights. We'd already begun the adoption procedures. That's where we met Alice Braxton, ah . . . Hamilton. The nurses were good to us; they made sure we knew everything that was going on."

He paused and swallowed, pinching the skin between his eyes beneath his forehead. "The adoption was final before she left the hospital. But the happiest day of my . . . our lives . . . was the day we took Abby home."

A smile crept across his face. "She's a fighter, that little one."

"And how is her health?"

"Oh, she's—"

Suddenly a shriek filled the courtroom. Peter turned and saw Suzanne rising from her chair, and behind her light streamed through the open door into the courtroom from the windows across the hallway outside.

"Dada!" And Abby charged down the aisle toward her father, slipping past the bailiff as he bent to catch her. She'd spotted her father on the witness stand and her little legs beat a path toward him. Peter had to smile—Abby still held Shauna's doll.

"Daaaa . . .!" she wailed as she ran, and then Suzanne swooped her up just before she reached the gate and just as suddenly, looking wide-eyed at her mother, she was silenced. She looked at her mother, then she turned her head and looked at Kenneth and Peter, and then her gaze traveled on and stopped on the judge, the huge man in black sitting high above her father.

Peter turned to the judge. Calvin Morrow was speechless, for once.

"I'm so sorry," Suzanne stammered as she looked at Peter, blushing. Peter was speechless too.

Then she turned to Calvin Morrow, bracing Abby on one hip, and said, "I apologize for the disruption, sir. I'll get her out of here right now. Please excuse—"

"Wait." Morrow's voice was calm, as he held up one hand. "Are you Mrs. Gordy?"

Suzanne hugged Abby to her. "Yes, sir." Abby leaned against her mother, that finger hooked into her mouth again. The doll dropped to the floor.

Morrow nodded toward the bundle in her arms. "Is that your daughter? Abigail?"

"Yes, Your Honor." Suzanne gave the judge a proud smile and moved a little so that he could see her child. Peter stood still, watching them and was amazed. He couldn't have planned this if he'd tried.

Suzanne inched closer to the rail gate, looking only at Judge Morrow. "This is Abby."

Artificial overhead lights can sometimes be cruel to beauty, and Peter and every lawyer who'd ever worked in this particular courtroom had noted that fact at one time or another. But today the lights seemed only to illuminate Abby and Suzanne. In that moment, the little girl's smile shimmered with the knowledge that somehow she'd become the center of attention. Her eyes were shining, bright and alert—inquisitive as she looked back and forth between her father and the judge.

She allowed inspection for only a moment, and then suddenly Abby looked at her father, threw out both arms, and strained forward in her mother's arms, with a wide smile as she cried out for him.

Judge Morrow coughed. He cleared his throat. Seconds passed and then he said, "Thank you, Mrs. Gordy. She's a fine little girl, but perhaps now you should take her out."

Kenneth turned to Judge Morrow and said with a little laugh. "As you can see for yourself, Judge, Abby made it through intensive care. She's a lively, healthy little girl."

"Objection, objection, objection!!"

Vince was on his feet, storming toward the bench. "This is clearly a stunt, Your Honor. Choreographed entirely by the prosecution, I'm sure. The defense demands a recess." Flailing one arm toward Peter, he added, "The defense moves for mistrial."

Judge Morrow peered down at McConnell. His tone was dry as he said, "Don't bother, Mr. McConnell. There's no jury to be swayed. Pull yourself together. I won't stand for a mistrial after all the time we've spent on this case, so save it for your closing argument, which"—he included Peter in his glare—"I assume will be tomorrow."

"Yes, Judge," Peter said.

Peter watched Suzanne walking back up the aisle between the spectators, carrying in her arms the best evidence he'd ever had the good luck to present in a murder trial.

55

ABIGAIL GORDY'S STORY MADE FRONT-PAGE HEADLINES the next day. Any hope of keeping Alice's past from Dr. Matlock was gone; her cover had been well and truly blown.

She'd told Dr. Matlock the day before that she'd need the morning off again today. His response had been somewhat surly, but she was determined not to miss the closing arguments.

She took one last look at herself in the mirror, put on her hat and pulled the half-veil down over her eyes, slipped on her best white gloves, and went downstairs to wait for the taxi.

She'd done the right thing with Abby, and no matter how the verdict came out for Baby Chasson, they had all proved that during abortions sometimes babies were accidently born alive. And given a chance, those babies could survive.

At the end of any trial Peter thought how lucky he was that his office was located in the courthouse building. To avoid the press his only hurdle was a brief elevator ride and a short dash through the hallway to the courtroom.

As he entered the courtroom, he saw the gallery was filling up. The Chasson family were sitting in the first row, up front and to Mac's left, in the seats just behind the prosecution table. He'd spoken with Glory Lynn last night and she'd sounded happy, and relieved that the trial was almost over. Behind him, Dooney walked in with the Gordys and Alice. The witnesses filed into the first row on Mac's right side, and Peter and Dooney continued on through the rail gate. The hotel had found a sitter for Abby for the day, Dooney had said.

Mac had saved a seat for Rebecca too, but Peter told him to give it up. Rebbe wanted that same place near the back. The baby was really active these

days, and she had to be able to come and go with ease. Again, Molly elected
to sit in the back with her.

The bailiffs took their positions at the doors and he glanced at his watch,
his stomach beginning to roil, like an early warning earthquake tremor. The
judge would be here soon. He ran through the first few lines of his closing
argument in his head.

Dooney edged around behind him and pulled out her chair. "Just a few
minutes and it's all over. Except for the verdict. How are you feeling?"

"Pretty good," he said. "I think we did our best."

"All rise," the bailiff called, and he heard the excited murmuring and shuffling behind him as everyone stood, but the blood rushing through his head
drowned out everything else. This case was a part of him now. Gooseflesh
rose on his forearms. He had to win. He had to expose to the world the secret
of what was happening to these children.

He thought of the tender shoots of new faith he'd observed in Rebecca.
She hadn't mentioned this to him, but he'd noticed. He thought that perhaps,
besides the baby, that this trial might have had something to do with that.
Now, as he stood watching Judge Morrow enter the courtroom, Peter took a
long breath and said a little prayer to God to help him say the right words.

When he'd settled back, Judge Morrow's eyes swept the courtroom and
the bailiff said that everyone could now be seated. Morrow's eyes landed on
Peter. "Is the State prepared for the closing argument?"

"The State is ready. Thank you, Your Honor."

Peter rose, glanced at Dooney and stood. She gave him an encouraging
smile. Ordinarily, if a jury had been present, Peter would have moved directly
to the jury box. He'd have stood about five feet from the rail, and he'd have
looked into the eyes of each man and woman in those twelve seats the entire
time he talked.

But today was different.

Today only one juror was present in the courtroom. So he walked to
the lectern instead, and stood before Judge Morrow. Yesterday Peter thought
he'd glimpsed a slight change in the judge, for the first time a slight softening
around his eyes and mouth as he'd looked at Abby Gordy in her mother's arms.

Resting both hands on the lectern, he looked up at Calvin Morrow and began.

"Despite what any person in this courtroom thinks about when life begins, as instructed by this court, the State is not here today to challenge the law of the land," he began. "But we are here to uphold the right of one small child to live—a right that was denied him by the Defendant."

He paused and took a step back, shoving his hands into his pockets. "The State has introduced evidence to the court through an autopsy report, a pathology report, and testimony of witnesses that Baby Chasson was born alive on the evening of May 13, 1982 at the Alpha Women's Clinic. The Defendant was the only physician in attendance.

"After the infant was born, Glory Lynn Chasson, the mother, heard the infant cry.

"After the infant was born, Nurse Clara Sonsten heard the infant cry. Nurse Sonsten also testified that she saw the infant, a boy, breathing, and moving various limbs while still in the Defendant's hands. And then, the Defendant handed the infant over to Nurse Sonsten, still in the delivery towel. When she asked the Defendant's permission, as the physician in charge, to suction the child's air passages so that he could breathe, and then to call an ambulance for help, the Defendant said no. Instead he took the infant back from her and wrapped the towel tightly around the infant's head and face as if it were already dead, and then handed the bundle back to Nurse Sonsten and told her to take it away . . . to the utility room, where medical waste was kept."

Peter held the judge's eyes as he spoke. Morrow did not look away.

"Those actions of the Defendant were deliberate and intentional." Peter lifted his finger, emphasizing his next words. "When Dr. Charles Vicari ordered Nurse Clara Sonsten not clear the baby's throat, not to call an ambulance, but to take him out of there, to take him away to the clinic's utility room after wrapping a towel around his face so that he could not continue breathing, Dr. Vicari understood *exactly* what he was doing." He paused. "And what was kept in the utility room?"

He answered his own question. "The evidence tells us: medical waste." He held the Judges eyes. "Oh, yes. The Defendant was fully aware that his actions would result in the infant's certain death, as he intended."

He dropped his hand back onto the lectern and waited a beat. "But, Nurse Clara Sonsten defied the Defendant's orders. Instead of abandoning the infant in the utility room, she testified that she unwrapped the towel from the infant's face, and attempted to clear the air passages with her fingers. She took it to an empty room at the clinic, and there she held that infant in her own arms until it died. He struggled to breathe, she said. He fought to live. For—over—an—hour, the evidence shows, Baby Chasson *fought* to live."

Peter dropped his arms to his sides, and, despite his earlier resolve, he began pacing back and forth before the bench as he went on, describing Melanie Wright's testimony that she'd seen the infant in that back room with Nurse Sonsten; that she'd seen the infant breathing, moving. And he repeated Stephanie Kand's conclusions from the autopsy and the pathology report that the infant could possibly have lived for over an hour.

Here he halted, looking at the judge. "Dr. Kand further testified, and the autopsy shows, that Baby Chasson presented no apparent anomalies. The heart was beating. The infant was breathing. The skull formation was normal for the infant's age. The circulation system was well developed and healthy and normal for the age."

He paused and took a breath. "The State's witness, an ambulance driver, testified that it would have taken only twenty minutes to get that baby to a hospital neo-intensive care facility. It's clear from the evidence that if an ambulance had been called, but for the Defendant, Baby Chasson might be alive today. Like Abigail Gordy." He felt threatening tears and forced them back.

His voice rose as he resumed "Your Honor, the Supreme Court of the United States has never considered the crime that we have before us today, the possibility that an infant surviving an abortion might be burdened with his mother's prior choice and charged to die because of that. And there is a reason that decision did not cover this situation. That is because this crime is already covered by another law. The governing law before us today is not *Roe v. Wade*. The law governing this crime is murder. Because under the laws of the United States of America and the State of Louisiana, once Baby Chasson was born and breathed and his heart continued beating, he was a living human being with the right of every other human being in this country and this state to live, to fight for life."

The courtroom was silent. Seconds passed before he continued.

"*Roe v. Wade* may have asserted the woman's control over a fetus within her body, with some exceptions at the point of viability. But after birth?" He raised his fist, and his voice. "At birth, the line is clearly drawn." He heard murmurs in the gallery behind him and paused, gathering his thoughts.

"After birth the child is no longer a part of the woman's body; no longer a charge on her reproductive system. We are asking this court to recognize that—accidental or not, unwanted or not—the birth of Baby Chasson brought with it 'personhood.' From that point on every decision made with regard to that infant should have been made in the best interests of that child—a full medical assessment should have been performed. And the State has shown that there was plenty of time for that."

He turned, looking at the defendant now. Peter's hands curled into a fist. Charles Vicari met his look with sheer disdain.

"The evidence shows beyond reasonable doubt that this Defendant's actions caused the death of Infant Chasson. The Defendant not only refused to provide medical assistance to the infant, but he refused to allow anyone else to do so either. And then he went further. He deliberately, knowingly wrapped the towel around the infant's head while, according to Nurse Sonsten, Infant Chasson still struggled to breathe, and then he ordered his nurse to take Infant Chasson to the clinic's utility room, knowing that alone and uncared for, there he would die."

"He *intended* to kill that baby."

Peter turned back to Calvin Morrow. "Second Degree Murder in this state requires as one element of proof evidence of an *intent* to kill. The defense will argue that Dr. Vicari was surprised by the live birth of Baby Chasson. The defense will argue that Dr. Vicari's failure to anticipate such an event, his so-called surprise, destroys any idea that he might have harbored ahead of time an intention to let the infant die. Mr. McConnell will say that Dr. Vicari was convinced that any twenty-three-week fetus—as he believed—could never survive an induced labor abortion.

"But what Mr. McConnell has *not* told the court is this." Peter leaned forward, bracing his arms on the lectern holding Morrow's eyes. "The defense has not told this court that Charles Vicari has done this before. He was well aware of the risk of live birth during abortion. The State has presented evidence in this case that the Defendant refused to provide medical assistance to a live-born infant before, three years ago in New Hope Hospital in Chicago, Illinois. That infant was Abigail Gordy."

In the silence of the courtroom, Peter turned, looking at Alice Hamilton. The nurse had shown great courage, then—three years ago—and now.

"Through the testimony of Nurse Alice Hamilton, and Abby's father, Kenneth Gordy, the State has established that this is not the first time that the Defendant has faced this situation. Therefore, he could not have been surprised. By any standard, the Defendant was aware of the risk. He cannot now claim surprise and confusion as a defense—"

"Objection!" Vince's voice rang out.

"—because Abigail Gordy's very existence condemns him."

"Your Honor," McConnell shouted, standing beside Vicari. "Counsel is doubling down! Now he's using the Gordy child as evidence?"

Judge Morrow turned red as he leaned forward over the desk with a hawk-like glare, his voice a staccato beat: "I remind you, Mr. McConnell, that this is a closing argument during which objections are *strongly* discouraged."

Vince stared. Seconds passed, and slowly the judge turned his eyes on Peter. "Mr. Jacobs, what have you to say?"

"I'm referring only to Kenneth Gordy's and Alice Hamilton's testimony on record, Your Honor. Not the presence of the child in the courtroom."

"See you keep it that way." Morrow turned toward Vince McConnell. "Objection overruled. Defense counsel will take a seat. You'll have your turn soon, but until then I expect you to extend to the State the same courtesy you'd expect for yourself."

"Yes, Judge." Vince sat.

Peter was finished, but he decided to push it one step further. "Your Honor, the State hopes that when the court takes this case under consideration, that you will consider the case of Abby Gordy as a living example of what I believe the Defense might agree is a meaningful life."

He paused to let those words sink in, seeing Abby in her mother's arms in the courtroom yesterday, the child's face shining as she reached for her father. That memory wouldn't be erased from the judge's mind anytime soon, he knew, and that memory struck something inside, a feeling that was somehow connected to his love for his own child yet to be born.

Lifting his head he held Judge Morrow's eyes. "The evidence in this case proves beyond a reasonable doubt that the Defendant, Charles Vicari, is directly responsible for the death of the infant born of Glory Lynn Chasson on May 13, as charged."

56

VINCE STOOD AND WALKED TO THE lectern, hands clasped behind his back, head down. He brought with him no notes. When Vince reached the lectern, he sidestepped it, dropped his arms to his sides and looked up.

"Imagine yourself in the Defendant's shoes in this case. A young woman comes into the clinic looking for help. She's distraught, alone . . . fragile. She has come to you because she's chosen to terminate a pregnancy that is, uninvited, unwanted, day by day stealing her dreams—her entire future."

He held out his hands in supplication. "And so she has come to you because the law of the land says that she doesn't have to go through that nightmare, she has a choice. And you agree to help her. But she's confused about her date of conception. Having fought the reality of her situation from the beginning, she can't remember now, she can only guess."

"First, you do everything in your power to determine the gestational age of the fetus. "Next, you must determine whether you believe the fetus is yet viable, and given the information you've put together, you conclude in good faith and using your best medical judgment, that the fetus is twenty-three weeks and not yet viable. You recall that *Roe v. Wade* placed likely viability at twenty-eight weeks, with some possibility of moving down to the last and most remote risk at twenty-four weeks."

Vince halted for an instant, turned to the judge, and shrugged. "As the autopsy later confirmed, the calculation of gestational age wasn't far off. But, of course, that information was developed after." He shook his head, sadly. "Hindsight makes it all look so easy."

"As we've learned from testimony in this courtroom," he said, "and as you will discover if you're of a mind to read papers published by physicians and academics in the field of obstetrics and pediatrics, there is no medical consensus as to the point at which viability occurs. It is a moving concept determined partly by medical advances, and partly by each individual woman's body and health, and the accuracy of the woman's own memory.

No physician could have done better than the Defendant in determining the gestational age with the information that he had.

"So, putting yourself in the Defendant's shoes, your next challenge is to determine the safest method to use with your patient, Miss Chasson. Here courts have held that the physician's best medical judgment will prevail. You choose the most conservative method available, induced labor abortion. It is the safest method to use because the fetus is expelled intact. For the most part, instruments aren't necessary.

"However, as the State has pointed out, with induction the fetus arrives intact, and on a rare—rare—occasion a fetus may survive for a minute or two with the heart still beating, breathing, still always . . ." He stopped, spun toward the gallery, raised one finger, and shook it. "Always, it expires within minutes."

He paused and spread his hands. "But a few minutes does not equal viability. The defense has placed into evidence testimony that the Supreme Court in *Roe v. Wade* recognized this when the Court added the condition that such a life must also have a certain quality, a certain level of meaning and awareness.

"The circumstances of Abigail Gordy are unique, Your Honor."

Vince turned back to the judge, and began pacing again. "It is against this background that the Defendant handed what he believed was fetal tissue to Nurse Sonsten that night. There was confusion in the room; his patient was hysterical, he was concerned about her health, and he was unaware of the live birth. The State has presented witnesses who claim that the fetus, the infant, was born alive, that they saw it breathing, moving, and heard it cry. The Defendant denies that he was aware of this at the time not only because of the confusion around him, because also his examination of the patient had convinced him that the fetus could not yet be viable. That was his mindset when he wrapped the blanket fully around the fetus and handed it back to the nurse."

"And let's make this clear." He stopped in the middle of the triangle, turned and pointed at his client. "The infant's death was inevitable. And in those moments, Dr. Charles Vicari's first and only duty was to his patient, Glory Lynn Chasson.

Dropping his hand, slowly McConnell walked back to the lectern. "We are asking this court to consider that when the fetus arrived, the Defendant was fully engaged and distracted by his primary concern, the health and safety of his patient who required immediate medical attention. Imagine the irony, Your Honor, that the State, with blindingly myopic hindsight, would come along to second-guess the Defendant's judgment. It is ironic that had the fetus expired one second earlier and one inch further back within the birth canal, we would not be here today."

There was a gasp in the courtroom.

"We ask the court to consider this. Courts have consistently protected a physician acting in accordance with his best medical judgment in an operating room. In the operating room, the physician is the captain of his ship. A verdict against the Defendant in this case would be unprecedented; it would cast shadows over every physician and abortion provider in this country whose judgment tells him or her that induced labor is the safest method of abortion for his patient. Such a verdict would shift the slight risk of a live birth to the patient rather than the physician.

"And it would cast an undue burden on every woman in this country exercising her constitutional right to have a late-term abortion."

"The defense now asks this court to find the Defendant in this case, Charles Vicari, innocent of the charge of murder in the second degree, and of all lesser included charges. That is the only way to protect the constitutional rights of women and physicians in this country."

He dipped his head and sat down, looking drained. "Thank you, Your Honor."

As Vince sat down and Vicari leaned toward him, whispering, Peter turned, seeking Rebecca's face and smiled at her.

Judge Morrow cleared his throat. Peter looked up and the Judge said, "Any rebuttal, Counsel?"

Slowly Peter rose. "Since this is a bench trial, your Honor, the State merely asks the court to remember this in consideration: Testimony in this case established that it would have taken an ambulance only twenty minutes to reach a hospital from the clinic." Seconds passed.

Morrow looked up. "Legal briefs by noon tomorrow," he said as he stood.

57

BEFORE EVERYONE LEFT THE COURTHOUSE, PETER made certain that Morrow's clerk had his office and home phone numbers and his secretary, Molly's, phone number. If Rebecca went into labor before the verdict was handed down, he'd let Molly know his whereabouts so she could contact him.

Dooney and the Gordys left to pick up Abby before heading off to the airport. Alice made them promise to keep in touch and let her know how Abby was doing. After they saw Dooney's group off, Mac and Peter went up to their offices. Mac was working another case. Peter had another hearing scheduled for the following morning in an upcoming trial.

So, Alice and Rebecca, left to themselves, strolled two blocks down from the courthouse to Common Grounds café for lunch. They passed city hall with Christmas lights strung over the doors and around the windows and roof. A cold damp wind blew from the river and they both buttoned their coats.

Rebecca, feeling heavy and out of breath, rested her hand on Daisy and walked along so slowly that Alice had to slow her step.

They halted inside the door of the café and looked around. The place was warm enough that fans swirled overhead, even on this chilly December day. They stopped before a blackboard near the door, looking at the day's specials: shrimp-stuffed eggplant, po-boys, spaghetti and meatballs—heavy food. Rebecca wanted something light.

"It's certainly busy in here," Alice said.

Rebecca glanced around. Even the tables in the large back room were full. Two waitresses glided between tables, carrying plates high above their shoulders as they skinnied from side to side avoiding collisions. Rebecca recognized a few people from the courthouse, lawyers in suits; some from the DA's office.

One of the waitresses appeared at their sides. "We've got an open table in the corner," she said, moving fast. Rebecca and Alice followed.

Rebecca thanked the waitress, who flew on by, and she pulled out a chair for Alice, then another one for her. "How long do you think it will take?" Alice asked as she sat down.

"The verdict?"

Alice nodded.

Rebecca placed the napkin in her lap. "You never know. Even with a jury it can take days. Sometimes longer. But with a trial to the bench—one man with all that on his shoulders?" Rebecca shrugged.

"I'd have liked to have been on that jury," Alice said.

Rebecca looked at her and smiled. "I was picked for one once. You wouldn't think they'd want a lawyer, so I arrived with my summons, just certain I'd be home in a couple hours." She snorted. "Boy, was I surprised. But something about being in that jury box brings out the best in most people, I think. Everyone took the job very seriously. There were long arguments, a lot of passion."

"I imagine a case like this one would be traumatic for most people." Alice eyed Rebecca as she picked up a menu. Her voice broke, and Rebecca turned to see a tear slowly sliding down the older woman's cheek.

Rebecca rose, gave her a quick hug, and returned to her place. "It must have been difficult for you in Chicago, knowing what Vicari was doing and sticking it out. But, Alice . . ." She bent her head toward Alice and lowered her voice. "Look what you've done. You saved Abby Gordy's life. You've given Kenneth and Suzanne a child."

Alice swallowed, nodding. "I know. It's just, remembering all the others . . ."

"Yes." Rebecca rested her arms on the table. "But because of your courage, coming to see me, if Peter gets his verdict, it'll be because of you."

Alice managed a slight smile. When the waitress arrived at their table, she ordered a ham sandwich on regular bread, she said, not French bread. Rebecca ordered a tomato stuffed with tuna salad.

The waitress brought a glass of iced tea with lemon for Rebecca, and water and a cup of hot tea for Alice. Then they settled back.

At the next table Rebecca noticed two young women, animated, talking with excited gestures. Both wore skirted suits that told Rebecca they were probably lawyers taking a break from the courthouse melee. They reminded her of herself and Amalise a few years ago, when they were getting started. Despite the long hours, the deadlines and demands and challenges, she'd been so happy with her life.

And now?

She'd thought partnership at Mangen & Morris was what she'd always wanted. She had worked so hard to get to that point. Thinking back to the day of that phone call inviting her to join the firm, it all seemed so long ago. So far away. She smiled to herself; she'd thought that becoming partner was the meaning and purpose of her life.

A wave of contentment ran through her at the thought of the surprising new direction her life seemed to be taking, and she thought of Daisy and Peter and the years they'd have ahead of them. The baby was going to change everything in her life, she knew. The decision had been forming slowly over the last few months. Suddenly, it had crystalized.

Everything was going to change.

And it was going to be okay.

"Your happiness is contagious," Alice said.

She leaned toward Alice and said, "Why don't you take some time off before you go back to work? Let all of this go." She waved her arm to encompass not only the room, but the courthouse and Charles Vicari. "Go somewhere. Have an adventure."

"I had actually been thinking about your trip with Peter to Italy. To Positano." Alice laughed. "Maybe I will go."

58

THAT EVENING REBECCA SAT WORKING ON the State's brief for Judge Calvin Morrow. Soothing piano music came from the stereo, Chopin's Nocturnes. Peter had lit the fire for her and the only light on in the study was the one on the desk that lit the page of the brief she'd drafted for Peter. Not good for her eyes she knew; but best for her soul.

Peter was upstairs in their bedroom, already asleep. He was exhausted. While the judge was considering his verdict, Peter had gone back to his routine of hearings and depositions. She shook her head thinking of the hundreds of cases on his calendar in any year.

And her life, ordinarily, was just as hectic. Somehow seeing the two women in the café had worked its way past her guard. The jolting rogue thoughts made her put down the pen and lean back. Adrenaline surged as she called up memories of the good times at Mangen & Morris, how she loved the work, the camaraderie, even the fast pace. It had taken so many years to get where she was today, to partnership. And there was so much still ahead—what was she thinking!

Still.

She didn't want to go back to working long hours, days, nights, weekends. She wanted to stay home with Daisy. She wanted to watch her child grow up, but she wanted to work too. She loved the practice of law.

She looked at the computer that Peter had bought for her and thought of the work that she'd done for Brightfield right here at home. Brightfield had mentioned once the idea of starting an appellate section at the firm. That was something she could build on, and, perhaps some of that work could be done right here at home, with Daisy at her side. She was good at this, he'd said— good at winding her way through the cases, good at the analysis required to write these briefs, and maybe someday even argue them in court. She could pick and choose her cases—take only those she really cared about.

She watched the fire burning low. The research for Brightfield's briefs was like digging for clues, solving a mystery, she'd found—and each time she turned up an answer, something new, a new holding, or some particular reasoning by a court that applied to her case, she felt good. It was a feeling of victory, as though she'd helped to change someone's life for the better.

Rubbing her hand over Daisy, she imagined the baby in a bassinet beside her, with the fire blazing and the baby dozing under a blanket while Mommy worked. For a moment—just a few seconds—she closed her eyes and let herself drift with her imagination. And then Daisy moved, kicking, and burst the bubble, pulling her back into reality.

She shook her head. What a crazy idea.

Rebecca looked back down at her draft. Vince had made a statement in his closing argument that had been nagging her. She thought about the problem, then looked up the Roe decision on the computer again. She'd read the opinion so many times while writing this brief that she was certain she had it memorized.

But now, she started again at the beginning, reading line by line, concentrating on that worrisome point. Vince had seemed to imply the constitutional right to choose an abortion declared by that Court also burdened a born-alive infant like Baby Chasson. When she came to the end of the decision, she sat back, looking into the flickering fire, thinking about what she'd just read. She'd missed it before. The answer was there. It was subtle, somewhat oblique.

She read through the section she'd remembered, and smiled. Then she went back through the case law dealing with the issue. At last she sank back in the chair, stunned at the clarity and simplicity of the answer. All bets were off after a live birth under *Roe v. Wade*. The mother's consent was extinguished.

By the time she'd finished and put down the pen, it was two o'clock in the morning. She closed her eyes, and exhaled. When she opened them again, she saw the fire had died down to ashes and glowing coals. Minutes passed as she sat there thinking about Peter's case and the raw irony of an accidental life.

One would think that knowing a live birth was a risk at least the clinic would have prepared for that event, but somehow that hadn't seemed to matter. The most obvious evidence of that fact was the lack of crash carts and provisions for postnatal emergency care in even the most expensive abortion clinics. But it hadn't mattered at New Hope Hospital either, when Abby was born. It was only Alice that had made the difference.

Live-birth survivors of abortion were the best-kept secret in the world.

59

ALICE HAD RETURNED TO WORK THE next day with a promise from Peter that he would call her as soon as he heard from the judge's clerk, but he'd said he thought the one-man jury would be out for days. She was on her way home now, still hoping he'd call. She'd be in court to hear the verdict, one way or the other, she'd promised herself. And she would call the Gordys as soon as she'd heard, as she'd promised.

Promises, promises. Charlie had promised to come back to her after the war, and look what had happened.

She'd made promises to herself, too, from time to time. Promises to enjoy life. Promises to travel, to see the world.

The streetcar slowed for the turn from St. Charles to Carrollton Avenue, and Alice looked up at Camellia Grill and saw her stop was near. She was tired, and hungry. When the car stopped at Oak Street, Alice got off. Ahead she saw Ciro's Christmas lights blinking, and she veered toward the grocery store to find something good to eat to make up for the lackluster day. Through the large plate-glass windows she saw Ciro's girl, Franchesca, standing behind the register, and a customer talking to her as she made change.

A bell rang over the door as Alice entered the grocery store. The customer turned to go and Franchesca looked up and greeted her. Ciro's daughter was a pretty girl, Alice thought as she nodded and walked on past. She wandered through the shelves and vegetable stalls for a minute and then decided on an alligator pear for dinner, and some sharp cheese for a sandwich. She picked out a large ripe avocado, soft to the touch, and selected the sharpest cheese and took them both to the counter where Franchesca waited.

The girl rang up the purchase, making friendly chatter while making change. Alice studied the framed photographs on the wall behind the counter while she waited. There were pictures there of Ciro, his wife and their children, and of an older woman, his mother, she supposed. Nearby were younger boys on a rocky beach eating gelato, and behind them green hills rose to the sky.

"Your family?" she asked as Franchesca handed her some change. She nodded toward the pictures as she put the money in her pocketbook.

With a glance over her shoulder, Franchesca pulled a brown paper bag from under the counter and placed Alice's purchases inside. "Yes, m'am. That's from two years ago, in Santa Margherita, in Italy. Dad's family is from Genoa, up in the north of Italy, near Milan. Have you ever been to Italy?"

"No."

"Well, I want to go and Dad says he'll take me there after my first year of college. But I'm just a junior in high school. That's a long time to wait."

"I'd love to go someday."

"Dad won't let me go alone. He says it's a place to fall in love, and I'm too young." She planted her hands on her hips. "Can you believe that?"

Alice laughed.

Bells tinkled overhead as Alice walked through the glass door framed in colored Christmas lights, heading across the street to her lonely apartment.

60

PETER WAS ALMOST FINISHED WITH BREAKFAST when Rebecca walked into the kitchen, still wearing her robe. She swiped hair back from her forehead, blew out her cheeks, opened the refrigerator door, and stood there peering in.

"Tired?" Peter's voice was too cheerful.

"Exhausted." She pulled out a bottle of orange juice, shut the door, and turned toward Peter. "I couldn't sleep last night, worrying about the verdict. I can't understand what's taking him so long."

"It's a big responsibility."

Judge Morrow had had the case now for over a week. She took a glass from the cabinet over the counter and filled it with juice. Returning the bottle to the refrigerator, she trudged toward the table where Peter was and sat down in a chair across from him. The baby was due any day now Dr. Matlock had said and she was more than ready.

"Daisy's developed a different sleep cycle from Mom's," she said, making a face. Lifting the glass, she drank a few gulps of the orange juice, and then set it down.

"What are your plans today?"

She lounged back, arms dangling at her sides as she looked at Peter. "Brightfield's got something new for me. Another appellate brief. He says it can wait until after Daisy arrives. There's no big hurry. But I'd just as soon get started now; thought I'd start checking out some cases this morning." She rubbed her stomach. "She was restless last night. I think she's getting bored in there."

"Promise not to call him Daisy when he arrives. In fact, why don't you practice? Just say it once—Gatsby." He reached across and she swatted his hand away, laughing.

"Not a chance, my love." For a few minutes she watched Peter drinking his coffee and reading the paper. Then she leaned across and pushed the paper down, so that she could see his face.

He raised his brows.

"I've made a decision, Peter."

"Uh-oh."

She sat back, looking at him. She'd been thinking about how to break this to him for the past week. He set the paper aside and looked at her, so she just came right out with it. "Listen. I've made a decision to resign from the firm, Peter."

His brows shot up.

"My plan is to set up a law firm of my own, handling only appellate briefs at first, and later on, when Daisy's older, I'd like to be able to do the arguments in court too once in a while. But here's the best thing: the firm will be headquartered right here at home, in our study." She hesitated. "With the computer, I can do it. What do you think of that?"

He leaned back, stretching his arms, wrists loosely resting on the table. "I think it's a great idea, Rebbe. In fact . . ." he nodded, "I think it's a smart move." He chuckled. "Bill Brightfield wanted to set up an appellate section at the firm anyway, so this way you can provide those services, do the same work, and take the profit."

Rebecca smiled. She'd thought of that, too. Brightfield would sulk for a few days, she was certain.

"Won't you miss working downtown, the action?"

"No. This way I can be with Daisy." She shook her head and gave him a somber look. "I didn't like a single one of those nannies I interviewed, Peter. Finally figured out why. It's because I can't stand the thought of not being around when she takes her first step, or speaks her first word. Can't stand the idea of being away all the time. So . . . I'll use the study." She gave him a sideways look. "You can have a corner."

He laughed. "Sure . . . *now* you say that."

"And while Daisy and I are still getting used to each other, well, I'll stick to what I know—the Mangen & Morris work, but I'll work as an independent contractor. I'll hire an assistant if I need one. This way I can set my own schedules. Then later on, when she's in school, well, I'll go national. Plenty of firms don't have appellate expertise. It's an opportunity."

"And Gatsby will love having Mom around."

"The name is Daisy." She smiled. "Mothers know."

Then she fell back in the chair, hands clapped together. "This is exciting, Peter."

Just then she felt a sharp kick from Daisy. "Come feel this!" She looked up, motioning to Peter. "Hurry. The child never sleeps. She's moving around more than usual this morning. I think she likes the idea."

Peter rose, walked to Rebecca, knelt beside her, and put his hand over the baby. A grin instantly split his face as he looked up. "He's busy today." His eyes met Rebecca's and lingered. Then he lifted his hand, cupping her neck as she bent down for his long slow kiss.

Straightening again, Rebecca looped her arms around his neck, looking down into his eyes. "I've always known we have something special together Peter. But . . ." Her expression turned grave as she searched his eyes. "Now, we've created this miracle between us. At least, this little life growing inside seems a miracle to me."

Peter was silent.

"Just think, we've made a child together. And, well . . . I think our love's grown stronger and deeper through this bond. Everything's changed! Even our relationship has changed."

He nodded. "We are a family now. Not just two people in love, living separate lives, Rebbe."

"I think someone is listening when we pray. I think . . . I think that Daisy's a gift. A gift from God, like Amalise has always thought."

"I know. I've been giving thanks."

She bent and touched her forehead to his, as they held onto each other. When, after a few seconds, she drew back, she caught Peter blinking, and wondered if those were tears.

Peter drew back and rose, giving her a long look. Suddenly he glanced at his watch and his eyes grew wide. "I've gotta get going." He picked up his coffee cup from the table and drained it, setting it back down, and turned. "But I'm one hundred percent on board with your idea, Beauty. It's better than anything I could have dreamed, really."

Then he gave her a look. "Are you certain you want to do this? Give up the partnership you've worked for all these years?"

"I'm sure. I'll have you and Daisy, and home, and work that I'll love. What could be better?"

"Well. I'm excited. I'll be married to the managing partner of a national law firm. That and Daisy; what more could a guy ask?" He picked up his briefcase from the chair. "I'm off now." But as he held the door handle, he turned quickly back to her. "Call the minute anything happens, Rebbe?"

"I will."

"Even a twinge. Promise?"

"Of course."

"The numbers are on—"

"I know. On the bulletin board beside the refrigerator."

As she heard the car door shut, the telephone rang. She pushed herself up with a groan, and walked over to the phone on the wall near the door to the living room, hearing the engine starting up in the garage.

"Hello?" she said, leaning against the wall.

"Rebecca? This is Molly. The verdict's in!"

A beat went by. Then she dropped the telephone, letting it dangle from the curling cord as she hurried to the door and flung it open. Leaning out, "Peter!" she called.

He was already backing the car out of the garage, but he spotted her.

"We've got a verdict!" she shouted.

61

ALICE HUNG UP THE PHONE. THE judge had reached a decision. She'd taken the call at the desk in the file room, and now she sat there looking down at the stack of files that must be put on the doors of each examination room right away for the first wave of patients.

The verdict would be read at ten o'clock this morning.

Dr. Matlock walked up and looked over the counter. "I need the file for Miss Waddington, please. She's already in the room."

Clutching the files, Alice told Dr. Matlock that she would have to leave the office for a while.

"Impossible," he said in a sharp tone. "Nonsense. We've got a patient already waiting in the room, and a full schedule this morning." He tilted his head, his brows drawn together. "What's gotten into you lately, Miss Hamilton?"

For a minute she thought about telling him about the trial and about how she'd been involved and what this meant to her. He seemed to have completely missed all that news in the papers. But the look on his face told her that nothing mattered to him right now but his work, his patients.

So she nodded and picked up the stack of files on the counter near the file room. "I'll get these ready, Doctor."

"Fine. And hurry, please. I need you in room one." He gave her a puzzled look and turned, walking briskly down the hallway to the room where Miss Waddington was waiting.

"All rise."

A shiver ran through Peter as he stood. Dooney stood beside him. Never in his career had he cared so much about the outcome of a trial. Turning, he glanced over his shoulder at Rebecca. She was standing also, in the back row near the door with Molly beside her. Again, just in case. She smiled and wiggled her fingers. Mac, sitting right behind Peter, gave him a thumbs-up and grinned.

The courtroom wasn't crowded, not yet. Word hadn't gotten around, but it soon would be and anyone working in the building who could escape would manage to find their way to this courtroom, he knew. He looked around and saw that Stephanie Kand was here, a few rows back.

As he turned back to face the bench, he noticed a dark-haired woman with a frozen expression on her face. She stood alone, directly behind Charles Vicari. He wondered if she was the doctor's new wife, Eileen Broussard. Across the aisle Vince McConnell was getting to his feet. He slipped his hand under Charles Vicari's elbow as he rose, and Vicari, with a sharp movement shook him off.

Judge Calvin Morrow's face, when he appeared in the doorway behind the bench, was expressionless. He lifted his arms from his sides like a great blackbird flapping his wings before he sat, adjusting the sleeves of the long black robe. There was a rustle as everyone sat back down, and then a heavy silence as the judge took his time settling into his place.

Morrow picked up several pieces of paper from the desktop before him. A few seconds ticked by as he looked at what he had written, then he turned his eyes toward the back of the courtroom and began speaking, almost as if to himself.

"I will admit that considering the verdict in this case has been the most difficult duty I've ever undertaken. A trial to the bench is a great responsibility." His eyes seemed to drift toward the press, and then lowered, sweeping over the defense, then the prosecution. "I've read both briefs submitted by the parties." He looked down and sniffed. Tapped the papers on the desk and looked up again.

The room was silent, except for a muffled cough from somewhere in the back.

"In the matter of the *State of Louisiana v. Charles Frank Vicari,*" he began.

"The Defendant, Dr. Charles Vicari, comes before this court charged by the State with having committed the crime of second degree murder under Louisiana Revised Statutes 14:30.1 against an infant born of Glory

Lynn Chasson. Under Louisiana law second degree murder is the killing of a human being with specific intent to kill or to inflict great bodily harm.

"The evidence before the court, supplemented by briefs filed by the prosecution and defense indicates the following:"

Peter listened, his heart beating, beating, as Judge Morrow slowly and carefully described each fact in the case, in the order that it had occurred.

At last Calvin Morrow came to the decision. He looked up and recited the next lines without even glancing at the pages in his hand. "In reaching this verdict," he intoned, "I considered the following questions to be appropriate:

"*First*, whether the expelled fetus was a 'human being' for purposes of Article 14:30.1. And if the answer was affirmative, then;

"*Second*, whether actions or omissions of the Defendant were directly responsible for the death of the infant Chasson. And if that answer was affirmative, then;

"*Third*—Did the Defendant have the requisite intent to kill or inflict great bodily harm on the infant Chasson when he failed, or refused, to provide medical assistance immediately after birth, and then wrapped a blanket around the infant's head, covering his face?"

He cleared his throat and shuffled the papers, putting the top one down on the desk beside him. "As to the first question—was Infant Chasson, once expelled from his mother, a 'human being' for purposes of Louisiana law?

"Evidence leaves no question that Infant Chasson, a member of the specie *homo-sapien*, was born alive in that after complete expulsion from his mother, he began to breathe, his heart continued to beat, and two witnesses testified to seeing movement of voluntary muscles continuing for minutes after the birth. It is clear from testimony and the autopsy and pathology reports that Infant Chasson sustained life apart from the mother for an undetermined period of time."

Here Morrow paused and looked up. "Except for the Supreme Court decision in *Roe v. Wade* nine years ago, that finding would be conclusive with regard to this first question. But the *Roe* Court overrode all Louisiana abortion laws when it enunciated a woman's right to terminate her pregnancy. The question then becomes, what does the Court in *Roe* have to say about this small human being born alive, when the mother has chosen otherwise?

"In my consideration of this issue, the State's brief submitted after closing arguments provided an answer."

Peter looked up, elated. Rebecca's brief!

Morrow went on. "Although the majority of the decision rendered in Roe does not deal with rights of an unborn child, the prosecution in its brief has pointed to several statements made by the Court in dicta seemingly acknowledging by implication that a line is, as the State has argued, drawn at live birth."

Here he looked up. "One particular passage from *Roe v. Wade* quoted in the State's brief was particularly persuasive in consideration of the verdict. It is stated in the negative and it is subtle, but it is there and it is clear. I quote: 'The law has been reluctant to endorse any theory that life, as we recognize it, begins *before live birth* or to accord legal rights to the unborn, except in narrowly defined situations and . . .'" Here Morrow paused, looking up as he emphasized each word distinctly, *"and except when the rights are contingent upon live birth.'"*

He looked up and out, over the gallery. His voice was clear and firm. "Second degree murder in Louisiana requires in relevant part, at this point, the killing of a live human being. Infant Chasson's rights as a human being to protection of his life under laws of the State of Louisiana arose immediately upon live birth, thus, they were *contingent upon live birth.*

"Under the reasoning of *Roe v. Wade* as described above, Infant Chasson's legal rights—including the right to life—having been vested upon him at birth, are entitled to protection by the State, and they supercede the woman's right to choose his death. After a live birth, the woman's right to choose life or death for the newborn infant ends. Any decision made from that point on must be made solely in the best interests of the child, and following—in this court's view—a full and professional medical assessment of the child's medical condition."

Peter heard a low hum rising in the courtroom behind him.

"I am persuaded that this subtle, but clear, exception in the *Roe* decision is applicable in this case, and it creates for us a governing rule. Regardless of what any one of us may believe about when life begins, the Supreme Court has made it clear that *after live birth* an infant is a 'human being' and is entitled to all the rights of any other human being born alive in this country."

Here Judge Morrow looked up and for an instant, caught Peter's eye. "This principle is well established. In *Weber v. Aetna Casualty & Surety Co.* for example, on certiorari to the Supreme Court of Louisiana, and in other decisions, the law is clear that the guarantees of the Fourteenth Amendment of our Constitution protect the right to life of all infants born under its jurisdiction, not merely those that are wanted.

Again he paused, seeming to take a deep breath before adding, "Based upon the foregoing, this Court finds that under *Roe v. Wade* a line is drawn at birth, and that after separation from his mother, Baby Chasson was a living human being free of his mother's choice, with a right to life. And this is true, whether the victim drew ten breaths or a thousand."

Peter listened, stunned at this first small victory, yet frustrated. In reality, why should the line be drawn at birth? Gatsby, and every other child on earth existed, lived, from the moment of conception.

But that was an argument for another day.

When Morrow glanced up as he spoke these last words, Peter saw suffering reflected in the judge's eyes. This conclusion probably conflicted with everything that he'd believed before this trial; it was something the judge had never thought about before. Peter just stopped himself from shaking his head at the finding that should have been so obvious. Behind him Peter heard the reporters scribbling the news: *The line is drawn at birth. Roe v. Wade offers protection for accidental live-birth infants.*

Judge Morrow continued. "Having concluded that Infant Chasson was a human being, and a person upon birth for purpose of meeting the first requirement of the State's charges, we must now determine the *cause and manner* of Infant Chasson's death to answer the second question.

"The coroner's reports do not give us an answer as to whether the Defendant's actions directly caused Infant Chasson's death—they merely state the medical cause of death as respiratory failure. But testimony of Nurse Clara Sonsten at trial was that the Defendant refused to allow her to render medical assistance to the infant, refused to allow her to call for an ambulance to obtain medical assistance for the infant, and then wrapped the blanket around the infant's head, covering his face and rendering him for that moment unable to breathe. The Defendant then ordered her to take the infant out of the room and to leave him in the utility room."

He looked up. Morrow's face was tense, strained. "And," the judge continued, "the witness was concise and clear as to what she saw and heard, and she spoke under oath. Furthermore, I am persuaded that the subsequent circumstances in this case also lend support to her testimony. For what other reason would Nurse Sonsten have held the infant for over an hour in an empty room in the clinic after she left the procedure room, other than the Defendant's refusal to render medical aid? In that regard, a second witness testified that she saw Miss Sonsten holding the infant in that room twenty minutes after the time of birth, long enough to have cleared the infant's air passages and call for help."

Peter sucked in his breath and across the aisle he heard Vince McConnell do the same. Judge Morrow looked up and said, "Therefore, I am persuaded that the Defendant's actions in covering the infant's face with the towel, and instructing the nurse to take it to the utility room, and his inaction—his failure to render medical assistance or to permit his nurse to do the same—all led to one certain consequence that night, Infant Chasson's death. It is therefore the opinion of the Court that the Defendant's actions and his deliberate inaction, were the direct causes of the death of Infant Chasson."

He exhaled. From the corners of his eyes Peter saw Charles Vicari turning to Vince McConnell and grasping his arm. Again Peter heard the murmuring behind him. He turned his head slightly to the right and saw the press corps bent once again over their notepads.

Morrow picked up the last piece of paper. "And now, we are bound to consider the last element of the charge of second degree murder against the Defendant, that is, whether Charles Vicari specifically intended to kill Infant Chasson when he covered Infant Chasson's face with the towel, and failed to render assistance to the infant, or whether this was all due to negligence."

62

IN THE GLOW OF THE JUDGE'S praise for the brief she'd written for Peter, Rebecca felt a deep radiating pain, at first an aching pain, and then a sharp stabbing pain. Perspiration bloomed on her face, and then a glistening rose over every inch of her flesh, covering her in a delicate sheen of moisture. As the pain continued and deepened, she muffled a cry and drawing her arms across her middle, she doubled, resting her head on the back of the bench in front of her.

"Rebecca, are you all right?" Molly's voice, whispering into her ear. Raising her head she could see Peter at the front of the courtroom, his attention riveted to Judge Morrow. She nodded, half-straightened, and put a finger over her lips.

"I think it's time," she whispered.

Molly's eyes widened as she reached her arm across Rebecca's back, holding onto her waist.

"Can you help me up? I don't want Peter to know. I don't want him missing this."

"Well sure." Molly's voice trembled as she spoke, but with a glance around, she tightened her grip and said, "Lean on me and see if you can stand. If we can make it to the lobby, I'll get my car. It's close by, and we'll go on to the hospital."

Rebecca sucked in a deep breath and nodded. "Let's go. We'll leave word at the desk downstairs. They can call Shauna or someone, and she'll make sure Peter gets word when this is over."

"Shauna can call your doctor, too."

Despite the pain, Rebecca smiled. "Good idea."

From the bench, Judge Morrow asked the last and final question: "Did the Defendant cover Infant Chasson's face, and withhold medical attention with the intent to kill the infant, or to inflict great bodily harm?"

With Molly's help, Rebecca made it through the exit door without Peter noticing.

Judge Morrow stopped, pulled a Kleenex from a box on his desk, and wiped his brow. He looked to his law clerk. The clerk rose, left the room and immediately returned with a glass of water. The judge took a swallow of the water and set the glass down on the desk beside him.

The room was silent as Morrow picked up the page again. "First, we have concluded that Infant Chasson was a human being, a person, under the law, with a right to life. Second, this court has held that Infant Chasson's death was due to the Defendant's action in covering the infant's face with a towel, and his refusal, or failure, to render medical assistance when the infant's life was in imminent danger and he was struggling to breathe, to live.

"And now . . ." Peter watched as Judge Morrow took a deep breath. They'd reached the most difficult part of the court's decision, he knew. "And now we must determine whether the Defendant's action or inaction resulting in the infant's death occurred with an intent to kill or to cause bodily harm. Specific intent, under Louisiana law, is a state of mind, and as such need not be proven as a fact, but may be inferred from the circumstances and the actions of the accused.

"The Defendant claims that he could not have harbored an intent to kill Infant Chasson because he had no reason to anticipate the live birth of the victim. He claims to have been taken by surprise by the live birth. Further, Defendant claims that he had no reason to believe that medical assistance would keep the infant alive. In that regard, again, Defendant claims that Abigail Gordy's survival was an extremely rare event.

"Finally, the Defendant claims that he was distracted at the time that Nurse Sonsten asked permission to clear the infant's passages and call for help, and the subsequent manner in which he wrapped the infant in the towel. His claim is that he was distracted not only by the medical needs of his patient, but also by the noise and confusion in the room caused by . . . as defense states in their brief . . . Miss Chasson's hysterical behavior. For all these reasons, Defendant argues that it is unreasonable to believe that his actions in withholding medical assistance to the infant exhibit an intent to kill.

"But this court finds the Defendant's claim of distraction to be an insufficient reason for refusing to allow his nurse to clear the infant's air passages and call an ambulance. If the Defendant was initially distracted by the confusion in the room, he was certainly alerted to the needs of the infant by Nurse Sonsten's questions, her request to suction, her request to call an ambulance. And it was after Nurse Sonsten's questions alerting him that the infant was still alive that he took Infant Chasson back from her and wrapped the towel around his head, covering his face.

"As to the defense argument that the Defendant was taken by surprise by this live birth, I find that to be contradicted by testimony at trial that live birth, however occasional, is a known risk in a late-term induction procedure as testified to by Dr. Mortimer Stern, and conceded by defense witness, Dr. George Barnett. In addition, the testimony of Nurse Hamilton and Mr. Kenneth Gordy established beyond reasonable doubt that the Defendant had previous experience with a similar situation while practicing at New Hope Hospital in Chicago.

"The evidence presented at trial establishes that when the Defendant refused to provide or allow medical assistance to Infant Chasson, and then covered Infant Chasson's face as he wrapped him in the blanket, and further ordered Nurse Sonsten to take him out of the room, to the utility room, those actions were taken with deliberate and specific regard to that particular living human being. If he'd had any doubt as to whether the infant was alive, Nurse Sonsten had advised him otherwise. And in fact, Nurse Alice Hamilton testified that the Defendant had used almost the same words to her with regard to Abigail Gordy in another live birth three years earlier."

Morrow looked up, frowning. "As stated before, the Defendant's order to Nurse Sonsten could only lead to one result. Death. Infant Chasson was a human being with a right to life. The Defendant stripped that from him."

Judge Morrow peered out over the courtroom. "It is a basic precept in law that we are all responsible for the reasonably foreseeable consequences of our actions." Not a sound invaded the courtroom. "Therefore, this court finds that the evidence in this case establishes beyond a reasonable doubt that the actions, and inaction of the Defendant, Charles Frank Vicari, directly, wrongfully, and intentionally deprived Infant Chasson of his life."

He looked down at Charles Vicari. "The Defendant will rise."

Turning his head toward the defense table, Peter saw Charles Vicari still sitting, seeming to sway toward Vince McConnell. Beside him Vince reached out and caught him, bracing a hand under his client's arm. The bailiff standing beside the jury box gave Vicari an anxious look and took a step forward. McConnell pulled his client to a standing position, and then stood beside him. With a dazed look, Vicari stared straight ahead.

Judge Calvin Morrow looked at them both. He read the charges. Then he said, "In light of the testimony and evidence presented to this court, it is the judgment of this court that the Defendant, Charles Frank Vicari, is guilty of the crime charged of second degree murder of the Infant hasson under Louisiana Revised Statute 14:30.1 of the Criminal Code of the State of Louisiana." He paused and motioned toward two uniformed sheriffs now standing at the door beside the jury box, where the bailiff had just been.

"The Defendant will now be remanded into the custody of this court. Sentencing will occur on Tuesday of next week, on December 21."

Morrow's words seemed to hang in the air as the gavel banged one final time, the words lingering for minutes . . . hours . . . days . . . until the sheriffs began moving toward Vicari. The dark-haired woman who'd sat behind him reached in vain across the railing.

And then Peter heard the bailiff's call: "All rise . . ." and he swung back toward the bench just in time to catch a glimpse of Calvin Morrow's ravaged face as he rose and turned away.

Peter turned, searching for Rebecca. Mac reached across the rail and slapped his shoulder. But as he peered through the crowd behind him, looking for Rebecca, he realized she wasn't there. And neither was Molly.

The baby was coming! But these thoughts were quickly submerged as he turned, pushing through the gate. Even as he moved through the crowd, even with the lifting hope that this verdict would draw attention to other accidental lives needing protection in the future, even with all of that—deep inside he felt no celebration. Too many had suffered too much, for that.

And now, all he could think of was Rebecca—already at the hospital with Molly and the doctor, he hoped.

63

ALICE SAT IN THE WAITING ROOM of Baptist Hospital. She'd asked Dr. Matlock if she could assist with the delivery, and he'd said fine. So, she still wore her uniform and the white cap and her comfortable shoes. In the room with her were some of Rebecca's friends, Amalise and Jude and their son Luke. And there was Molly who'd driven Rebecca to the hospital from the courthouse.

Detective McAndrews, Mac, was there too. And Mac had given Alice the verdict. It had taken time for the news to really sink in after all those years of living with the memories of that night. And now, a verdict.

She closed her eyes and thanked God, at last free of the great weight. The feeling lifted her. She rose, put on her hat, slipped on her gloves, and feeling as though she were walking one inch above the floor in the waiting room, she said her goodbyes and left humming . . . *Things are never bad as they seem, just believe in God.*

She walked down to Napoleon Avenue where she could catch a bus to St. Charles. The bus rolled up and she got on, dreaming. She paid her coin and took her seat, looking straight ahead through the front windows of the bus. Rebecca had once mentioned the beauty of the harvest moon rising between the Faraglioni—two mystical rocks sculpted through time and wind and waves just off the coast of the island of Capri.

She would do it, she decided. She would start in Europe—she'd see Paris and London of course, and Geneva, Vienna, and Rome. And maybe one day even Bangkok, Singapore, Beijing, Tokyo.

Why not? She smiled. What was she waiting for?

In the room, alone at last with Daisy, bundled in a soft blanket and cradled in her arms, with Peter sitting on the bed close beside her, Rebecca nudged her lips against her baby's silken forehead. Peter pressed against her, silently watching his daughter sleep.

Unable to express her feelings in this moment, all she could do was hold the baby close and look from one to the other, from Peter to baby and back again. She'd never known such love.

I have called you by name, you are mine.

The words flowed unbidden into her mind, and she knew them now. When she'd first fallen in love with the baby, back then, months ago, those words had come from nowhere. But she'd looked them up, finally found them one day in Amalise's Bible. And she'd finally understood. She'd found them in the book of Isaiah. In this moment, she and baby and Peter were encased in those very words, encased in a circle of love greater than the three of them by far, eternal love of a kind that she could never have imagined before.

Peter was silent, stroking his daughter's tiny head, her back.

She would be baptized with her daughter, she decided.

Then lifting her lips from the top of baby's head, she looked at Peter and he looked back at her. "I have a name," she said in a tentative voice.

His hand flattened, covering their daughter's back. "Let's hear it. I'm hoping it's not Daisy."

She smiled. "There's nothing wrong with Daisy. But, I'd like to call our girl, Elise."

He gave her a long look. And then he reached up, slipping his hand behind her neck and brought her close. After a soft, sweet kiss, he pulled back and said,

"Elise it is. How about Elise Rebecca Jacobs."

Epilogue

(A little lagniappe)

ALICE SAT AT A SMALL WICKER table outside a bar on the piazza, fanning herself with the loose, wide-brimmed straw hat that had replaced her small black veiled one somewhere along the way about five months ago. Perspiration gleamed on her rosy cheeks; she was flushed from the long trek down from Villa Jovis. She was slightly browner from the sun now, too. And she wore lipstick, a bright coral color that made her skin glow. Her hair was a bit longer, still brown with pepper and salt, and right now wispy curls from the humidity framed her face. On the long walk up to the ancient ruins she'd picked a bright yellow flower from a bush and stuck it in her hair just above her ear.

The ancient ruins of Villa Jovis fascinated Alice. The island of Capri fascinated her, the history, the fragrances, the sound of the sea, the waves crashing against the cliffs. The water here was as clear and beautiful as Rebecca Jacobs had said. She'd walked up to the ruins around four o'clock this afternoon, after the day-trippers were gone and you could wander alone through the secretive stone passages of the palace, and up and down the stairs, all through the cool, hulking rooms, imagining things as they were two thousand years ago when the Emperor Tiberius's palace was new.

It was a forty-five-minute climb up those steep rocky steps, but she'd been drawn back to the ruins every day. Sometimes, on the way up she would stop and rest on a bench she'd found at the edge of a cliff, looking out over the sea. There, she'd let the wind blow through her hair, breathing the cool fresh air.

Back in the village center now, the piazza, she fanned herself with the straw hat and looked about. She'd been here for four days and had not yet decided when she'd leave. She looked about the Piazza d'Umberto I thinking how lucky she was that Rebecca had told her of the Amalifi Coast and this island.

At this time of evening, dusk, the piazza was almost deserted. In the harbor below she heard the last ferry whistle. A waiter ambled over to the table, wiping his hands on his apron, and asked if she would like something. Alice slapped the hat back on her head and asked for a bottle of cold still water, and a dish of sliced peaches. He nodded and disappeared without comment.

Lights in the piazza were beginning to glow, even though the sun just touched the sea's horizon. Fog was sinking into the village from the peaks above, from the top of the mountain at Anacapri, and the air was turning cool. She tipped back her head and searched the sky for the first stars. The sky was lavender now. Soon it would turn purple, then black, and the stars would seem so close that you could almost reach up and touch them. The latitude creates that effect, the hotel manager had said.

The waiter brought the peaches, water, and a glass to her table and put them down. No ice, but she'd grown used to that. She'd just cut into a slice of the peach and was lifting it to her mouth, when suddenly she noticed that man, again. She'd seen him here in the piazza every night since she'd arrived.

Studying him, she ate the peach. Tall and lean, gray hair, attractive—she guessed that he was older than her, but only by a few years. Tonight he wore loose linen pants that just touched the tops of his sandals. He wore a collarless blue gauze cotton shirt hanging out over the pants, reaching to his hips, and a straw hat pushed back on his head. He was American, she was certain, although she'd only heard him speaking in Italian.

She watched him while she ate another slice of peach. He seemed to know everyone in the town of Capri. The piazza was the center of social life here after dark; it seemed everyone in the village and the hotels and villas descended on the place at night. One evening she'd watched from this table as the man had played chess for hours, totally focused, completely absorbed in the game.

He stood under the clock tower in the corner of the piazza now, talking with a man who, as she recalled, owned the art gallery in the two-storied building right behind her. The gallery was on the second floor. She'd wandered through it several times. The stranger seemed to be glancing her way, so quickly she transferred her gaze to the bowl of peaches.

But while she ate, she studied the stranger from under her lashes. He had a good solid way of moving, and he held himself straight with the posture and confidence an old soldier never forgets. And he had a good, hearty laugh. She ate another slice of peach and then closed her eyes, enjoying the tangy sweet juice sliding down her throat. This was heaven. She could hear the sea, everywhere on Capri you could hear the sea. And she could smell flowers in the air. As she swallowed, the bells in the tower struck the hour.

"*Buena Sera.*"

Startled, she opened her eyes, fork still hovering midair, and stared at the man she'd been watching. He stood before her now, holding his hat in his hand. "I think I recognize a fellow American," he said. "I've seen you here for several nights, Signora, and would like to introduce myself." Motioning the hat toward her table, he said, "May I sit?"

She set the fork down on the plate and patted the corners of her mouth with the napkin in her lap. "Yes, of course. Please."

"*Grazie tanto!*" he said, pulling out the chair across from her. Then he lowered himself into the chair.

"Are you enjoying the island?" He cocked his head, studying her.

"Yes." She patted her hair and smiled. "It's lovely."

"I'm always happy to see someone from the States." He smiled. "Trevor Morello," he said, with a two-fingered salute. "At your service, ma'am." He reached his hand across the table and she hesitated, then gave it a shake and drew back.

But his smile was infectious.

"Alice Hamilton," she said. "I arrived four days ago on this lovely island, and am finding it difficult to leave."

"This is the land of the lotus, you know. It's best not to make plans."

Morello settled back then, resting both hands on the table. "Where are you staying?"

"La Luna." She motioned in the direction of the hotel. "It's small, with a perfect view of the Faraglioni. Just what I wanted."

"Yes, I know the place. The owners of La Luna are friends. They provide me with escargot from their gardens occasionally. The snails live in the vegetable gardens alongside the grape arbor, the walkway. Have you run into those yet?"

"No. I haven't met them."

He smiled.

"Besides," she added. "If I got friendly and then found them on my plate one night . . ." She made a face.

"Are you here alone, Miss Hamilton?"

"Call me Alice. Please."

He nodded. "And for you—he pressed his hand over his heart and bowed—"I am Trevor. But am I right that you're here alone, Alice?"

She nodded.

"I've been traveling through Europe for the last few months." She'd begun her travels in Paris, she told him. From there she'd taken the *Orient Express* to Venice. From Venice to Athens, from Athens to Venice and then on to Florence, Rome, Naples.

"And now . . ."—she spread her hands—"here I am."

"Where are you from?"

"New Orleans."

She saw the spark in his eyes. "Have you been there?"

He smiled. "Sure have. It's a fine place. I like a city with a soul."

"When were you there?"

His eyes drifted off. "Oh," He flipped his hand vaguely. "A couple years ago. I was there on business for a few weeks."

Alice slid her hands into her lap. "I lived there when I was growing up. My family's gone now. My husband died in the war, and after that, I left."

He looked her up and down. "Unfortunate man. He missed a delightful life," he said.

She shrugged. "You were a soldier too, I'll bet."

He nodded. "How'd you know?"

"The way you carry yourself."

He thought about that, and then said, "When you've been through war, after that, for a while nothing seems real. You have to keep pinching yourself, until finally one day you realize that you really made it through."

"What did you do in the war?"

He hesitated, then gave a slight shrug. "Paratroops, WWII. Europe—France, then Germany." He tilted his head and seemed to be studying her. "I was a jumper."

"I can't imagine doing that. Jumping out of planes midflight." She paused. "Was that fun?"

"Oh, very rewarding," he said in a strange tone, and with a little smile. After a moment he seemed to settle in the chair, relaxing. "How long will you stay with us on Capri?"

Alice turned her head and looked about. Colored lights glimmered around the square, and strings of twinkling white lights framed striped canvas above the diners in every cafe. She looked back at Trevor. "I'll stay here until I'm bored, I suppose. Or until some other place calls."

"Let's have dinner, shall we?"

She put her hands in her lap. "Yes. Let's do."

"Gianno's going to play," he said. Across the piazza she saw the young man with his guitar. He sat off to the side, in a chair far from the cafés and tables.

Trevor stood, turned to her, and stretched out his hand. "Will you dance? I think you might remember this song. It's from our time, back then."

Alice stood up and smoothed her skirt. They walked to a spot near where Gianno played, away from eyes. With one hand on her waist, he took her other hand in his and they began dancing.

Over his shoulder she looked at the colorful scene: the old men playing chess, the younger men in their work shirts and jeans, the children and dogs, and cats outnumbering the dogs. The women in flounced dresses the color of a sunset, and everywhere the lights.

And then Trevor took one step back and lifted his hand high overhead and with a quick, sharp motion sent her spinning, whirling, and the lights streamed in circles around them and the stars winked high overhead and she found herself laughing as he pulled her close again, and she thought to herself—

Yes. This is life.

Author's Note

THE STORY IS FICTION, BUT BASED on fact. That many infants have survived abortions is true, and there are thousands living now. Before 2011 I had never heard of infants born alive after surviving an abortion. Below is the shocking testimony given by Jill Stanek, a registered nurse working at Christ Hospital in Oak Lawn, Illinois, before a House Committee in the United States Congress in 2001 that inspired this book:

> One night, a nursing co-worker was taking an aborted downs syndrome baby who was born alive to our Soiled Utility Room because his parents did not want to hold him, and she did not have time to hold him. I could not bear the thought of this suffering child dying alone in a Soiled Utility Room, so I cradled and rocked him for the 45 minutes that he lived. He was about 21 to 22 weeks old, weighed about ½ pound, and was about 10 inches long. He was too weak to move very much, extending any energy he had trying to breathe. Toward the end he was so quiet that I couldn't tell if he was still alive unless I held him up to the light to see if his heart was beating through the chest wall. After he was pronounced dead, we folded his little arms across his chest, wrapped him in a tiny shroud, and carried him to the hospital morgue where

> all of our dead patients are taken. (*Testimony of Jill Stanek,*
> *R.N. Christ Hospital, Oak Lawn, Illinois*)

I first heard Jill Stanek speak of this on a television show one night in 2011, and afterward began researching the issue. What I found was almost unbelievable—live births during abortions, particularly induction abortions, had been occurring for years. It was, and still is, one of the best-kept secrets in the country (despite Kermit Gosnell, who is considered by many as only an abberation).

In 2001 Congress enacted the Born-Alive Infant's Protection Act as a response to Ms. Stanek's and many other witnesses' testimony. This law established that for federal purposes, an infant completely expelled or extracted from the mother and who is alive is a "person"—regardless of whether the child's development is believed to be, or is in fact, sufficient to permit long-term survival. The Act does not mandate medical treatment where aggressive treatment would be futile. It only establishes a fact—a baby born alive is a person with the constitutional rights held by any other person in this nation.

But this law does not bind the states; it governs only federal hospitals, administration, and facilities.

The need for the law was obvious by the time of those hearings before the Committee on the Judiciary in the House of Representatives in 2000. In a rational world, it would seem self-evident that infants who are born alive at any stage and under any circumstance are "persons", and are therefore entitled to protection of the law.

But the Congressional hearings concluded that "recent changes in the legal and cultural landscape have brought this well-settled principle into question." Live birth had become the new frontier. In a Supreme Court decision in 2000, *Stenberg v. Carhart*, the Court concluded that an infant's location in the mother's body was irrelevant to the unborn child's status—his or her right to protection under the law is extinguished if the mother intends to abort the child. As the court made clear, this is true even if the infant's crown is inches from the cervix and birth.

Given that the infant's location had just been made irrelevant, Justice Scalia's dissent from that opinion argued that the result was to give live-birth abortion a free rein.

Testimony from many witnesses before the committee made it clear that in hospitals and clinics around the country infants born alive in abortions, like Baby Chasson in the story, were being left to die on their own. Somehow, the committee concluded in its report, what had developed in our country was a situation where "infants who are marked for abortion but somehow survive and are born alive have no legal rights under the law—no right to receive medical care, to be sustained in life, or receive any care at all."

The Committee Report is publically available—Report 107-186/107th Congress, 1st Session/House of Representatives. The belief systems of those who would bind an infant born alive with the mother's prior choice that he or she should die, as reflected in this report, is almost beyond belief. Confusion over the rights of a born-alive infant really reached a peak when Princeton University Bioethicist, Peter Singer, in his 1993 book *Practical Ethics*, advocated the idea that "a period of twenty-eight days after birth might be allowed before an infant is accepted as having the same right to live as others." Any infant!

In the committee hearings in 2000, many other witnesses testified to the plight of infants surviving abortions. Nurse Allison Baker, R.N., B.S.N., also working at Christ Hospital, testified about three live-birth abortions that she witnessed there. Here is a portion of her testimony.

> The first occurred on a day shift. I happened to walk into a "soiled utility room" and saw, lying on the metal counter, a fetus, naked, exposed, and breathing, moving its arms and legs. The fetus was visibly alive and was gasping for breath.

Christ Hospital's ultimate response to the allegations was that although it had performed late term abortions on infants with nonfatal birth defects, it was changing policy and would henceforth use the procedure to abort only fatally-deformed infants.

And then there is the story of Baby Hope in 1999. The mother's abortion procedure was initiated in a clinic, but when she experienced severe pains she reported to the emergency room of Bethesda North Medical Center in Cincinnati. The infant was born alive at twenty-two weeks, although some doctors believed that she was older. As reported by the *Washington Times* on May 17, 1999, she was a perfectly formed newborn. Baby Hope lived for three hours without the benefit of an incubator or other intensive care. Initially the attending physician placed the infant in a specimen dish. A technician saw the child gasping for air, realized that she was alive, and held the baby until she died three hours later.

There are many, many stories like this, and sadly they continued after the Born Alive Infant's Protection Act became federal law in 2001. As I said, reader, the federal law did not bind the states. As of the date of writing this note to you twenty-six states have laws creating a specific affirmative duty for physicians to provide medical care and treatment to born-alive infants at any stage of development: AL, AZ, CA, DE, FL, GA, IL, IN, KS, LA, ME, MI, MS, MO, MT, NE, NY, OK, PA, RI, SC, SD, TN, TX, WA, and WI.

Three states have laws creating a specific affirmative duty for physicians to provide medical care and treatment to born-alive infants only after viability: IA, MN, and ND. As the House Judiciary Committee Report noted, however, the limitation requiring a finding of viability presents a conundrum, since true viability can only be determined retrospectively. One state protects born-alive infants at any stage of development from "deliberate acts" undertaken by a physician that result in the death of the infant: VA.

Today, away from the eyes of the world and the media this crime continues. Data is difficult to come by—no surprise there. Facts generally come to light only when a dramatic crime is covered by reporters. For example, the abortion doctor Kermit Gosnell was recently found guilty of murder of three infants born alive during induced labor abortions in his Philadelphia clinic. The bodies of other infants in the sixth, seventh, and eighth months were found in the clinic during the investigation. A similar case in 2011 in Maryland was dismissed on a technicality, but over thirty little bodies were found in a freezer at that clinic.

So, this remains an ongoing horror despite a finding in the House Judiciary Committee report over ten years ago that an infant born alive as of 2001 at twenty-three weeks had a 39 percent chance of sustained survival, and at twenty-four weeks, a greater than 50 percent chance of sustained survival, with the odds improving all the time. With medical advances, imagine what the chances of survival for a live-birth infant after medical assessment could be today.

It's past time to hold this fact up to the light. Turn the page and read Melissa's story. Melissa Ohden is a voice for the voiceless. Melissa survived a saline infusion abortion in 1977, and has now established The Abortion Survivors Network online, reaching out to survivors and their loved ones to let them know that they are not alone. The network provides current information about live-birth survivors, as well as an opportunity for those who wish to tell their stories to do that privately, or publically. The network offers comfort, companionship, understanding, and plenty of love. Melissa says that based loosely on figures by the Center for Disease Control, as of 2012, there are tens of thousands of failed abortion survivors in the United States alone.

The pain, of course, is not limited to infants born alive in a failed abortion. If you are a woman hurting and confused after an abortion you can find immediate confidential assistance, and compassion and understanding twenty-four hours a day by calling The National Helpline for Abortion Recovery at 1-866-482-5433, or by going to the helpline website at www.nationalhelpline.org. The National Helpline is a nonprofit organization which provides counseling, referrals for medical services, and accurate information.

So turn the page and read Melissa's story. And following that, check out my website www.pamelaewen.com for some of the source materials—studies, articles, books—which formed the basis of the medical testimony for witnesses in our trial.

Melissa's Story

MELISSA OHDEN IS THE FOUNDER OF The Abortion Survivor's Network, (www.theabortionsurvivors.com), a nonprofit organization which seeks to provide support to abortion survivors while also educating the public to the reality of abortion and abortion survivors. After experiencing her own struggles with feeling alone as a survivor and journeying through healing over many years, Melissa felt driven to establish this network to be of support to other survivors after witnessing the sheer number of abortion survivors out there and their needs.

Melissa's biological mother was a nineteen-year-old college student when she had a saline infusion abortion in 1977. Although her biological mother thought that she was less than five months pregnant when she had the abortion, the fact that Melissa survived and weighed almost three pounds indicates that her biological mother was much further along in her pregnancy than she realized. In fact, when Melissa obtained her medical records in 2007 that detail the abortion procedure that she survived, one of the first notations by a doctor after she survived was that she looked like she was approximately thirty-one weeks gestation. Despite the initial concerns that doctors had regarding her ability to survive, and the quality of life she would experience if she did, today Melissa is a healthy wife, mother, speaker and writer.

Although Melissa grew up knowing that she was adopted and loved, she didn't find out the truth about being an abortion survivor until she was fourteen years old. Needless to say, finding out the truth about her life changed her and now the world forever. Melissa ultimately went searching for answers about her survival and her biological family, and since 2007, has had contact with both sides of her biological family in varying degrees. Through this search and reunion, Melissa has experienced firsthand what she calls the "intergenerational impact of abortion." The reality is that abortion doesn't just impact a woman's life. It ends a child's life and it forever changes the lives of everyone it touches, including women, men, extended family members, friends, and our communities.

Melissa is a mother, a wife, and a speaker and advocate for survivors of abortions and their loved ones. More information about her story, and about The Abortion Survivor's Network, can be found on Melissa's personal website: www.melissaohden.com.

Acknowledgments

THIS BOOK COULD NOT HAVE BEEN written without the assistance and support of many friends. Profound thanks to each one of you.

Dorinda Chiapetta Bordlee is a wife, a lawyer, the mother of four children, and a founder and Vice President and Senior Counsel of the Bioethics Defense Fund, an international legal advocate for human rights at all stages of life. Dorinda was not only instrumental in guiding me through the legal evolution of rights, or the lack thereof, for infants born alive during an abortion, but she was also my role model for Rebecca's inspired choice at the end of An Accidental Life. She is an example of a woman who made a difficult choice, and through that has found a happy and fulfilling balance between her family and a demanding career. Like many women today, Dorinda illustrates that there are alternatives.

Scott Schlegal, a former Assistant District Attorney of Jefferson Parish, Louisiana, led me through the winding corridors of the courthouse in Gretna, introduced me around, and explained the pressing demands of every prosecutor's life. He answered my numerous questions with good humor and held my feet to the fire on the burden of proof in the trial portion of the book, without judgment, in his cool, collected way.

Julie Gwinn's editing of *An Accidental Life* was magical, seamless. I am thrilled to be working with her. Thank you, Julie, for believing in this book and for peeling back the onion. Without you the story of these children might not have been told and this book might have been just a (very long) manu-script sitting on my shelf. Special thanks also to Kim Stanford, Managing Editor, B&H Book Production for her patience with my constant revisions and her insight. And, as always, thanks also to the entire B&H team—Diana Lawrence, Matt West and the sales force, and everyone else who worked so hard to help get this book out to readers.

Jill Stanek's testimony described in my Author's Note before the Judiciary Constitution Subcommittee of the U.S. House of Representatives, and thereafter in various public forums, inspired this book. Thanks, Jill, for the time you spent answering my endless questions, and for your courage. And thanks also to Melissa Ohden for telling her story to the world, and her strength and courage.

Thanks to both Dr. Hal Scholen and Margo Scholen, one of my former law partners who is also a registered nurse, for your friendship, advice, and help. And to Cheryl Schleuss, who walked me through the medical systems and protocols back in 1982, and to Dr. Mike DeFatta, Chief Deputy Coroner and Chief Forensic Pathologist of St. Tammany Parish, Louisiana. Big thanks also to Peg Kenny of the Archdiocese of New Orleans, Robert E. Winn, founder of Louisiana Right to Life and a former partner of a major law firm in New Orleans. And thanks to Cindy Collins, Louisiana State Director and member of the National Advisory Board of Operation Outcry, a ministry of The Justice Foundation for her support, advice, and introductions.

Reader, please understand that the opinions and conclusions set forth in this book came from my own research, including case law, articles, and published studies in journals, and are not necessarily the opinions and con-clusions that any one of these fine people would have reached.

Finally, I want to thank my husband, James Lott, for his love and patience and understanding. Jimmy is in every sense my true love and my partner, and like Jude, I always know he has my back.